I0600276

HEIR OF DARKNESS

THE HEIRS SERIES
BOOK 1

LEJLA MURIC

TABLE OF CONTENTS

Copyright © 2025 by Lejla Muric

This is a work of fiction. Names, characters, places, and incidents are the product
of the author's imagination or are used fictitiously. Any resemblance to actual
persons, living or dead, events, or locales is entirely coincidental.
All rights reserved. No part of this book may be reproduced or used in any manner
without written permission of the copyright owner except for the use of
quotations in a book review.

Copyediting by Misha Carlstedt of Verity Ink Editorial
Proofreading by Gabby D'Aloia of GCD Editorial
Cover Design by Georgia Stove of Pixel and Quill Studio

ISBN 979-8-9926679-1-2 (paperback)
ISBN 979-8-9926679-0-5 (ebook)

TRIGGER WARNINGS

Depression, Harsh Mental State, Guns, Violence (Gruesome), Murder (Graphic/On Page), Suicidal Ideation, Fighting, Abuse (Parent to Child), Mentions of Domestic Abuse, Mentions of Homophobia (Parent to Child), Arranged Marriage, Primal Kink (Consensual), Mild Mentions of Body Image, Consensual Sexual Activity, Mature Language.

To anyone who has ever found comfort in the darkness.

PROLOGUE

SEVEN YEARS EARLIER

THE WHITE GOWN Luna wore was too similar to a wedding dress, but that was the intention behind it. Her father wanted potential suitors to see what his sixteen-year-old daughter would look like walking down the aisle to them. It made her sick to her stomach.

She attempted to drown herself in the champagne the bar offered considering they wouldn't give her anything else, but it wasn't enough. When she saw an opening at one of the patio doors, she made a run for it, nearly twisting her ankle in the obnoxious heels her mother forced onto her feet earlier in the night. She couldn't escape the party completely considering every inch of the grounds were guarded, but she could slip out for some air. At least that was what she would tell anyone who asked why she wandered off.

Preparing for an arranged marriage at sixteen was the last thing Luna wanted to do. The contracts would be signed, the parties would happen, and at eighteen she would be married. Her life would be over.

She walked between the statues lining up the fake grass. The marble on the naked men and warriors with swords on their backs still in pristine condition as if they had never been exposed to the harsh New York weather before.

She didn't care about those. No, her attention caught the only one with chips and a yellowing tint on it. It was a statue of a woman clutching her dress in fear. Luna studied it closely for a moment, noticing one single tear that had been carved out on the woman's cheek. There was no mention of who the woman was or who had carved her.

Such a horrible moment to have frozen in time.

Wasn't that Luna's predicament? That this moment, in all its awfulness, would be a moment she would remember forever. She would become another nameless woman whose identity was stripped away, left to serve a husband that would never truly love her.

"I think everyone is expecting you inside."

She turned around. It was Valerio Vitali. The heir of the family her own family despised. She didn't know why he was invited tonight, but she assumed it was so her father could make a point of showing off the various connections people were trying to make with him just to have his daughter.

Luna hadn't even realized she was crying. Quickly, she wiped the tears, sniffling in an attempt to cover up her vulnerability.

They had never talked before, but she had seen him at events here and there considering he was Gianna's cousin. He was older than her by a year. Mysterious, handsome, and terrifying. Another way to say he was out of her league. Not that it mattered anymore anyway.

"Tell them you don't know where I am," she told him. Her eyes took in every inch of his face, memorizing the blue in his eyes that looked like the frigid Norwegian water she'd stayed next to only a couple of months ago for spring break with her best friends. He always looked like he was thinking about something terrible, the way his lips held a permanent frown.

"Why are you crying?" He sat down at the base of the statue, staring at her intently. She sat down beside him, laughing bitterly.

"Why do you think?"

"I'm guessing getting married isn't your idea then?" Valerio asked.

"Is that what you would want when you have your whole life ahead of you? When you know that every dream you've ever wanted is never going to come true now?" She wished she didn't sound so bitter, but there was no use.

"When you put it like that, no."

"He's going to pick the highest bidder—doesn't matter if they treat me right or not," Luna said. She threw her head in her hands. "I wish I could run away. Make this nightmare disappear."

"Running never solves anything."

"A bullet to the head does."

She lifted her head, her eyes wide. She couldn't believe that she told him something so dark, something she had considered but hadn't even told her best friends about.

Valerio's face morphed into something between anguish and desperation. It stunned her for a second, but no more than when he grabbed hold of her chin with a solid grip. "Don't ever consider taking your life over something like this ever again. Do you understand me?"

She nodded her head, too shocked to answer.

That wasn't good enough for him. "Use your words."

His growl had her muttering, "Yes."

He stared at her for a long moment before finally letting go. She took a deep breath, keeping her eyes locked on him in case he reached out for her again.

His voice broke the silence once more. "You want out of that contract?"

She could only nod her head. "More than anything."

A pair of footsteps walked up to them. It was Dante Vitali, his suit wrinkled and shirt unbuttoned. Luna didn't bother to fix her appearance or move away from Valerio. She didn't care anymore if their position looked improper.

"Father wants you for the meeting," he told Valerio.

Valerio stood up, turning back to Luna one last time. "Drink some water and go inside."

"Drink some water and go inside," she mocked in a quiet tone, currently annoyed with all men.

Even if he heard her, he pretended he didn't, but still kept the slightest hint of a smirk on his face. When she was alone once again, she looked up at the statue behind her, running gentle fingers over the unnamed woman's hand. Luna stood up, walking back into the party that continued on without her.

By the time she found her father, he was already shaking hands with Valerio and his father, Cesare Vitali.

A contract had been signed just like they wanted. One more influential and groundbreaking.

Luna Kingsley was set to marry Valerio Vitali.

ONE

LUNA

THE LAST PLACE Luna should have been on a Sunday night was the Vitali mansion. Finn had made her promise she would be staying in bed tonight, getting a full night's sleep before her first day of school tomorrow. Unfortunately for both of the Kingsley kids, Cecilia Hart was far too convincing when she wanted to party.

Luna hated the Vitali mansion. The home itself was beautiful and spacious. The walls were a soft cream, the floors a deep oak. The couches in the living room looked far too fancy to be sitting in the center, vulnerable to the drunk partygoers who overfilled their cups and danced erratically. One known fact about the Vitalis: They were loaded. Hosting a party of this size, they must have had a cleaning crew booked and replacement furniture on the way.

But that wasn't why Luna hated the mansion. Rumor was *he* was living here again, back from his time abroad for the last seven years. She had been at the party for a couple of hours and he was still nowhere to be found. A relief for her and her best friends, who were able to continue partying until Luna was ready to leave.

Although the rivalry between the Kingsleys and the Vitalis rang strong, Luna was best friends with Gianna Moretti, cousin of the devil. It meant she was excluded from the petty fights that the boys got in to. She still had her own rivalry with the devil himself though, but it was personal and went beyond the rivalries their families had had for generations.

All night, she felt his shadow watching her like a predator stalking its prey. Her mind told her it wasn't real; he wouldn't have wasted time to make his presence known to her if he was actually there.

But it was his coming home party, a fact Gianna had conveniently left out until Luna walked through the door. That meant he had to be here somewhere, waiting for his moment to pounce.

She hadn't intended to come, but when Gianna brought up the party to her, Cecilia, and Blair, the latter two jumped at the offer and forced Luna to come along.

She wished she'd stayed home.

Still, Allister Moretti and Dante Vitali knew how to throw a party. Gianna danced on the table, drunk out of her mind. Blair Adler, one of the top students at Grand Willow University, sat in the lap of some poli sci student who stood absolutely no chance with her, and Cecilia was lost somewhere in the sea of bodies. They were all in a state of carelessness, or maybe they were just drunk. She would have been too if she wanted to wake up with a pounding hangover for the first day of classes.

Any other night, Luna would have been dancing alongside them. Tonight, she hid against the wall, hoping the crowd of people covered her.

Until she had to pee.

Luna sighed, pushing herself off the wall. She shoved her way through bodies covered in sweat, making her way over to the bathroom beside the kitchen. The house was abnormally large, and yet, the number of people inside made it feel like she was walking through a tunnel. The floor was sticky and covered in gold glitter decorations, forcing her to kick off one that had stuck on her shoe.

The line for the bathroom was long. Luna wasn't even sure where it ended and the urge to pee only got worse. She groaned.

Ducking under a fallen "Celebrate" sign that had been lazily hung up with tape, she climbed the stairs quickly, her heels clicking on the polished floors as she walked. Her feet were killing her and the straps of the black dress she wore dug into her shoulders. She was ready to go home and take it all off, turn on a show, and pass out on her bed before her anxiety about the new semester kicked in.

The upstairs was clear just as she knew it would be. There was a bathroom in Gianna's room down the hall, but there was also one directly across from the study. Since *he* had been gone, the doors remained shut. She always passed by it when she came over to visit Gianna, and the room felt so much colder than the rest of the home. She assumed that any room he occupied frequently, like his bedroom, was probably just as cold.

This time, the mahogany doors were cracked open. Loud laughs escaped, drifting down the hall. Someone muttered something incoherently, stupidly—most likely drunk. Dante and Allister would be in there, but she wasn't sure if *he* would be.

The last time she had seen him was for a second at some gala they both attended with their parents years ago. Seven years ago, to be exact. He had been young and boyish-looking, with black hair that was brushed back neatly but could be unruly at best. He didn't smile back then, and she was sure he probably still didn't.

That was when they first brought up the possibility of their union—her parents and his father. And it was for that reason she avoided him like the plague. It was also for that reason that she shouldn't have been at his homecoming party either.

Another loud chuckle stopped her. Was there something really that interesting happening inside?

Luna's curiosity was piqued. There may have been a small part of her that wanted to see if he was actually back. If she was quick with it, she could take one glance into the room and then continue her way to the bathroom. She huffed. Why did she even care if he was back?

Another howl of laughter rang through the hall.

One peek wouldn't hurt. Luna looked around, making sure no one lingered before she approached the door silently. Her breath hitched as she leaned in.

The first person she saw was Allister, who carried a bottle in his hand as he walked with unsteady steps to the desk. His golden-blonde hair was lit up by the warm lights of the room, a big grin on his face. The other was a man she recognized for his dark black hair and the carefree smile. Dante. The youngest son of Cesare Vitali. He considered everything in life to be a joke and was known to be the life of the party.

Their leader was nowhere to be seen. Perhaps he ditched the party thinking he was above being celebrated.

Luna turned away from the door, but hands grabbed on to her hips, pushing her up against the wall. She gasped.

A big hand clenched her chin, lifting her head up so she would be forced to stare into the same electric blue eyes she hadn't seen in years. His brows were narrowed, a permanent frown etched on his lips. There was a hint of satisfaction in his eyes, knowing he had caught her.

"Looking for me?" he asked. His voice was rough and reeked of power.

Valerio Vitali.

The man her brother hated. The man who had more rumors than truth surrounding his name. And the man her father had arranged for her to marry.

For the past seven years, she had prayed and pleaded with every God to ensure he wouldn't come home. She even called different embassies, creating lies about him so he wouldn't be let back into the country. Somehow, he had defied it all because there he stood in all his menacing glory.

Her words were lost on her as she stared at his beauty. He was older now, his face more stern, body more chiseled. Of course he was beautiful, but it was a dangerous type of beauty.

"I was looking for the bathroom," she told him.

"And stopped to look inside my study? Were you disappointed I wasn't there?" he asked. He moved his hand along her neck, settling it against the skin like a necklace.

Luna ground her jaw. "As if. I went years without seeing you. I can go for a lifetime."

Valerio's eyes narrowed. "Lucky for you, you won't have to."

"So you're back? For good?" she asked, swallowing harshly.

"Don't sound so disappointed." He smirked, trailing his thumb along her skin. She hated the goosebumps that rose on her skin.

"You know what they say about hope and misery," she said, pushing against him.

He gave her a sinister grin. "Oh, come on, Luna. There must be a part of you that is at least a little bit happy to see me." He leaned in, his lips brushing against her ear. "I didn't take you for a liar."

Luna closed her eyes, before opening them again, realizing where she was and who she was with. She pushed him again; this time he moved away from her. "Sorry to break it to you, but I don't want your disgusting hands or your miserable energy anywhere near me."

"Is that why you came to my party?" he asked, crossing his arms.

Luna rolled her eyes. "If I had known what this party was, I wouldn't be anywhere near it."

"Here I thought my fiancée would have helped throw this party for me," he said.

Luna's face fell. She was completely over the conversation.

"I'm going home," she said, walking past him.

He grabbed her arm, forcing her to fall against him. She quickly composed herself, pushing his hand off. "Is there an issue with that word?"

"You know why I hate that word," she spit out, her composure completely derailed now. She tried so hard to act and look proper, the way her parents raised and expected her to act. There was something about Valerio that was always able to send her into a spiral. She'd had peace for seven years. Why did he have to come back? "I will never be your wife."

"Let me make this clear for you, Luna. I gave you seven years to come to terms with the inevitable. Fight me all you want; I don't care. I'm not going anywhere. You will be my wife and that is final." Valerio's voice sliced through the hall, loud and promising to anyone who listened.

Luna narrowed her eyes. She wouldn't bow down to anyone; she never had and she wouldn't start now.

"Over my dead fucking body, Vitali," she hissed.

His eyes lit up with a dangerous gleam as if he wanted her to fight back.

He leaned down, his lips only a hair strand away from touching her ear. The goosebumps rose on her skin without control, coming alive with his presence near.

"Then so be it, Kingsley," Valerio whispered.

Then he pulled away from her completely, leaving her frozen in space. She only snapped out of her daze when his stare traveled down the length of her body, taking in every inch of skin exposed from the dress.

"Run now. You know I'll find you, fiancée."

And Luna did. She wasn't going to hang around to give him another chance to touch her. She wanted to stay as far away from him as she could.

Her skin crawled the entire way down the hall, knowing he stood there and watched her the entire time. She hated him. That was the one thing she knew for sure. There would never be any other word to describe the way she felt toward Valerio Vitali.

The air rushed back into Luna's lungs when she could see the stairs once again. The music from downstairs engulfed her like a blanket, reminding her she wasn't alone. Her need for the restroom was gone. All she wanted was to get the hell out of that house and never return.

"Where were you?" Blair asked, grabbing Luna's arm when she spotted her. Sweat coated her tan skin, highlighting the tops of her cheekbones.

"Bathroom," Luna lied. "I'm thinking about going home."

"They're about to bring out the guest of honor," Gianna said, a random boy hanging off her hand. Her blue eyes were glazed over, a big smile on her face.

"We have to stay for that!" Cecilia squealed. Her makeup was smudged, her long black hair matted in the back. She stumbled and held on to Blair, who wrapped an arm around the drunk girl.

The man in question walked onto the balcony that over-looked the living room. Allister stood at his left, Dante at his right. Everyone was silent until Valerio lifted a bottle of alcohol, allowing the cheers of celebration to begin.

Dread settled in Luna's stomach the moment his eyes landed on her. She stared back before she turned around, walking out of the Vitali home.

She desperately wanted to run, but suddenly it felt like there was nowhere to go.

TWO

LUNA

LUNA WASN'T A MORNING PERSON. Not in the slightest. Even when she was a child, she preferred to stay up all night when the house was silent and she could play alone. When the sun rose, she was forced to slap on a smile and become the perfect daughter to Reece and Eleanora Kingsley.

She was also forced to remember what happened the night before.

God, that was the last time she listened to Cecilia.

She rolled out of bed to get ready for the day—a start to the new semester. She'd spent most of her school years in all girls' schools with Gianna, Blair, and Cecilia. The four of them met at a private elementary school and had stuck by each other's sides ever since. It was only natural they would be drawn to each other considering their parents, except for Gianna's, worked together at one point in the past.

When it was time for Luna to start applying to universities, she really only had one option: Grand Willow University. The same place her brother attended.

It was miserable having her brother breathing down her neck constantly, making sure she wasn't getting into trouble. But Finn wasn't always *that* bad. He stood up for her occasionally, and usually he was busy getting himself into trouble, so really, Luna was able to do whatever she wanted.

Not to mention that for the past three years of being in college, it was better to have Finn around than the devil himself.

Except now he was back.

Maybe she could transfer schools.

Luna huffed, burning her red painted fingernail while she curled her hair. It was tough putting makeup on with only one hand, but she got it done. She slipped on a soft white sundress, smoothing out the wrinkles, before grabbing her bag and leaving her room.

Voices were already coming from the kitchen. Gianna sat on a kitchen stool, her blonde hair perfectly curled and her jeans hugging her legs. There wasn't a single trace of a hangover on her face.

"Good morning, sunshine," she said with a bright smile.

Luna returned it. "I don't know how you're functioning right now."

"I agree," Cecilia said with a groan. "I feel like I'm dying."

Her long black hair was pulled into a messy ponytail, a pair of leggings and an oversized T-shirt on. She held the cup of coffee up to her nose, waiting for her hangover to miraculously leave.

"It's the Moretti blood in me. I actually need alcohol to function fully," Gianna said, shrugging. "I want to know why you decided to leave suddenly last night."

Luna stared at her, dumbfounded. "Are you seriously asking me that right now?"

"Okay, okay. But at least you didn't see him, right?"

"No, I didn't. And I don't want to." The lie slipped out before she could stop herself. If she had told them about the run-in, then she would be forced to explain the entire conversation and Luna wasn't prepared to get into it this early in the morning.

"Well, good. At least the night was a little bit of a success." Gianna smiled.

"You would have missed a fun night if you stayed in," Cecilia said.

"Who would have missed a fun night?" Blair asked, walking into the kitchen. She opened one of the cabinets, pulling out some medicine and handing it to Cecilia. "Take some medicine and drink water. You'll be fine." Cecilia grabbed the pill bottle from her hand, swallowing two pills right away.

"Luna would have."

"Right, because seeing the man you're being forced to marry is so much fun," Blair said with a snort.

Luna gave her a big smile. "Thank you, Blair." She turned back to Gianna. "Do you know how Finn would have reacted if he knew I was there last night? He's already going to lose his mind when he finds out Valerio is back."

Gianna rolled her eyes. "Your brother is too tense. It's not like he can do anything about Valerio."

Luna huffed. No, he couldn't. It just meant their petty little attacks on each other would start up again, both trying to prove they were better than the other.

"Finn could kill him." Blair took a sip of her coffee, an eyebrow arched.

Gianna gave her a sarcastic smile. "Just like you could kill Allister?"

Blair shot her a dirty look. "I can and I should."

"Let's go before we're late," Luna told them. A second longer and there would be a fight brewing between the two of them.

"Cecilia, go get dressed," Blair told her.

Cecilia narrowed her eyes. "I am dressed."

"Oh," Blair said. She plastered on a fake smile. "You look great." Blair's short skirt and matching light pink blazer complemented her title as being one of the top students of her class in the pre-law department. Not a single strand of honey-colored hair was out of place.

"Are any of your classes in the King building?" Luna asked before any bickering could start.

Gianna nodded. "I'm headed that way."

"I have a meeting so I'll join you," Blair said.

"Ugh, so I have to walk to the science building all on my own?" Cecilia asked, standing.

"You're the one who decided you wanted to go into medicine," Gianna said.

"I'm sure Augustus will be waiting for you," Luna told her with a small smirk. "Maybe this time he'll have a box of donuts instead of the lips of someone you made out with at the club."

She rolled her eyes. "Even worse. And that was one time. I didn't know they knew each other."

"Let's go. I can't be late," Blair said, clapping her hands.

"God forbid Allister get there before her," Gianna said.

"Exactly," Blair said, giving her a bitter look.

Luna shook her head, grabbing her tote bag and entering the elevator to go down to the lobby with everyone else. The sun warmed her skin as they walked outside. The sky was a bright blue without a single cloud to be seen. The trees were blooming and bright green, the summer plants and flowers still blooming. The rest of New York City looked nothing like this, but Grand Willow University was outside of the city. The founders found it necessary to keep the private school on neutral acres of land as an attempt to keep civility between all the influential students and their families. That was the only way students could attend the school; otherwise, every day would be a bloodbath.

Even though it was farther from the city, the campus itself had more than enough amenities for students: apartments, cafes, restaurants, clothing stores, bookstores.

The girls' apartment wasn't far from the actual campus, so the walk didn't take long. In no time they were saying goodbye to Cecilia, who groaned while walking to the science building.

Luna couldn't focus in any of her classes for the life of her. Her mind constantly replayed the night before, how Valerio had put his hands on her as if he could, how he just spit out that annoying word, not caring who heard or that it wasn't true.

She practically ran out of the lecture hall when her last class ended, starving after missing breakfast that morning. She and the girls would be going to a restaurant on campus once they finished, but there was still another hour until then. With the list of books her professors required for the semester, she thought it would be smart to get them ordered before the rush swept through.

Surprisingly, the library was busy for the first day, but it would die down eventually. Most of the students that came to school only did it because their parents forced them. They had trust funds and future businesses they would be inheriting no matter what, so they showed up the first week and partied for the rest of the semester, living off of their parents' money.

"The books will be delivered to your apartment in a couple of days," the woman behind the counter told her. Her glasses hung low on the bridge of her nose, her hair perfectly wrapped in an updo that Luna wouldn't have known how to do herself. "It also looks like the payment will be taken out from the card on file."

She nodded, giving the woman a smile. "Thank you for your help."

Her dad probably wouldn't blink at the cost of the books, so Luna threw in a couple extra for her own personal reading. It was the least he could do.

She walked farther into the library, desperate to find a way to spend another forty minutes. Most of the tables were taken, so she found herself in the fiction section, losing herself in the tall book-shelves filled with multiple editions of books she had never even heard of. She ran her finger across the spines, feeling every indent and crack in them.

The library smelled old, comforting in a way. It felt lived in like most of the books were, and Luna couldn't help but smile.

She wasn't a book nerd by any means, but she enjoyed the craft enough to want to study it.

"*Wuthering Heights*? I would have pegged you for a *Pride and Prejudice* type of girl."

Luna's eyes widened as she turned around frantically. Valerio leaned on the bookshelf opposite of her, his arms crossed over his chest. She caught the way his eyes trailed her body.

"What are you doing here?" Luna asked.

"Looking at books."

His voice was nonchalant. Valerio moved to the bookshelf beside her, skimming the books as if he cared.

"As if you read."

"Of course I read. I keep up with all of those smutty books you buy at the bookstore. I have to say, Luna, some are far too scandalous for a girl like you," Valerio said. She hated the smirk on his face.

"So you follow me around?" she asked, her voice hard.

"No. I was in Italy," he said, shaking his head. "I had you followed and it was reported back to me."

Luna's mouth dropped open. "Are you serious?"

She tried to move around him, falling short when Valerio grabbed hold of her arm, pushing her back against the shelves. "You should have answered my calls and texts."

"I don't owe you anything," Luna bit back. "And your number is blocked."

"I'll get a new number."

"I'll block that one too," she said, crossing her arms. "Can you move back? You're invading my personal space."

"I like having you so close to me," he said, stepping even closer. His chest pushed against hers, allowing her to feel the rigid muscles he held under his plain white T-shirt. His body emanated too much warmth for Luna's already burning body.

"Well, I don't," she snapped.

"How were your classes? Anyone I have to take care of for bothering you?" he asked, changing the subject.

Luna grinned. "I don't know. I wouldn't really call all the cute guys *bothers*. They were more of a distraction if anything."

Valerio's face fell in an instant. "Which classes?"

"I'm not telling you," she said, acting innocent. "I deserve some eye candy this semester. Don't you agree?"

"Are you trying to make me jealous?" he asked, cocking his head to the side.

Luna shrugged. "I'm not trying to do anything."

"Let me remind you that I have nothing to be jealous of. You're going to be my wife. With one bullet in those little boys' heads, they'll be taken care of. Wiped from the face of the planet," Valerio said. His voice was darker, the banter completely gone.

Luna clenched her jaw. "I want a copy of that contract."

"Why?" he asked. "Eager to fulfill it?"

"I'm going to find a loophole in it," she said. "I know there has to be one in there somewhere."

Valerio's eyes narrowed for a moment before his face switched back to being emotionless. It was strange how often he was able to change his facial expression. It was even stranger how he was able to choose when he showed emotion and when he didn't.

"Good luck with that," he said. He leaned in, placing a kiss on her cheek. Luna's eyes widened, her mouth dropping open. Her cheek tingled from where his lips had touched her, and for a tiny second, she imagined what they would feel like on her lips. She blamed the shock and exhaustion on that.

He pushed away, turning to leave before he stopped mid-step. "Oh, feel free to buy a couple more of those smutty books you like. My card is on your account; you might as well get used to using our money."

Rage blossomed through her. She swore she could feel steam escaping out of her ears. She needed to find a way to expel the devil, and quickly, before his claws sunk deeper into her.

THREE

VALERIO

AS THE OLDEST son and heir to the Vitali Empire, Valerio always got everything he wanted while growing up. His mother had tried to teach him to be a gentle, loving, compassionate boy. Her death when he was nine years old meant that he was left to his father's reins. Cesare made sure Valerio was ruthless, unforgiving, and emotionless. It was a liability to feel emotions; it showed others there was a weakness to exploit.

Valerio was a monster. He could admit that much. Still, part of him considered himself Luna's hero—he saved her from some freak her father would have arranged for her to marry. For her, he was willing to look deep into his soul for the things his mother had taught him about how to treat someone you loved.

He didn't even need to attend school. Hell, he was already done with any and all studies he would ever need while he was in Italy. But as long as a certain brunette lingered on campus for another year or two, he had to keep an eye out.

She was his fiancée after all.

Arranged marriages were how connections were made in their world. It was the strongest contract any family could create. Maybe it was something about loyalty and the kind that only stemmed from family. Valerio wasn't sure. He just knew that when the offer fell—or more like was forced—into his hands, to marry Luna, there wasn't a single thought about it. He signed without a second to waste.

Most people would have killed for their daughter to have a chance to marry Valerio Vitali and benefit from what it meant to have attachments to the Vitali family. He could have had a multi-million-dollar deal in place just to marry some wealthy asshole's daughter, but he chose Luna. He didn't want money, land, or part of their businesses. Just her.

The contract was written, signatures signed, and it was filed away.

There was only one small issue with the contract. If either died, the contract would be void. Death was truly the only way out and Valerio didn't doubt Luna would be willing to stab him to death if she found out.

Once they were married, the contract wouldn't matter. They would have the marriage certificate tying them together instead.

Valerio threw his head back, leaning in his desk chair. He ran a hand down his face. Why the hell did she have to be so stubborn?

Wasn't that what attracted him to her in the first place?

"Who wants to go out tonight?" Dante asked, slamming the door of Valerio's office open. With loud steps he made his way to the couch, slumping down on it as he lit up a cigarette.

Valerio snapped out of his daze.

Allister followed in after Dante. "I thought you would have been done after last night."

"Are you fucking kidding me? Last night was just a warm-up for the rest of the semester," he said, puffing out a cloud of smoke.

Valerio shook his head. "I'm praying your liver gives up on you soon."

"Rude." Dante scoffed.

"What could you possibly be preparing for now?" Allister asked. He leaned against the black bookshelf filled with random business and legal books.

"Did you both forget that initiation weekend is coming up?"

Dante asked. More smoke escaped his lips, making Valerio's turn up in disgust. He hated the smell.

"Put it out, jackass," he said. Dante rolled his eyes, crushing the cigarette on the rectangular mahogany table in front of him. Valerio clenched his jaw at the mess. "And I haven't forgotten. I've been preoccupied."

"Oh, right, you're reunited with the woman who hates you," Dante said. "How romantic."

"She doesn't hate me."

"No, she just refuses to be anywhere near you," Allister told him. "I'm sure that means she's in love."

"I could shoot both of you in the neck and no one would utter a word," Valerio said.

"Who would be your wingman then?" Dante asked. He grinned. "You seem to forget that I'm actually friends with those girls."

Allister snorted. "With who? You know Gianna because she's your cousin. You know Luna through Valerio, and the other two don't talk to you."

"I'm fun," Dante said. He shrugged. "They like fun."

A murderous feeling stirred inside of Valerio. What kind of fun could he possibly be talking about?

"She would never let you near her," Valerio told him. "She has standards."

"Clearly. That's why she doesn't want you," Dante muttered.

Valerio's gun was pulled out in a second, aimed perfectly at the space between Dante's eyebrows. One shot, and it would be done.

"He's being a dumbass, Valerio," Allister said, walking over to the desk and pushing the gun down so it was angled at the floor instead. "You can't kill your own brother."

"Talk about initiation night before I reconsider," Valerio told him. He set the gun back on his desk, leaning back in his chair once again. If there was one person other than Luna that knew how to drive him fucking nuts, it was his brother.

"Well, I don't know about you guys, but I'm in the mood to chase some newbies." Dante had a smirk that only led to reckless actions, ones that Valerio usually cleaned up.

"I have to say I agree," Allister said. He took a seat on one of the chairs that sat in front of Valerio's desk.

The Chase was fun. Members who wanted to be recruited into the Vitali family always started their loyalty to the heir while in their younger years, usually when they were just beginning to get into their careers. It secured their connections to the family.

The rules were quite simple. The Chase required that everyone wear a flag that was strapped around their waist. The whole point was to see who naturally fell into the predator and prey roles, meaning the people who collected the most flags joined the group. It was a free for all, every person for themselves. Natural pacts were created, but most of the time everyone kept to themselves and ran for their lives. If they made it to the edge of the forest where a post was set up with a bell attached to it, they were safe. Didn't mean they got in though. Anyone who couldn't fight for the flags wasn't worth keeping. That meant the actual event always ended up bloodier and more violent than anyone intended.

If there was something a person wanted enough, there wasn't a single thing they wouldn't do to get it.

Valerio knew that all too well.

He enjoyed taking part in The Chase himself—running wild in the forest and forgetting who he was for a moment so he could resort to his natural instincts. There was something about the way his heart would beat, the adrenaline built up in his body; it was all addicting. The last time he had been a part of The Chase was when he was seventeen, right before he was sent to Italy.

This time Valerio would be a part of it.

"The Chase is always on Saturday night, so what's happening on Friday?" he asked.

"We started throwing our party on Friday since that's when

Fight Night happens," Dante told him. "It got boring sitting at home."

"You're not canceling that party, right?" Allister asked. "A lot of people look forward to it."

"Go ahead, plan the party. I have a special guest I'm inviting to The Chase," Valerio said. He walked out of the room, not bothering to wait for their replies.

"Does that mean you'll be in attendance at all of the events?" Dante called out from the study.

Valerio smirked. He would be. He would make sure he spent adequate time with his fiancée, showing her exactly what type of man he really was.

FOUR

LUNA

"THIS HAS BEEN the longest week of my life. Did I tell you guys I already have an exam to start studying for? An exam. It's the first week," Cecilia cried out, frowning at her ice cream.

Luna patted her on the back. "You'll get through it. Probably."

They had officially reached the end of the week. One whole week. God, Luna didn't know how she had done this for the past three years, but she was completely and utterly exhausted. All week she had been taking different routes to class to avoid running into the devil.

The sweets shop they had decided to visit was new to campus, packed to the rim, and wonderfully delicious. There was a variation of cookies, brownies, frozen yogurt, ice cream, milkshakes. It was overwhelming.

"I have a paper due in a few weeks that I need to start," Blair said. "I'll probably start it this weekend. Hell, I'll probably be busy working on it the next couple of weekends."

"What the hell? When did we get so boring?" Gianna asked, her eyes wide.

Luna took a spoonful of her cake batter frozen yogurt. "I've always been boring."

"Ugh, cover your mouth," Cecilia said, feigning gagging.

"We're in college. We have to do our work to graduate," Blair told Gianna. "Well, the ones of us who actually want to do something with our lives."

Gianna glared at her. "I'm going to ignore that dig at me, and instead bring up how initiation weekend is in a few weeks and there's a shit ton of parties happening every weekend until then."

"No way," Luna said, shaking her head. "First of all, I'm never going to a party you recommend again. Second, I'm not going to initiation weekend events. One event is hosted by my brother, the other by the devil. There are no events for me to attend and enjoy."

"I'm sure Valerio would make you feel good at The Chase." Cecilia grinned, pushing her brows up and down.

Luna smacked her shoulder. "What the hell are you talking about? Isn't The Chase some barbaric, violent thing with weirdos playing tag in the forest together?"

"I thought you were into that," Gianna said with a smirk.

She reached over the booth to smack her this time. "I told you that in confidence."

"Well, this is news to me," Blair said, raising her brows in shock. "Little Luna, do you want to be chased and manhandled?"

"I'm done talking about this," Luna said. She could feel the heat on her cheeks at their comments, desperately trying to ignore what they said.

So what if she fantasized about something as primal as that? It wasn't wrong to think about her being taken desperately and roughly. And it wouldn't happen anyway; it was just something she read in a book and maybe searched to watch on her computer when she had some alone time. God, leave it to them to make her feel flustered about it.

"Any run-ins with your future fiancé this week?" Cecilia asked, changing the subject.

Luna rolled her eyes. "No, thank God. Like I've said, I can go without seeing him."

"Marrying him couldn't be that bad," Gianna said, shrugging. "I mean, he's related to me, so he has some redeeming qualities."

"Not enough to let me enjoy a lifetime being married to him," Luna said, shaking her head. She shoved another spoonful of cake batter frozen yogurt into her mouth.

"Well, think about it like this. There had to be something you liked about him in the first place to have a crush on him," Blair said. "I don't know, maybe you can find that thing in him again?"

"Why do you guys want me to like him so much?" she asked.

"Because you're stuck with him," Cecilia said.

Luna rolled her eyes. "I thought he was hot and mysterious, not to mention he was my family's enemy. I was like fifteen at the time. Of course I was into him because of it."

"Into who?" a deep voice asked from beside them, making all the girls turn their heads to the two intruders who now stood in front of the booth.

"Oh, it's you again," Luna muttered.

Valerio grinned. "Miss me?"

"In your dreams," she growled.

"That's where I see you," he said, leaning against the table. Dante stood behind him, looking at the menu behind the counter as if he was going to order something. "Now, who were you talking about?"

"Wouldn't you like to know," Luna said sarcastically.

"I've never seen people flirt like this," Gianna said. "It's interesting."

Luna kicked her under the table. There was no flirting. No, there wouldn't be anything with the devil in front of her because she couldn't stand him.

"We were just talking about some guy Luna used to have a crush on," Cecilia said. Luna sent her a glare, one she conveniently ignored.

"Doesn't matter now because that boy is dead to me," she said, taking a bite of her frozen yogurt. It didn't taste as good now that the energy had been sucked out of the room by Valerio.

"So you were talking about me," he said, leaning closer to Luna. "I'm flattered you think about me, fiancée."

"Where is my copy of the contract?" Luna asked, ignoring his words and how her body stood up in goosebumps because of them.

"At my house," he said. "You'll have to come over to get it."

"You can mail it to me."

"It's top secret. Safer being viewed in person."

"What flavor is that?" Dante asked, pointing at Luna's frozen yogurt.

"Cake batter," she said.

"Ugh, I hate that one."

She looked at him dumbfounded, turning back to Valerio. "I'm not going to your house."

"My house is the only place you'll find the contract," he told her.

She clenched her jaw. "I'll get my hands on it one way or another."

"I hope you do," Valerio told her. "Maybe seeing it in person will help you come to terms with our arrangement quicker." He grabbed the spoon from her hand, tracing his fingers on hers. He took the scoop that was meant for her into his mouth, clearing off the frozen yogurt in a way that made her skin tingle. She hated how her mouth became dry watching it.

He stood at his complete height that towered over Luna's sitting figure. She looked up at him, taking in his natural frown, his furrowed eyebrows. She hated the way her eyes traced his plump lips, the way they drifted down his body, stopping in front of his crotch, eye level to her. "Oh, I hope you'll accept my invitation to The Chase in a few weeks. I would love to have you there."

With that he walked out, leaving Dante—who now had an ice cream cone in his hand—to follow after him. Luna could feel the heat on her skin, and she didn't know if it was from anger or something unusual and strange she didn't want to bring attention to.

Luna turned to Blair. "How good are you at getting what you want?"

"Excellent. Why?" she asked.

"I need to see the contract. There has to be some kind of loophole or something," Luna said. No matter what it was, she would find it. She couldn't stay with him, and she wouldn't.

Until then, she had to do whatever she could to get him to break the contract first.

"When's the next party?" she asked Gianna.

Gianna grinned. "I'll find out. Why?"

Luna got up, smoothing out her clothes. "Because I'm going to find a handsome stranger and make out with them."

She grabbed her cup of frozen yogurt, tossing it in the trash and walking out of the sweets shop.

Would Valerio still want her if she was with someone else? She wasn't sure, but dammit if she wasn't going to try to make him hate her.

FIVE

LUNA

WITH HOW BUSY Luna had been, she wouldn't have even known a whole week had passed if Valerio didn't insist on sending flowers to her apartment every day like clockwork. The kitchen counters, the dining table, and the floors—save for a little walkway—were covered in roses, peonies, and other flowers Luna couldn't identify and didn't care to. The entire apartment smelled like a greenhouse. It was overwhelming.

"This has to stop," Cecilia muttered, kicking dead petals out of her path. "Talk to him."

Luna scoffed. She picked up a few of the vases, setting them on the floor to clear up counter space. "Absolutely not. Not until I get that contract."

She had been actively avoiding his calls and texts all week as well. And without the contract in her hands, she would continue to do so.

"Jeez, does it ever stop?" Gianna asked, walking through the front door. One of the vases fell to the floor, water spilling. She ignored it, walking farther into the apartment. Blair followed in after her, moving to open a window immediately.

"Tell him to stop," Luna told Gianna. "He's your cousin."

"You think he'll listen to me?" she asked with a raised brow. "That man doesn't know how to listen to people."

"Luna, I think this is something you'll have to solve on your own," Cecilia told her.

"Actually, I might have gotten something that will help you," Blair said. She reached into her bag, pulling out a crumpled piece of paper.

"What is that?" Luna asked. Her eyes were wide. For a second she thought it could have been the contract, but no way it was a single piece of paper crumpled up beyond repair.

"It's one page of the contract because I couldn't get access to all of them, but it's an important one," Blair said, handing it over to her.

Luna took it, skimming over every word.

"How exactly did you get a copy of that?" Gianna asked, crossing her arms.

"Allister left his laptop open in class when he went to the bathroom," Blair said. "I just happened to stumble across it when I was walking to my seat."

"And you just got it? That easily?" Cecilia asked. Her tone held apprehension.

"I feel like they wanted you to find it," Gianna said. "How the hell would you have found the file that quick and managed to send it to yourself all while he's peeing? Boys use the bathroom in like a minute."

"That's gross," Luna muttered, still reading.

"Why would they want me to find it?" Blair asked.

Luna threw down the paper. "Because they want me to see that the only way out of the marriage is death."

"Simple, just kill him," Cecilia said, shrugging. "If you hate him that bad then it shouldn't be that hard."

Luna shook her head. "I can't kill him. I want to, but I can't."

"Because a small part of you feels something for him?" Gianna asked.

"No. Absolutely not. I'll kill him just to prove a point," Luna threatened.

Blair took a seat on the barstool with a disturbed look. "I can't believe I got played by Allister of all people."

"We all got played," Luna muttered, patting her shoulder for comfort. "If I can't kill him though, I need him to hate me."

Maybe there was a way that she could pull on his hatred for the Kingsleys. If he hated her father and brother, then maybe he could hate her with the same scope. She just had to do something that would send him off.

"Let's be honest, I don't think Valerio could ever hate you. But if you make his father hate you, then maybe he can break the contract," Gianna said.

"How could I make Cesare Vitali hate me?" Luna asked, frowning.

"I don't know. Do something crazy? Destroy his things, become a burden, hook up with other guys? Become someone Cesare Vitali would never want his son with," Gianna said.

"That sounds ridiculous," Blair said with a scoff.

Cecilia cut in. "No, think about it. Think about your mom, Valerio's mom—they both had clean reputations; they were essentially the perfect wives. Now, look at how you were raised. You were practically groomed for the position. You've never been in trouble at school or received a bad grade, you've never been on a date before in your life, you've never even had serious conflicts with people because you always resolve things right away. I mean, hell, you even stopped fighting your father when you should have been giving him hell for what he's making you do. Anything you do outside of that would tarnish your reputation."

Luna looked at Cecilia in complete astonishment. Everything she said was exactly on the nose and it hurt way more than it should have. From the moment she was born, she was shaped into someone who could bend to someone else's whim. It worked in her father's favor when Luna went down without much fight, then he could gain connections and business deals.

She couldn't understand how Valerio was the exception. With him, it felt like she didn't need to hold on to that version of herself that Cecilia described. She fought against him continuously, and of course it made her consider if her anger was misplaced. The harsh truth was that neither one of them was innocent.

But where Valerio had never raised a hand to her, her father did. Things like that made fighting painful, figuratively and literally.

So if her father wasn't willing to let her out of the contract, and Valerio promised to never let her go, tarnishing her reputation and hoping it got back to her potential future father-in-law might be her only hope.

"What do you recommend I do?" Luna asked.

Blair groaned. "This is going to end in disaster."

Gianna squealed, probably excited that she would get to see Luna live out her wild side for once. "Well, initiation weekend is coming up, but I remember some losers saying they weren't going."

"You know The Chase is happening this weekend," Luna said. "I don't want to be anywhere around *him*."

"Then we can go to parties that are affiliated only with the Kingsleys," she said. "But otherwise, I fear I see a white dress in your future."

Luna felt her internal panic set in. What choice did she really have at that point?

"Fine, we can go," she said, giving in.

As soon as she saw the sinister smile on Gianna's face, she almost wished she hadn't. God save her.

SIX

LUNA

SOMEHOW GIANNA and Cecilia had managed to find a party that filled every single one of Luna's requirements. The most important being no sign of Valerio anywhere. That was hard to do considering he was everywhere, but according to Gianna, he had too high of standards to go anywhere near a dingy, gross frat.

Still, Luna couldn't stop herself from cringing at every sweaty body that passed by her. She couldn't tell if it was because they were actually gross or if she was grossed out at herself for being willing to kiss anyone here. There were red Solo cups everywhere, the floor was sticky, and people were already drunk out of their minds.

"Was there seriously no other party we could have gone to?" Luna asked Cecilia.

She attempted to hold down the bottom of the dress that kept rising dangerously whenever she walked. It was shorter than she would have preferred, but as the girls pointed out, there was a mission tonight. Luna couldn't show up in just anything, so instead she showed up in a strappy, sparkly lavender dress. The sweetheart neckline showed off her cleavage, and the dress managed to make her legs look longer than they were.

"You specifically said no party with any affiliation to the Vitalis," Cecilia said. "I did the best I could without asking the devil."

"Augustus will probably end up showing up anyway," Luna pointed out.

Cecilia turned around with a glare. "Then you better hold me back so I don't end up locked up."

Gianna led them to the kitchen where the alcohol lined up the counters. She made them their drinks, opening a new bottle and not trusting anyone else to touch it for them.

Luna took a sip of the drink, nearly spitting it out. "Geez, did you pour the whole bottle in here?"

"Enough for liquid courage." Gianna winked, drinking from her own cup. She tapped Luna's cup for encouragement. "Come on, you have to be a menace tonight."

"How am I even supposed to do this? I just go up to them and ask? And then what?" Luna asked. "I don't know how to kiss."

"Oh shit, I forgot you haven't been with anyone."

Luna rolled her eyes. Her lack of experience had never made her feel as terrible as she did at that moment.

"Making out is easy," Cecilia told her. She wrapped an arm around Luna. "Especially when they're drunk. Watch out for the tongue though."

Luna could only imagine what that meant.

"This is the worst crowd I've seen. At least try to pick someone with a little bit of class. Preferably someone who doesn't have throw-up on their clothes." Blair grimaced, moving out of the way when someone covered in it walked past them.

"You don't come to parties to meet the love of your life. You come to find the hottest guy here and make him bow down to you," Gianna said. She placed a hand on Luna's shoulder. "I'll help you find someone."

"How are we so sure anyone will even approach me?" Luna asked nervously. "If they know who I am, then they know my baggage. And how will Valerio even know I kissed someone?"

"God, you ask so many questions. Everything will be fine. In case he doesn't find out, which I'm sure he'll hear from someone anyway, I'll take a picture," Gianna told her.

"And you'll what? Send it to him?" Blair asked, dumbfounded.

"You can send it to Finn. He'll probably send that shit out so quick," Cecilia suggested.

"You're involving my brother in this now too?" Luna asked, her brows furrowed in concern. Now, she was starting to feel queasy.

There was no way the plan was going to end up working in their favor.

"I'm not going to send it to him, just don't worry about anything. Focus on making out and having a good time with someone tonight," Gianna assured her. "We can handle everything else. Remember, it's this or marriage."

"Are you sure Valerio and Allister won't kill you for being a part of this?" Luna asked.

"He has his loyalties, I have mine. Now drink up. It'll make everyone hot."

Luna took a deep breath, praying everything worked out. Then she took her cup and downed as much of it as she could. Her gag was unattractive, but she managed to get the liquid down.

Everything that happened after that moment was a blur to Luna. She was thoroughly drunk after two cups of whatever Gianna poured and lost herself on the dance floor. Her little mission was completely abandoned at that point while she danced with Cecilia. She only remembered it again when unfamiliar hands wrapped around her body, pulling her into a mildly firm chest.

Luna grinned, turning around to see who it was. Her smile faltered slightly when she realized it was a stranger. He was cute— light brown hair and brown eyes. A couple inches taller than Luna, his body lean. He would have been fine for any girl there, but for some reason, she felt nothing. Not a single butterfly in her stomach, not a single wink of attraction, nothing. She couldn't understand her disappointment or why she felt the need to compare this boy's light, subtle features to a certain devil that looked the complete opposite.

She also didn't recognize him at all. "Do you go here?" she asked, wrapping her arms around his shoulders.

He shook his head. "No, I'm just here for initiation weekend."

She nodded. Good enough. That probably meant he didn't know who she was either or what baggage she carried with her.

Luna continued dancing with him, desperately trying to have fun with his hands on her body. It didn't feel right and she finally figured out why.

He was boring. He was normal. He wasn't—

She stopped herself. No way. She was drunk out of her mind and her brain was trailing into dangerous territory, all of which was false and dumb.

The boy didn't need to have any substance or be any better *or worse* than the devil; he just needed to kiss her. The thought almost made her feel guilty. She felt worse about betraying her psychopathic fiancé than she did using this boy.

But what did it matter? She saved herself for marriage while Valerio probably slutted it up with any and every girl in Italy. How the hell was that fair?

Maybe because she wanted Valerio to be here kissing her?

Her eyes widened. God, she needed to get him out of her head.

"What's wrong?" the cute boy asked.

She shook her head. "Nothing."

"Do you want another drink?"

"No, let's just keep dancing."

Maybe then she could muster up the courage to push her lips onto his. It was just a kiss. Just mouth on mouth. Nothing more.

Sure, it was her first kiss and she would remember that

moment for the rest of her life, but the alternative was to have her first kiss with Valerio at their wedding.

With that thought, she found herself leaning in, spotting Gianna from the corner of her eye. The blonde was shaking her head frantically. She was there to take the picture. One kiss and it would all be done.

Two shots rang out through the room, the boy in front of her screaming out in pain. Luna moved away from him as he fell to the floor, blood pooling on the ground from the back of his knees.

Luna raised her head in shock, locking her eyes on Valerio who seemed to have appeared out of nowhere. Goosebumps rose on her skin, an icy feeling enveloping her completely.

Valerio stalked up to her. He stepped over the boy on the floor, stopping until his chest touched Luna's. He towered over her, his power menacing.

She hated the murderous and lethal look on his face. Finally, she understood all the rumors about his violent nature. Gone was the bantering Valerio. He was hunting, looking for his perfect prey.

"Let's go," he said. His voice was eerily calm, but it did nothing to soothe the terror she felt.

"No," she protested. Not a single thing in the world could get her to leave with him.

She looked behind him, trying to see if the boy was still there, but he had been dragged off somewhere.

His lips turned up in a sneer. "Who are you looking for? Care to have me finish him off?"

Luna shook her head, her mind dizzy. "No. He disappeared so quickly."

"Let's go now. You don't get a fucking choice," he told her. His face was a mere couple of inches away. Her eyes betrayed her, trailing down his nose and leading her straight to his plump pink lips. They looked a lot better than the other boys'.

Her eyes narrowed. "You love that, huh. Taking all of my choices from me."

"And if I do, what then?" he asked viciously. "It doesn't change the fact you're *my fiancée.* So when I say let's fucking go, you better start walking."

"No," she said, standing her ground again. She crossed her arms, swaying slightly.

That was the wrong answer because in the next moment she was thrown over his shoulder, seeing the world upside down. She gasped, worrying about her dress riding up. He grabbed it and held it down. She resented the wetness that leaked from her pussy from his hand being that close to her.

He carried her out of the party, stopping in front of his obnoxiously nice car. He finally set her down, but trapped her between the open passenger side door and the inside of the car, leaving no other place to go. She stood with her arms crossed.

He rolled his eyes. "Get in the fucking car."

"I'm not obligated to go anywhere with you. It's not in the contract," Luna said. Sure, she was being a brat, but he deserved it. For as long as they both lived, she was going to make sure she never made anything easy on him.

"Don't give me a list of things to add to it," he hissed. "Now, get in the car before I take you back in the party and fuck you in front of everyone to make sure no one ever fucking touches you again."

She frowned, finally sliding into the car in an attempt to ignore his barbaric language. She didn't doubt he would attempt to actually do it, and she didn't doubt she might like it. The leather was cool on her skin, a relief to her heated skin.

Valerio walked to the other side of the car, getting into the driver's seat and slamming the door shut behind him. Without so much as a warning, he started the car and drove away from the party.

Luna crossed her arms, ignoring his presence completely. All she could do was brace herself for her impending doom.

They had to have been driving for fifteen minutes when she realized the lights from the city were gone, leaving them in complete darkness except for the headlights.

"Where are we going?" she finally asked. Her voice was panicked. All she could think about were worst-case scenarios for why Valerio would be taking her into the woods and none of them ended with her leaving alive.

She was completely sober now.

He didn't answer her. Instead, he tightened his hands around the wheel, turning his knuckles white. Luna wanted to blurt out some sarcastic reply, but she thought it might be best to keep quiet for the moment.

If she was smart, she might have started to beg for forgiveness the way she had been taught to. Beg him to forget about what happened, for him to consider her perfect reputation and still want to marry her. But she didn't and she wasn't going to.

Eventually, he pulled in front of a small cabin. It took too many turns to get there and was too far from any main road. If she made a run for it, she would get lost in the woods. At this point, that might have been her best chance at survival.

Valerio turned off the car, submerging them into darkness. "Get out," he said, opening his door and stepping out. He walked around the front of the car to get to the passenger side. She made no effort to move. She wasn't planning on leaving the comfort of the car.

He opened her door, waiting for her to get out.

"Either you do it yourself or I'll carry you out again," Valerio said, his patience clearly wearing thin.

"Are you going to kill me?" she asked in a quiet voice.

"Don't tempt me."

Luna took a deep breath, undoing the seat belt and getting out of the car. The cool air bit at her skin. Valerio closed the car door, and together they walked to the front door. He pulled out a key to unlock it before throwing it open.

She looked at him, trying to plead some reason to him, but his emotionless face remained. With cautious steps she entered the cabin, greeted with the scent of fresh wood surrounding her. Luna couldn't see anything around them, except what little light from the moon slipped in from the window, showing there was a small couch.

His heavy footsteps walked past her, arranging something she couldn't see. A match swiped against the striking surface of the box before the small flame was thrown into a fireplace that lit the living room up. Only in the warm light could Luna make out a small kitchen behind the couch that only had a small stove, oven, fridge, and a tiny counter. The fireplace was made from red bricks, stretching the entire way up the wall while the rest of the walls were covered with wood panels.

There was a small hallway that ran between the kitchen and two doors that were closed. The space was small and modest compared to what she normally associated with Valerio.

"What is this?" Luna asked.

"A cabin," he answered, standing. He turned to look at her now.

She bit back the urge to roll her eyes. "It's fitting that someone like you would have a cabin in the woods. Is this where you're going to kill me?"

"I don't kill people here," he said. "I do that at the warehouse."

She gave him a disgusted look. "That's not funny."

"Who said I was joking?"

A sharp chill ran down her back, the unease in her gut intensifying. "I want to go home."

"Do you? It seems like leaving you by yourself is only causing problems."

"I told you I don't want to be a part of this contract." She took a step back, trying to cover the fact a part of her feared him. He noticed it; of course he did. He moved forward a step.

"And I told you that I don't care."

Her same frustration returned. "You don't even know me."

"Oh, I know you," he said, taking another step forward.

"No, you don't. You were gone for seven years."

"Did you miss me?"

Luna caught her mistake. "I didn't say that."

"Are you upset that I was gone for those seven years? I did it for you, you know. To give you a chance to come to terms with this."

She threw her hands up. "Is that how you think this works? That I would just wake up one day ready to give up my life? That I would call you home, ready for marriage? Is that why you came back now? Huh? Got too impatient waiting for me to come to terms with something I never wanted?"

The words left her mouth like venom. She couldn't stop herself from trying to push him back, but his hand caught her arm, interweaving his hand with hers.

"I missed you," he said. "You know I did. That's why I'm here."

"You'll live," she told him. "But I won't if you force me into this marriage."

"I'm not the only one who wants this contract," he told her. "You're forgetting about my father and yours."

She sighed. "You can talk to them. Do something. If you cared about me, you would."

"No."

Luna's face hardened. She snatched her hand away from him. "Then I don't know how much more clearly I can tell you that I will never love you."

Pain ripped through his face. He covered it up in the blink of an eye. "Never say never."

She shook her head. "I can promise you I will never fall in love with you. No amount of contracts or rules you force against me will ever work. It would all be for the contract. All fake for the rest of your life."

"Do you remember what was happening that night all those years ago?" Valerio hissed. "I did this to save you. You asked me to do this for you."

"What are you talking about?" Luna asked, confused

"Think back to the night of the gala," Valerio told her.

She forced her mind to return to that night, the one where she realized her life was over. It was a night she desperately tried to forget, but it was forever etched into her memory. A defining moment in her life that made her realize that there wasn't a single decent man to be found out in the world. "I didn't ask you to marry me. I told you I didn't want to be married at all. I wanted out of any contract my father was going to put me in."

She was sixteen, vulnerable, drunk, and beyond miserable. He used her moment of weakness to swoop in like a falcon.

"Do you know who your father was thinking of marrying you off to? Some fucking freak of a business partner older than himself," he pointed out. "You would have been walking down the aisle at eighteen, probably on your second or third child at this point."

Luna swallowed harshly. "My father wouldn't do that to me."

"You know he would because he almost did."

She knew he was right. She wanted to believe her father was above doing something like that to her, but she wasn't actually naive enough to think that was the reality.

"Is that what you want? A thank you?"

"I don't want anything from you but a chance."

"That boat sailed a long time ago."

"Did it?" His permanent smirk came back. "There used to be rumors, you know. About your little crush on me. I remember catching your longing gazes at events and in passing."

Her cheeks heated. She hated the dark look in his eyes, and hated the tingling in her stomach even more. Here she thought she had been completely lowkey about everything the whole time, only to have given him ammunition. "They call it a schoolgirl crush for a reason. I grew up and found out who you really were."

"I think you're lying."

"I don't care," she bit back.

Valerio shook his head. "I watched you too, you know; it was when you turned away, a blush on your cheeks, that I took my time to study you. For years I observed and memorized the way your eyes narrow when you're mad, or how when you're surprised your mouth drops open, or how when you're nervous you chew on the inside of your lip. You've been mine since the moment I laid my eyes on you, but I can play along. If you need to pretend you don't care about me anymore so you can prove a point, then go ahead. But I won't pretend. You're mine, Luna. With this engagement intact or not."

Luna's lip wavered. She sucked in a deep breath, trying to calm the rapid beating of her heart. "There's still one way to get rid of it."

His lips turned up into a wicked smile. He leaned in closer, forcing their faces within inches of each other. The warmth of his hand covered hers until it was replaced with something cold and made of metal. Luna's eyes widened; he'd placed a gun in her hand.

What the hell was wrong with him?

"I know you read the contract. You want to kill me? Do it. I'll offer you the bullet, the gun. Hell, I'll stand completely still, right in front of you so you don't miss. Kill me if you can," he told her, his rough voice kissing every inch of her exposed skin.

If she could just lift the gun in her hand and aim it at him, she could end this and be free.

But she couldn't.

Of course she couldn't. She didn't believe in harming others just to get what she wanted.

He knew it. She knew it.

She pushed the gun back into his hand. "Fuck you," she hissed, turning around and walking out the front door. She marched over to the car, slamming the car door closed once she was in.

Her skin burned, making her squirm in her seat. She hated how he got under her skin, how she fell for it. Suddenly, he knew her better than she even knew herself. How the hell did that happen?

And why did she like it?

SEVEN

VALERIO

VALERIO BEGRUDGINGLY DROPPED Luna off at her apartment. If she was trying to act more stubborn than usual, then she was succeeding. She refused to talk or even look at him, slamming the car door when he wished her a good night.

She drove him over the fucking edge, and yet, he couldn't get her out of his mind for even a second. It was like he was wired while around her, and then as soon as she was gone, he just crumbled into himself. Not healthy, but that was his life now.

The exhaustion hit him as soon as he walked into the house. He didn't think his night would include crashing a party and nearly killing some boy his fiancée was trying to kiss, but that was his life now. He should have shoved a bullet through that boy's head for even touching Luna in the first place. Valerio shook his head. He needed to talk himself out of killing, not pushing himself to do it.

"Finally, you're home," Dante called out from the living room just as Valerio was closing the front door.

"Why are you still awake?" he asked with furrowed brows.

"Wasn't sure what your plan was tonight," Allister admitted, sitting up on the couch. He rubbed his eyes. "If you were coming back to finish the job."

"Where is that boy now?" Valerio asked. He slumped down onto the couch beside Dante, letting his body sink into the soft cushion.

"Dropped him off at the hospital," Dante said. "You're paying for the detailing on my car by the way."

"Get over it. The asshole had it coming for touching Luna like that," Valerio muttered. "I should have just finished the job."

"You've been back on campus for a couple weeks. Give it a little longer until the university is forced to kick you out." Allister shook his head.

"I'd like to see them try." Valerio snorted.

"How was your night with the Mrs.?" Dante asked. "Hopefully it wasn't all screaming and crying."

Valerio let out a deep breath. "Gave her a gun to shoot me."

"And she didn't? Wow, that is progress." Dante shook his head. "I see a hopeful future for the two of you."

Valerio grabbed the small couch pillow, throwing it against Dante's chest with a thud. He loved his brother, but he always talked too much at the worst times.

"Why are you torturing yourself with all of this?" Allister asked. "You could have anyone, anything."

They were right, of course. He could have anyone. But there was only one person he wanted. Luna had always been his, just like he had always been hers. Valerio didn't understand how it worked or what fucking laws of the universe made their paths cross, but they were destined for each other, no matter how cruel it seemed now.

"She's mine," Valerio told him, shutting him up in a moment. And because of that, he would go through this hell a million times over again if it meant one day she would fall in love with him the way she was before. Valerio leaned back on the couch. "Just talk to me about what is going on for initiation weekend."

"Glad you asked. While you've been out and about, frolicking with your future wife, I decided I could use a good fight," Dante said. He took out a cigarette, lighting it as if it was muscle memory.

Valerio watched him in confusion. "Since when do you want a fight?"

"Since I feel like causing some chaos," Dante told him. "I think the Kingsleys can use it."

"Not to be the voice of reason around here, but I think it might be a good idea if you didn't choose chaos for once. Your brother is marrying a Kingsley. Maybe you could try to build better bonds with them," Allister said to Dante.

"But Augustus isn't a Kingsley," Dante pointed out.

Valerio thought about it for a second. Every initiation weekend had two events: the Chase for the Vitalis and Fight Night for the Kingsleys. Valerio knew that Luna had attended every single Fight Night for the past three years, going to support her brother. But maybe there was a way he could join the Fight Night himself, make a little wager with his future wife.

"We're crashing it," Valerio told them. "Tomorrow night."

"What the hell do you mean we're crashing it?" Allister asked. "Are you forgetting that the contract is supposed to bring peace to the two families? How the hell is this peaceful? I swear to God, I feel like I'm losing my mind around you two."

Valerio smirked. "I never said I wasn't keeping the peace."

"So I get to beat the shit out of Augustus?" Dante asked.

"Do what you want. Finn is mine though. I need Luna to bet against me," Valerio told them. He stood from the couch, letting his body stretch. In the morning, he would have to train, but for tonight, he would pray he could get a couple hours of sleep. "I'm going to sleep. See you both in the morning."

They waved him away, getting up to go into their own rooms for the night.

He took the stairs up to his room, the silence overbearing. He had become used to it, but there had always been a part of him that wished for that silence to be filled. Valerio ripped his shirt off, throwing it into the closet. His mind immediately went back to

Luna, but it wasn't like he had stopped thinking about her anyway. His mind had her on repeat, thinking of the next moment he would get to see her again.

It didn't help that she looked absolutely fucking perfect tonight, but she hadn't dressed up for him. She was dressed for someone else and was willing to give herself to someone fucking random. It wasn't going to happen. Not when Gianna had let it slip to Allister that they were going to the party in the first place. Of course Valerio had followed them, and of course he had kept an eye out on Luna all night.

And of course as soon as he saw some little boy put his hands on her, Valerio pounced. He would have gotten to the scene sooner had Dante and Allister not held him back, but once he got free of their hold, the damage was done.

If she tried it again, he would do the same thing. He didn't care how many bodies he left in his wake. Until Luna understood she was his, he would have to do whatever was necessary.

He was a patient man. Maybe that was a semi-redeemable quality of his. His ability to sit and wait, to weigh out his options for the perfect time to strike. It made him an excellent business-man, the perfect hit man, and he thought it also made him a better choice for a husband.

He gave her seven years when most wouldn't have given her a single second to wrap her brain around it. He saved himself for her. He waited and waited until he couldn't wait anymore.

Until he got too antsy just looking at photos of her. Until he started daydreaming about her during all hours of the day and night. Until the fear of losing her became suffocating.

She was an obsession, a drug he couldn't stop taking now that he had gotten a hit. Nothing and no one would compare to her. No way in hell.

Valerio took off the rest of his clothes, turning on the shower. He let it heat up before sinking under the stream of water, finally feeling his muscles relaxing.

He thought about her frown, the anger in her eyes, the sweet

"Fuck you" she hissed at him. His hand was already reaching down, wrapping around his hard cock. He leaned against the shower wall, letting his mind wander, but of course it led him back to her. Luna fucking Kingsley. All it took was imagining it was Luna's hand on him that sent spurts of cum onto the tile shower wall.

He turned the shower handle to the cold side, desperately cooling his body.

It seemed his patience was officially gone.

EIGHT

LUNA

SOFT KISSES DRIFTED from her neck to her collarbone, taking their time to taste her skin. Luna's eyes fluttered closed, the sensation feeling like heaven. He stroked along her body slowly, tracing down between her breasts before grabbing the right one. His mouth met her left breast, sucking and biting the skin, forcing her to wither in pain and pleasure.

It didn't take him long to make his way between her thighs. He placed kisses along her inner thigh before taking one single taste of her pussy with the swipe of his tongue. Luna moaned, throwing her head back and arching her spine. Instinctively, her thighs closed around his head, keeping his head in place as his tongue continued flicking against her clit, sucking and making a mess of her.

God, she would do anything to make the feeling never end, but her orgasm was crashing into her the minute a finger slipped inside. With one more kiss on her lower abdomen, he was moving so he was hovering over her.

"Look at how ready you are for me." Valerio smirked, stealing a kiss from her lips.

"Stop teasing," Luna begged.

"I like having you like this for me—wet, moaning, a mess," he said, entering her swiftly. A gasp escaped Luna, the fullness completing her. "Look how perfectly you fit with me." His rhythm was brutal, hitting every part of her that yearned for him.

He was right, and she wanted to hate him for it.

The thrusts continued, pushing her to another orgasm she wasn't sure she could handle. Valerio reached down between them, running his thumb over her clit. "Come for me, baby."

Luna gasped awake. Her body tingled, covered in a hot sweat. She looked around her room, checking where she was. God, it felt so real. The way he touched her, the way she moaned for him. She swore she could feel the phantom touches lingering on her skin as a reminder.

She was soaking wet. A reminder of how good the dream felt. Her mind drifted back, replaying every moment of it.

Why Valerio? Why was it that she couldn't escape him in her daily life and now she couldn't escape him in the safety of her dreams?

She hated him, for God's sake. She couldn't be having dreams about him where she rode his cock like there was no tomorrow.

Sure, she found him attractive. Of course she did; she was just a girl, after all. And sure, maybe the crush she had on him before had snuck its way into her mind and made her think about him more often than not. But it didn't matter and it wouldn't because she would not fall for the one man who was attempting to destroy her life.

Valerio Vitali was bad news.

He shot a boy in the legs over her. He was wild, possessive, obsessive.

But the dream felt so *good*.

Luna groaned, throwing a pillow over her head. Why couldn't he have been disgusting? Or better yet, why did he have to stumble outside all those years ago when she was in the midst of a breakdown, trying to play the savior?

He wasn't her hero.

He didn't have any good intentions.

But would marriage to him really be that bad?

She sat up in bed, her eyes wide in shock. How could she even think that? God, she needed to get it together. The dream was over. It was fake—just her subconscious being a bitch.

The sun was barely rising over the horizon, but Luna knew she couldn't go back to sleep. She had a feeling her mind would try to return to the dream, and she couldn't handle that again. This time, she might not wake up from it.

She got up to get ready for the day. She didn't have class since it was Friday, but it was also initiation weekend and if she knew anything about her best friends, she knew the weekend would be packed with parties. Her best bet was to get some homework done while everyone was still sleeping.

Tonight, she was attending Fight Night to support Finn, who kicked ass every year. It was bloody and gruesome, but over the years she got numb to the violence and attempted to enjoy it.

Tomorrow night was The Chase, and in honor of not getting caught up in it, she would be locking herself in her apartment. There was no doubt in her mind that if she was out and about, the devil himself would snatch her up and force her to run for her life, or whatever the hell they did during it. She never attended and she wouldn't start now.

She threw on a pair of sweats and a gray T-shirt that said 'Grand Willow' on it. She grabbed her backpack, deciding to go to a cafe to get some work done. She slid on a pair of sneakers and left the apartment, closing the door carefully behind her.

The air was crisp and fresh; the grass and windows covered in a fresh layer of morning dew. Everyone seemed to still be sleeping, probably trying to conserve their energy for the parties later tonight, leaving campus unusually quiet.

Her walk was peaceful until she noticed a black sports car following suspiciously close behind her. She took small glances over her shoulder, frowning when she realized it was trailing her. When she walked, the car moved. When she stopped, the car stopped. She had pepper spray in her bag that she could reach for, but hopefully no one was dumb enough to really kidnap Reece Kingsley's daughter.

Her breathing turned ragged once the car pulled up right beside her.

"What's up, sis-in-law?" the voice called out from the car, the window now rolled down.

Luna's face scrunched up in confusion. Only one person was obnoxious enough to call her something like that. She rolled her eyes, looking at the two men who associated themselves with her alleged fiancé. "What the hell are you guys doing? Have you lost your mind?"

"Where are you going?" Allister asked.

"Why is that literally any of your business?"

"Making sure you're not rushing off to meet some other man again," Dante told her bluntly.

"Are you kidding me? He sent you to follow me?" Luna asked. "Talk about insecure."

"No," Allister answered. "He doesn't know we're here. Get in. We need to talk to you."

"Why would I get in the car with you?" Luna asked. "I'm going to a cafe, if you must know. I have homework to do because we're in college and most people do that instead of stalking."

"I've never done a lick of homework," Dante said. "Now get in before I actually kidnap you."

Luna rolled her eyes. She opened the back door, sliding into the cool leather seat. The door barely closed behind her before Dante took off down the street, speeding like someone was chasing him. "Can you slow down?" Luna barked, holding on to the seat for dear life.

"No time," he told her. They continued speeding down the streets, passing right by the campus cafe.

Luna's eyes widened. "Where the hell are you taking me?"

Dante looked at her from the rearview mirror. "What you did yesterday was fucked up."

She rolled her eyes. "Oh, and forcing me into a marriage isn't?"

She recognized the road they were driving down immediately. The neatly cut lawns, intricately shaped bushes, and the large, gated fence. They were at the Vitali mansion. Why did they come here? She couldn't face Valerio, especially after the dream she had. Her body was still coming down from that high. "I'm not getting out of this car, so you might as well just drive me back home."

Dante pulled up at the front door. Both him and Allister turned around to look at her. She crossed her arms, trying to cover how uncomfortable she was under their scrutiny.

"What do you think Valerio was doing for those seven years he was gone?" Allister asked.

Disgust filled Luna. She didn't want to think about all the gross things he was doing out there, catching any and all diseases he could. "I don't care."

"Nothing," Dante answered. "He did absolutely nothing because he promised himself to you."

"He's really pathetic if he made you guys pick me up just to lie to my face," she said. "I don't care what he's done with anyone. It's not my business, just like whatever I do isn't any of your business."

"You're marrying him. What you do is his business," Allister said. "And what you did last night was low."

Luna narrowed her eyes in rage. "What I did was low? Do you even hear yourselves? He shot someone in the legs!"

"We didn't say he was normal," Dante said, shrugging. "He cut himself off from any fun in life, too busy plotting how to rule the world and staying loyal to your contract. The least you could do is the same."

"You know he cares about you," Allister said. "I don't know why he would damn himself to marriage, but either way he chose it."

"Well, I didn't," Luna spit out. "I don't owe any of you a single thing, especially not him."

"You should be grateful, considering the alternative. He's willing to live a life of misery with you just because he's in fucking love with you." Dante spared her no sympathy, speaking his mind regardless of the fact Luna was ready to break down into tears. "He's my brother, so that means I look out for him. If it was up to me, you would have had a bullet in your head for that stunt. Next time you hurt him, I won't be so forgiving."

Luna could only stare back at him. They all had reputations, but Dante was always thought to be the careless, fun one. That had to be a lie because the man that sat in front of her seemed just as lethal as his brother. It was a whole family of unforgiving souls.

"Is that a threat?" she asked.

"No, no threats. It's a promise," he said. "I want to like you, Luna. Don't ruin that."

She clenched her jaw hard, begging herself to not let the tears fall. At least not in front of them. She wouldn't let them see her weakness, not now and not ever. "Protect your brother all you want; I don't care. But remember, I am a Kingsley and if you ever threaten me again, you'll wake up with a fucking army at your door."

With that, she got out of the car, slamming the door behind her. She didn't have anywhere to go, except inside the house. Gianna was home, but she was likely still sleeping. For now though, her room would be the safest place.

Luna let herself into the house, the front door thankfully unlocked.

She needed to go somewhere to cry. After she cried, then she could call someone to pick her up. Her driver or her brother. Whoever—it didn't matter. The lump in her throat was suffocating and her eyes burned with unshed tears. She couldn't even pinpoint why she wanted to cry so bad. Was it because she was threatened or because no one cared about the situation she was in? Why was she being punished for almost kissing a boy, but no one else was suffering for all of their actions?

That had to be what it was. Frustration. She was so frustrated that every action, every word, every movement she made was being judged and scrutinized. Every day, more and more, the small freedoms she enjoyed in her life were being ripped from her hands.

There was one place where she needed to go. The place she would sneak out into during sleepovers when she couldn't sleep.

She walked through the kitchen, hurrying to make her way to the backyard where a gazebo stood, surrounded by wildflowers. They were beginning to lose their petals, but still, their colors blended seamlessly, creating a picturesque scene.

She sat down on the small bench inside of the gazebo, looking out into the flowers. The sob tore through her throat before she could swallow it down. The next one followed after and then another one. She gasped and choked on her tears, but they wouldn't stop.

She must have been cursed. That was the only explanation. Maybe Valerio was a better option, but she never got an option. She was human; it was natural for her to fight when she was trapped. The minute she stopped fighting and gave into the marriage was the minute she lost herself. She saw what happened to her mother, what happened to countless numbers of women she met at galas and balls. They became a shell of a person, stuck in an endless cycle of infidelity and violence. There wasn't real love in their world; it didn't exist. Maybe she was naive for still believing in it and yearning for it, but what was the alternative?

She didn't want that life for herself. She didn't want the wars, and the violence, and the targets on their backs, never having anyone to turn to. That was her own personal nightmare.

She wanted to go on dates and fall in love. She wanted the option to break up if the relationship didn't work out or to take it to the next level if it did.

And yet, her life would have none of that.

She wiped her tears off her cheeks. So much for getting up early to get some work done.

A sigh escaped her lips. Crying was pointless; it wouldn't

change anything. She needed to take control of her life. Luna didn't have a single clue on how to do that, but she needed to think of something.

Finally, the sun made its way up into the sky, coloring everything in a multitude of blues and pinks. Eventually she stood and walked into the house once again. She entered the kitchen, stopping in her tracks at a shirtless Valerio chugging a water bottle. Her throat became dry and immediately the dream from the night before clouded her mind, her breakdown forgotten for the moment.

She couldn't stop her eyes from drawing down his body, following the trail of hair that disappeared under the low hanging gray sweats.

She snapped her eyes back to his face and his narrowed look. In a split second he set the water bottle down on the counter and stalked over to where she was standing. He grabbed her face, wiping away any tears that lingered from the chilled skin of her cheeks.

"Who made you cry?" he asked. His voice was dark and bordering on anger.

She couldn't answer, suddenly so aware of his half-naked body pressed dangerously against hers. "No one," she answered in a weak voice.

She needed to get out of the kitchen and sort her emotions because her mind was taking her to too many places at once.

"Don't lie to me," he said. "Who brought you here? Was it them?"

"I need to find Gianna," she said, trying to sound more firm that time.

"I'll take care of it for you."

"It's not serious," she told him, shaking her head.

"It's serious enough if you're in my house crying." His plump lips fell into a frown. His eyes held a dark gleam, one that promised some sort of punishment. "No one in this world has the right to disrespect you. Tell me what they said."

"Have you ever been with anyone else? During our engagement or before?" she asked. She didn't even know why she was asking, but the words slipped out before she could stop herself.

"No," he answered without hesitation. "Never."

She swallowed harshly. Dante and Allister were telling the truth? Valerio hadn't been with anyone the entire time they were engaged. Was it possible he wasn't like the other mafia men she knew?

Her mind swirled bitterly with a new possibility she hadn't wanted to discover. She pushed him away from her before regretting letting her hands touch him. She felt the goosebumps that rose on his skin from the contact, snatching her hands away as if he burned her.

Her legs pushed her out of the kitchen. She climbed up the stairs, nearly running down the hall to Gianna's room. She slammed the door open, waking her up in a confused panic.

"What the hell? Luna? What are you doing here?" Gianna asked, sitting up with her eyes still nearly closed. "It's too freaking early for this."

Luna closed the door behind her, walking closer to the bed. The look on her face must have been alarming because Gianna sat up more awake now.

"What happened?" she asked more urgently.

Luna could only throw her hands up in the air.

Something felt like it had changed, and she didn't like it one bit.

NINE

LUNA

AFTER HER BREAKDOWN earlier that left her feeling especially fragile, Luna needed a night out.

Her leather pants were tight around her hips, but they made her look extravagant. She wore a cropped black long sleeve shirt, knowing the arena was always freezing inside. Cecilia helped her curl her hair and she decided to wear a little extra makeup to hide the redness around her eyes after her cry session earlier.

After Luna had spit out the nonsense from her mind to Gianna earlier that morning, the blonde forced them into the car, where they drove back to the apartment and woke up Cecilia and Blair. Luna confessed the dream and everything Dante and Allister had said, blurting out a million thoughts per minute. She was confused and just needed someone to listen to her, and that was exactly what they did. They let her get everything out before they reassured her that she wasn't losing her mind.

"You can't control your dreams, but also, it doesn't mean anything," Blair told her.

"How do you know?" Luna asked.

Blair looked over at Gianna before leaning into Luna. "Because I may have had a dream or two about someone I deeply despise. It doesn't mean anything."

"What?" Gianna screeched. "Oh my God, I knew it."

"You know nothing," Blair cut her off. She huffed, crossing her arms.

"You just need to forget about him for the night," Cecilia reassured Luna. "You were in an emotionally vulnerable place and then seeing Valerio's juicy body sent you over the edge."

"Literally, according to the dream." Gianna laughed. Luna threw a pillow at her. She threw it back. "Even if you are attracted to him, what's the issue?"

"That's how feelings start," Cecilia said.

"Not necessarily. Maybe if you did sleep with him, you would get him out of your system. You already think he's a bad person. Once you realize he sucks in bed, you'll be completely over him. Then the fight can continue," Gianna said with a shrug.

"What makes you think he's bad in bed?" Blair asked.

"He's a virgin," Gianna said as if it was self-explanatory.

Luna shook her head. "I'm done talking about this."

And that was where the conversation ended, leaving her with too much to think about. A night out was necessary.

Gianna's driver drove them to the arena because none of them were willing to make the trek out to the middle of nowhere in their own cars. The arena had to be off campus to ensure the school had no affiliations to it as they claimed no liabilities. It made it extremely inconvenient to get to.

The inside of the arena was dome shaped. The seats went up the walls so that even the nosebleeds had a view of the ring. It was already packed inside, people rushing to their seats with their drinks in hand. The girls always sat all the way up front, a way for Augustus and Finn to keep an eye on them.

The boys usually became too consumed by their fights to notice anything though, which meant the girls partied hard. By the time they entered the arena, Augustus was already waiting by their seats. He had a permanent smirk that only intensified when he saw Cecilia.

"Oh great, my night is ruined," she muttered.

Luna placed a hand on her shoulder. "Act like he's not there."

"Easier said than done."

Blair and Gianna ran off to go get drinks for them while Luna took a seat beside Cecilia who was trapped on the other side by Augustus. He whispered something in her ear that sent her off, putting them in their own little bubble. Luna turned toward the ring, wishing she had gone to grab drinks too.

The entire event was professionally set up. Security guarded the doors, the betting table busy and loud. Every Fight Night, Finn walked away with a huge pocket of cash because he always won. People loved betting on him for that reason. They got to watch a good match and make good money on it.

Luna had never actually bet money on any of the fights before, but tonight felt different. Maybe she could make a couple bucks betting on Finn.

The lights dimmed and the announcer came on. "Welcome ladies and gentlemen to Fight Night!"

Cheers erupted around the arena. Luna's stomach filled with butterflies, excited for the night. The first few fights passed by in a blur. Quick ones that usually ended with a knockout or they fought until neither one was left standing. She felt sick when the latest fight ended and a mop and bucket were pulled out to clean up the blood in the ring.

Augustus's name was called next. They were almost at the most anticipated fight of the night: Finn's. Augustus practically ripped himself away from Cecilia, who huffed and crossed her arms. He blew her a kiss, entering the ring.

Luna sipped on her drink, looking over at Gianna and Blair who were already getting up again. "We're going to get another. Do you want one?" Blair asked. Luna shook her head.

"Bring me a couple," Cecilia told them, sinking into her chair. Luna could feel the anxiety coming off her as she bit her lip and tried to act cool. She placed a comforting hand on her shoulder, squeezing it before she let the girls go get the drinks.

Luna took her time to look around the arena. She recognized

a couple of girls from previous classes, waving at them. So far, Fight Night was a success.

"Now give it up for the first time, Dante Vitali!" the announcer called out, dragging out his name. Luna's head whipped around in confusion. What the hell was he doing there?

Dante walked out from the back and down the pathway, already shirtless. Bruises covered his body, and he sported one on his cheek. He high-fived people as he walked, winking here and there. Luna was turning around to ask Cecilia about it when a familiar warm body sat down next to her, wrapping an arm around the back of her chair.

"Who are you betting on?" Valerio asked. "Personally, I'm betting on Dante, but I'm not sure what his chances are after I trained with him earlier. He might still be sore, but I figured he could handle it if he was brave enough to threaten you."

"What are you doing here?" Luna asked.

"Why didn't you tell me about what happened this morning?" Valerio asked.

She frowned. "Don't ignore my question."

He didn't budge. "I answered your question this morning and then you ran away. Now, what did Dante and Allister say to you that made you cry?"

Luna turned away from him, focusing on the fight. Both men were already bleeding. Cecilia was up by the ring, worry etched on her face. Blair and Gianna were standing beside her, sneaking glances over at Luna.

His lips were right beside Luna's ear, causing a chill to go down her back. "So help me, Luna, I will force you to talk if I need to."

She snapped back to him. "And how exactly will you do that?"

He smirked, looking at her lips before looking back up into her eyes. Luna gulped, hating how attractive he looked. His dark hair was messy, his clothes overly casual for such an event.

"I have my methods."

"They said that what I did to you last night was despicable. That because you weren't with anyone, I shouldn't be either," she blurted out. "Which leads me to the point of why that is any of their business?"

"It's not their business. They had no right to comment on any of that," he said. "I'm sorry they made you cry."

Her hard exterior softened for a moment. He was apologizing for something he didn't do.

Luna shook her head. "You don't have to be sorry for that. And you shouldn't have hurt Dante because of it."

"No one deserves to make you feel that way," he said. "They won't do it again."

Luna nodded. She took her time to study him, focusing on his lips. The same ones that trailed along her body in her dream. Her cheeks burned.

"Why haven't you been with anyone?" she asked. "You were gone for seven years."

He smirked, leaning in closer. This time their lips were only a few millimeters away from each other. "Because I only want to fuck you."

Her cheeks heated. She moved her head away, trying to regain her composure. "Why are you here?" she asked again.

"I'm here for Fight Night," Valerio told her. "Curious to see your brother in the ring once and for all."

She frowned. "Why do you care?"

"I have a bet going on. If he loses, I'm a lucky man," Valerio told her.

"You do realize Finn is basically a professional. He's never lost a match before."

"I think tonight he might."

"Doubtful."

Valerio's eyes lit up. "Want to bet?"

Her eyes narrowed in consideration. She was thinking of betting anyway, and at least she knew it would be a sure bet. She didn't know who Finn was fighting, but he was good—no, he was the best out there. Luna nodded. "Only because I'm confident he'll win."

"Let's make it interesting then. If he wins, I'll stay away from you forever," Valerio said.

Luna's eyes widened in shock. "You're lying."

He shook his head, putting his hands up. "I swear. If he wins, I'll void the contract."

Her mouth went dry. "And if he loses?"

"Then you come with me to the cabin tomorrow night."

Tomorrow was The Chase. She didn't know where it took place, only that it was somewhere in the forest with plenty of space to run and hide. It was a wild bet to make, but she had full confidence in Finn.

"That's all you want?" she asked. Her gut told her he was up to something, that there was no way Valerio would make such a bet. Unless he finally decided he didn't want to be with her either.

"Simple bet," he told her. "Do you accept?"

Luna nodded. "Sure."

As long as Finn won, she would rid herself of Valerio. It seemed almost too good to be true.

He held out his hand, and she shook it. She ignored how warm it was and how perfectly it fit in hers, letting go after a moment. He turned back to the ring. "Huh, looks like Dante did get his ass beat. Serves him right."

Luna looked at the ring. Sure enough, both men were bleeding, unwilling to stop fighting. They were pulled apart from each other, Allister grabbing Dante and Finn grabbing Augustus. They kicked them out of the ring, Finn continuing to stand there while they introduced him. Screams lit up the arena from fans of his.

Finn was good at what he did. She didn't blame them for enjoying his fights.

Luna waited anxiously to hear his opponent get called. It was silent while the announcer cleared his throat. "Another first for the night and surely an epic fight that beats the one we just watched!" the announcer declared. "Give it up for Valerio Vitali!"

Her face fell as Valerio stood next to her. He took off his shirt, ignoring the cheers that erupted at the action. She felt like an idiot, her face heating up out of anger this time.

He leaned down, setting his shirt on her lap. His lips found her ear once again.

"I never lose either," he whispered. His lips lingered there for a second before he stood back up and began walking toward the ring.

Luna watched him, dread filling her once excited body.

Fuck.

TEN

LUNA

THE FIRST PUNCH was thrown before the bell had even rung. Valerio blocked it, throwing one of his own at Finn. Just like that, everything around them disappeared and they were immersed in the battle between themselves, keen on destroying each other.

Luna could only watch in horror. She was long out of her seat, standing right beside the ring now while she watched the two massacre themselves.

This wasn't just any fight; it was personal. She was nauseous as soon as the first drop of blood hit the already dirty floor. She didn't know if it came from Finn or Valerio.

Allister stood beside Dante, an ice pack against his cheek. She stomped over to them. "Get Valerio out of that ring."

"Why? He's doing fine," Allister told her.

Luna clenched her teeth. That was exactly the issue. He was doing fine and she needed him to lose. As long as the deal was still up that he would disregard the contract if he lost, Luna needed to do whatever she could to make him lose.

"Let them fight it out. They both need it," Dante told her. "I just hope you didn't bet against him."

"I'm glad you got your ass kicked," Luna said, walking back to the girls.

"I can't explain it now, but I need Valerio to lose," she told them.

"I don't think there's a single thing you could do to make that happen," Cecilia said. "I feel like he's got this in the bag."

"Valerio is good, but my money is on Finn," Gianna said.

"Bet on who you want. I need Valerio to lose." She desperately tried to ignore all the thumps and sounds of fists meeting with flesh coming from the ring. "I need to distract him or something."

"Well, kissing someone didn't really work last time," Blair said. "Just enjoy the fight. Seriously, what could be that bad?"

Luna took a deep breath. "If he loses, the contract is gone."

"Oh, shit," Cecilia was the first to say.

"I think he's about to get a knockout, so your time is running out," Gianna said, pointing to the ring.

Luna turned back to the ring in a panic. Finn was already kneeling on the floor, desperately trying to catch his breath. Valerio was leaning against the ropes, his chest moving rapidly. He straightened himself out, stalking over to Finn.

Luna caught his gaze. He smirked, knowing he was about to get the winning blow.

Before she could think, she used the one asset she had that she knew Valerio wanted. She grabbed the bottom of her shirt, lifting it up. All she wore underneath was a lacy lilac bra, but enough could be seen through it.

Valerio's eyes widened before they narrowed, becoming lethal. Luna pulled the shirt back down, her cheeks flaming. The damage was done.

"I guess when in doubt, show your tits," Gianna muttered, laughing.

"Oh, Luna," Blair said, shaking her head.

"I had to think quickly," Luna hissed.

It was enough of a distraction to get Finn to stand back up, about to send out a punch, but Valerio blocked it. He didn't throw one back though. He jumped out of the ring, marching over to Luna. He didn't give her a chance to react or say anything before he was pulling her with him.

She struggled to keep up, stumbling over her legs as he hurried to the locker room. He slammed the door behind them, pushing Luna against some of the lockers. The locks dug into her back, but it was the least of her concerns.

Valerio's eyes were dark and terrifying. She had never seen him look that way before, and she hated that it was centered toward her.

"What the fuck were you thinking?" he practically growled, pushing into her.

"You have to go finish the fight," she said, trying to change the subject.

"I don't give a shit about the fight," he hissed. "What do you think you were doing?"

She swallowed harshly. "You never said I couldn't distract you."

"So you decided the best fucking solution was to show your tits to everyone in attendance?" he asked mockingly.

"I had my bra on." She tried to justify herself, but he wasn't having any of it.

"How many fucking times do I have to remind you that you are mine? My fiancée, and soon my fucking wife." His voice sent a chill down her spine.

"I'm not—"

"Don't fucking finish that sentence," he spit out. "I have been patient. I have given you time to accept, but I'm done fucking waiting."

Her eyes widened. "What do you mean?"

"I'm talking about our engagement party. A chance for me to declare to everyone, including you, that you are mine."

Her jaw clenched. "If you force me, I will hate you forever."

He leaned in closer to her. "You already hate me. What more do I have to lose?"

"Maybe you have nothing to lose, but you have everything to

gain if I end up loving you," Luna said. "This is a sure way to ensure that will never happen."

"How I see it, that doesn't seem like even a remotely close possibility."

Luna wanted something that would give him hope. She didn't want to dangle anything in front of him, but if it would buy her time before he began moving along with their wedding, then she had to try anything.

She thought of the one thing that was a good enough incentive.

Luna lifted her arms, wrapping them around his neck to pull him closer to her. She had no idea what she was doing, but she had read enough books and seen enough movies to attempt it. She closed her eyes, took a deep breath, and then pressed her lips against his.

The minute she did it, she regretted it.

His lips were softer than she'd expected, similar to how they felt in her dream. Only this time, she was tasting him for real, and he was intoxicating. She pulled back, shocked.

She opened her eyes to find Valerio looking back at her with just as much shock and puzzlement. This time he was the one forcing their lips together.

He led the way, allowing her to follow along and lose herself in the process. For just a second, she would indulge only enough to realize it wasn't good. All she needed was just a second. One uninterrupted second where she shut her mind up and let the moment happen.

So she did.

Valerio's lips moved with ferocity, all of his frustration towards her slipping into their kiss. Luna accepted it, pulling him impossibly close. She tangled her hands in his hair, tasting the blood that escaped from the cut on his lip. If it hurt him, he didn't give any indication. Instead, one hand found its way into her hair, pulling her head back so he could get more access to her.

She pulled on his hair back, his groan against her lips enticing her even more.

Luna hadn't even noticed his other hand was sitting on her ass until he squeezed and forced a gasp from her. He took the opportunity to slide his tongue in, allowing her to finally taste him.

She was dizzy and out of breath by the time he finally pulled away. His eyes were wild. He felt it all too, just like she did.

The door to the locker room opened. Luna looked behind Valerio's shoulder to see who it was, while he refused to acknowledge anything besides her.

"Fight Night's over," Allister said, looking at the wall instead of the couple pressed against the lockers in a compromising position.

"I don't give a shit," Valerio said.

"Your friends are waiting for you," he said, this time to Luna.

She pushed Valerio away but he was like a magnet trying to grab onto her again. "I have to go," she said in a rush, wiping her lips and trying to fix her hair.

Valerio watched her go, not saying a single word, which she was thankful for. She skirted past Allister, attempting to regulate her heartbeat. She must have looked wild with her messy hair, bruised lips, and wide eyes.

Luna walked out of the room, meeting up with the girls who looked at her suspiciously. "Not a single word," she muttered to them, walking ahead.

She wasn't sure who won the fight or how long they had been in the locker room for. Most of the arena had already been cleared out at that point.

But she was sure about one thing that she would never admit to a single soul—one taste wasn't enough. She needed more.

ELEVEN
VALERIO

VALERIO HAD NEVER FELT SO alive in his life. Maybe that was why despite the fight he had just been in, he still made his way into the gym to burn off the adrenaline that lingered. His knuckles were raw, his body covered in cuts and bruises, including the small one on the outside of his lip, but he didn't care.

Only one thought kept floating through his head and it had to do with the woman who was going to drive him into the grave. He was positive of it.

One fucking kiss. That was all it took. One kiss to completely destroy him, to bend him to her will. She had initiated it too. The thought shouldn't have made him as excited as it did, but he couldn't help himself.

His mind replayed the kiss, every moan and gasp, the taste of her. He groaned, landing another punch against the punching bag. It flew back and forth, on the border of completely falling apart from his abuse.

Valerio caught it, leaning his head against it.

Someone had finally done it. They had finally broken Valerio Vitali. And it was his fiancée of all people. Her first kiss had been him, and his had been her. It was a beautiful sentiment if no one looked too closely into their relationship. All he knew was that he had been deprived for far too long and now his body yearned to make up for past time.

God, he needed a cold shower.

Valerio rolled his shoulders, deciding it was enough for the night. He still wouldn't be able to sleep no matter how hard he tried, but his body deserved a break before the events tomorrow. He had the house to himself. Allister and Dante were out at some party and Gianna was over at the girls' apartment. The security cameras at Luna's apartment building showed she had made it home safely. Despite how much he wished he could see what she was doing, there weren't cameras in her actual apartment and it was a good thing anyway.

As long as she was safe at home, Valerio didn't need to worry about shooting some asshole in the legs again. He still couldn't believe she had exposed herself just to distract him. It worked. Of fucking course it did, but her body wasn't for anyone else's eyes. The anger that had rattled him when she lifted her shirt and he realized everyone else could see it too was instantaneous. What the hell was she thinking?

She was perfect, every inch of her. He had always known she was. For years he had dreamed of how her body looked and it was better than he expected. Then the moment was soiled because he was in the middle of beating the shit out of her brother.

But then there was the kiss and the tight fucking leather pants she wore. He sighed, walking upstairs to his room. He needed the coldest shower he had ever had.

Just as the sun was rising, he slipped into sleep, only to be awakened by a phone call from his father demanding he look at some new contracts. From then it was a long workday that only added onto Valerio's exhaustion.

Every night, he begged his mind and body to go to sleep, but most nights it never came. It had been that way since his mother died. He was haunted by waking up in the middle of the night to the sound of a gunshot and then proceeding to find her dead in the bathtub. That moment played through his mind late at night when he lay alone, and it was enough to keep him awake. He buried himself in any work he could do, keeping his mind busy.

His schoolwork was easy, but it was unnecessary. He would be taking over his family business no matter if he got his degree or not. The only reason he really attended was to be close to Luna and get some sort of college experience before he was thrown into the working world completely. It was his last chance to fuck around before then. It wasn't like Valerio knew how to completely let go anyway. He was always on the lookout, making sure everyone was safe, making sure he was the upstanding heir his father had raised him to be.

He wished he could be careless like Dante and Allister, who got away with everything because they had Valerio to cover for them. But he didn't get that luxury, and he never would. In his defense, he wasn't interested in doing the wild shit they did. He had his responsibilities, and at this point in his life, he'd preferred a night in with his Luna over anything else.

Except that was also a complicated shitshow now.

He closed the laptop, giving it a break for the day. Valerio got up, showered, and changed into a black T-shirt and black jeans. He could already hear Dante's and Allister's anticipation when he finally got down into the kitchen as the sun was only an hour away from setting.

"I don't know that I've ever seen you this excited before," Valerio told them.

"Since you've missed a couple initiation weekends, you don't fully understand just how exciting the night is. The adrenaline from running, beating the shit out of people, getting drunk and fucking someone later, that's the dream," Dante said. His eyes gleamed.

"I need a fucking night off," Allister said. He massaged the back of his neck with his hand. "Blair has been driving me up a fucking wall these past couple of weeks."

"You both would benefit from fucking it out," Dante said.

"Shut up," Allister told him.

"I might meet up with you guys later," Valerio said, unable to listen to this conversation any longer.

"What? You're not joining us?" Dante asked.

"I have my own chase going on." He gave them a final smirk before walking out of the house and to his car. He listened to the purr of it for a moment before speeding off into the night to collect what was his.

She'd refused to answer any of his calls or texts all day. He knew she would try to avoid him today after what happened the night before. No doubt she was freaking out about the kiss, struggling to understand why she liked it so much. He could read her like an open book. Her face when Allister walked in told him everything he needed to know. But Valerio wasn't giving up so easily.

The drive to her apartment was engraved into his memory, and in no time he was pulling into the parking garage. Usually it was blocked by security and only opened for people who lived in the complex, but Valerio had a way in. He even had a spot reserved just for him right by the elevator so Luna wouldn't have to walk far.

Energy was buzzing through him by the time he entered the elevator. When he looked at the cameras earlier, the other girls had left for some party or maybe they would be attending The Chase themselves. Valerio wasn't sure and he didn't care. All he knew was that Luna was home alone, hiding out from him.

The thought made his skin burn. Too bad for her, he would chase her down to the ends of the Earth if he needed to. And knowing Luna, she would make him do it just to spite him.

He found himself in front of her apartment door, taking his key out of his pocket. He'd had one made just in case there was ever an emergency, but also so she wouldn't be able to keep him out.

He unlocked the door, closing it quietly behind him. He walked slowly through the apartment, taking in the white couch in the center of the room, pink pillows and what seemed like hundreds of blankets covering the thing. Magazines sat on the table with some nail polish, the odor still lingering in the air. He looked at the kitchen table, his heart stopping when he saw a bouquet of flowers still sitting there, looking like they were on their last leg. It was one of the many bouquets he had ordered for her. He was going to need to keep sending her some every week to replace the dying ones.

He continued walking, passing the big windows in the living room that showed off most of the campus. Could his house be seen in the distance? He moved slowly, careful not to make a sound. He was skilled enough to enter completely undetected, but he also didn't want to give his future wife a heart attack.

He passed several different doors, all decorated to indicate whose door was whose. Luna's was at the end of the hall on the right side, little moons and gold stars surrounding her name. He opened the door, hearing music coming from the bathroom.

Surely he should have called out to her by now, but he couldn't stop from taking a moment to surround himself in her space. The entire room smelled like her. He took a deep breath: the perfect combination of coconut and something sweet. Big bookshelves lined one entire wall, books of all genres sitting on them. Her bed was unmade, too many pillows lining the headboard. Small twinkling lights lined the room, casting it in a warm glow. Her room was peaceful and fit her perfectly.

The bathroom door was ajar, so he pushed it open farther, seeing Luna with a towel around her body leaning against the sink and looking into the mirror. She screamed when she saw him standing there. She turned around with wide eyes, clutching the towel closer to her.

"What are you doing here? You scared the shit out of me," she told him, her chest rising and falling.

"I tried to be quiet to avoid that." He couldn't help the way his eyes dragged along her body.

"You could have knocked on the door like a normal person," she said.

"Where's the fun in that?" he asked. "Get ready, we have to go."

"Go where?"

"To the cabin."

She crossed her arms. "You didn't win."

"And whose fault is that? Unfortunately for you, I didn't lose either."

"I should have known that bet was too good to be true," she said.

"You knew I was going to win," he said.

"I guess we'll never know for sure," she muttered. "Now, get out. I need to change."

The door was slammed in his face before he could come up with some smartass comment. He rolled his eyes, taking a seat on her bed. He continued looking around her room, obsessed with memorizing every inch of it. Once they moved in together, he would let her decorate the house however she deemed fit. As long as every inch of the space felt like her, he wouldn't mind.

His eyes landed on the nightstand beside the bed. It was a light brown color, scratches and marks covering it. On it lay a book, some kind of romance. The man and woman on the cover held each other passionately. Valerio could only assume what the book was about. He had read a few she purchased at bookstores over the years, wanting to get a better sense of his future wife. All he could say was that she might have been innocent, but her mind was far from it.

There was a picture of her and the other girls, all with big smiles. She even had a picture with her family. Her father wasn't smiling; neither was her mother or Finn, but Luna kept her smile big. That was the only picture of her family in her entire room. All of the other ones only included the girls or were random prints she had purchased. Beside the small picture frames was a single little rose in a small vase, also on the verge of drying out completely.

He was snapped out of his daze by the door opening. Luna walked out with her hair down, freshly brushed. She wore a big hoodie and gray sweats, her face bare of any makeup. Valerio's breath hitched. He would never get used to her beauty no matter how many times he stared at her face.

"Hope you don't mind me going in my worst clothes," she said sarcastically.

"You've never looked more perfect," he told her, drinking every inch of her.

Her face fell, stunned. "Let's just go before it gets too late."

He stood, letting her lead the way. She grabbed her purse and her phone, sliding on a pair of sneakers. They exited the apartment, walking all the way to the elevator and then back to Valerio's car. He helped her in, closing the door before rushing to the other side. Like a routine they had unconsciously established, he drove quickly through the dark night and she turned on the heat, leaning her head against the window.

Luna had dozed off, but finally woke up when the car came to a complete stop. Valerio turned it off, but she was already ripping off the seat belt and leaving the car before he could say a word. He made his way after her, unlocking the cabin and letting her enter first.

It looked the same as it did last time. The only difference was there were snacks on the counter and new blankets on the couch. Luna made her way to the couch, settling down while Valerio began lighting the fireplace.

"You don't have to make a big fire," she told him. "I'm already warm enough under these clothes."

"You could always remove them," he said with a smirk. "I wouldn't want you to overheat."

"I bet you would like that," she muttered, crossing her arms.

"What? You overheating or you taking off your clothes?"

She rolled her eyes. "Where did you even find this cabin?"

He lit a match, throwing it into the fire before standing and wiping his hands on his pants. The fire was small, but it lit up the room and warmed it. "I built it."

"Since when are you a builder?" Luna asked, surprised.

"Since I needed a hobby outside of killing and being terrifying."

"Does that mean the roof is going to fall in on us?" she asked him.

"If it does, I'll save you," he told her.

"When did you build it?"

"A few years after my mom died," he said, walking over to the kitchen. Luna turned around on the couch, watching as he took out two glasses from the cupboard.

No one ever talked about his mother. After her funeral, not a single thing was whispered about her out of respect, but it didn't mean they didn't have questions.

"I can hear your mind working a million miles per minute. If you have questions, just ask them," he told her, opening the small fridge to pull out some kind of juice.

Luna bit her lip. "How old were you?"

"When what?"

"When you built the cabin?"

"I was sixteen. But I was nine when I found her dead in the bathtub." He grabbed the two glasses, bringing them over to where Luna was sitting. He placed them on the table, sitting down on the couch. "She shot herself."

"I'm sorry," she told him.

"There's nothing to be sorry about," he told her. "She made the decision herself."

"Who else have you brought here?" Her attempt to change the subject wasn't subtle, but he appreciated it.

"Not a single soul outside of us in this room knows about this cabin," he told her. "And it's gonna stay like that."

She frowned. "Why did you bring me here then?"

"You know why."

"This feels like too personal of a thing for me to know about," she told him.

"You're going to be my wife one day. If anyone is going to know my secrets, it would be you," he said.

"I wouldn't be too generous with giving away your secrets," she warned him. "Things could change."

"And if they don't?"

"You know that answer," she said.

He stared at her for a long minute. She reached for the drink on the table, taking a sip. "Good juice," she muttered, setting it down.

"What do you want from your life?" he asked out of curiosity.

"That's a loaded question."

"Just answer it."

She was quiet for a moment. "I want to graduate college, travel the world, write some books, fall in love, do anything and everything that would make me happy. I want what all people want in life: true and genuine happiness."

"Happiness is overrated," he told her.

She shrugged. "Maybe it is. But that's what I want from life."

"And you could never have those things with me?" he asked.

Her breath hitched. These were not the types of questions he was expecting to be asking tonight, but they seemed necessary.

"Men in our world take what they want without caring about who they hurt in the process. They lie, they cheat, and they destroy you until you are just a shell of a person unable to find meaning in life. I'm sorry if it hurts to hear I could never be happy trapped in a life I didn't choose, but that is my reality," she said. "It's time you understood the reality too."

"Why fight me? Why not fight your father?" Valerio asked.

Luna let out a sardonic laugh. "Do you really think I haven't? It earned me a slap to the face and a month forced on lockdown. I can't fight him. I have no power to fight him." She shook her head. "You've seen what this world does to women. How it tears them away from their identity, leaving them with nothing."

"Is that how you see me? Capable of ever doing something like that to you?" Valerio asked.

"Do you want the truth?"

"Always."

"Yes," Luna said. "And maybe it's because I know my father was capable of forcing me into something I didn't want, but I didn't think you were capable of doing the same."

The silence was suffocating. For the first time in his life, Valerio was at a loss for words. There was the truth—the ugly, horrifying, foul truth.

In her eyes, he had committed the same crime as her father. She equated the two to each other. But whereas her father did it for monetary gain, Valerio did it because he wanted to be with her, to stop her from being with anyone else.

That made him as much of a selfish bastard as any other.

"Don't ever compare me to your father," Valerio growled, disgusted at the comparison.

"What does it matter anyway? You've proved there's no way out. You'll take what you want, kill who you want, and destroy me in the process." She shook her head. He could finally see the vulnerability in her eyes. "I'm tired of the fighting. It's not getting me anywhere. It never has."

That broke Valerio worse than it should have. Suddenly, he was his father and she was his mother forced into a marriage she didn't want. Would she birth his children just to end her life with a gunshot to her head in the middle of the night? Valerio loved her more than anything, but he didn't know if loving her could keep history from repeating itself.

If he trapped her and she harmed herself because of it, he would never be able to live with himself. But that was what she had been trying to tell him all along, wasn't it? That she wouldn't give him a chance to trap her. She would take any opportunity necessary to escape.

He saw the signs in his own mother once upon a time. She fought and fought, until one day the fighting stopped. And it was the minute that the fighting stopped that he lost his mother forever.

Luna was already there. Her fighting was over, so if the marriage to him was the one thing that could send her over the edge, then he would set her free.

It was no secret that Valerio was an asshole, selfish, and obsessive, but above all that, he loved Luna far too much. More than he loved himself and more than he would ever love anything else, so he wouldn't do that to her. He loved her.

He stood. "Let's go." All the emotion he once held was wiped clean, leaving a shell of the Valerio she knew.

Luna stood along with him. He threw the juice in the fire, leaving it a smoky mess. He stomped to the front door, leaving Luna to follow.

He sped the entire way back, ignoring the way Luna held onto the seat in anxiety. He swerved in front of the apartment building, stopping there instead of going into the garage. It was necessary to cut the routines out now. It would make the transition smoother. Luna grabbed the door handle, pushing it open, only for him to reach over her body and slam it closed.

"Tomorrow morning, the contract will officially be void. You and I are no longer together," Valerio said, cutting straight to the point like they were talking business. And maybe they were. That was all this could be from now on. "Good luck, Luna. I hope you get everything you want from life."

Luna stared back at him in shock.

With shaky hands, she opened the door. He could only assume she finally got what she wanted. And when the door closed, he took off down the street, leaving her to stare at the disappearing brake lights.

TWELVE
LUNA

THE CONSTANT KNOCKS on the front door at eight in the morning were enough to wake even the deepest sleeper. Luna covered her head with the pillow, trying to drown out the sounds.

Her bedroom door opened, heels clicking along the wooden floor. The pillow was ripped away from her face. Luna groaned, finally opening her eyes.

She expected Blair or Cecilia, maybe even Gianna, though that was rare this early in the morning. Instead, it was the one woman whose face was permanently carved into a scowl—her mother.

"Get up, now."

Luna's eyes widened as she sat up. Her mother didn't say another word before she left the room, leaving her stumbling out of bed in a hurry. She grabbed a robe, tying it, and then stopping dead in her tracks when she saw that her mother wasn't alone. Her father was there too.

Finn looked like he had gotten hardly any sleep, sitting on one of the armchairs in the room. Eleanora Kingsley sat at one end of the L-shaped couch, while Reece Kingsley stood beside her, his arms crossed over her chest.

He was a scary man. His hair was beginning to gray and

wrinkles covered his face; anyone would have assumed he was just an aging man. But when he got angry, his entire face twisted into a monstrous expression that used to terrify Luna when she was younger. Now, at twenty-three, she felt that same fear.

"Good morning," Luna told them, sitting on the couch. She was on edge, trying desperately to remain unfazed, but it was impossible.

"Do you want to tell me why Valerio Vitali canceled the contract?" her father shouted, his voice echoing through the living room.

It had been an entire week and she was wondering when her parents would not only find out, but when they would finally confront her about it. She just assumed she could run away before the day came, but it came far sooner than she hoped.

Luna swallowed harshly. "I don't know."

"Don't lie to me!" he bellowed, making her flinch. She looked down at the ground, avoiding his gaze.

"I have been in meetings with them for the last week trying to get him to reconsider. Do you understand what their connections would do for our family? And then you go and completely screw it up! Have you lost your mind? Is this school making you this way?" he hissed.

Luna shook her head. "I didn't do anything."

"For seven years the contract was undisturbed," Eleanora spoke up. "He spends a couple weeks with you and now he's backing out? If it's not you, Luna, then what is it?"

"Maybe he realized who I actually am and that I'm not the person you spoke me up to be," Luna said, looking up in defiance.

"Watch your mouth," Eleanora snapped.

"He is absolutely done with the contract. Wants nothing to do with this family. Luckily for you, there is a list of men who were quick to ask for you because Valerio assured us your purity is still intact," her father said. "I am finishing sorting out arrangements with one of them this afternoon. Your engagement party will be within the next couple of weeks; your wedding within a few months."

"Why the rush?" Luna asked, her eyes wide in fear.

"So there's no chance of another contract falling short as well." The icy malice in her father's voice should have been enough to get Luna to shut up, but the panic built up before she could stop herself.

"Please don't do this," Luna begged, standing. "Please. Let me fix this; let me do something."

Reece's hand connected with her face before she could blink. The impact sent her falling to the floor, the burn of her skin forcing tears out of her eyes.

"You have done enough," he hissed. "Focus on finding a wedding dress."

Luna didn't have the guts to look up at him. She held her cheek, looking at the floor until she was sure she heard him leave. Her mother followed him out immediately, not bothering for a second to check on Luna before the door shut behind them.

Finn walked up to her, taking a knee beside her as he squeezed her shoulder. Luna looked up at her older brother, finding a similar broken look in his eyes.

"I tried to pick someone else," he told her.

"What did he do to you?" Luna asked, already knowing that the defiance would have warranted some kind of beating.

"Ten lashes on my back." Finn said.

She swallowed harshly. "Then he went easy on me because of all the events coming up." He could have done worse, but he held back for the sake of her physical appearance.

"They're keeping you on lockdown for the next couple of weeks. You won't be allowed to leave unless they give you permission," Finn told her.

Luna nodded her head, the tears already gathering in her eyes. "I figured."

"I'll stop by tomorrow," he said, standing up. He gave her one last look before walking out the front door as well. From a stranger's point of view, no one would have known that his back was probably raw and destroyed, but the Kingsley siblings were good at covering it up by now.

Luna's shoulders fell. The apartment was silent until the first choked sob escaped her lips. Blair and Cecilia ran into the room once they heard it, knowing Luna was suffering.

They hugged her and whispered hopeless promises, but none of it mattered. Her life was set and she would never have any say in it. To her father, she was nothing more than something to sell off. She had always known that, but in that moment, it struck her more than anything else. She had blamed Valerio, cursed his name day and night for the past seven years, and yet, he wasn't here now to be blamed.

Her father was at fault. He always had been. And she wished she could stick a knife so deeply into his heart and watch the life fade from his eyes the way he did to her. The thought struck her so vividly, she was shocked by her own rancid hatred towards her father, but it wasn't new. It just festered and grew worse with every passing moment.

Her life was a clusterfuck of mistakes and consequences to the actions she had never decided on. The thought was enough to send her down the darkest spiral she had ever experienced in her life.

One she wasn't sure she would be able to pull herself out from.

THIRTEEN

VALERIO

LIFE WAS TRULY BLEAK. Two weeks had passed since Valerio had seen her, spoken to her, but not since he thought about her. He thought about her every day, destroying his mind with the constant cycle of wondering what she was doing, knowing he had to let her go, fighting the urge to kidnap her and keep her all for himself, and then falling back into his spiral. It took all of his willpower not to run back to her, begging her to take him back. But he didn't. And he wasn't going to.

He couldn't be the reason she found misery in her life. After his mother, he'd learned desperation could push people into the worst situations. If Luna ever hurt herself because of him, he wouldn't be able to handle it. That night, he saw the brokenness in her eyes, the exhaustion she was facing after having fought against him for so long.

So he released her.

Now all he heard about her were rumors that swirled through the people in their world. Her father had allegedly found someone else, but Valerio wasn't sure how legitimate that was. He couldn't pry into it either because it would only raise suspicions on whether he was trying to reinstate the contract or not. If there was someone new, it was better he didn't know who it was.

He didn't have time to start a war over it.

So he surrounded himself with work and beat the shit out of the punching bag, having to replace it too many times to count at this point. Only when he could hardly keep his eyes open did he make his way to his bed where he lay, begging sleep to overcome him. Rarely did it.

Valerio sat at the kitchen counter, his second cup of coffee in his hand. He hadn't slept the entire night and felt like he was on the verge of a caffeine overdose at any moment. Still, no matter how badly he wanted to sleep, his nightmares shifted into finding Luna in the tub instead of his mother, making it impossible.

The first night that happened, he woke up in a cold sweat, barely making it to the bathroom where he threw up everything that was in his body.

He was absolutely terrified, his hands shaking, having to convince himself it wasn't her. She was alive.

Valerio ran his hands through his hair. He was seriously losing his fucking mind.

Gianna stumbled into the kitchen on the phone, Allister following in after her. His brows were furrowed as he listened to his sister's conversation.

"Tell her to stop freaking out. We'll figure something out," Gianna told whoever was on the phone. "Ask her if she has a passport with another identity."

She rummaged through the fridge, taking out a water bottle. Valerio watched her, having a clear indication of who she could be talking to. He looked over at Allister, who had a look of worry on his face.

The hair on his body stood up in anticipation of some sort of bad news. Something bad was happening; he just didn't know what it was yet.

"Maybe I can ask Dante if he knows someone who can create one for her," Gianna said, running a hand through her hair. "Give her the phone."

Valerio wished he had super hearing so he could listen in on whatever was being said on the other side of the phone. He craved to hear her voice one more time even if it was her telling him to go fuck himself. He tightened his hand on the coffee mug.

Gianna looked at Valerio before turning away from him to face the kitchen cabinets. "Luna, listen to me. We will get you out of this. Give me a couple of hours to figure out something. Give the phone back to Blair."

She was silent for a second before she whispered into the phone, "Make sure she doesn't do anything stupid. Don't leave her alone."

With that, the phone call ended and Gianna let out a deep breath. She turned around, a bright smile on her face that didn't match her eyes. "Good morning." She was a great actress; he would give her that.

"What's happening?" Valerio asked immediately.

"Nothing you should concern yourself with," she told him, crossing her arms in defiance.

"Gianna, now is not the time," Allister said in a stern voice. "Tell him or I will."

"Why do both of you know something I don't?" Valerio asked.

"Because she didn't want anyone to tell you," Gianna said.

Valerio's eyes narrowed. "Speak now."

"If you must know, but you didn't find out from me, Luna is having an engagement party tonight," she said quickly and quietly. "Her parents found someone else."

Valerio was sure his heart had stopped for a second. Or maybe it was longer than that because time seemed to have stopped so quickly, he didn't understand how long he was silent for.

The rumors were true then. She was marrying someone else. He shouldn't have cared.

Something murderous rushed through him in an instant. The mug in his hand shattered, leaving a mess of spilled coffee and ceramic pieces on the counter.

"It's better I didn't know."

"No one is expecting you to do anything about it," Gianna said. "You let her go, and that's great for you, but I'm wasting valuable time talking to you right now."

Valerio let her leave the room, his heartbeat so loud in his ears that he couldn't hear anything else.

Allister turned to him, only when he was sure Gianna was gone. "What's your plan? You're not actually going to let her go through with another marriage, are you?"

"There's nothing for me to do. She didn't want me to trap her, so I let her go. We all knew this was the alternative," Valerio said, standing.

"Despite all that, you still love her. You know you do. She cares for you too. She did before and I'm sure she still does."

Valerio froze in his spot. In the next second, he had his hand around Allister's throat, holding him against the wall. "You don't know anything," he spit out.

He didn't need false promises about whether Luna cared about him or not. She told him she never would. She promised she never would.

But what if she did?

Allister gasped for air. "I won't be surprised if you crash that party tonight."

Valerio released his neck and left the room. He made his way into his office, attempting to take in a deep breath to calm himself, but it didn't work. He leaned against the desk, letting out a scream before he swiped all the items on the desk on the floor. Valerio turned around, lifting the coffee table off the ground and throwing it at the wall.

He felt disastrous, destructive. Something dark swirled inside him, wanting to destroy something—someone. Over his dead body would Luna be marrying anyone other than him. He gave her a chance, an out. He did something good.

But that wasn't who he was. He wasn't good. He wasn't the hero. He was the one that took what he wanted and destroyed those who denied him.

He was coming back to take his wife, and this time, he wasn't ever letting her go.

FOURTEEN
LUNA

LUNA HATED the white dress she wore. The straps were too tight on her shoulders, and it showed off too much of her legs. Her hair was pinned back, curls flowing down the length of her back. The pearl necklace hung around her neck like a collar; a gift from her mother to celebrate her engagement.

Her cheeks were pink as if she were a young blushing bride, but really it helped to hide the fact Luna was as pale as a ghost.

The ballroom her parents had rented out was decorated with white doves hanging from the ceiling, the tables covered with food and drinks. Luna didn't recognize most of the people there, but they weren't her focal concern right now. She tried to find a way out, a window or door, but security stood at every entrance, keeping her locked inside. Her parents had assumed she would try to run, so they made sure there was no place to go.

Soon she would be meeting her future husband for the first time. The thought made her feel sick; everything in the room made her feel sick. The music, the bright lights, the fake smiles from the guests even though she was practically being sold off. It was all disgusting.

"There you are. We've been looking for you," Cecilia told her, rushing up. Blair and Gianna followed her.

"Here I thought I was blending in," Luna said.

"You're the only one wearing white, you stand out like a sore thumb," Gianna said.

"Have you met him?" Blair asked.

Luna shook her head. "Not yet."

"I can look at the contract again. Try to find anything that forces Valerio to stay in it," she suggested.

"No. I'm not forcing anyone into anything," Luna said.

"What's your plan then?" Cecilia asked.

She didn't answer the question. Her mind had gone to a dark place far too many times in the past week, but she didn't dare voice that out loud. If she was truly trapped with no way out, then she would have to do whatever was necessary.

She just feared it might be sooner rather than later.

"Have you seen your parents anywhere?" Blair asked.

"My mom was down here talking to some people, but last I saw my father he was upstairs," Luna told them. She didn't have to think hard to know who he was meeting with or what he was discussing.

"Speaking of your parents, they're literally over there with some old dude," Gianna said. Her eyes were wide, her face pale.

Luna turned around for a moment. Her mother shook hands with the older dude, her father stood beside him with a bright smile. She recognized him as one of her father's business friends that attended the same galas and balls they did. Someone that had been in her father's life since she was a child. That was all Luna knew about the man, other than that he was single with no children of his own.

She turned back around with horror. "They want me to marry him?" she asked, her voice fearful. A panic attack was on the horizon, building and building until it hit completely. "I need to get out of here." Her hands reached for her neck, rubbing at the skin with brutal force that shocked her. She felt like she was suffocating, the pearls around her neck starting to choke her.

Cecilia grabbed her hands, pulling her along.

"Where are you taking her?" Blair asked. "There's no way out of here."

They were able to hide in between the crowds of people and away from her parents' sight.

"She needs to get out of here," Cecilia said. "I just don't know how. Maybe we can cause a distraction?"

"Finn is over there," Gianna said. He stood right beside Augustus, sporting a black eye. Luna had to assume there were more bruises where that came from. He shot back another glass of some dark liquid.

"No," Luna disagreed. "I don't want to drag him into this."

"He's your brother. He'll want to help you, and if he doesn't, then he's more useless than I thought," she said.

Luna wanted to shake her head because Gianna didn't understand. She didn't understand that her brother had probably already taken another beating trying to stop the events of tonight just because her father couldn't put his hands on her himself. If he wasn't in the meeting earlier, then he had to have seriously pissed off their father. She didn't want him putting himself in harm for her any more than he already had.

Gianna stomped over to Finn and Augustus, shoving his shoulder. "Tell security to let Luna out of the building for air." Of course he knew they weren't just going out for air, but it was an alright lie for the moment.

"They've been given strict orders not to let her out anywhere," Finn said. "You can thank my father for that."

"Is that who fucked up your eye?" Blair asked.

Finn's mouth turned up into a snarl. "Watch your mouth."

Luna could feel her time running out. She was going to break. It was only a matter of time. "Please, Finn," she begged. "I can't do it. I swear to God, I can't."

He looked at her for a long moment. "You know what he'll do to us."

"Grow the fuck up," Augustus said, shaking his head. "I

would send a bullet through his head for every time he put his hands on you if I was you."

Cecilia placed her hand on Finn's shoulder, which was quickly pushed off by Augustus. She ignored the latter and instead focused on the issue at hand. "No woman deserves to suffer like this, especially not Luna."

Luna hated hearing the desperation in everyone's voices. How quickly it seemed that the situation had turned into life or death.

"I didn't say I wasn't going to help," Finn said. He looked at Luna, setting his glass on the table. "Come on. You all stay here."

She followed after him, walking as fast as she could in her heels. They maneuvered through the crowds, narrowly missing their parents that were still engaged in conversation but would probably be looking for her soon. They made their way into the hallway where the bathrooms were. The first place in the entire building that seemed bare of people. Had they not been in a rush, she would have asked him a million questions, but silence was the best option. Once they made a sharp turn entering a more desolate hallway, Luna ripped the heels off her feet.

She left them in the hallway, the cool marble floors relieving her feet. Finn opened a door at the end of the hallway. It was another entrance into the kitchen. Cooks were rushing around, plating food and carrying it out to the ballroom. They paid no attention to the two people who had no business being there. She narrowly avoided running into any of the chefs but slammed against Finn's back when he stopped abruptly.

He held open a thick, silver metal door, letting in the frigid night air. She stepped out apprehensively, wishing she had more on her than what she currently did. She turned to look at her brother, wondering if that would be the last time she would ever see him again.

"I never took you back here and I didn't see anything. You got it?" Finn asked.

She nodded. "Thank you."

"Do what you have to do."

He didn't say anything else, but she had learned that he wasn't one to comfort anyone. The fact he gave her an out was enough for her at the moment.

With that, he shut the door in her face, leaving her outside all alone. That was all the sign Luna needed to start running. She ran away from the building, trying to get to the back lawn of the property. Her lungs burned and her feet ached with every step she took on the uneven concrete, but she kept running. She ran down the hill, seeing the statues and decorated bushes in front of her.

Her legs took her as far as the last statue before she fell. How she was able to get all the way down here all those years ago in a drunken stumble was a mystery to her. Pebbles dug into her hands as she held herself on all fours, her knee burning from scraping it. She sat up, leaning her back against the statue's base, staring at the blood that dripped down her leg.

It was when her mind finally stopped that everything hit her all over again. When the first tear fell, she wiped it away furiously, angry at herself for crying so much. All she had been doing for the past two weeks was crying and she was sick of it. She didn't want to cry anymore. She didn't want to feel so helpless, and yet, she couldn't help it.

She had nowhere to go, no money, nothing to her name. That was why her father kept her isolated and under his wing her entire life, so she wouldn't know how to live without him or without a man.

She looked up into the sky, letting her tears and sobs escape as she looked at the moon. Most nights, it gave her comfort. Tonight, it did nothing for her.

She looked over at the large pile of rocks that sat off to the side at the edge of the forest. One of them would be able to do enough damage to her, maybe even end everything.

Could she really go through with it though? The brutal strength and force it would take to end her life that way was horrifying to consider, but really what were the alternatives?

Maybe there was a body of water somewhere close by.

"I think congratulations are in order."

Luna turned her head in shock. Valerio's large figure stalked out of the darkness slowly, allowing the little light from the moon to finally immerse him into visibility.

"I don't need them," Luna said. She wiped her fingers under her eyes, collecting the tears and makeup trailing down her cheeks.

"Who knew that white was your color?" he asked, his voice full of sarcasm. He kept walking until he stood directly in front of Luna, forcing her to look up at him. She hated how handsome he looked; his face menacing, the black T-shirt tight around his arms.

More than anything, she hated how familiar he felt and how relieved she was to see him. How quickly he could calm the chaos in her mind and silence her demons.

"What are you doing here?" she asked. "I'm not your problem anymore."

Valerio gave her a small smile before letting it slip off his face. "You weren't ever a problem, but you just had to run off and get another husband."

"Don't call him that."

"Why? Looks like a decent enough guy if you ignore his age and the fact he'll be taking Viagra to get it up on your wedding night. Bet he'll make a great husband."

"Shut up," she spit out. "You can leave."

"No, I can't," he muttered. She hated the way he was looking down at her, knowing he had all the power in the world at that moment. "I came to collect."

"Collect what?" Luna asked, looking down at the ground. She couldn't stand the intensity that shined through the blue in his eyes.

Valerio kneeled in front of her. "My wife."

His hand found its way under her chin, lifting her head so she had no choice but to look at him. The butterflies returned in her stomach at his touch. She hated the effect he had on her, despised it.

"You know what I hate? I hate that even though I shouldn't

be here, even though I let you go, even though you're not my problem, I still couldn't help but run over. I hate that I haven't been able to rid my mind of you for seven years and that I would do anything you asked," he said. His voice was hardly more than a whisper, but every word sounded like it was being amplified in her ears. "I want to make you a deal."

"What is it?" she dared to ask.

"You ruined The Chase for me, so I want a redo. This time, if you win, I will get you out of the country, away from any marriage prospects," he told her, trailing his thumb under her eye to wipe a tear away.

"And if I lose?" she asked in a whisper.

"Then you are mine for the rest of our lives."

A sharp chill ran down her spine. Another game where the chances were stacked against her, but he promised her things only he could grant her. She had no chances otherwise. The stiff reminder that she had nothing left to lose, but potentially everything to gain was enough motivation to agree to the insanity he was proposing.

"Okay."

Valerio's grin was sinister. He grabbed her hands, helping her off the floor. He turned them around to the forest, pressing her back against his chest with his hands on her hips and his lips grazing her ear.

"I'll give you a fifteen-second head start," he said. "Run like your life depends on it."

He gave her hips a squeeze before he moved back. She waited for him to say the words that would send her sprinting into the forest.

"Go."

And just like that she was off, fleeing like a lamb trying to escape a wolf. All she could think about was the one thing he had told her before: He never loses.

FIFTEEN
LUNA

THE HEARTBEAT in her ears thumped loudly, drowning out all other noise in the forest. Her legs burned and ached, but she kept running because she had no idea where he was. With how long his legs were, he would have no problem reaching her. If she wanted any chance at winning, she had to push herself.

In the dense forest, the moon's light was limited. Sticks and leaves scraped against the bottom of her feet, while she held her hands out in front of her as a second line of defense against the trees. She barely avoided colliding with them multiple times, her hands taking most of the abuse.

Despite her fear, her adrenaline was at an all-time high. She couldn't remember the last time she had ever felt so alive, let alone on a night as awful as this one.

Running for her life was proving to be a perfect distraction for everything that was going on a couple hundred feet away. And she needed it. Especially after what she had contemplated moments before Valerio showed up.

"Where are you, my little moon?" he called out through the forest. Panic rose inside of her. She couldn't tell which direction his voice was coming from, the echo jumping from side to side.

She forced herself to move quicker, only to find herself

running directly into a clearing. The trees were positioned in a circle, creating a fence around her. She was completely exposed, while anything hiding in the forest line would be able to watch her without her knowledge. A single large boulder sat in the center of the clearing and that was it. The strange setup felt odd, but it didn't matter when his voice called again, this time so much closer than before. Luna stopped for a second, trying to decide on a direction to take.

A branch cracked from somewhere in the tree line. She ran behind the boulder, holding her hand against her mouth to quiet her breathing. It was silent, too silent. Luna stepped around the boulder, trying to look out into the area she had just come from to see if he was there or not. She saw no one.

Her shoulders dropped. She released a breath of relief. She could make a run into the forest again, going until she got up to the main road. She turned back around.

Two hands pushed her against the rock, locking her in place. Luna gasped. Valerio had found her.

His eyes were wild, his breaths harsh.

"I found you," he growled, pressing against hers.

"What now?" she asked. She had to have looked as wild as he did. She waited in anticipation for his answer, her skin itching for the scratch only he could provide.

She should have pushed against him, fought him, told him he needed to get her out of the country even though they had made a deal. But she did none of it. Maybe he would have helped her too if she pleaded with him. She could have blamed it on her confused state of mind, on how hopeless life seemed just a few moments ago and now it seemed hopeful again, or even on the adrenaline coursing through her body.

But there were no excuses for the way she felt now around him: protected and safe. His presence felt so familiar, so good to be in again, she almost felt guilty allowing herself to relish in it when she had only pushed him away. For the past couple of weeks, all she had felt was unsafe and in danger. Now, it was the opposite, and it was thanks to him. And maybe it was always his presence in her life all these years that kept the lingering protection there. The moment he was gone, so was everything else.

The overwhelming sense of longing filled her. She hadn't even realized that she missed him until he showed up once again unannounced in her life. Maybe that was the real reason she didn't fight him.

"Now," he said, drawing it out. He traced the skin of her neck, feeling the quick pulse under her skin. "You're mine."

And then his lips were on hers. One hand found its way into her hair, pulling on it so he could have more access. Luna melted in his hold, trying to keep up with his kiss. It was violent, angry, but exactly what she needed.

He grasped her neck like a necklace warming her skin. He grabbed it firmly before he let go of it again, but it was enough for Luna to feel the dampening in her underwear. His lips replaced his hand, biting and sucking on the soft skin, leaving bruises in its wake. Luna wasn't sure she would be able to cover them up. She lifted her leg, wrapping it around his waist while he grinded against her.

His free hand yanked the straps of the dress down her shoulders, exposing her nipples to the now freezing night air. Valerio stared at them, looking up at Luna who looked at him with wide eyes. The eye contact didn't last long; a moment later he pressed a kiss against her left breast, wrapping his mouth around the nipple.

"Absolutely perfect," he told her, before digging back in.

Moans slipped out. He paid attention to the other nipple, pulling and squeezing, mixing pleasure with a little bit of pain. He played with her as much as he wanted, as if he were entitled to it, as if her body was his.

Luna wrapped her hands into the back of his hair, pushing his head into her chest.

He fell to his knees, trailing his hands along the smooth skin of her thighs. She looked down at him this time, feeling overly powerful having someone like Valerio on his knees for her. "What are you doing?" she asked breathlessly.

"I want a taste of my fiancée."

"We're in the middle of the woods," she said. She attempted to close her legs, but his hands held her open.

His boyish grin sent her mad—teasing her, making her wish he would put that mouth to good use instead. "This wasn't where I imagined I would eat your pussy for the first time, but no time better than now."

He trailed his fingers up her thighs, finding the lacy thong she wore underneath the dress. Her breath hitched in her throat as he pulled on it, forcing it down her legs. "Unless you want me to stop?" Valerio asked her.

"What?" she asked. Her mind was only occupied with his hands too close to the place that was now drenched for him.

"Do you want me to stop?"

She shook her head.

"Use your words," he said.

"Don't stop," she muttered. "Please."

He grinned, slipping the underwear down and off her feet, sticking it in his pocket. "When you beg so sweetly for me like a good girl, I have no choice but to play with your pussy. Hold your dress up."

She did, looking at him with wide eyes. He threw her leg over his shoulder, allowing him to be at eye level with her pussy. Valerio lifted his other hand, moving his pointer finger through her folds, collecting the slickness. He trailed his finger up, circling her clit for a moment. Luna whimpered, feeling the need growing inside of her.

"Look at how wet you are for me," he told her in awe. "So fucking perfect."

He circled her clit again, putting more pressure on it. She thrusted her hips forward as a response. Valerio looked up at her with another grin, one that was so rare for him but fit his face perfectly. "I wonder how you taste," he said. "Probably delicious."

He lifted the finger to his lips, sticking it into his mouth for a few seconds before pulling it out. Luna's mouth went dry. "I was right. Delicious," he groaned.

Then he leaned his head in, licking a strip from her slit to her clit. Luna gasped, holding on to his head. He continued to lick around her clit. Luna nearly lost her mind the moment he decided to suck on it, putting the most intoxicating pressure on her clit. She threw her head back, gasping for air and choking on her moans. She had never felt a feeling like it. Sure, she had masturbated before, but nothing compared to the way he made her feel.

He gripped her ass, pressing her into his mouth. She tensed the leg around his shoulder, thrusting her hips forward before she came. She wasn't ready for it, but it crashed through her body without another thought.

Waves after waves of euphoria swept through her body, forcing her to go silent. Her legs shook and threatened to crumble under her. He helped her ride it out until she was completely spent. He pulled back, but not before leaving one last kiss to her clit that had her twitching.

Valerio looked up at her. "You look like an angel."

She let out a laugh, a real and genuine one. "I probably look like I crawled up from hell," she told him, lowering her leg. She dropped her dress, lifting the straps back over her shoulders.

"Don't be so quick to get dressed," he told her. "I can go for round two."

She shook her head. "I can't." She stared at him for a few moments. "You didn't have to do that, especially since it left you with that." She looked down at the bulge in his jeans, before returning back up with red cheeks.

"I did it because I wanted to. Don't worry about me," he said. "You know what this means now?"

"Means we're engaged," she said, swallowing harshly. "I know."

He grabbed her hands, pulling her into him. "Don't think about it for tonight. We can talk about it later."

Luna nodded, relieved. "Should we go back?"

"I have to tell everyone you're my fiancée," he said, pressing a kiss to her lips.

They began walking back, Valerio holding onto her hand the entire time. Her legs were weak, so she appreciated it. His hand warmed hers, and it wasn't unpleasant. It didn't feel wrong walking with him like that either. It felt oddly comfortable and it silenced her mind.

"I wasn't expecting you to come out tonight," she told him. "I didn't expect you to ever want to see me again."

"Unfortunately for you, you can't get rid of me that easily," he said. "Why were you outside?"

"I was starting to lose it. I saw who my parents picked and I needed to leave. I needed to do something," she admitted. "I was trapped."

Valerio stopped in his tracks, turning to face her. His eyes were hard. "What were you planning to do?" he asked.

"I don't want to say it," she whispered. The thing in question being something she couldn't take back—a more permanent fix. She couldn't look at his eyes, the intensity in his gaze was overbearing.

Valerio grabbed her chin, holding her in place. "If you ever reach that point again, you call me. Don't ever even think about harming yourself, killing yourself. I will find you a solution, something else. Do you understand me?" he asked. His voice was stern, and all Luna could do was nod. "Use your words."

"Yes, I understand. I won't ever do that. I promise."

Valerio nodded his head, seeming to accept her promise. With that, they kept walking. Finally, Luna felt like she could breathe again.

SIXTEEN

LUNA

LUNA'S FEET were absolutely killing her by the time they returned to the building where her engagement party took place only a few feet away. Being with Valerio had been a pleasant distraction, but she was right back to having the same crippling anxiety from earlier.

"I can't go in there," she told him, pulling on his arm. "I look awful."

And she did with the cut on her knee, the dried-up blood on her leg, her hair ruined, makeup smeared, and the white dress covered in dirt. Not only that, but the man her parents wanted her to marry was in there, probably wondering where his future bride had run off to.

Valerio turned to her, pushing her hair out of her face and running his thumb against her bottom lip. "You look perfect," he muttered. "You're incapable of ever looking less than perfect."

Something in her stomach fluttered so violently. He spoke with such conviction that she almost believed him herself. Instead, she said nothing as he grabbed her hand and walked them inside the busy room. Luna made an effort to brush out her hair with her free hand and wipe the mascara under her eyes, which did help her appearance a little bit.

Everyone looked at the couple with wide eyes. She could have crumbled under their stares, but when her eyes moved over to Valerio, she saw how confident he looked. None of the stares seemed to faze him in the slightest. He walked with his head straight ahead, his eyes holding a newfound determination. It was almost like he didn't care what anyone thought about him and she wished she could share that quality, but even now her skin crawled wondering what everyone would be saying about her. The rumors they would come up with seeing Luna looking this way, walking in with Valerio Vitali, wondering if their engagement was back on.

She saw the girls staring back at her with eyes wide in shock. Gianna had a wicked smile on her face as if she could see right through her. She owed them the entire story as soon as she got back to the apartment, but for now all she could give them was a small nod in reassurance. She was okay—or at least she would be.

Finn stood beside her parents, his eyes narrowed on Valerio. He most likely wasn't expecting that Luna would have returned with his enemy of all people, but then again, Luna hadn't expected it either. Hell, nothing made much sense anymore. But not thinking about it proved to be a lot easier than destroying herself about it. At least for the moment.

Her energy needed to be reserved for her father, who looked ready to kill someone. He was ready to pounce. She swore she could see steam leaving his ears.

He stomped up to the couple, his face red. "What the hell do you think you're doing?" he spat out, forcing Valerio to push Luna behind him.

"I came to get my fiancée," Valerio said in an oddly calm voice. Luna stood on her toes, trying to see over his shoulder. Then she wished she hadn't. The second her father's eyes locked on hers, she wanted to run and hide.

"You ran off to find him?" he asked. His hand twitched.

She shook her head. "I didn't look for anyone."

"I sought her out. The contract is back on," Valerio said.

"No! For weeks I tried to get you to agree again. Luna is marrying someone else. That is final," Reece hissed.

"Who is her fiancé then?" Valerio asked, his head tilting to the side.

Reece ushered with his hand for the other older man to step forward. The same nauseated feeling returned to Luna when her alleged fiancé locked eyes with her. To think her father wanted her to marry him.

"This is Edward Barnes," Reece said. "He owns large stocks in oil and is a member on several of the same boards I'm on. He can take care of Luna."

Edward had a large bald spot in the center of his head, creating a big, shiny sphere when the lights reflected off it. His eyes were dark, holding secrets that Luna wanted to know nothing about. Everything about him seemed off and gross, and it wasn't just because he was her father's age.

Luna looked at her father in disgust as well. This time her hand twitched out of instinct. A fierce burning rushed through her body.

"You wanted me to marry him?" She stepped out from behind Valerio, confronting her father. His eyes widened in disbelief at her outburst. She didn't care. Not when he didn't give a shit about her.

"Watch it," he warned, his voice low.

Anger rushed through her. It consumed every thought she had. Even Valerio's hand on her back wasn't enough to pull her out of it. "You're a vile, disgusting excuse of a man. A coward—"

"Watch your mouth!" His hand swiped through the air, attempting to connect with Luna's cheek, but the sting of pain never came. Instead, another broad hand stopped it in a frighteningly tight hold.

Luna opened her eyes, not even realizing she had closed them out of instinct to see Valerio's murderous glare on her father as he towered over him. "So, this is what you've been doing? Putting your hands on my wife?" His voice was deathly eerie calm, nearly a whisper but judging by the look of fear on her father's face, he heard every word loud and clear.

"You don't know anything." Reece tried to smooth out the situation. His eyes widened when Valerio pulled his wrist back, not stopping despite the protests from the older man.

"You're right, I don't. I have my ways of finding out though," Valerio told him. With a loud snap and a scream from Reece, his wrist laid at an awkward angle, broken like it was nothing.

Luna looked at the scene with wide eyes. She couldn't dwell on the moment for long. Valerio pushed her behind his back once again, attempting to block her view but it was too late.

His hand reached behind him, pulling out the gun that sat in his waistband. The gun was pointed and aimed before anyone could blink, but when he pulled the trigger, that was when the chaos actually erupted.

Luna screamed, watching as Edward fell to the floor, blood spewing from the center of his forehead. Valerio had taken the perfect shot.

Reece turned to look at his dead friend and then back at Valerio with a look Luna couldn't decipher. Something between horror and shock.

"Well, it looks like that contract isn't valid anymore. I'm willing to re-sign when you are," Valerio told him. "This time with Luna's signature as well."

She couldn't process his words. She could only stare at the dead man on the floor who had been living just a minute before. And Valerio had killed him without a second thought. The nightmare seemed never ending at that point.

But it wasn't a nightmare; it was real life. As real as the enlarged vein that stood out from her father's forehead in fury and threatening to burst. Still, Reece Kingsley had no choice but to nod in agreement, allowing Valerio, with the gun still locked in his hand, to do whatever he wanted.

Reece took out his phone, calling who she assumed to be his

lawyer. Luna saw Finn in the corner of her eye. His eyes were narrowed, but he didn't move from his spot.

Just in time, her father's lawyer was walking in with a stack of papers prepared. In that stack stood her fate, her future.

Luna hadn't even realized how much of the room had cleared out by then, but it was understandable. No one wanted to get caught in the crossfire between the Kingsleys and Vitalis, but it didn't seem like a fair fight anymore. At least with this battle, there seemed to be a clear winner and everyone knew who that was.

The lawyer laid out all of the papers, clear indicators on where everyone needed to sign. Her father went first, grabbing the pen with shaky hands. He signed it messily with the hand that wasn't broken, but it was there, in ink, for the rest of their lives.

Valerio was next. He traded the gun for the pen. He signed his name far more confidently, engraving his signature into the pages with how harshly he pushed the pen down.

There was only one person left: Luna. The lump in her throat nearly choked her. She swallowed harshly, grabbing the pen that her father's lawyer held out for her. Luna turned to the girls, looking for Blair in particular. The latter seemed to have understood what was needed because she stepped forward, her face changing into the emotionless future lawyer she was so good at being.

"I need to read over this first," Blair told the lawyer.

"We don't have time," he told her.

She rolled her eyes, grabbing the papers anyway to skim over them. Luna saw all of the men eyeing her aggressively, but Blair didn't care. That was one thing Luna admired about her. She didn't care when she upset the fragile egos of the men around her.

When she got to the end of the contract, she set the stack down and looked at Luna. "Are you sure about this?" Blair asked, whispering so no one else heard.

"You know what the alternative is," she whispered back. "I have no choice."

"I'll explain what everything means tomorrow," Blair said. "I'm making sure you're protected."

Luna nodded, feeling more thankful for her than ever before. Her father's lawyer laid out the papers again, giving Blair a dirty look as he did so.

Luna could feel all eyes on her. She wiped her hand on her dress, securing a grip on the pen. She looked at the first page, where both her father's signature and Valerio's sat.

> *Both parties agree to the aforementioned agreement set in place.*

Her hand shook violently.

> *Both parties agree to hosting a wedding, ensuring the unity is presented to the public.*

She leaned over the paper, using her other hand to steady the one that held the pen.

> *Both parties agree to bring an heir into the world; one holding the blood of both families and holding the title of heir for the Vitali name.*

She dropped the ink point of the pen onto the paper.

> *Both parties agree to stay in the contract until one of them succumbs to death, releasing the other from the contract.*

Luna signed her name.

A tear fell onto the paper, smearing the ink slightly, but it didn't matter. Her father's lawyer took the papers the moment the pen lifted from the page.

"I will get these filed and sent to both parties," the lawyer said.

"We need a copy," Blair said.

He nodded reluctantly, walking away from the group. Reece looked at Valerio once again. He didn't say anything before he was stomping out of the door. Her mother followed after him, not saying a single word to Luna on her way out. It should have hurt, but her mother choosing her father never surprised her anymore.

"Be my date to the gala next week," Valerio said, pulling her out of her own thoughts.

She could only nod her head. It gave her time to think and to reflect.

"Then it's a date," he said, leaning down to press a kiss to her lips, ignoring her look of surprise.

Luna's signature was on the page now, officially.

Forever, until death did them part.

SEVENTEEN
LUNA

EVERY YEAR, the University hosted a party to honor the families that donated all the millions of dollars that funded the school and paid their incomes.

For the past two years, Luna and Finn attended the party alone because their father and mother were never able to make it due to other business requirements. Really, they didn't want to make the trip down. They threw a check at the Dean and didn't care about anything else as long as their children remained out of headlines.

Not that it mattered anymore since her parents refused to speak to Luna after what happened at the engagement party. In Reece Kingsley's eyes, her reputation was tainted and destroyed. He couldn't care less what happened to her. Her mother also made that abundantly clear when she followed her husband out of the party without so much of another glance at Luna. She couldn't tell if their silence was a good thing or a bad thing.

The girls attended the party as well, but their parents actually showed up. Well, those that weren't absolutely horrible. Gianna's and Allister's father mingled and talked business with some of the others in the room but not before giving Gianna a kiss on the cheek and Allister a slap on the shoulder. Blair's mother stood beside her, looking elegant in their matching emerald dresses. Her mother's skin was slightly tanner than hers, but otherwise they were so similar with their caramel colored hair and deep brown eyes. Her father, on the other hand, never showed up to anything unless it had to do with Blair being recognized for something specifically. Even then, the excuses came too often.

Cecilia's parents had walked in with her, but now they talked with Augustus' parents at the bar. Friends since the two were born, the two parental couples were close, which made Cecilia's life hell when she tried to stay away from Augustus himself.

It was embarrassing not having parents there, but nevertheless, Luna and Finn walked in together. The navy silk of her dress dragged on the floor behind her as she walked down the stairs. She didn't pick this dress; her mother sent it before she stopped speaking to her. Considering she had no time to prepare otherwise, the dress was the best option. The halter top neckline wrapped around her like a noose and it was purposefully tight on her body until it flowed out at her knees. The back was open, so she wore her hair up. The dress was beautiful, she had to admit.

She didn't like wearing the color blue though, especially not when it resembled a pair of eyes she was becoming too familiar with, and especially when they darkened like they did now. Valerio stood by the bar talking to Dante, but the moment he saw her, his gaze skimmed her body. She turned away, forcing herself to keep her composure. She knew people would be watching them—they were all the talk lately. Especially after the spectacle at the engagement party.

Everyone latched onto Valerio walking over to her looking undeniably handsome in his all-black tux. She held her breath, her body tensing.

"Luna," he said, grabbing her hand and placing a kiss on the back of it as if he were some kind of gentleman. "You look beautiful."

"Thanks." She pulled her hand away, pretending to fix his tux instead. Her voice got quiet. "I know what I agreed to in that forest, but this doesn't mean I'm suddenly okay with everything."

His eyes darkened dangerously. "I never said you had to."

She went to open her mouth, to call for Finn, but he was already long gone. Valerio wrapped an arm around her waist pulling her along to the bar. "Where are your parents? I saw you only brought that little rat with you."

"My parents never come," she told him, ignoring his jab at Finn. "Where's your father?"

"Who fucking knows," he muttered. "He's never attended a school event in his life and he won't start now."

"Great future ahead for any children we'll have."

He looked over at her with a small smile on his face. "Was that a joke?"

"I think it's more of a foreshadowing."

"At least you're acknowledging a future between us." He leaned against the bar, motioning for the bartender to come over to them. "I would say that's considerable progress in our relationship."

"I think you're missing the point completely. And this isn't a relationship," she muttered. Valerio ignored her, ordering drinks for them. She looked around the room, her eyes catching on Gianna who was walking over to them.

Relief filled her immediately. Finally, someone normal enough.

"I didn't know you were here," Gianna told her, a bright smile on her face. "I just saw Blair with her mom and Cecilia is hiding out somewhere. I'm sure you'll see her eventually."

"I just got here," Luna said. "Unfortunately, I was stopped before I could find any of you."

Valerio smirked, leaning into her. "Don't sound so bitter about it. You agreed to be my date after all."

He handed her the drink. The rim was lined with sugar that she didn't hesitate to lick off before taking a sip of the drink. He watched the whole time and she would have thought it was amusing if the hunger in his gaze didn't send a shot of pleasure up her spine.

It was easier to pretend she wasn't attracted to him when she remembered that they were in an arranged marriage she didn't want. But even that line was beginning to blur more and more as they spent time together.

He had substance and she hated it. Why couldn't he be like the other assholes in this room that bragged about how much money they had and couldn't hold a conversation?

Luna turned back to Gianna completely ignoring him. "Would you like to sit and hang out with us?"

"No." Valerio's answer was immediate. "I think she has to go mingle."

Despite the pleading look Luna gave her, Gianna shook her head. "As much as I would like to sit in this weird sexual tension the two of you have going on, I would actually rather be anywhere else. Sorry." She walked away without another word, shooting Luna an apologetic look.

"Bitch," Luna muttered under her breath.

"I'm not that terrible of company, you know?"

She sighed. That was exactly what she feared. She swallowed down her entire glass sitting it down on the bar a little too aggressively. "Order me another one," she told him.

He did just that, giving her a cautious look. "We still have to go say hi to people."

"I know. You seem to forget I've been doing this my whole life. I know how to play nice with people I hate," she told him.

"Everyone except me."

She thought for a second. "Well, if I'm stuck with you for the rest of my life, I might as well learn to play nice."

He handed her the drink once the bartender set it in front of them. She began walking away, but his hand grabbed her wrist stopping her. He frowned, a deep intensity in his gaze.

"On second thought, don't. I don't want anything from you

if it isn't authentic. I would rather you hate me but know it's real, than have you pretend to tolerate me."

His hand intertwined with hers and they walked into the crowd of people as if what he said hadn't squeezed Luna's heart in the most uncomfortable way. She couldn't understand why he would ever want hatred over tolerance, but as they mingled with people and accepted congratulations, it hit her. They were surrounded by inauthenticity. People smiling and playing nice for the sake of closing deals and keeping their reputations.

There was one thing Valerio had asked of her: honesty.

That felt like the hardest thing to give when she couldn't even offer it to herself.

Valerio talked with the couple in front of him, but she was long done with the conversation and with her drink. The only interesting thing was their reflection in the mirror that hung on the wall in front of them.

She looked like the spitting image of her mother; so much so it made her stop, her breath catching in her throat. She looked every bit like the dutiful mafia wife standing beside her powerful husband.

Valerio found her lower back, his hand heating the skin. They looked so good together. Every bit like the powerful couple everyone wanted them to be.

A part of her hated it. Hated how much it made her feel like her mother, hated how powerless she felt. Why? She wasn't even sure herself. Maybe it was the entire notion of their relationship catching up to them. It wasn't her choice. The foundation of their relationship was built on force, on an arrangement making her feel like she was an object to be bought in the first place.

The other part of her made her feel sick because a part of her didn't mind standing beside him.

She didn't mind how he introduced her first and seemed so proud that she was his fiancé. He held her like they were meant to be together, acknowledging how perfectly their bodies fit against each other as if he had always known.

He listened to her talk and cared about what she had to say and it shouldn't have seemed so groundbreaking, but no man in her life had ever done the same for her.

She was confused beyond belief.

If she gave in and if she tried, what was that saying about her? That she was just willing to accept whatever anyone did to her?

But she had signed the contract this time. She agreed to it. He would have let her go, so why didn't she let him?

She watched his full lips speak, a graceful smile on his face. Luna excused herself, feeling sick to her stomach. She rushed into the empty bathroom, leaning on the sink as she took in deep breaths. Her hands trembled when she turned on the cold water, soaking her hands first before she patted her face.

Had he actually done it? Had Valerio Vitali actually snuck his way into her heart?

No.

Fuck, maybe.

Her hand collided with the mirror, shattering it. The hiss of pain was immediate and it did nothing to soothe the madness in her mind. Blood leaked from her knuckle, dripping into the sink.

If anyone walked in and saw her with a bloody hand and the broken mirror, they would assume she had lost her mind. Maybe she had. She wished she could blame it on the alcohol, but she wasn't even sure if it was affecting her anymore.

She turned off the water, reaching for the paper towels to hold against her hand. The door opened, loud footsteps echoing in the empty restroom.

In the shattered mirror Luna locked eyes on the most stunning blue ones she had ever seen in her life. Valerio looked at the mirror, her hand, and then back at her eyes.

In three steps he reached her, his body pulling hers into his as his mouth met hers in a collision that calmed all of the chaos. She wrapped her arms around him, pulling him closer as she opened her mouth for him.

Luna bit his lip, forcing a growl as he lifted her hips onto the sink, running his hands over her legs, pulling her dress up as he did so. His tongue slipped its way into her mouth, forcing her to let out a gasp as she lost herself. Her mind was silent for the first time that night and all it took was his lips on hers. Ridiculous.

One hand wrapped its way around her neck, squeezing gently before he pulled away.

"Are you going to tell me what happened in here?" he asked.

"No."

"Well, I need to take care of your hand." Valerio pulled away completely, grabbing her hand in his. His lips were swollen, lipstick smeared on them. His hair was messy, clothes disheveled, but he looked too handsome for his own good. Luna was sure she looked just as guilty now.

"It's fine," she told him, but still allowed him to pull the paper towel away and look at the cut.

"It's not deep but it needs to be cleaned," he said. "I'll clean it at your house."

"We're done with the party?"

"Do you really want to stay?"

"Absolutely not," she said. "But I need to tell Finn."

"He'll live."

"You should probably let Dante know."

"I'm sure he'll have more fun at the after party."

"You're not going?

"I'm not going anywhere without you."

He helped her off the counter, grabbing another paper towel for her while she attempted to fix her hair. She wiped the corners of her lips, but the damage to her look was done. She didn't look nearly as put together as she did earlier and she really didn't mind.

Luna ran her thumb along his lips, wiping the lipstick off.

"What? Not my color?" he asked, cracking a boyish grin.

And for the first time that night she let out a genuine laugh. It made her forget who they were and how their relationship began.

Dare she say that their relationship even felt a little bit ... *normal*.

"Take me out on a date. A real one," she said, fixing his tie once again. She felt vulnerable even asking for it, but if she was going to make this relationship with him work, this was a start.

"How does next Saturday sound?" he asked, desperately trying to hold back his grin.

She nodded her head, feeling the tug of her lips up into a smile.

"Sounds perfect."

EIGHTEEN
LUNA

"THIS CONTRACT IS RIDICULOUS," Luna said, throwing the papers onto the table. "How could you let me sign this?"

"Um, I asked if you were sure," Blair said. "Besides, it's not the worst contract I've ever seen."

Gianna picked up the papers, skimming through them. "I don't even understand what most of this says." She paused on one section, nodding. "Have you read the cheating clause?"

Luna's brows furrowed in confusion. "No, what does it say?"

"Basically that if you or Valerio cheat, then the other can get out of the contract," she told her. "Get Valerio to fuck some other girl and you'll be free."

Cecilia laughed. "Yeah right, as if it would be that easy."

Luna laughed awkwardly, trying to ignore their comments. The thought of her own husband being unfaithful to her made her feel gross. If Valerio ever chose to break their vows, then she truly wouldn't want anything to do with him.

"Doubtful he'll want to cheat considering he then owes her half of everything he has," Blair told them. "And believe me, he has a lot."

"What do I get if we both stay in the marriage?" Luna asked.

"I don't know. You need to discuss that with your future husband. The contract doesn't specify any of that," Blair said.

"You should probably set up a separate type of agreement with him," Cecilia told her. "Something on paper that both of you agree to. At the end of the day, you two are the ones who are actually in the marriage."

Gianna gasped. "We can help you create it."

Luna thought about it for a moment. It was a great idea; some things that both of them would have to follow in order to ensure their marriage remained respectful to both parties. It would also allow Luna to hold some of the control in the relationship.

It was definitely a reach into trying to accept their new arrangement, but as long as she was trying, she considered it a win. After the donation party the other night, him taking care of her hand and being obnoxiously kind, she thought she might owe him that at the very least.

"Okay. I need something to drink while we do it," Luna told them.

"Say no more. We have some vodka in the fridge," Cecilia said, standing.

"I'll type it out," Blair said. "If you're getting drunk, someone has to be sober."

"Boo! You can drink and type, Ms. Pre-Law. How do you think most lawyers work?" Gianna asked.

"Hopefully not drunk," Luna said.

Blair rolled her eyes. "Fine, but only because I don't want to be left out."

Cecilia came back with red Solo cups, a bottle of vodka, and orange juice as a chaser. "We have to go grocery shopping soon."

"Are you kidding me? This seems like the essentials to me," Gianna said. She grabbed the cups and the vodka, distributing it out to all of the girls. Luna asked for orange juice in hers, unable to handle the taste of vodka by itself. A couple of sips down and they were ready to start creating their list.

"To start, we should mention that there can be no mistreatment of either party. Maybe something about communication too," Blair told them. "That way you both are open and honest with each other."

Luna nodded. "Along with that, no forcing each other to do things they don't want to do. AKA, not rushing me to have children when I'm not ready."

"Oh, add something about being allowed to travel. We still have breaks coming up and trips booked," Cecilia said.

"Kind of weird we have to mention any of this," Blair grumbled, taking another sip of her drink.

She was right. It was heartbreaking that they lived in a world where their girls' nights were spent having to write up a contract for how her future husband had to treat her. Luna took another sip, pushing the thought from her mind. It was a necessary precaution, something to protect her.

"Better safe than sorry," Gianna said. "Add something about mandatory foreplay. If you're going to be stuck with the same man for the rest of your life, you might as well have a good time when you do fuck him."

Luna choked on her drink. "I can't put that in the contract."

"Actually, you probably should. Especially if he doesn't know what he's doing," Cecilia said.

Her cheeks heated. Unfortunately, he did know exactly what he was doing, much to Luna's relief, but there was no way she was going to tell any of them about it. Luna cleared her throat. "On to more important subjects, add something about how no matter the sex of the first born, they're still the heir. I won't allow them to push aside my child."

Blair nodded, typing frantically on her laptop. "What about your living accommodations?"

"Oh my God, you're going to have to move out, won't you?" Cecilia asked. She gave a puppy dog frown, causing Luna to grab her hand in sympathy.

"She's going to be a married woman. She needs her own home," Gianna said. "Or Valerio can move into here."

Luna let out a laugh. Picturing him amidst the pink and fluffy whites of their apartment was hilarious to think about. "I don't want to move out."

"I can bet you money that you won't be living here when you're married," Blair said.

"Well, I don't want to live with Dante and Allister either," Luna said. "No offense to you, Gianna."

"Can't say I blame you. The only reason I still live there is because all of these apartments were too small. Where would I put all my clothes?"

Everyone rolled their eyes at that. "Fine, I'll put something about the two of you buying a home of your own, but it has to be close to us and we have to be able to come over whenever we want and have rooms of our own."

"Perfect," Luna said.

The drunker they got, it seemed that the more outrageous the list became. But she was going to dinner with Valerio the next day, so it had to be typed up with spaces for the two of them to sign. And as soon as Blair printed out the papers, they all passed out in the living room, promising to regret their hangovers the next day.

Luna gasped awake, holding her head when the hangover struck her just as violently. For the past few nights, she woke up with nightmares of marrying Edward and ending up with the bullet in her own head. Last night, she was shackled to the altar screaming for help, but no one came. They made her feel so helpless and alone. She hated that feeling more than anything.

But with the morning sun came the reminder that at least one nightmare was over. Edward was dead and she wasn't going to be marrying any strangers ever.

The sun also brought along the reminder that they had had far too much to drink the night before. All she remembered were fuzzy memories of a new contract they were typing up. When she finally looked at her phone, she was reminded of the date she had with Valerio later that night. She roused the girls up, forcing them into looking decent enough for a trip to the mall so she could find an outfit for the night.

She wanted a dress she would feel beautiful in and the moment she put on the silky, pastel yellow dress, she knew it was perfect. The fabric draped down her body like a waterfall, hugging her hips and stopping at the middle of her calves. She finished the look with some diamond earrings she got for her birthday a few years ago and a pair of white kitten heels she stole from Blair's closet.

She stuck the typed-up stack of papers in her bag and made her way out of the apartment. With prompt orders from Luna, Valerio waited downstairs in the garage. It felt too romantic to have him come up to the apartment and pick her up.

She ignored the comments the girls made and opened the door to leave, only to find Valerio waiting in the hallway. Luna's eyes widened as she closed the door behind her. "I thought I told you to wait in the car."

"Why? Are you trying to hide me?" he asked, his brow raised.

"No, I'm trying to save you the embarrassment of my best friends," she told him. "Are you ready to go?"

He didn't say anything for a moment, his eyes trailing up the length of her body before moving to her face and locking eyes with her. "Now I am."

"What was that about?" she asked, shifting uncomfortably.

"Trying to save the way you look into my memory," he said. "You look magnificent."

A blush crept onto her cheeks. "You could always just take a picture."

"I know. I'll be getting on to the cameras later to rewatch this moment," he told her, a grin on his face.

"Which cameras?"

"I have no idea what you're talking about." He grabbed her hand.

Luna rolled her eyes, a snort escaping as she tried to hide the butterflies that fluttered in her stomach from his warmth.

When they reached the garage, Valerio was opening the door for her, making sure her seat belt was fastened before he made his way to the driver's side. They began driving and this time he drove the speed limit.

"Where are we going?" she asked.

"I made a reservation for an Italian restaurant," he said. "I hope you like it."

"I love pasta. Maybe it's a place I've been before."

"I don't think so."

"Why not?"

"Because I own it."

"So you're in the restaurant business too?" she asked. "Are there any fields you haven't nudged your way into?"

"Real businesspeople diversify their investments," he said. "How else do you think I can afford my luxurious lifestyle?"

"Hope you can afford mine as well." The words slipped from her mouth before she could even register them, but before he could say anything, they were pulling up to the restaurant. It was a beautiful brown stone building. A man in a black uniform came to open her door for her, but Valerio was practically pushing him away to open it himself.

"Thanks," she muttered, fixing her dress as she got out of the car. They walked through a set of double doors held open by people in black tux uniforms.

The actual interior of the space was lit up by warm, ambient lighting causing a cozy feel to envelop the space. The tables were lined with white tablecloths and brown barrel chairs. There wasn't a single person sitting and having dinner, which seemed odd for such a beautiful space. Luna began walking into the large dining room, but Valerio pulled on her hand, leading her through a hallway lined with gold sconces on the walls. He pushed open a door that opened up into the most extravagant room Luna had seen.

Large windows lined the wall directly in front of them, allowing the city lights and the setting sun to stream into the room. The warm lighting carried into the room, and along the windows were green vines. She wasn't sure if they were real or not, but the space felt like they were in a villa in Italy.

Valerio pulled out a chair for Luna, allowing her to settle in before he pushed it in for her. "This place is beautiful. When does dinner start?"

He sat down as well, scooting his chair so he was beside her rather than across. "I closed the place for the night. You said you had things you wanted to discuss, so I thought it would be best if we had privacy."

"You didn't have to do that." She shook her head, completely shocked at the action. "This room is private enough."

"I wanted to," he said. "Order anything you want, but I also want you to try my favorites."

She grabbed the menu, eyeing through it but finding it was completely in Italian. "I can't read the menu."

"I could get you an English one."

She shrugged. "Or you could just read me the items?"

Valerio nodded. He took it, moving even closer to her so they could share the menu. He went through each item, pronouncing the names slowly. Luna couldn't help but look at his lips, watching as they changed and moved to fit the pronunciations, putting emphasis on specific parts of the words.

Her mouth was suddenly dry, mesmerized by him. He did have beautiful lips. Only a week ago, they were on hers in a heated frenzy. The thought brought a blush to her cheeks.

A waiter entered the room asking for their drinks. Valerio glared at him, causing the waiter to shift uncomfortably. It knocked Luna enough out of her daze to realize where they were.

They settled on some bottle of wine, but Luna also ordered a lemon drop martini. Valerio also made sure to order a little bit of everything on the menu, giving her a chance to experience just how delicious his food was. He spoke with the waiter in Italian, and she hated to admit it, but it was incredibly attractive. Something about how his voice became deeper, ordering authority in a language she didn't understand did it for her.

She shifted in her seat, waiting until the waiter left. "Should we get into the contract?"

He nodded, sitting back in his seat and throwing his arm around the back of her chair. "Go ahead."

"I know we both signed the contract my father's lawyer wrote up, but I think it's important for us to also establish ground rules for each other," Luna told him. She grabbed her purse, taking out the stack of papers and handing it to him. "I had Blair type this up last night, but I agree with everything that is in this and I hope you will too. If we're going to be in this for the long haul, I think we should be civil with each other and this is a good place to start."

He looked at her unamused, his brow raised. "It's a marriage, not a business deal. What the hell do you need this many rules for?"

"Just read them," she said. "I want to make sure we're both understanding what this marriage means."

He rolled his eyes, reading the first page. His face didn't shift until he read the second page. Suddenly, his eyes were lit up and a shit-eating grin replaced his frown. "Did you read it over before giving it to me?" he asked.

Luna looked at him, confused. "No, but I told Blair what to write, so I'm pretty sure I know the contents of it."

"Oh, so you told her to write, 'Adequate foreplay is necessary before any intimacy takes place, including, but not limited to, cunnilingus?' You know what, I think I can get behind some of these rules."

Luna's eyes widened in horror. "Oh my God, she did not write that." She tried to grab the papers from his hands, but he held them over his head.

"Before I sign, I like to make sure I read through all terms of the agreement," he said, flipping to the next page. He laughed.

"These just keep getting more crude and less legal sounding as we go through it."

Luna's cheeks were burning. How drunk did they get?

"Oh, so you'll only let me put it in your ass when we're married? I can agree to that," he told her. "I can agree to living in a house close to your friends, granted you're living with me and we're sleeping in the same bed."

"You should stop reading," she told him, completely embarrassed. "We got drunk last night while we were doing it so I don't remember half of the things written."

"So this was a group effort?" he asked, flipping to the next page. "I agree with the first child clause. I would never take anything away from my child. I'm assuming you thought of that."

She nodded, ignoring how her body responded to hearing him talk about their future children. "That one I did."

"Did you also write the one about guaranteeing your orgasms?" he asked, his brow raised. "I think I have a fair enough score considering what happened in the woods. What do you think?"

"I'm not commenting on these anymore," she muttered, looking down at the floor. The waiter entered the room, setting their drinks on the table before leaving quickly again. Luna grabbed her martini, taking a big drink from it.

"If you're so concerned about me taking care of you, you could have just told me," he said. He grabbed the bottle of wine, pouring her a glass before moving onto his own.

She shook her head. "Listen, there are actual important rules in there that I care the most about. We both signed the contract; we both understand we're stuck in this for the rest of our lives. If there are some you don't like, we can discuss that. Just like if you decide you want to see other women while we're married, I can't stop you, but I would prefer to at least know about it. I'll pay you that same respect if I decide to see anyone else too."

"What the fuck are you talking about?" Valerio asked. Luna was shocked by how quickly his tone had changed. "Neither one of us will be seeing anyone else. I'll follow your rules, but that's one I want in there. No extramarital affairs. I'm not marrying you just so you can go fuck someone else."

"But you can?" Luna asked, testing him.

"I would never. God, woman, I fucking tracked you down at your own engagement party and killed the man you were supposed to marry. I'm fucking obsessed." He ran his hand through his hair. "Tell me you didn't like what happened in the forest. Tell me you didn't feel anything or that anyone else could make you feel that way." He leaned in close, his lips only a couple inches away from hers. Her breathing turned heavy, her body responding to him immediately. "Tell me you hated coming all over my tongue and I'll let you have all the whores you want."

She couldn't because despite how hard she tried to keep hating him, her cold exterior toward him was already beginning to melt. She was sure that part had to be because of how easily he got down on his knees for her, making sure she came and was taken care of without worrying about himself.

And maybe her thinking about him on his knees had sent her over the edge more than once over the past couple of weeks, forcing her to wish it could happen a second time. Her eyes glazed over his lips, wanting to feel them all over again.

So she did. Luna met his lips, wrapping her arms around his neck to pull him closer. He tugged on her head so he could taste her deeper.

Valerio pulled back for a second, his lips in a menacing grin. "Say you don't want me. Say it."

Luna clenched her jaw, angry that he was asking her such stupid questions in such a heated moment. She tried to pull him to her again, but he didn't let her, keeping her at a distance.

"Say it," he muttered, his eyes blazing with lust and possession.

"Shut up," she said, instead.

"Not good enough." He shook his head, grabbing her chin with his hand. "Say you don't want me the way I want you."

She finally gave in, completely soaked and over his teasing. "I can't," she whispered.

His lips were back on hers, devouring them all over again. Why did he have to be good at touching her, kissing her? Why couldn't he be ugly and suck at making her come so she wasn't so drawn to chasing that same feeling of pleasure again?

She hated him. But she hated him because of how badly she wanted him. The feeling came out of nowhere, clouded her judgment in every respect of the word. But something had shifted in her. Maybe it was him killing the man her father wanted her to marry. Maybe it was him giving her another out when he didn't have to. Maybe because he wasn't as bad of a person as she thought he was.

Or maybe it was because she knew he actually cared about her. No, he loved her. That feeling terrified her, made her anxious and sick to her stomach. He hadn't said it, and he didn't have to. But she felt it. She knew it was there. Everyone did.

He stood, pushing his chair out before he got down on his knees, swiveling Luna's chair so she was facing him.

"What are you doing?" she asked, breathless. "Anyone could come in here. Stand up."

He gave her a devilish smirk. "Guess you'll have to stay quiet then."

He started at her calves, collecting the dress up her waist. She grabbed the chair, clutching for dear life.

He hooked his arms around her thighs, pulling her body towards the edge of the chair. He hooked his fingers into her underwear, slowly pulling them down her thighs and off her legs. Her breath hitched when he looked up at her, his eyes a dark shade of blue.

"Your pussy is just as perfect as I remembered it to be," he told her. He spread her legs apart, leaving her completely open to his eyes to his hands to his mouth. "I don't know how I went this long without it. One taste and I'm obsessed."

"Someone could come in at any moment. Our food will be here soon," she reminded him.

"Do you want me to stop?" he asked, his brow raised.

She smirked. "If you're okay with that waiter seeing your fiancée's pussy, I guess I am too."

His eyes turned deadly. "Then I think I have to make sure my fiancée comes quickly."

And then he leaned his head down, licking a strip up her core. She jumped off the seat, completely not expecting he would actually do it—again. Still, she didn't make a sound, terrified of someone walking in. Valerio looked up at her, spreading her folds apart before he placed his tongue directly over her clit, adding pressure onto it.

Luna grabbed the chair with a death grip, biting her lip to stop herself from moaning. She watched him the entire time. The way he sucked on her clit before trailing his tongue back down to her slit, letting it enter her.

The moan was on the tip of her tongue, waiting to slip out, but she held back. He pulled away, letting her inhale a deep breath. It was short-lived once his hand replaced his tongue. He moved his thumb in circles around her clit, forcing waves after waves of pleasure up her spine. Her eyes closed and her head fell back. A small moan escaped her.

Valerio trailed his hand down, putting one finger inside her. Luna whimpered, looking back down at him. "Look how fucking tight you are." He groaned, moving his finger in and out of her. "My cock is going to destroy you."

Luna let out a louder moan. His dirty talk made her feel something deep inside, igniting her further toward her orgasm. He slipped in another finger, connecting his lips back to her clit. Her body screamed in pleasure, everything building up so suddenly that she crashed through her orgasm with full force. She closed her thighs around his head letting him feel every shake of her body, every pulse of her pussy as she came.

Luna let out a shaky breath, unlocking her legs so Valerio

could come up for air. He pressed one last kiss to her inner thigh, pulling his fingers out of her. He gave her a bruising kiss, biting her lip.

"So much for being quiet," he said with a small laugh. He stood up, stretching his back out. Luna stared at him in amazement. How the hell was she supposed to recover from that?

She slid her dress back down just as the door was opening. The waiter brought in a tray of food, setting it down on the table for them, promising more was coming. Valerio took his seat again, his eyes locked on Luna. She avoided his gaze until he lifted his hand to his mouth, pushing his fingers inside. She gulped at the thin sheen of herself covering his lips.

She didn't understand what overcame her, but Luna leaned over, pressing her lips against his.

It seemed like he was expecting it, because his hand was locked on the back of her head, pushing her closer so she was practically out of her chair. He let her taste herself.

She pulled away, breathless. "So you'll sign the papers?"

He nodded. "I'll send you a final copy. There are some things I want to add."

Luna sat back in her seat. She fixed her hair and adjusted her dress. She grabbed the water on the table, taking big gulps.

Suddenly, she was more hungry than she had ever been in her life.

NINETEEN

LUNA

"IT'S SURPRISINGLY WARM," Luna said as they walked to the car after they had finished their meal. Her skin had felt feverish ever since Valerio had gotten on his knees. It got worse with every lemon drop martini she consumed. The drink didn't taste like alcohol, so she assumed there was barely any in it. She was wrong. "I wish I could go swimming right now. Being in the water sounds so nice. Don't you have a pool at your house?"

"Is that your way of asking to come over?" Valerio asked with a smirk. He opened the car door for her, letting her get in and making sure her seatbelt was secured before going over to the driver's side. He started the car once he was situated.

"Is that a no?" she asked.

"We can swim, but I know a nicer place that's more private than the house I share with the three most annoying people in the world," Valerio said. He entered the street, steering carefully between the slight traffic that had built up.

"You know you love them," Luna muttered, leaning her head back on the seat. For leather seats, they were surprisingly comfortable. She could also feel the heat under her butt from the seat warmers.

"Unfortunately."

"So, where are you taking me?"

"We're going to one of the hotels my family owns," he said. "There's a penthouse reserved for us that has an indoor pool."

She snorted. "I didn't know I signed up for the Vitali business tour."

He shrugged. "Not my fault my family owns a big portion of the city."

"How much money do you have?" she asked. "That has to be illegal."

"Who are you? The Feds?" he asked.

"I don't think I'm cut out for that type of job," she told him, looking out the window. "I'm built for something less stressful."

"Like what?"

She was silent for a moment. "I've never actually thought about it. Once I was told I would be getting a husband, I just kind of assumed I wouldn't get to do anything with my life just like my mom. She just kind of exists, it seems. I didn't tell you that to make you feel bad or anything," she added. "I just want to be honest and I'm sick of hiding how I feel. And maybe that's more of a hit on my father than on you. Truth is, I don't know if I'll ever forgive him for what he did to my life. If given the choice, I think I would prefer to put a bullet into his head." She gasped, opening her eyes that she hadn't even realized she'd closed. She turned to Valerio. "Please don't tell anyone I said that. I didn't mean it."

"I would never tell a soul, even if you decided to do it," he told her.

"Have you ever thought about it?" she asked.

"Killing your father?"

"No, killing yours."

"One time, but even that was too dark for me," he told her. This time he focused his gaze on the road, speeding up.

"When?" she asked. She was always too curious for her own good.

"When my mother killed herself because she couldn't handle

being married to him any longer," Valerio admitted. The words felt like venom leaving his lips, but the truth was out in the open for the both of them to deal with.

"Were they arranged?" Luna asked, but her voice was more of a whisper.

"She was pregnant with me," he told her. "My father couldn't have his heir out in the world unprotected. He couldn't have the mother of his child open to the same dangers either. AKA your family if they found out. The story sounds too familiar, huh?"

She shook her head. "I wasn't thinking that."

"It's hard not to compare you to her, and me to my father," Valerio said. There was a bite to his voice, but she knew it wasn't intended for her.

"I'm not pregnant," she said. "There's one difference."

"One day you will be."

"If you're so scared of that happening, why did you decide to marry me?" she asked in genuine curiosity.

"Maybe it's the hope that we'll be different," he said.

Luna was silent for a second. "My mother and father were arranged too. I wonder what she would have been like if her life had been different."

"I guess we'll never know," he said. "I'm sorry."

"Me too," she said. She stared out the window, her brows furrowed in thought. "You should know I would never leave you like that." She would never let him find her body one day, completely void of life. It would be too cruel, especially for him.

"I would never stop you from doing what you want in life," he told her. "Whatever career, however much schooling you want to do, if you want children or not, I'll never force you."

She turned toward him with a small smile. Maybe they would defeat the odds after all.

Valerio pulled into the valet of the hotel, put the car in park, and turned it off. He turned to face Luna. "Are you still up for that swim?"

"You promised me a pool," she said, unbuckling the seatbelt. "I want my pool."

He let out a small laugh and got out of the car. He made his way to the other side, opening the door for her. "Then let's go for a swim, baby."

He took her to the elevator, pulling out his wallet to retrieve the key from it. Luna didn't pay any mind to the grandiose hotel, too busy ripping off her heels once they entered the elevator. Her feet were stinging and she was sure there was a blister already forming.

"What are you doing?" he asked. "You can't be barefoot."

"Is that a rule?" She raised her brows in defiance. "Am I going to get kicked out?"

"Let me carry you. I don't want you accidentally stepping on something dangerous," he said, moving toward her.

"I'm fine," she said, pushing him away. She wasn't the smallest girl ever, and she didn't feel like dying of embarrassment if Valerio couldn't carry her. He was incredibly built, sure, but still.

"Don't think so deeply about it. Let me carry you," he said. His voice held no options, and besides, her feet were killing her.

She swallowed harshly under his intense gaze. "Fine, I'll accept a piggyback ride but only because I don't want to bring dirty feet into the penthouse."

He accepted his win, kneeling down so she could hop on. She lifted her dress, allowing her legs to stretch apart farther, but it didn't work unless she lifted her dress all the way up her waist, which wouldn't have been an issue if Valerio hadn't stolen her underwear.

"Get on, Luna."

"I can't without exposing everything," she said, pushing the dress down. "You never gave back my underwear from earlier or from the other night, by the way."

"And I'm not going to," he said, standing. He turned toward her, putting one arm around her lower back and the other under her knees, lifting her into his arms bridal style. She yelped, wrapping her arms around his neck to balance herself.

"What are you doing with all my underwear you've been taking?" she asked.

"Are you sure you want to know?" He looked down at her with a smirk that promised it was something naughty. The elevator finally opened on the right floor. Valerio got out, still carrying Luna.

"Well, now I'm curious," she said.

He leaned in until his lips were grazing her ear. "I wrapped it around my cock and jerked off imagining it was you instead."

"Oh," she squeaked. She cleared her throat. Immediately, the thought of him laying back on his bed, muscles out and flexing as he worked his hand up and down his cock, entered her mind. She assumed he was probably big, veiny.

"It's okay if you're picturing it in your head right now," he told her, knocking her out of the daze. They had arrived at the door, but it didn't stop Valerio's dirty mouth. "I imagine you touching yourself to the thought of me. Now reach into my pocket and grab the key from my wallet."

Luna reached down to try to find his front pocket. She realized her mistake when she brushed against his zipper instead. "Oops," she said, quickly, navigating her hand to the right. She reached in, grabbed the wallet and pulled her hand out. She didn't bother looking at his face as she took out the key and unlocked the door for them.

"What? You're not gonna return it back to my pocket?" he asked.

Valerio set Luna down, letting her feet touch the cool wood floors. "I wanted to snap a few pictures of your credit cards first," she said, taking the wallet with her as she walked through the penthouse.

The floors were a dark mahogany, spanning the length of the room. Floor-to-ceiling windows covered two full walls, with thick black velvet curtains drawn halfway over them. A brown leather

L-shaped sectional sat in the center of the room. There was a set of stairs by the piano on the right side, leading to an additional floor upstairs. On the left side was what Luna assumed to be the kitchen hidden behind a small wall and then another dark hallway.

"Where's the pool?" she asked.

He grabbed her hand. "Down the hall." He led her down the hallway, letting her eyes graze the abstract art that lined the walls.

"What's upstairs?"

"A bedroom if you're interested," he said.

She rolled her eyes. The entire space felt romantic and very unlike a space for someone like Valerio. He opened a glass door that entered into the pool room. The room was surrounded by glass, giving a clear view of the rest of the city. Now in the darkness, the lights twinkled like stars.

"This is incredible," she said in awe. "Are you proud of yourself for having things like this?"

"Of course," he said. "I've worked my ass off for so long. It's nice to have someone to enjoy it with now."

She remembered the wallet that was still in her hands. "I should probably give this back." She tossed it, and he caught it effortlessly.

"Hold onto it if you want," he said, throwing it on the pool lounger. "Everything mine is yours."

"Not until we're married."

"I don't need a paper to tell me you're mine."

He undid the buttons of his shirt, pulling it off. Luna's mouth went dry. She knew he was built and had gotten a glimpse of it at the fight, but back then she had been more freaked out about him fighting her brother and had too much at stake with their bet. Now, she was able to stare, and she did, suddenly completely sober as if she hadn't had a sip of alcohol.

His abs were chiseled and defined as if he had been carved by Michelangelo himself. With every movement he made, his muscles pulled and strained, locking Luna into a daze that she couldn't get out of. Her gazing only felt sinful when she caught the small trail of hair that disappeared under his slacks that he was already removing.

"Why are you getting undressed?"

"To swim," he said, confused. "Remember, the thing you insisted on doing."

"That was before I realized I don't have a swimsuit," she said. And before she realized what a distraction his body was proving to be.

He slipped out of his shoes, letting the pants fall to the floor. He picked them up, setting them on the pool chair. He threw off each sock, letting them fall as well. "Suit yourself. I'm swimming," he said, smirking as he pulled down his underwear.

Luna's eyes widened, eyeing the dick that stood rigid in front of her. She shifted her eyes quickly, waiting until he was in the water.

"The water is perfect," he said.

She stared at him for a long moment before she approached the pool chair herself. "Turn around," she told him.

"It's nothing I haven't seen before," he said.

She knew that, but this felt oddly intimate. She hadn't ever shown anyone her naked body in this type of environment, let alone someone she had been sexual with or who she found dangerously attractive.

Still, he turned around. She pulled the dress up and over her head, feeling the cool air of the room hit her. She dropped it on the pool chair, removing her bra after. With quick steps she entered the pool, submerging herself into the warm water.

He turned back around, his eyes immediately falling to her body under the water.

"My eyes are up here," she said.

"I know. I'm trying to engrave your body into my memory."

She swam past him, making her way to the edge of the pool to stare out at the city. It was oddly freeing swimming naked, not caring who saw her. She relaxed for the first time in so long.

That was why when he moved beside her, she didn't fight it.

"The moon is so bright tonight," she said. It was a full silver moon and from where they were, she swore she could see the little dark spots and crevices on it.

"Is that where your name comes from?" he asked.

"According to my mom, I was always the most active at night while she was pregnant with me. She didn't get any sleep at night for the entire nine months," she said. "She was the one that decided Luna would be the perfect name."

"It is the perfect name," he said.

"What were you named after?"

"My grandfather on my mother's side. I heard he was a wonderful man, but I never got to meet him. He passed while my mother was pregnant," he said. "So now I'm stuck with an old name."

"I like it," she said. "It fits you."

She turned toward him, studying his face while he stared ahead. He had a little mole beside his right ear and long black eyelashes she was jealous of. She saw the faintest hint of a scar on his chin, but it wasn't bigger than an inch. There was a story there and she realized that one day she would probably end up hearing it because he was the man she was set to spend the rest of her life with.

Her breathing increased as she realized that for the first time, dread didn't fill her at that thought. Instead, something akin with familiarity and serendipity filled her.

Maybe that was why she found herself leaning into him, setting her head against his shoulder. And maybe that was why when he wrapped his arm around her, she accepted it. The same butterflies returned and so did his warmth.

And she didn't fight it.

TWENTY
LUNA

LUNA DIDN'T KNOW what time it was, but she was exhausted. After swimming around for a little bit, her hair was flat and wet, but surprisingly her makeup stayed intact thanks to whichever setting spray Cecilia had used.

They lay on the pool chair now, right in front of the glass window. Valerio had a towel around his waist and Luna had one held securely around her. She didn't feel like throwing on her dress again, and the heat had been turned up to make sure she didn't get cold. Plus, laying on Valerio's warm body was like laying by a furnace.

His chest rose up and down under her head, and she could hear his heartbeat. It beat normally now, but earlier it had sped up.

"Valerio?" she asked, looking up at him.

"Hmm?" he replied. His eyes were closed as if he were dozing off, but his grip around her body was still as tight as ever.

"Are you sleeping?" she asked.

He opened his eyes this time. "I guess I was dozing off," he said, his voice surprised.

"Why do you sound so shocked?" she asked him.

"I can't sleep at night," he told her. "I usually get work done at this time."

"That can't be healthy for you." She sat up, adjusting the towel. "What keeps you up?"

He shrugged, keeping his hand on her hip. "I don't know, a lot of things, I guess."

"Do you do anything to help you fall asleep? Like a nighttime routine?"

He laughed. "Like what?"

"I don't know. Maybe you should drink some tea, read before bed, something."

"Maybe you should just sleep next to me." He leaned into her, burying his head into her neck. She laughed. "That seems to let my mind rest."

She pushed his head away. "Until I wake you up with all my yapping."

"I could listen to your voice all day and night. Sounds like a melody."

She snorted. "No, it doesn't."

"It does. I wouldn't lie to you about that," he said.

Luna rolled her eyes. "Do you really not sleep at night?" She felt worried about his health, she couldn't help it.

"I don't," he said. "Most nights at least. Sometimes the exhaustion takes me out against my will."

"How long has it been since you slept?" she asked. She ran her hand against his arm, watching as goosebumps rose on his skin.

"Since we both signed the contract," he admitted. "That was the first night I got sleep in a long time."

She felt a little guilty. It didn't help that she was probably one of the things keeping him awake at night, especially when she was fighting the contract as hard as she had been.

"I'm sorry for being one of the things that kept you up," she said.

"Don't apologize for anything. You can help me sleep now."

"If you weren't with me, would your father have set you up

with someone?" she asked. "I know Finn will probably get set up one day."

He sighed. "Yes, my father brought it up at one point. Had someone picked out, but I was quick to sign another contract instead."

"And you picked me?" she asked. She couldn't help but feel like maybe she was the bad decision. If Cesare Vitali had picked someone for his son, it had to have been someone beautiful, smart, and most likely more understanding of her role in his life. Probably someone less stubborn.

"I would have always picked you," he said. "You're loud, wild, beautiful, stubborn—"

"Is this list supposed to make me feel better?" she asked.

He grabbed her hands, pulling her against him. "You are so unapologetically you. It's not my fault that I've been enthralled since I was seventeen."

"Who knew you were so mushy?" She smirked. "Imagine if any of your men heard you speaking this way."

"I don't give a shit. You're going to be my wife; you deserve the mushy side of me. Let everyone hear it."

Her heart shouldn't have thumped the way it did, but it seemed to betray her at this point. He said all the right things, everything she wished he wouldn't say because it made her melt more and more. Who knew the future mafia don was such a romantic?

"So you have a mushy side, a possessive side, a violent side. Any other versions of you I should know?" she asked.

"I'm sure you'll learn them all one day, but something tells me you might like all versions of me, even the bad ones."

"Like the version of you that shot not one but two different men on two occasions?" she asked sarcastically. She could feel the heat creeping up her cheeks.

He nodded. "Absolutely. Maybe you don't want to admit it to yourself yet, but I think you enjoy the side that would go to extreme lengths for you. The version of me that remains on your side no matter what," he said, cocking his head to the side.

"And if I don't?" she asked, trying to hide the fact she did. She felt entirely too exposed in front of him and it wasn't because she wasn't wearing any clothes.

"Then you'd be lying to both of us."

She nodded her head slowly. "And if I do?"

"You should. I'll always be on your side," he said, running his hand up and down her back.

She looked at him, exposing her vulnerability. "You promise?" The words tumbled out of her mouth before she could stop herself. For some reason, she cared a great deal about whether or not he would always be on her side.

He wrapped his pinkie finger around hers. "I swear."

"You're a little too good at this romance thing." She let out a breathless laugh, trying to lighten the intensity of the moment. As if sensing exactly what she was doing, Valerio gave her a small grin.

"It comes naturally with you." He shifted on the chair so he was sitting up, but now his towel had ridden up, exposing his upper thigh.

That brought her a sense of satisfaction. Her hand rested on his upper thigh, testing the waters and enjoying when his muscles flexed under her hand.

"Are you sure you've never been with anyone else? Never touched anyone but me?" she asked him.

"Only you," he said.

"Has anyone ever touched you?"

She felt bold enough to move her hand up, looking up at him. He swallowed harshly.

"No."

She enjoyed that fact a little bit too much. It gave her a power she didn't realize she could have, an edge on the fact she was his first everything, making her feel dizzy with need. She felt daring and bold.

So she asked, "Could I?"

"Oh, fuck," he groaned out. "Only if you want to."

"I want to," she said, reaching for his towel and undoing it so he was exposed once again. Her eyes fell on his cock before going back to his eyes. He was completely naked, extended on the entire length of the pool chair.

Luna swallowed, already feeling the familiar heating in her core. She leaned over him, pressing her lips against his softly, but it seemed like soft and gentle weren't in his vocabulary because his hand was tangled up in her hair, crushing her lips against his. She trailed her hand along his neck before tracing the skin of his chest. His skin lit up in goosebumps from her touch, his body immediately becoming in tune with it.

Luna pulled away slightly, placing a kiss against his jaw, then the skin of his neck, gradually making her way down. His breath hitched, letting her do whatever she wanted.

She left open-mouthed kisses along his chest, hoping that it would leave a mark on him like all the ones he left on her. She moved lower, now running her mouth over every ab that lined his stomach. He flexed when her lips moved closer to the hair that created a trail to his now obviously hard cock.

Luna looked up at him, a little grin on her face when she saw he was in pain from her teasing. "You're going to kill me," he groaned.

She had never touched a man before, but she had read enough books and seen enough videos to have a general idea of what to do. With that, Luna sat up, reaching her hand out to grasp him. He tensed when she wrapped it around his cock.

She needed two hands to cover the length of him, which left her feeling intimidated. There was no way he was going to fit inside her mouth. She tightened her hands, moving it up his shaft and then back down.

"Fuck," he gasped. "Just like that, baby."

She took that as her cue to lean down, using her tongue to lick his tip. The salty pre-cum touched her tongue and she didn't hate the taste. She continued licking him, using his groans as an indication she was doing something right.

Then she took him into her mouth, only fitting a couple of inches, but it was enough to have him wrap his hand into her hair. She pulled back, taking in a deep breath. "Can you guide me?" she asked.

"Yes," he said without hesitation. "Absolutely."

Her mouth surrounded him again, but this time he lowered her head until his cock hit the back of her throat, forcing her to cough. He let up, forcing her to get some air before he did it again. She got the routine down quick, sucking when he pulled her head up and using her hand on the space her mouth couldn't reach.

"Fuck, just like that. You're such a good girl," he praised.

Those words sent dopamine straight into her brain, encouraging her movements all the more. Her jaw was already becoming sore, but she forced herself to push through it for him. Every groan out of his lips, the tensing of his muscles, pushed her to send him over the edge—to watch the big bad mafia heir lose control.

He lifted his hips, thrusting into her mouth when she came back down. It pushed his cock deeper, nearly suffocating her. Saliva dripped out the sides of her mouth, tears slipped from her eyes, but he didn't let up.

And she didn't want him to.

Luna could tell that he enjoyed the way she choked on his cock—something about being able to own her mouth, knowing that he was the only one who would ever fuck it.

He pushed his cock deeper into her mouth, keeping her there as bead after bead of cum erupted out of him. Tears stung her eyes and her lungs burned from the lack of airflow.

"That's it," he moaned. "Take it all, my good girl."

So, she did.

And finally, when he emptied himself, he pulled out. A

mixture of spit and his cum dripped out of her mouth, creating a mess on his stomach and thighs.

Luna took in deep breaths, wiping her mouth with the back of her hand. Valerio grabbed the back of her head again, kissing her. Lack of air forced Luna to push away. He wiped the remaining tears from under her eyes.

"How was it?" she asked.

"Fucking perfect," he told her. "Can you spend the night?"

"What time is it?"

He reached for her phone that sat beside them. "Almost three."

Her eyes widened. "In the morning?"

"What? Do you have somewhere better to be?" he asked with a grin.

"Yeah, asleep."

"Then let's go," he said, sitting up.

"Are you taking me home?"

"Do you want to go home?"

Luna nodded her head. "I didn't intend on sleeping in a hotel room."

"Fine," he said with a huff. "Next time, you'll be falling asleep beside me."

And she was looking forward to it.

They got dressed, not bothering to fix themselves up before they were walking back to the car downstairs. Luna had dozed off during the drive and only woke up when they got to the apartment. He got out of the car and walked to the passenger side, helping her unclip the seat belt.

"We're already here?" A loud yawn escaped her lips.

"Yes. Go back to sleep. I'll carry you up."

She shook her head, pushing him away. "I can walk." Her feet touched the cold ground, only to be swept up when Valerio was carrying her once again.

"I thought we had an understanding earlier," he told her, closing the door behind them.

Luna groaned. "I forgot about it."

"Then I'll add it into our contract," he said. They made their way into the elevator. Luna's eyes closed once again, only opening when she felt him start walking, this time to their door.

She took the key out of her purse, opening it for the two of them. When they made their way inside, he finally set her down. "Want me to tuck you in?" he asked.

She shook her head. "I think I can make it to my bed."

He nodded. "I'll see you on Monday."

"Why Monday?" she asked.

"So I can drive you to school," he told her. When he saw her opening her mouth to protest, he stopped her with a kiss. "Good night."

She frowned but accepted it. "Good night."

He turned to leave before stopping again. "I need to give you something before I leave."

"What is it?" she asked, confused.

He reached into his pocket, taking out a small black box. He grabbed her hand, setting it in her grasp. Even in her drowsy state, she knew exactly what was inside of the box.

"Don't think too much about it," he said, pressing a kiss to her forehead. "Good night." He finally turned around, leaving the apartment and closing the door behind him. Luna stood there in shock, the door locking and his footsteps leaving.

She opened the box, her heart threatening to jump out of her chest when she saw the ring. Her engagement ring.

If the contract didn't make everything feel official already, this certainly did.

TWENTY-ONE

LUNA

FOR TWENTY-FOUR HOURS Luna had been unable to take her eyes off the ring that still sat in the little black box. It stared back at her, glittering when the light hit it. She hadn't even bothered to take it out, too afraid it would somehow slip onto her ring finger as if it had some kind of magical powers.

Actually, maybe it did. The moment she put it on, it transformed her from Luna Kingsley to Luna (almost) Vitali. The thought sent a nauseous wave over her.

"It's not going to disappear if you keep glaring at it," Blair told her.

"I'm not glaring at it," she said. "I'm just looking."

"That's all you've been doing. Do you not like it or something?" Cecilia asked. "I think Valerio would be willing to buy you another one if you wanted."

Luna shook her head and closed the box. They were waiting for Gianna to get there, all wanting to take advantage of Valerio driving Luna to school. She hoped he didn't mind the additional guests on their ride. It had been raining all night and had yet to stop, so the ground was covered in mud and none of the girls felt like going to class soaking wet.

"The ring is beautiful, magnificent. I mean, the diamond is huge. Who wouldn't want it?" Luna said.

"Then what's the problem?" Blair asked.

"The moment I put this ring on, everyone knows I am engaged. It's like a flag is getting waved and that's all anyone will know about me when they look at me," Luna huffed.

"Why does that bother you so much?" Cecilia asked. "I'm sure everyone already knows you guys are engaged. I mean, news spreads like wildfire on campus."

"Not to mention you signed the contract yourself. You had to have known this was coming," Blair said.

They were both right. Of course they were. "I know." Luna sighed. "But we just had our first real date. It's like we're skipping a million steps and rushing into marriage when we should be getting to know each other."

Before either of them could respond, the door opened, and a huffing Gianna entered, shaking off her umbrella. "Your fiancé is an asshole. He parked across the street, claiming he couldn't get into the garage, so I had to walk in the rain."

"That sounds like a legit problem," Luna said.

"Well it would be if he hadn't driven into the garage as soon as I got out," Gianna said, crossing her arms. "I don't understand how I'm related to that freak."

"Hey, that's Luna's future husband you're talking about," Cecilia said, laughing, only to stop when Luna shot her a glare.

"Can we stop using those types of words?" she asked.

"What's the issue?" Gianna asked. "Was the date bad?"

"No," Luna said, keeping it short. Her mind flashed the images of that date. It wasn't bad at all.

"He gave her *the* ring," Blair said.

"What?" Gianna screeched. "Let me see!"

She extended it to her, watching as Gianna opened it in a hurry. "Now this is a ring," she said, her eyes practically glowing. She took it out of the box, going to put it on her finger.

Luna snatched it from her. "You can't put it on."

"Why? You won't," Gianna said. "I want to see how a rock that size would look on my finger."

"Doesn't matter. It's my ring," she said, placing it back into the box and closing it.

"Oh, so now you want it." Blair gave a pointed stare.

"Just because I'm hesitant to wear it doesn't mean it doesn't belong to me now," Luna told her, crossing her arms.

"Well, the date must have been really good since he gave you his mother's ring," Gianna said. "She kept it on lock and key when she was still alive, never wanting Cesare to get his hands on it."

Luna's eyes widened. "This is his mother's ring?"

"Not her wedding ring. It was passed down from her grandfather, so Valerio's great-great grandfather," Gianna said.

"That was actually sweet of him," Cecilia said. "That means he wanted you to have something special."

Luna swallowed hard. "Yeah."

She placed it into her bag, having every intention of giving it back to him. She couldn't take something that important from him, let alone wear his mother's ring. If she lost it or if anything happened to it, Luna would feel destroyed, especially if that was all he had left of her. She would never forgive herself.

She could settle for any ring at the jewelry store, something less meaningful so it wouldn't matter if it got lost.

"Let's go before he leaves us walking in the rain," Gianna said, opening the door.

Blair snorted. "He'll leave us, but take his bride."

Luna was the last to walk out of the apartment, taking smaller steps than everyone else. They made their way into the garage where Valerio was already waiting with his car running. A smile lined his lips when he saw Luna, but she couldn't return it.

His smile fell. "What are the rest of you doing?" he asked.

"We're Luna's cargo," Gianna said sarcastically.

He rolled his eyes, walking up to Luna. He pressed a kiss to her lips. "Good morning," he said.

"Morning," she said. "I hope you don't mind them coming since it's raining outside."

"Only for you."

He opened the passenger side door for her, letting everyone else fend for themselves as they all packed into the back of his car. Valerio got in, placing his hand on Luna's thigh as he began to drive. Her cheeks turned red, knowing her best friends saw the movement.

"So, Luna got back pretty late on Saturday," Cecilia said. Her tone was mischievous and Luna could see where this was going. "I wonder why."

She turned around, her eyes telling her to shut up.

"I wasn't aware she had a curfew," Valerio said.

"Since she's marrying you and we're her best friends, I think it's only fair we are compensated in some way," Blair said. "For example, I like going on yachts."

"Oh, me too," Gianna said. "And vacationing in Italy."

"Don't you already get all those perks?" Cecilia asked.

"Yeah, but I want to be included."

"Keep this up and I'll kidnap Luna so none of you see her again," Valerio told them.

She slapped his arm. "Be nice."

He looked over at her. "I only want to be nice to you."

Luna sunk into her seat at the *awws* that erupted from the back seat. He was being sweet now, but just the other night he had fucked her mouth and made her suffocate on his cock.

And then he gave her the ring.

The same anxiety filled her again. He pulled the car into the closest parking spot next to the building she had class in. Luna turned around, motioning for the girls to get out of the car with her eyes.

"We'll see you later then," Blair said, knowing what Luna was going to do. She was sure they all knew, which was why they hurried out of the car.

It was silent in the car for a moment. Luna turned to look at

Valerio, who had his gaze tied to her bare ring finger. She covered up her hand quickly.

"You're not wearing it," he said, flicking his eyes back up to hers.

She sighed. "It's not all why you think." She reached into the bag, pulling the small black box out. "You didn't tell me this was your mother's."

"Why does that matter?" he asked, leaning back in his seat. "I would have told you eventually."

"If something happened to it, like if I lost it or damaged it in some way—" She shook her head. "Is this the only thing you have left from her?"

"It is the only thing I have left from her. That's why it means so much to me and why I want you to have it. She would have wanted me to give it to you," he said, grabbing her hand that held the box.

"But maybe you should hold on to it. I can get any other type of ring. Seriously, I don't need this one," she said quickly. "And I know this isn't a romantic marriage, so maybe she wanted you to save it for someone you loved like that."

"I don't want you to have just any other ring," Valerio told her. "And this isn't just a contract. You know my feelings, and if she was still alive, she would have also understood my feelings for you. It has never felt like just a contract to me, Luna. I've never treated it as such, and I won't start now."

She had to look away, too intimidated by the intensity of his gaze. His authenticity and rawness made her uncomfortably vulnerable.

Quickly it was becoming more than just a contract—he already knew it, but it seemed like she was finally getting the memo.

He sighed. "Do you not like this one?"

"No!" she shouted, looking at him again. "I love it. I mean, look at it. It's absolutely beautiful."

"Then it is yours," he said. He leaned closer to her. "You're going to be my wife. This ring is just as much yours as it is mine."

"Are you sure?" she asked again. "I won't be offended if you decide to take it away."

Valerio rolled his eyes, kissing her to shut her up. She responded, missing the feel of his lips against hers. It had only been a couple of days and already she was starving for him. He pulled away. "The ring was made for you," he said. "There is no one else more worthy of wearing it."

Luna let out a shuttered breath. "Okay, I'll wear it."

Valerio took the box, opened it carefully, and grabbed the ring. He set the box on the dashboard, grabbing her left hand in his own. Luna watched in a daze as he slid the ring onto her finger, the cold silver touching her feverish skin. It fit her perfectly, as if it truly was made for her hand.

Luna flexed her hand, feeling out the weight of the ring. She didn't wear rings usually, so it was different. Not bad, just different.

She expected to feel transformed, different, dreadful, but she felt none of it. The butterflies still swarmed her stomach, but it was more about what the moment signified than anything else. She was officially an engaged woman—well, at least to anyone who now looked at her finger and could figure it out.

Valerio lifted her hand, pressing a kiss on the ring. He looked up at her, his eyes darker than before. She saw that same possession swirl in his eyes from before, only this time he had something physical claiming her as his.

"Perfect," he muttered. "Absolutely perfect."

A chill erupted up Luna's spine. One moment she felt like she was losing her mind and then Valerio showed up and suddenly she was completely calm. It made no sense to her.

A knock on the car window was the only thing that took them both out of their daze.

Valerio rolled down the window, allowing Dante to lean in casually. "What are you lovebirds up to?"

"What the fuck do you want, Dante?" he asked.

"I have class like everyone else on campus," Dante said. He lifted his hand to wave at Luna. She rolled her eyes, waving back.

"Since when do you attend class?" Valerio asked.

"Speaking of class, I have to go," she said, gathering her bag in her hand. Valerio turned off the car, pushing Dante away so he could open his door and walk with her. "You don't have to walk me," she said, closing her door behind her. "Plus it stopped raining."

He grabbed the umbrella from her hands, opening it and holding it over their heads while the light drizzling continued. "I have to head that way anyway."

"You don't have a bag or any books with you," Luna said, her eyebrow raised.

"He keeps all his knowledge in that big ass head of his," Dante said, laughing. It turned to a cough when Valerio smacked him in the stomach.

He grabbed her bag, holding it in one hand while he held the umbrella in the other. Luna walked close to him to avoid the drizzle of rain still falling. The stares from people on campus startled her, but that was the effect Valerio had on people. He made them stop and look.

"Did you invite her yet?" Dante asked Valerio, walking beside the couple. "Or can I do it? I already called dibs on inviting the others."

"Invite me to what?" Luna asked.

"My birthday party next weekend," Valerio said, almost sheepishly. "It's not a big deal."

Her eyes widened. How did she not know his birthday?

"Of course it's a big deal," she said. "Isn't it your quarter-life crisis?"

"I hope I don't have any crisis at twenty-five," Valerio said.

"So are you coming? I'm throwing the party, so you know it's gonna be good," Dante said. "We'll have fireworks, drinks, food, and strippers."

Luna's head snapped over at that word. "Strippers?"

Valerio shook his head. "I already said no to it."

"How can you have a party without some sort of entertainment?" Dante asked, groaning in protest.

She eyed Valerio suspiciously. Was it his idea to have strippers? Was that why she hadn't been invited to it sooner?

"If you want strippers, get strippers," Luna said, a fake smile on her face. "Don't let me stop you, especially if you had plans to get them anyway."

"I never agreed to it because I don't want it," he said. "When we went over it this morning, I shut it down immediately."

She nodded, feeling embarrassed. What was the sickening feeling that built up inside her? It felt murderous, unlike anything she had ever felt before. It was such an ugly feeling. One that left her wanting to grab Valerio and make sure everyone knew who he belonged to.

Was she *jealous*?

She couldn't be. To be jealous meant she considered Valerio hers, which she wasn't even sure that she did. Sure, things had definitely shifted since their date, but still, she couldn't already be feeling that way. It was too soon. She hadn't even known when his birthday was, for God's sake.

They were outside the building already, but Valerio grabbed her hand, stopping her from going inside. "I swear I don't want anything to do with Dante's plans and I'll make sure nothing like that happens. I didn't even want the stupid party, but him and Allister were already planning it before I could tell them I only wanted dinner with you that night at the cabin."

There it was. In a second, Luna's heart was melting once again. "I wouldn't mind still doing that. We have an entire weekend."

He smirked. "I think you're starting to enjoy spending time with me, my little moon."

"Little moon? What is that? My new nickname?" she asked, letting out a small laugh.

"I think it's fitting. You're able to brighten up my darkness like no one else." The grin on his face made him look so much younger and eased all the worries that usually overtook it.

"That's cheesy, even for you," she said, her grin matching his. It was cheesy, but she couldn't help but like the nickname. It was from him and sounded damn good leaving his lips.

"Have a good day. I'll text you," he told her. "Make sure you answer." She took back her bag, ducking under the cover of the building while he closed the umbrella and handed it to her.

"No promises," she said.

He rolled his eyes, wrapping his hand in her hair and pulling her lips to his. She wrapped her arms around his neck, standing on her toes. Every kiss left her completely breathless and wanting more. This had to be an addiction at this point.

She pulled away with a small smile. "I have to go to class."

"Go, before I change my mind," he muttered, slapping her ass when she turned around to walk away.

She looked back at him one last time, swirling the ring around her finger and disappearing past the doors.

TWENTY-TWO
VALERIO

"SO ARE you going to tell me when all of that changed?" Dante asked while they drove to their father's office. "I thought she hated your guts."

Valerio could only roll his eyes. He didn't think she felt that way anymore, or at least he hoped she didn't. "I'm not telling you anything."

"You're no fun. Like at all."

Valerio sighed. "We've been communicating and it's been good for us."

Dante looked at him suspiciously. "Nah, it's something else."

"I'm not going to gossip about my relationship with you."

"Oh, so it's officially a relationship."

"I'm marrying the girl," he said. "Of course it's a relationship."

"I should have known something changed. You've been nicer than usual," Dante told him, propping open the window. He grabbed the pack of cigarettes out of his pocket, sticking one in his mouth and lighting it.

Valerio grabbed it, throwing it out his own window. "No smoking in here."

"Never mind, I take that back," he said. He stuck the box back in his pocket, crossing his arms. That was until he saw the small ring box on the dashboard. His eyes widened. "You gave her the ring?"

Valerio nodded slowly. "I did."

"And she accepted it?"

"She did."

"So she's really in this then?" Dante asked, looking over at his older brother. "She's actually giving you a chance?"

"I'm pretty sure she is," he said, letting out a long breath. Finally, it seemed that she had accepted it. Or at the very least she stopped hating him enough to attempt to give him a chance.

"So you'll be showing off your fiancée at your party?" Dante asked. "Perfect timing."

"Yeah, the fucking PG party that you're going to throw," Valerio said. He drove wildly through the streets, trying to get to his father's house for the random meeting he'd called.

"She's just jealous; that's why she's so against it," Dante told him.

Valerio turned to look at him. "Wow, who would have thought that she wouldn't want her fiancé having half-naked women dancing around at his birthday party."

"Whatever. It kinda sucks that you're engaged now," Dante said. "You were so much more fun before."

"No, I wasn't. And I was always engaged to her," he said. They pulled up at their father's mansion, stopping at the guard stand where their identity was checked before the gates opened for them. Valerio drove in, parking right in front of the door.

He turned off the car, getting out. Dante followed after him, muttering something he couldn't hear and didn't care to. He loved his younger brother, but Dante had the annoying quality where he always poked and pried more than he wanted. Everyone knew Valerio was a private person, but Dante was one of two people who could truly get him to open up against his will. And now, Luna was the second.

They walked the familiar halls they grew up in, but instead of family portraits that once lined the white walls, random artwork replaced them. It made the space feel completely foreign even after spending seventeen years of his life in this house. Was it his mother dying that left this foreign feeling or finally leaving for Italy that drove the final nail in the coffin?

They made their way up the stairs, walking down the long hallway to get to their father's study. His loud voice echoed through the halls as he screamed at someone he most likely believed had betrayed him.

His father was that type of person; fragile with his loyalty. He shot first and asked questions second. If he even smelt an inkling of betrayal or traitorous behavior around him, he eradicated it. But never head on. Everyone knew Cesare Vitali's specialty was a bullet to the back. If anyone turned their back on him, he paid them the same respect.

The one thing he could admire about his father was his strong sense of loyalty, but his specialty always screamed cowardly. Valerio never shied away from looking someone in the eyes when he took their life away. He wanted his face to be the last thing a traitor saw before they went straight to hell.

Valerio knocked on the door, waiting to hear his father bark the usual "What?" When it came, he pushed the door open, walking into the room with Dante following.

Cesare Vitali eyed his sons for a long moment before he turned to look at the man that sat in front of him. All it took was a flick of his wrist to have the man stumble out of the door. Valerio could only stare at the man running out in pity, before he took a seat on one of the chairs in front of the grand mahogany desk. Dante closed the door, taking the seat right beside Valerio. The leather of the chair whined under his weight, leaving the room in silence.

Valerio was the one to break it. "Why have you called us here?"

Cesare took his seat finally. He stretched the time, making sure he was in control of the situation as much as possible. He finally leaned back in his seat, representing a calm demeanor, but there was an edge in his eyes. "I received a copy of the contract. I didn't realize you re-signed it."

Valerio stiffened, but he covered it up effortlessly. "It must have slipped my mind."

Cesare's eyes narrowed. "And you shot one of the Kingsleys' allies for it? What was that about?"

Valerio cursed himself. Sure, he had acted a little bit irrationally, but at the time he hadn't thought about what his father would think about it. A simple mistake on his part.

"You were so adamant about ending the contract, just to jump back into it. What game are you playing, boy?" Cesare spit out, slapping his hand against the desk. Gone was the faux calm exterior.

Valerio didn't even flinch. After years of dealing with the man in front of him—twenty-four years to be exact—he didn't feel anything toward his father, especially not fear.

"There is no game," Valerio said. He kept his voice leveled.

Cesare turned his gaze to Dante. "Are you in on this too?"

He jumped in before Dante could. Their father wouldn't do anything to Valerio because he was the heir, but that didn't mean he wouldn't give Dante double the beating instead. "He had no part of it. He wasn't even there."

"Don't tell me you actually care about the girl."

A cold chill drifted down Valerio's back. He didn't answer and he refused to give his father the satisfaction of the truth.

Cesare let out a mocking laugh. "Dear God, help me. What have I told you love will do to you? It gives you a weakness, something others will use against you—against us. That girl is a liability if you give a shit about her. Had I known about your little crush, I would have never allowed the contract in the first place."

"It's too late," Valerio told him.

Cesare shook his head. "It's not too late. I can take care of the girl. Sophia's father would be willing to sign again. I know he would."

Sophia, the girl his father wanted him to marry before he Luna. That night, all those years ago, when he found Luna crying, he had made up his seventeen-year-old mind. He brought up the contract to his father and hers, and made valid points for how much land, money, and power they would gain through the alliance. It was all bullshit. Even the numbers Valerio created on the spot and had Dante back up so that his father would let him enter the contract with Luna. It had to look strictly business and it had to look more profitable than any other proposition. And it did. Valerio did a good job, but now it was unraveling quicker than he could get ahead of.

He was always a planner. Always two steps ahead.

And now, for the first time in his life, he wasn't.

Valerio moved quicker than he could even comprehend. He grabbed the bottle of whiskey on the desk, slamming it against the tabletop to create a sharp edge. He was behind his father's desk in an instant, towering over him with the sharp edge against his jugular and his hand wrapped around his father's neck, directly under his chin.

"You will not touch my girl," he hissed, his entire body seething with anger. "She is going to be my wife and there isn't a single thing you, or her father, or even God could do about it. Do you understand me?"

Cesare continued choking, his face becoming increasingly red by the second. "Do you understand?" Valerio spit out again.

This time Cesare nodded, slumping into his chair to catch his breath once Valerio let him go.

He dropped the top of the bottle on the floor. "If you ever threaten her again, you will be answering to me, only this time I'll leave you bleeding to death on the floor. Don't ever make that mistake again."

The room fell into a tense silence. Cesare didn't say a word, but Valerio took that as his cue to leave the room. He swung the door open, hearing it hit against the wall violently. Dante followed after him, but neither one said a word until they were in the car, driving.

"What the fuck just happened?" Dante asked, a look of horror on his face.

Valerio just betrayed his own father. That was what happened.

TWENTY-THREE
LUNA

THE SUN WAS SETTING, lighting the sky up in blues, pinks, reds, and purples when Valerio came to pick Luna up for their date night and his birthday celebrations.

He had asked for a comfortable night, which meant comfortable clothing as well, declaring they would save the dressing up for tomorrow night. Luna walked out the door in some running shorts and an oversized sweatshirt. She still felt severely underdressed compared to him in his gray sweatpants and white T-shirt. Everything on him looked so much more luxurious.

She carried a little black gift bag in one hand and an overnight duffle in the other. His smirk grew, but she averted her gaze. When he called her earlier, he hadn't explicitly stated that she was spending the night, but he also hadn't said he was taking her home later. She just thought it was better to be prepared for anything. She also might have taken too long of a shower that included shaving everything and making sure her skin was smooth as butter, but he didn't need to know the details.

He grabbed the duffle from her, but she refused to give him the little black bag. "You'll see it at the cabin," she said, standing on her toes to kiss him. "Happy birthday by the way," she whispered.

He grinned, pulling her closer. "Best birthday by far."

She laughed. "We haven't even gotten to the cabin yet."

"I know, but I'm finally getting to spend it with you."

Warmth filled her. Before she could reply, he helped her into the waiting car. It wasn't his usual sports car. This time, he brought a SUV with him. Still ridiculously nice and expensive, but it just wasn't him.

"What happened to your car?" she asked.

"This is my car," he said.

She rolled her eyes. "The one you always drive me in."

"Dante smoked in it, and I can't stand the smell," he said. "So I'm getting it detailed and fumigated."

"I can't stand the smell either," she told him. They began driving, this time taking their time unlike how he usually drove. "This car is nice too."

"You like the other one more?" he asked.

"It's just the one we always use," she said. "Now, tell me what you did for your birthday today."

"I was just preparing the cabin. They've been setting up all day at the house, so it's like a circus," Valerio told her. His hand found her thigh, holding onto it while he drove.

She set her hand on top of it, sinking into the leather seat. "Everyone seems excited for the party tomorrow. Why don't you?"

He sighed. "It's not my thing. I've never been the type of person who wanted to be celebrated," he said.

Luna frowned. "Why not?"

"I don't know. The more powerful you get, you realize people just want to party with you for status, not because they actually give a shit about you. When I was in Italy, I made myself a nice dinner, went to whatever party Dante threw for me for a couple of minutes, and then ducked out."

"You should enjoy the little moments, which means even the annoying parties," Luna said. "Working so much will lead to burn out."

"I know that now. I just felt like I always had so much to prove being my father's firstborn. Too much responsibility comes with it and I had to dedicate my time to getting everything perfect, making sure the business was flourishing and everything was in order."

Valerio was young, but he lived his life like he had already experienced everything it had to offer. Luna couldn't imagine the pressure he was under, but she also knew that type of life wasn't sustainable. She was thankful she had her best friends that forced her to enjoy life and the little moments instead of the responsibilities that came with being her parents' only daughter. Without them, she would have sunk into her misery long ago.

Valerio needed that person too.

"Well, now you get to enjoy all these moments, including the stupid parties we're forced to attend," she said, giving him a smile.

He returned it, squeezing her thigh. "I do and believe me, I'm thankful for it." His eyes drifted down to the ring on her finger that shined under the bright setting sun's light.

The drive felt longer when Luna wasn't forced to go to the cabin. In fact, the drive and his presence were pleasant. They talked about random things, letting Luna tell him all about her birthdays over the years. On her fourteenth, her father gave her a diamond necklace, on her fifteenth he bruised her cheek for staying out late with the girls, and on her sixteenth, he set up an arranged marriage.

"How long has he been putting his hands on you?" Valerio asked. His knuckles were white on the steering wheel, his voice eerily calm.

"Since I could remember." It was hard to remember when it exactly started, but once it started it never stopped. "He kept it at slaps and minor punishments for me, but Finn always had the brunt of it. He took the heat off of me and placed it on himself so I never get it worse."

"Maybe there is something redeemable about Finn Kingsley."

"He's not a terrible person. He's misunderstood. I think a lot of you are," she said, looking up at him.

He was silent for a moment. "My father always went worse on Dante, finding any and all excuses to beat him. I always wondered if it was because I was the heir, but the older we get the more I realize just how much he looks like our mom. The eyes, the nose, the hair—identical. I think our father hates him for it, the constant reminder Dante serves," Valerio said. "Like your nightmare looking you in your eyes repeatedly."

Luna swallowed harshly. She never knew just how similar her and Valerio's lives were; how both their fathers made their lives hell. Even Dante, though she hardly tolerated him after what happened in the car that day when he threatened her, but she could understand now. Valerio was all he had.

"Maybe this is cruel, but I'm happy your father is tortured by Dante," she said. "Neither of you has ever deserved to be harmed by him."

Valerio grabbed her hand in his, pressing a kiss to the back of it. "You don't know how much that means to me," he whispered. The vulnerability struck Luna so deeply, she could only squeeze his hand tighter. "I hope you know that if your father ever puts his hands on you again, I will fucking kill him."

There was silence in the car as they pulled up to the cabin. Luna knew he would do it, and for some reason, she didn't hate that he would. "Thank you."

He kissed her, ending their conversation there as he exited the car. He helped her out before grabbing the bags. Luna walked up to the door, letting herself in when he let her know it was unlocked.

Immediately, she could tell that the space felt different. The cabin always felt cozy and comfortable, but tonight, the cabin seemed almost sensual. Maybe it was the fake candles that surrounded the space, the new cozy blankets on the couch, or maybe it was because something had shifted between her and Valerio. She assumed it was a combination of all of the above that left her with butterflies in her stomach as she removed her shoes and made her way over to the couch. Valerio dropped their bags into the bedroom that Luna had yet to see but she was sure that she would soon.

"This looks amazing, Val," she said. She took in every inch of the space, completely aware of the way he watched her.

"I wanted it to be perfect for you."

"But it's your birthday."

"And you're my girl. Are you hungry?" Valerio asked. "I bought some things to make us dinner while we're here."

Luna turned around on the couch, looking over at him in the kitchen. "You're spoiling me."

"It's my responsibility to make sure you're taken care of," Valerio said. "And I'm actually an excellent cook."

Luna laughed. "Since when?"

"Since I was in Italy," Valerio told her, beginning to grab ingredients from the fridge. She stood, walking to the sink to wash her hands. "What are you doing?" he asked.

"I'm going to help." She dried off her hands, rolling up her sleeves. "I can't guarantee I know what I'm doing, but I figured the expert can teach me."

The smile on his face made it worth it for Luna. Valerio leaned down and pressed a chaste kiss to her lips. "I'll prepare the meat; you can prepare the salad."

She nodded, getting started with washing the lettuce. It was quiet for a few moments, until Luna spoke up again.

"What was Italy like?" She looked over at him from the corner of her eye as he expertly seasoned the steak. "You never talk about it."

"There isn't much to say. All I did was work."

The answer wasn't good enough for her. "What type of work?"

He stopped what he was doing to direct his full attention to her. "The type of work I don't think you want to know about."

She chopped up the lettuce, ignoring his gaze. "Don't you

think it's important for me to know what kind of business you're involved in?"

He sighed, moving to the sink to wash his hands. He dried them off with a random dish rag, leaning against the counter right bedside Luna. "Yes, I do think it's important, but I would rather your opinion of me didn't change because of it."

They had finally reached a good place, one where she was finally starting to trust him enough to be around him willingly. In her mind, she knew she trusted him more than that, but she needed the communication and the honesty no matter how brutal that part of his life truly was.

Luna frowned. "You do know who my family is, right? I'm more used to this world than you think."

He was silent before he took a deep breath. "I sell *things*; ship them in, ship them out."

Luna stopped cutting to look at him. She could only assume the "things" he was referring to were deeply illegal.

"I have other businesses too, legit ones," he said. "And then I have the *physical aspects* of my job."

"So I can assume my father's friend wasn't the first person you killed?" she asked.

"No," he said. "And it won't be the last."

She stared at him. Rumors had told her this much, but still, having him confirm it made her feel odd. During the day he went out and committed felonies, and then at night he would come home and be a caring husband to her. Could both exist?

She went back to cutting the lettuce. Her mind was reeling about the dangers of his life.

"I would never hurt you," he said.

"I know," she said without hesitation. "But what if someone hurts you? What would happen if someone got their hands on you? All it would take is one bullet and you would be—"

She stopped herself, dropping the knife on the cutting board. Her mind had moved to that area without her even realizing. He could get killed, he could get hurt; it all made her feel extremely nauseous.

Only a couple weeks ago, she had still been fighting against him, praying for his demise. Now, it felt like the feelings she'd had for him at one point returned, perhaps even stronger than before. She didn't hate it, but she would be lying if she said it didn't scare her. The way her mind shifted and got whipped around confused her, made her dizzy.

She shook her head, trying to get rid of those thoughts. They were intrusive and disturbing.

Valerio grabbed her shoulders, turning her toward him. He had a deep frown on his face. "No one is going to get me. Don't underestimate how strong I am," he told her.

"It's not about strength," she said. Luna had the same fear with her own family. Every woman knew that every day their husbands left their homes there was a chance they wouldn't be returning. Some prayed for it, others lived in dread forever because of it.

"I will always come back to you, I swear," he promised her.

"Please," she whispered.

He grabbed her cheeks, stroking the skin with his thumbs. "I will never break my oaths to you, my little moon."

His lips found hers in a gentle reminder that he would always be there for her. There was no point in doubting it either; he hadn't left her alone before, she doubted he would ever do it now.

The moment was over when her stomach growled obnoxiously. He grinned, giving her one more kiss before going back to working on dinner. She finished the salad, which was too simple to really mess up, and the rest of the time she watched Valerio cook the steak in the skillet and make some type of Alfredo pasta to go with it. Luna made them drinks, adding a little bit of alcohol into each of the cups. At least she thought it was a little bit until he took a sip and began coughing.

"What is this? Straight vodka?" he asked, setting the cup down to stir the sauce.

"Just sip it slowly," she said, before gagging on her own drink. "Never mind, this is horrible." She emptied hers out and replaced it with some juice instead, grabbing another drink for Valerio as well. "I swear I know how to do some things in the kitchen."

"You don't need to know how to do anything," Valerio said. "I'll never let my baby starve."

She ignored the blush on her cheeks and set the table for them. She lit a couple of candles as well to set the mood.

Valerio plated the food, helping Luna into her chair. Her eyes widened at the explosion of flavor on her tongue, praising him for his skills to which he bragged about other skills he could show her. Her cheeks flushed, but she continued eating. When they both finished, they cleaned up the table and dishes and ended up on the couch.

The fire roared in front of them, immediately warming the cabin with a smoky essence. Luna relaxed against Valerio, closing her eyes in contentment. She accidentally kicked the small black gift bag that sat on the opposite end of the couch.

"Oh, I almost forgot," she said. She got up quickly, reaching for it and turning to Valerio in waiting. "I got you something for your birthday."

He shook his head. "You didn't have to get me anything. You being here was enough."

"I wanted to." She handed it to him, her eyes wide in anticipation. "I hope you like it."

He grabbed it, reaching in and pulling out the rectangular box. Valerio opened the box to reveal a silver chain with a silver "L" pendant at the center.

"This is the most thoughtful gift anyone has ever given me," he told her. "Thank you."

Luna's heart melted. She knew she did good when he pulled the chain out of the box. "I figured since you gave me a ring, you needed something from me," she said.

"Or something to tell everyone I belong to you," he said, looking up with her with darkened eyes.

Luna swallowed harshly, nodding. "Maybe there was a little bit of that component there too."

"You want people to know I belong to you?" he asked.

"You don't have to wear it if you don't want to." Her voice was close to a whisper.

Valerio clasped the necklace around his neck and ran his fingers over the chain. Goosebumps rose on his skin. "I'll wear it like a collar, a chain, a fucking rope around my neck that only you can pull around," he said. His voice was deeper than before, speaking with a conviction she had only heard a handful of times before. "You have me, forever and not a moment less."

Luna's breath hitched. A shiver shot up her spine, but her core was burning up with a new need. To be wanted, to be needed, to be *loved*—wasn't that all she had ever wanted in her life? And she had found it in the one person she didn't want it from, the one person she'd fought more than anything when she should have jumped into his grasp instead.

Luna reached out, trailing her fingers over the chain. She felt his heartbeat beating out of control. She grasped the "L" with her finger, pulling him towards her. He followed, completely and utterly stuck in her gaze.

She gave him a little smirk.

"Show me you're mine."

And he did.

TWENTY-FOUR

LUNA

THE FIRE BURNED BRIGHT, painting the room in a soft orange light when Valerio wrapped his hands in Luna's hair, pulling her lips to his in a frenzy. He pulled her onto his lap, drifting his hands from her hair, to the nape of her neck, down the curve of her spine. The movements stopped at her waist where he grabbed her sweatshirt and pulled it over her head.

They pulled apart so he could slip it off completely, but when he tried reconnecting their lips again, Luna pushed him back.

"Wait, I have a cute outfit I wanted to put on," she said breathlessly.

"Save it for another time," he growled, trying to reattach their lips again.

"I bought it specifically for tonight."

"I'm just going to end up ripping it off of you," he said, playing with the straps on the bra she currently wore. "I would prefer you without any clothes right now."

"I'll take two seconds," she said, getting up quickly. She could feel his heated eyes on her the entire time, only escaping them in the safety of the bedroom.

Luna was still attempting to catch her breath when she pulled the white teddy dress out of her bag, clutching it to her chest. The room was mostly plain except for the dark oak bedside tables that sat on either side of the huge bed, which took up most of the room. The headboard, darker than the other wood in the room, stretched up the wall and covered nearly half of the window behind it. Luna pulled the thick light brown curtains closed to cover the rest of the window before stripping. She slipped into the lingerie she'd bought knowing that their relationship was going to take this next step.

She grabbed the small mirror from her bag, checking herself over. She checked her teeth, fixed her hair, and made sure she was completely presentable. Her eyes were bright, cheeks flushed.

She was going to give him her virginity, and that felt so right to her. She didn't fight it and didn't hate it. She had always known it was going to be him, and that was why she got on birth control the moment they signed the contract again after their night in the forest.

Heat built up in her core thinking about that night and how he chased her, promising to make her his. She didn't want gentle. No, she wanted to be ravaged just like he had done before when she couldn't stand on her own legs.

She smiled at the thought. They had come so far, and she wouldn't change anything about it. Not a chance.

Luna walked out of the room, taking a deep breath when she saw Valerio standing by the fireplace, his shirt long gone. He stood in the dimmed light in only a pair of gray sweats. The sight left her breathless, and it only intensified when he looked at her.

His eyes traced her body, taking their time. She heard his deep inhale; it made the hairs on the back of her neck stand up. Being gazed upon like she was some magnificent painting or statue wasn't something she was used to, but when Valerio looked at her that way, he made her feel like that was the only way anyone should. Like she was the best thing anyone had ever laid their eyes on.

She took a small step forward, suddenly feeling like some little rabbit who had been found by a big bad wolf in the forest. He didn't look away from her, not for a moment.

"Do you like it?" she asked, taking another step forward.

He inhaled. "You look like an angel."

Her lips quirked up. "Is that a good thing?"

Valerio's eyes darkened. "Not when you have the devil's attention."

"And you're the devil in this situation?"

He smirked. "Haven't you always known that?"

She did. "Well, while we're on the topic, I wanted to ask you something. Make a deal, if you will."

This time his eyes lit up in curiosity. Valerio walked over to where she was standing, grabbing a strand of her brown hair in his fingers. "Ask away."

She traced his arm. "Do you remember the night we signed the contract?"

"I'll never forget it. What about it?" He cocked his head to the side, his eyes narrowed slightly as if he were analyzing her.

Her cheeks turned red. "You made a deal with me back then. I had a chance to run, but if you caught me, you would marry me."

"And I am," he said. "But I don't think you're referencing the terms of that deal. I think you want a chase again."

Luna's hand stilled and she bit her lip. She looked up at him, while his fingers dragged along her upper thigh pulling on the fabric of the lacy lingerie.

"I do want another chase, but this time if you catch me, you get to fuck me." She couldn't believe the words actually left her lips, but the minute they did, it felt like she was exposing a secret. Now he knew just how much she wanted him if he wasn't able to guess it before.

His lips pulled up into a lethal grin, one that promised he was going to win.

"Then you better start running."

Just like that, Luna turned around, ripping the front door open and started running for her life. The cold night air shocked her feverish body. Her feet had a mind of their own, leading her into the woods she had never explored before. The sun was long gone now, replaced with the barely visible moon and a couple of stars in the sky. These woods were uncharted territory, surrounded by dense trees and the rough ground. Her feet would be bruised and scratched up in the morning, but her mind could only think about what awaited her when he found her.

She stepped on top of overgrown tree roots, nearly twisting her ankle in the process. Sweat coated her skin and she wasn't sure how long she had been running for now.

Her thick breaths escaped while she attempted to keep moving to put distance between herself and the cabin. At this point, she was deep in the forest, unsure if Valerio would even be able to find her out here at all. She paused for a moment, trying to listen out into the forest, but the beating of her heart was loud in her ears, making it difficult to hear anything else. She slowed her breathing, listening in again.

A branch snapping had her taking off again. She couldn't be sure if it was an animal or Valerio, but at this point they were one in the same. The ends of the teddy dress whipped around wildly with every step she took.

The snapping of twigs and footsteps became more consistent and too close for comfort. She begged her legs to go faster, but it was no use. Valerio was catching up to her; she knew it. The hair on the back of her neck was sticking up, alerting her to the danger that was present.

She couldn't run anymore; she needed some kind of diversion. Valerio would expect her to continue going deeper into the forest, but he wouldn't think she would return back to the cabin. With that thought she made a sharp right turn, running straight like that for a few moments before turning back to run the opposite way she had been coming from. Hell, she didn't even know if this would take her back to the cabin but at the very least it could throw him off.

She started to slow down, her legs aching and lungs burning.

She could also see the lights, very faintly, from the cabin. She was close, but not nearly close enough. The trees around her were starting to become more sparse, leaving her exposed. If Valerio was anywhere around there, he would be able to spot her no problem. She pushed herself with one final boost of energy to get there.

Two arms wrapped around her waist, slamming her back into a chest. Luna let out a shocked scream, forcing Valerio to press his hand on her mouth to keep her quiet.

"I caught you," he growled out. He let go of her mouth, using his hand instead to wrap around her neck and press her into him.

"How did you find me?" she asked, gasping for air. She refused to turn around, knowing what was going to happen now.

"If you run, I will always catch you," he muttered into her ear, biting on the lobe. His hand drifted down from her waist to the bottom of the lingerie, running his fingers against the bottom of the lacy material. "Especially when the prize is so sweet."

He lifted the dress up, running his fingers against the exposed skin of her lower stomach where the waistband of the underwear sat. Luna's breath hitched when he dipped his hand into the panties, finding her clit without any hesitation. She gasped, dropping her head against his shoulder.

"Look how wet you are." He groaned, rubbing circles around her clit, slipping his fingers down to her slit to collect the moisture that leaked out of her. "Did you want me to catch you?"

She couldn't answer. All she could muster up were small moans while he slipped two fingers inside her, fucking and stretching her pussy. He bit her ear again. "Do you want me to fuck you?" he asked again, thrusting his fingers quicker.

"Oh God," she muttered. It was embarrassing how close to an orgasm she already was, but everything was stimulating her. His touch, his body against hers, his words. It was all too much.

"Answer me or I'll stop," he threatened, slowing his fingers down. Luna grabbed his arm, keeping it in place.

"Yes," she gasped out. "Yes, I want you to fuck me."

He paused his movements, forcing Luna to groan in frustration. Why was he stopping?

He slipped his hand out against her protests, turning her so she could face him now. A chill ran down her spine at the wild look on his face. His eyes were filled with lust. His hair was messy, small glitters of sweat decorating his chest, and the chain around his neck shined under the moonlight.

He looked perfect.

Valerio wrapped his hands under her thighs, hiking her up into his arms. She wrapped her legs around his waist, her arms around his neck. "What are you doing?" she whispered.

She could feel his hardness digging into her clit with every step he took, causing delicious pressure.

"I'm not fucking you for the first time in the forest," he muttered, kissing her. "I'm fucking you in a bed where I can take my time to savor the moment."

Luna gave him a soft smile, her heart melting at his sentiment. Of course, he wanted to make their first time special. And besides that, she didn't think losing her virginity in the woods was something she wanted to experience.

Although, she wouldn't mind doing it in the woods eventually. They had become somewhat sentimental to her.

She took it upon herself to press kisses against his neck while he walked them back to the cabin, torturing him. She was sure his neck was one of her favorite things about him, especially now that he wore the chain around it.

He kicked in the front door, carried her through, and then kicked it closed. He tried his best to avoid hitting anything while he made his way into the bedroom, setting Luna down on the bed. Valerio didn't leave them disconnected for long; he was back on top of her, connecting their mouths with a newfound passion. This time, however, the kiss was slower, more sensual.

Luna pulled him closer, running her fingers through his hair. He kissed down her neck, biting the skin as he made his way down. Soft moans escaped Luna. She arched her back, allowing him to grab the dress in his hands and rip it in half. Luna gasped at the archaic gesture, her breasts out in their entirety.

"I could have just slipped it off," she muttered, her eyes closing when his attention moved onto the raised nipples. His tongue swirled around the left one, licking and teasing before he bit down on it causing her to yelp.

"I prefer this more," he said. He continued kissing his way down her body, while pinching her right nipple. His teeth ran against the waistband of her underwear, igniting her in that same fire she always got around him.

He snapped her underwear off, throwing them to the ground with a grin. The grin only grew when he saw the unamused look on her face. "I'll buy you all the underwear in the world just so I can rip them off."

But when he looked down at her glistening pussy, his eyes dropped closed. "Fuck me," he groaned. He wasted no time digging in, spreading her open with his fingers and letting his tongue taste her. Luna leaned back on her elbows, watching him devour her. She nearly lost it when he looked up at her, sucking on her clit with a devious look.

Her head fell back and she gripped his hair to keep him in place. No matter how many times he ate her out, she would never get used to it. He held down her hips, forcing her legs open despite how hard she tried to shut them around his head.

And it left Luna shattering for the first time, her pleasure seeping through every inch of her body. She let out a loud moan, calling out Valerio's name.

Her body shuttered from the aftershocks as he moved back up, pressing small kisses along her body until his lips touched hers. She tasted herself on his lips, his tongue, letting him consume her mouth the same way he consumed her pussy moments ago.

When he stood, his eyes were covered in admiration and lust. Luna watched him with precision as he pushed the sweats down his legs, leaving him completely bare. His cock stood rigid, pre-cum leaking out of the tip. Luna sat up, pushing the lingerie the rest of the way off her shoulders, and crawled over to him.

"What are you doing?" he asked, his voice deeper than before.

"Having a taste of what's mine," she said. She felt mischievous from seeing the lust on his face. It drove her crazy to know he was just as affected by her as she was by him.

She wrapped her hand around him, moving up and down the length of his dick, squeezing slightly. "Fuck," he muttered. His eyes darkened when her mouth took him, her tongue swirling around the head of his cock before she attempted to take him further. She looked up at him with wide eyes when his hand wrapped itself into her hair, guiding her.

He pulled back, watching as a streak of spit connected from her lips to his cock. He gripped her chin, holding her mouth open. Valerio leaned down, spitting into her mouth before shoving his cock back inside her.

Luna looked at him in shock, choking when he hit the back of her throat. Her entire body hummed at the satisfied look he gave her. She could feel her core awakening again, wanting him as if she hadn't just had an orgasm. "Good girl," he praised. "Take my cock just like that."

The praise had her bobbing her head quicker, hollowing her mouth while he fucked it feverishly. Then he pulled out completely, leaving Luna confused.

"Why did you stop?" she asked, sitting up.

"Because as much as I love your mouth, I want to come inside your pussy tonight," he told her. His lips connected with hers again, pushing them both back onto the bed.

Luna's heartbeat quickened, realizing what was about to happen between them. She was giving herself to him, and he was doing the same. Nervousness settled in the pit of her stomach, but it calmed down when she realized Valerio would never harm her. She trusted him. Somehow, despite everything they had been through, she completely trusted him. He had grown on her quicker than she had even realized, and she was content with it.

His hips ground against her, pressing his cock against her clit. He pulled back, looking at her with a look that Luna had never seen before from anyone else other than him. She knew what the look meant; it was a certain four-letter word she was afraid to admit herself.

"Are you sure you want this?" he asked.

She gave him a soft smile. "More than anything."

His grin was infectious while he pushed her hair back from her forehead. Valerio leaned down, kissed her, and then he slid his cock into her.

Luna gave a small gasp, already feeling incredibly full. He stopped completely, looking at her for permission to continue. She nodded, gripping his shoulders while he pushed himself in further, stretching her to fit him. Luna forced her body to relax, but she couldn't stop the drops of tears that slipped from her eyes at the intrusion. She knew he was big, but inside her he felt impossible to fit.

"Do you want me to stop?" he asked.

"No," she said immediately. "Keep going."

He let her adjust before he pushed all the way in. Luna let out a cry, digging her nails into his shoulders.

He kissed the tears that slid down her cheeks, trying to distract her from the pain. "I wish I could feel the pain instead," he whispered.

"I know," she told him. And she knew he would if he could.

He pulled his hips back, and then pushed back in slowly, moving at a pace that would be more comfortable for her.

Slowly the discomfort subsided and the pleasure started faintly. Every time he pulled out, he brushed against something inside her that sent a wave of pleasure up her spine. It was a different type of pleasure though. One that made her feel full, completely connected with Valerio.

"You're doing so good, baby." He kept his slow, steady pace.

"Go quicker," she said breathlessly.

He listened, gradually building his pace. She let out a louder moan, her eyes falling closed when the pleasure intensified. She lifted her legs up, wrapping them around his waist. In this position, his dick slid in deeper, hitting that little spot over and over again.

They fit perfectly, as if she was made just for him. He thrusted into her harder, making her release moan after moan.

"Harder," she grunted.

Valerio let out a breathless laugh. Still, he obliged. His hips slammed against hers, balls slapping against her ass. He reached down, playing with her clit while he fucked her.

She let out a cry, digging her nails down his back. She had never felt anything like this in her life, not even when he fucked her with his tongue or his fingers. The orgasm snuck up on her, making her lose her mind when the pleasure crashed through her body.

Valerio leaned against her forehead, fucking her through her orgasm. Her eyes locked on his, leaving them in a moment of disbelief, of something new that connected them for the rest of their lives. And when he came inside of her with a loud groan, marking her as his, she knew she was tied to him forever.

They both let out heavy breaths, unable to move from their place of tangled limbs. Luna was the first to connect her lips to his, putting every drop of emotion that she felt into it. One emotion shined above all the others, but Luna couldn't admit it. No, she wasn't ready for that yet.

And when he pulled out of her, she didn't expect to feel so empty.

"Let me clean you up," he said, attempting to get up.

Luna shook her head. "No, stay or at least let me come with you."

He grinned, lifting her with him. They made their way into the bathroom, allowing Luna to use the restroom while Valerio took ample attention to cleaning her up. She could already feel the soreness between her thighs.

She held on to him tightly, even when he went into the

kitchen to grab them some water and then carried them back into bed. He tucked the blanket over them, pulling her into his arms impossibly close.

He stroked her back, lulling her slowly to sleep. "Are you going to sleep tonight?" she asked, her voice thick with exhaustion.

He pressed a kiss to her head. "I think I will. You can go to sleep, I know you're tired."

She let out a small laugh. "Whose fault is that?"

With that her breathing evened out, lulling her into a deep sleep. Not a single nightmare came.

TWENTY-FIVE
VALERIO

VALERIO STIRRED awake to the chirping of the birds outside and the sunlight streaming into his eyes from the crack in the curtains. He had no idea when he fell asleep, but being next to Luna must have relaxed his mind enough to actually knock out. She lay entirely on top of him, her hair wild and tickling his chin. A grin appeared in an instant once he heard her snores.

He couldn't remember the last time he had woken up feeling completely content, but he could get used to the feeling. All he could think about was the night before. Luna running in the woods begging him to catch her, letting him fuck her into oblivion, marking her as his with the necklace; it was the best fucking birthday he had ever had.

He looked down, pushing her hair from her face. He wanted to devour her just because she wanted everyone to know he belonged to her. That feeling alone made him dizzy, exhilarated with a shot of adrenaline swimming through his body.

Never in his life had he had a reaction like this with anyone or anything, but now his body only reacted to Luna and her call. She was his puppet master, pulling the strings of his body, mind, and soul. The power she held over him should have made him fearful and should have made everyone else in the world fear it because there wasn't a single thing he wouldn't do for her if she simply batted her eyes at him.

He had waited twenty-four years, and all he could say was that it was completely worth it. Was he addicted now? One hundred percent. There was no question about it. Luna was his favorite drug, and he would destroy his life just to have one more hit of her.

He hardened under her, cursing to himself. Was that all it took? One thought of Luna and he was at half-mast. He couldn't help himself; he was a man in love.

He played with the soft strands of her hair, waiting for her to wake up. It was the most beautiful color he had ever seen in his life. The hints of auburn amongst the strands of brown he hadn't noticed before. Like this he could even see the little freckles on her cheeks. Strangely enough, none of them stretched over her nose. Her eyes, that were always wide in disbelief at him, were closed, but he wanted nothing more to see them and the shade of forest green he had become obsessed with. They were similar to the color of the trees outside, the same ones she had grown to enjoy running around.

She groaned, stretching her body out before she finally opened her eyes. She looked around the room in confusion before she found him.

"Good morning, my little moon," he said.

"What time is it?" She rubbed her eyes. She tried to sit up, but he pulled her back down onto his chest.

"It's almost eleven, but if you're tired, go back to sleep," he said.

She shook her head. "No, I should get up. I'm sure you have a million things to do today to prepare for your party."

"Fuck the party. I think I know where I would rather be," he muttered, flipping Luna onto her back. He buried his head in the crook of her neck, relishing in the laughs she gave him. He could listen to that sound all day, every day.

"Is it safe to assume you had a good time?" she asked.

He pulled back, looking at her with a "duh" look on his face. "I think I'll have to fuck you again to make sure."

Luna raised her brow. "Just one more time?"

"Well, one more time after that, and then another after that, and then another one after that. Could be hundreds of times. I like to be thorough." He grinned, wrapping his mouth around her nipple before biting down softly.

Luna cursed, arching her back. "I need a shower," she said when he moved to the other breast.

"Perfect. I'll join you." He picked her up, carrying her into the shower. The water was scalding the way she enjoyed it, but he put up with it. Especially when he got to wash her hair and then move onto her body. He took his time gliding the soap over every inch of her skin, teasing her until she was the one kissing him first. He promised to go slow when she mentioned being sore, but when she was pressed against the glass door begging him to go faster, he couldn't help himself.

He buried his head in her neck while they came together and then rinsed off once again just as the water turned cold.

Valerio threw on a pair of sweats and went out into the kitchen to make her something to eat. He scrambled eggs on the stove, motioning to the water and pain meds he had set out for her when she finally made her way out of the room in only his sweatshirt and a pair of underwear.

He could feel her eyes watching his movements, staring at his body. He let her stare without bringing attention to it. She was free to look as much as she wanted; he was all hers. He plated the food and handed it to her, fighting the urge to feed her himself.

"Did you have a good birthday?" she asked. She lay with her legs on his lap when they finished eating.

"If every birthday is like that, I think I'll enjoy getting old," he told her. "How are you feeling?"

"Sore," she said. "But it's not bad."

"Was I too rough on you?"

Luna's cheeks turned red. "No. Actually you could stand to be a little rougher."

He let out a loud laugh. "Those books are rotting your mind."

"Well, if you don't, I know someone else will," she said in a sing-song voice.

He heard the joke in her voice, but he saw red before logic could meet his brain. He was on top of her in a second, tracing her chin with his fingers. "Try it," he said. "See if anyone could fuck you better than I could. Poor bastard couldn't even get within 10 feet of you before I intercepted him with a knife in the throat."

Judging by the way her eyes darkened, he knew she was turned on by it. Of course she was. Luna loved this side of him just as much as she loved the other sides of him. She was perfect for him.

"I wouldn't want to be with anyone else," she said, leaning up to trace her fingers around the chain on his neck. "Never." And just like that, he couldn't figure out what made him so mad in the first place. That was her effect on him. She ran her fingers through his hair. "Now, I need to go home because I have no idea what I'm wearing tonight."

He would have preferred to never leave the cabin and to keep Luna with him there for the rest of his life, but she wanted the party and he wanted her happy. They drove back to campus, and he walked her up to her apartment, only leaving once she was safely inside. He would see her in a couple of hours; it wasn't a big deal. Only it was to him. He had no idea how he ever went seven years without seeing her, but Valerio knew for sure he would never do anything like that again.

TWENTY-SIX

LUNA

LUNA SIGHED, a grin on her face when she turned around to go into her room. Blair and Cecilia blocked her in the hallway with looks of curiosity on their faces. Luna put on a more neutral look. "Good morning," she told them.

"I'm sure it's been a good morning for you," Cecilia said with a grin. Blair elbowed her in the side.

"How was your night?" Blair asked.

"Fine," Luna told them, walking into her room.

"I'm here!" Gianna called out from the living room, running into Luna's room. "Have you started talking about anything yet?"

Luna rolled her eyes. "I'm not sharing anything."

"Oh, so it wasn't good?" Cecilia asked. She had a frown on her face.

"No, it was more than good," she said, grinning. She gave into it easier than she wanted to, but she couldn't help herself.

"I knew it!" Blair squealed.

"God, that's disgusting," Gianna said, clamping her hands over her ears.

Luna indulged them in a couple minutes of gossip that ended up taking longer than she anticipated, leaving them rushing to get ready for the party. She threw on the dress she'd bought the other day with Cecilia: a lacy pastel-blue, mini dress. It had a little blue satin bow right at the neckline of the dress and held her breasts tightly. The bottom flowed freely with the uneven cuts on the end making it feel more whimsical and fairy like. She threw on white platform sandal heels and curled her hair. Luna loved the way she looked, even with the bruises on her neck and collarbone from Valerio.

After one of his drivers picked them up, they finally arrived at the mansion that seemed even more packed than it had been for his homecoming party. The space was crammed with people, music blasting through the yard. Luna, Cecilia, and Blair followed behind Gianna, who demanded people move out of her way—and they did.

Luna found Dante before she found anyone else. His shirt was ripped open, exposing his defined torso. Sweat coated his face as he left the middle of the dance group.

"Look who it is!" he cheered, walking over to them.

"Where are the others?" Gianna asked.

"Being losers sitting on the couches over there," Dante said, pointing in one direction. "Enjoy yourselves, ladies. I know I will." With that he disappeared into the crowd again. Luna shook her head, walking over to where he said Valerio was.

He was slumped against the couches, a look of indifference on his face and a drink in his hand. When his eyes caught hers he stood, ignoring whatever the people around him were saying and instead walking over to where she stood.

"You look beautiful," he told her, pressing a long-lasting kiss to her lips. "You get more and more perfect every time I see you."

"You saw me a couple of hours ago," Luna said with a little laugh.

"Too fucking long," he growled, kissing her again. "I want to introduce you to some people," he said, leading her over to the group at the couches. The girls had already made themselves comfortable, pouring drinks and mingling.

"This is Zahir," he said, pointing to the man who sat beside

Allister. Zahir had a defined beard covering his face and thick black hair that was pushed back. He was undoubtedly handsome. Luna wondered if Valerio was only associated with attractive people. "And this is Cass," he said, pointing to another man. This one had longer hair that reached down the length of his neck and big muscles covered in tattoos. He looked mean, but the smile he gave Luna made her feel better. "This is Luna, my fiancée," he introduced.

Her face flushed as she waved at the two other men as she took a seat beside Valerio and Cecilia. "How do you all know each other?" she asked.

"We went to high school together in Italy," Zahir said.

Luna raised her brow. "Any crazy stories you can tell me?"

Cass snorted. "About this grandpa? Yeah, right. The extent of his craziness included assignments from his father. Brutal, but this asshole doesn't know how to lose control."

Luna eyed Valerio closely. So much of his life was really spent in service to his father and to his duty. Had he truly ever had fun?

He leaned in close, his lips brushing her ear. "I think I did a pretty good job of losing control last night."

Luna felt a blush settle on her cheeks immediately. "You still held control. Let me tie you up and keep you completely powerless, and then we'll see if you can handle it."

"I'm never opposed." He bit her earlobe, pulling on it. "But I don't think you realize just how much power you already hold over me."

"Do they do that often?" she heard Zahir ask as Valerio moved away.

"Wouldn't know. They just started getting along recently," Gianna said.

"Man, Valerio with a fiancée. Who would have thought that would ever happen?" Cass asked with a mischievous smirk on his face.

"I've always been engaged," he said.

Luna didn't even attempt to hide the grin that settled on her face. He wore her initial around his neck proudly, claiming their relationship to everyone. God, it drove her wild.

He kept one arm wrapped around her shoulders and the other hand on her thigh. They chatted for what seemed like hours, telling stories about Italy and a younger Valerio. The one Luna never got to know but so badly wished she did.

Gianna gasped. "Oh my God, this is my song! Let's go," she said, ordering the other girls up.

Luna stood, practically peeling Valerio's hands off of her. "I'll be right back," she said with a grin when he rolled his eyes.

"Stay where I can see you," he said, kissing her.

Luna nodded, walking with her friends to where everyone else was dancing. Somehow Dante had managed to turn their home into a club and the atmosphere was perfect for her to lose herself to the music. Blair chatted with Cass, who joined them on the dance floor soon enough. Cecilia had disappeared somewhere, so it was only Luna and Gianna.

"Do you see anyone attractive here?" Gianna asked, eyeing the crowds around her. "Because I don't."

"I'm not going to answer that question," Luna said.

"I can't leave the party without someone," she said with a frown. "I need someone to dance with at least, and I won't dance with any of my brother's friends."

"Well, Cass looks available if you change your mind," Luna said, noticing Blair wasn't near him anymore. He was back at the table where he sat with Valerio, Zahir and a new person.

Her eyes narrowed at the blonde sitting next to Valerio, chatting with the group as if she had known them forever. She was beautiful. Her hair flowed down to her waist, her smile was sparkling white, and she gazed at Valerio with a little too much familiarity.

Luna's heart dropped, a bitter sensation coming over her. Immediately the dress she wore felt uncomfortable. Gianna was long gone dancing with some guy now, but she spotted Dante stumbling around instead.

She made her way over, grabbing him by the arm. "Who is that girl sitting next to Valerio?" she asked, her voice holding a dangerous edge.

"Hello to you too, sister-in-law." He hiccupped, slurring his words.

"Dante, look over there," she said, moving his head to the side so he could stare at the table. "Who is that girl?"

"Who, Sophia?" he asked. "She's the banging girl he was supposed to marry before you." He let out a ridiculous laugh as if it was the funniest thing he had ever said.

Luna's heart stopped. Her mind hyper focused on what he said, and it was enough to make her feel humiliated. Her body heated up from a deep-seated anger she had never felt before. That was the girl Valerio was supposed to end up with, not Luna.

If he had been freed from their contract, was she his second stop? The thought made her sick. She ditched Dante, walking up to the table now with quick, heavy steps.

Her hands shook, but the adrenaline was pushing through the moment she heard Sophia laugh at something Cass said. She sat between Valerio and Zahir, and even though he sat at least two feet away from her and drank out of his cup looking out at the crowd with a bored expression, Luna felt enraged. Just knowing who that girl was, knowing she probably had some sort of attraction to Valerio (because why wouldn't she), and knowing that she approached him when Luna wasn't there sent her off even more. Nothing could have calmed her mind at that moment.

Luna cut into the conversation between Sophia and Zahir, plastering on a fake smile. "Hi, I don't think we've met," she said, sticking her hand out to Sophia.

"Luna," Valerio said, trying to grab her. His eyes gleamed as if he was happy to see her, but she ignored him.

"I'm Sophia," the girl said, shaking her hand. Even her fucking hand was soft and perfectly manicured.

"I'm Luna, his fiancée," she said, shaking the girl's hand with too much intensity. "How do you all know each other?"

"We all go way back," Cass said with a wicked smile on his face.

Sophia gave an awkward smile. "It was nice meeting you, but I should get back to my friends."

She stood, slipping past Luna, who refused to move from her spot. Luna didn't say a word, just watched Sophia walk away, before turning to Valerio who already had his gaze locked on her.

"What's wrong?" he asked.

Luna huffed, walking away from him. She stomped through the dance floor and up the stairs, bumping her shoulder into people who refused to move. She knew Valerio was following behind her, but she didn't care. Her mind was already driving her wild with a million thoughts of how perfect of a couple Sophia and Valerio would have been. Both attractive, tall, perfectly built, not like Luna's shorter frame with more curves and bumps than she would prefer.

That made her even more mad. Why was she comparing her body to someone else? Why was she hating the way she looked because of another girl?

Because that wasn't just any girl; it was the girl Valerio was supposed to marry.

Luna stomped into the study, slamming the door behind her, just for it to be opened two seconds later by Valerio.

"What's wrong?" he asked, confusion on his face. He closed the door behind him, walking up to her. "Did someone do something? Tell me. I'll handle it."

She looked at him. "You were supposed to marry her."

He cringed. "Who, Sophia?"

"Don't say her name!" Luna screamed. Who had she become?

Valerio's eyes widened. "My father wanted to arrange something between me and her, yes, but I have never wanted her. It's always been you."

"Would you be getting married to her right now if we didn't sign the contract the second time?" Luna asked.

"No. I would still be marrying you either way. I was giving

you a chance to choose me. I don't want anyone else. I never have," Valerio said, walking closer.

"That doesn't change the fact you would have married her if we didn't meet," Luna cried out, throwing her hands up. "I didn't know about it either. I had to find out from your drunk ass brother. And on top of that, she's at your party talking to you."

The words fired out of her mouth like venom. The feeling engulfed her in flames, and she hated the feeling, but it made her want to mark him. Let everyone downstairs know he belonged to her.

"You're jealous," Valerio stated. His eyes were bright.

"Do I have a reason to be jealous?" she spit out.

"No, no," he reassured her. "You have absolutely no reason to be jealous. I was looking for you after you disappeared from the place you were dancing. She walked up and said hi and that was all. She talked to the other two because my focus was on looking for you. I'm so fucking obsessed with you, there isn't a single second you don't consume a thought of mine."

That seemed to simmer the thoughts slightly, at least enough for her to relax somewhat. "How do I know that?" Luna asked, her shoulders slumping. "I hate this feeling. I hate feeling out of control because I see some other girl talking to you. I wanted to kill her, and I probably would have and maybe I still will. Oh my God." Luna put her hand on her forehead, her eyes wide.

"Welcome to my life," he told her, approaching. "Do you know how fucking crazy I felt when I found out you were engaged to someone else. I wanted to slaughter your entire fucking family, and I still do. I feel that way every time someone's eyes graze your body, every time you speak to someone who isn't me."

He caged her against the desk. "How do I control it then?" Luna asked, her voice hardly more than a whisper.

He smirked, pushing her hair back. His hardening cock in his jeans pressed against her, forcing her to become flushed because of something different this time.

"You remember that I only love you. I'm only in love with you," he said.

He wrapped his hand in her hair, pulling her closer to him. Luna's eyes were wide, her mouth gaped open at his admission. He loved her.

She had known it from the way he took care of her, the way he spoke to her, touched her, but hearing him say it made her feel dizzy, drunk.

Valerio loved her.

Before Luna could respond, his lips were crashing into hers, swallowing whatever answer she was going to give. Luna jumped onto the desk, pushing things off to sit comfortably. Things clattered and probably broke, but neither one paid it any mind.

He fell in between her thighs, grinding against her underwear-covered pussy. She was already wet, leaking through the white panties. Luna ran her hands through his hair, destroying it to make sure everyone would know he was hers.

She gasped when she he slipped his hand into her underwear, playing with her already overly sensitive clit. She'd already had him twice in less than twenty-four hours, but her body sang for him regardless of how sore she was.

She was frustrated though. She didn't need his fingers; she needed him to fuck her.

She undid his belt, unzipping his pants in a hurry. He groaned when she brushed against his bulge. She freed him from his underwear, watching as his cock slapped against his stomach. Valerio lifted her, turning her around and forcing her to lay on her stomach over the desk. He pulled the dress up over her waist, giving him a clear view of her plump ass.

Luna whimpered when he ripped down her underwear, kicking her legs open. They shook in anticipation. A groan escaped when his cock rubbed between her folds, soaking himself in her wetness.

"You know what I love?" Valerio asked, leaning on her back so he could see her face. She turned towards him.

"What?" she asked breathlessly.

He smirked. "I fucking love that you're as much in this as I am now, willing to destroy people for me."

He slid inside her, forcing a gasp out of her. He wasn't gentle and didn't give her time to adjust before he started thrusting, holding on to her hips while he slapped against her. Luna gripped the edge of the desk, bracing herself while he fucked her mercilessly.

"It shows me you're mine, my little moon," he groaned. He tugged on her hair, forcing her head back. Valerio found her neck, biting the skin. He pulled away for a moment, licking the raw skin. "It shows me that you were made for me."

Luna was losing herself to his words, to the pleasure he was giving her. He slapped her ass, turning the skin red before he did it again. "Take my cock, my perfect girl. My good girl," he praised.

Luna clenched around him, letting out moan after moan. She didn't care who heard it—she wanted people to hear it, to hear he belonged to her.

He leaned back over her, pressing sloppy kisses to her jaw this time. Luna grabbed his chain with her finger, pulling his mouth to hers. He held her jaw and neck in one hand and reached down to pinch her clit with the other. She cried against his lips, riding out her orgasm brutally. He didn't slow down even when her body shook. Instead, he fucked her until her orgasm had subsided and then he came, filling her up.

He lined her back with kisses as she slumped on the desk, feeling completely spent.

She sighed contently, only standing when he pulled her dress back down. "How was that for rough?" he asked, biting her lip.

She wrapped her arms around his neck. "Do you really love me?" she asked.

"With my whole heart," he told her. "I'm madly in love with you, and I can't wait to marry you."

Luna could only grin, giving him another kiss. She lazily fixed her hair, adjusting the dress in the bathroom before they went back downstairs. They walked hand in hand, both flushed and satisfied.

Valerio held her the entire night, never once leaving her side. She basked in it, slumping in his bed at the end of the night. Only one thought swarmed her thoughts before she fell asleep beside him.

She was truly in love with him too.

TWENTY-SEVEN
LUNA

IT WAS OFFICIALLY one week after the party. Valerio had business in Buffalo for the night, Blair was going to a debate competition, Gianna and Allister were going back home to see their mother who stopped by once a year, and Cecilia, actually Luna didn't know where she was. All she did was clutch her duffle with a white-fisted grip, promising Luna that she would check in.

When Luna looked out the window, she could have sworn that it was Augustus's car that Cecilia was driving away in, but the idea was unimaginable.

Luna huffed, looking around the now empty and silent apartment. She wasn't used to silence while living with roommates, but there was something peaceful about it. With midterms out of the way, she wanted to make sure she rested up before finals approached quicker than ever. It was a perfect opportunity to spend the night doing self-care.

She started by cleaning the apartment, dusting and vacuuming the space. She danced around to some of her favorite songs to push off the dread of doing the multiple piles of laundry she had neglected over the past couple of weeks.

Then Valerio called her, demanding an update on what she had been doing.

"How was the drive?" she asked.

"I left before the sun was even up, so I've already been here for a while. I'm thinking I'll get home tonight, but if I don't, I told Dante to stop by and make sure everything is okay," he said.

"You don't have to rush home for me," she told him, walking to the drier to take out the last load of clothes. "And why were you up so early? Did you end up getting any sleep last night?"

He snorted. "Yes, I do. I can't live without you. And no, I didn't. You know I can't sleep unless you're next to me."

She couldn't help the smile on her face. "Well, make sure that if you come over tonight you have energy."

She could sense his smirk. "Oh? You plan on tiring me out?"

"I guess you'll just have to make it back tonight to find out," she said in a singsong voice. "I have the place all to myself."

"Tempting. I haven't fucked you in your bed yet."

"Let yourself in if you make it back tonight," Luna told him, setting the basket of clothes on her bed. "I know you have a key."

"I'll see you tonight then," he told her. "I love you."

Her breath hitched, still not used to hearing those words. She clicked off the phone, holding it against her rapidly beating chest. He said it so casually, as if he had been saying those words forever. She felt the same way about him, but saying the words out loud scared the hell out of her.

Admitting it to herself had been one thing, but admitting it to Valerio was a completely different ballpark. The first time she said it back wasn't going to be over the phone when he was miles away. It would be in person so that she would be able to see his face when the words finally came out.

She finished folding the laundry, preparing for a comforting bath afterwards. She soaked with a face mask, letting her muscles relax in the hot water. One of her little romance books sat on the edge of the tub, but she was too exhausted to pick it up and read. Her brain was already starting to shut off for the night, leaving her ready for bed.

She rinsed off her body and the mask, drying off and changing into her pajamas. She typed out a text to Valerio letting him know she was going to bed and to just meet her there when he got home. Somehow, the day had already passed her by. Taking care of herself was exhausting.

She made her way into the kitchen to grab a glass of water before she actually went to bed. She navigated through the dark apartment, turning on the light above the stove to grab a clean glass from the dishwasher.

With an ice cold water in her hand, she walked to the front door to make sure it was locked—a habit the girls deemed as part of the closing tasks in the apartment. One of them always checked the front door before bed.

The top lock was twisted to the side instead of straight up and down, meaning it was unlocked. Luna frowned. She hadn't left the apartment the entire day and she was sure she had locked it after Cecilia left. She reached out to turn the lock, double checking that it was actually locked this time.

Luna walked back toward her room, but never got there. A pair of hands wrapped around her mouth, pushing her against an unfamiliar body. She dropped the glass on the floor, struggling against the person behind her. She reached up, attempting to claw at the hands over her mouth, but it did nothing.

The person knocked her into the wall. She thumped against it, a groan escaping her lips at the impact. Luna reached her leg back, kicking it into the intruder's knee. The hands holding her let go, and she heard a man's voice cursing.

Her adrenaline kicked in in full force, forcing her legs into her room to reach for her phone. She screamed the entire way, hoping that someone in the apartment building would hear her. She grabbed the phone, but he knocked her onto the floor again. The phone slipped out of her hands, right out of reach.

Luna fought against the man at her back, thrashing any way she could to slip out from under him. He didn't budge. Instead, his hand found her hair, slamming her head against the floor.

Luna could feel the pain immediately, sensing the blood

already escaping her nose. "Please don't," she begged, but her face met the wooden floor once again. Luna reached backward, remembering what her brother had once taught her when they did self-defense training. She felt for the man's face, finding his eyes in a split second and pushing her thumbs into his eye sockets.

She put all her force into it, hearing his scream of pain as he let go of her hair. Luna twisted to the side, forcing him to fall off of her back. She reached for the phone again, gripping it and standing. She ran out of the room, her heartbeat going a million miles per second. She found Finn's number immediately, clicking on it and praying to God he answered. Valerio was too far away and she didn't have Dante's phone number saved, so Finn was her only option.

She heard him answer. All she could muster out was a "Help!" before the phone was pushed out of her hand, shattering on the floor. The man wrapped his hand around her neck, throwing her back onto the floor. Her back hit the edge of the table, a strained scream leaving her lips.

She attempted to move, but it was no use when he stood over her, leaning down so his body covered hers completely.

"You're more fucking trouble than I thought you would be, you little bitch," he spit out, his hands wrapped around her neck. She reached up immediately, scratching at his arms. It didn't faze him.

His grip tightened, suffocating her. When getting him to release his grip didn't work, Luna tried to reach up to his face again, only getting a single scratch before he moved out of the way, so he was just out of her grasp. His eyes were bulging and red, but she hadn't inflicted enough damage on him.

Luna heaved and gasped for air, black dots covering her vision. She slapped against his arm, all fight and strength slipping from her. Her eyes closed despite how hard she tried to keep them open. The only thoughts in her head surrounded Valerio, her brother, and her best friends. One of them would find her dead body right here, and she couldn't stomach the thought of it.

But it didn't matter anymore. No one would be coming to save her.

The door slammed open. She could faintly hear a pair of footsteps rushing toward them, knocking the man off her. She inhaled a deep breath, coughing uncontrollably. She could hear the fight happening behind her. The slam of a body into the entertainment center, knocking the TV to the floor.

She mustered up the energy to lift her head, seeing Finn now standing over the man who was seconds away from killing her. Finn's gun was raised, and he didn't hesitate to pull the trigger. Luna's eyes widened, turning away when the splash of blood covered her body like the drizzle of rain during a storm.

She continued gasping for breath. Finn reached out for her, placing it on her shoulder while he spoke to someone on the phone. Luna sat against the floor, unable to turn around to witness the man's dead body in her living room, staining the cream-colored rug she had vacuumed only a couple of hours prior.

"Luna!" Finn yelled, shocking her out of her daze.

"What?" she whispered, her voice strained and painful.

"I've been calling your name," he said. "What the fuck happened?"

"I don't know. I don't know." It hurt to speak, it hurt to breathe. Everything hurt. Her head, her neck, her face, her back.

"I'll have someone look over your neck," Finn said, moving away from her to walk toward the door. She could feel the thumps of footsteps against the floor. He grabbed a blanket off the couch, wrapping it around her shoulders.

Dante walked in first, his eyes wide and frantic.

"Did you call him yet?" He directed the question to Finn.

"He's on his way," Finn said. "I shouldn't have even fucking called him. Where was he tonight? He's her fiancé. This falls on him."

Valerio. That was who was coming.

Luna let out a tear, desperately massaging her throat. It felt raw and destroyed, the pain unimaginable, but it was nothing compared to the fear that entered her body.

They waited until she was completely alone before they attacked.

This wasn't random.

Someone wanted Luna dead.

TWENTY-EIGHT
LUNA

DANTE GRABBED another blanket off the couch, covering the dead body on the floor. He made his way over to Luna, kneeling down in front of her. "Are you okay?" he asked.

She shook her head. "Do you want an honest answer?"

"Why didn't you call me?" he asked. "I was supposed to be keeping an eye on you. Valerio is going to kill me."

"I didn't have your number, and you couldn't have known. No one could have known."

At least she didn't think they knew. But judging by all of their reactions, they seemed just as puzzled as her about it.

Dante looked at her for another moment. "Don't talk. Your throat sounds destroyed. You'll only make it worse." He stood, looking over at Finn. "Valerio has some men coming over to help move the body. Any idea who it is?"

Finn shook his head. "No idea. It doesn't make sense. Who the hell would want to attack her of all people?"

"She's not completely protected yet," Dante said. "She's just as much of a target as the rest of us if someone wants her gone."

The fear entered her once again. She tried to keep their voices out. The sound of shoes hitting against the wooden floors of the apartment as if someone was running before they flung themselves on her nearly had Luna freaking out. Only when she saw the familiar black head of hair clutching her with a death grip did she slump into Cecilia's hold.

"Oh my God, as soon as I heard we came over," she told her. She spit the words out frantically, panic coating her voice. "I can't believe this happened to you. I should have never left you here alone. Oh my God, can you imagine what would have happened if Finn didn't show up?"

She chose not to think about that scenario. "I'm sorry you had to come."

"Nonsense," Cecilia said, waving her off. "Do you need a doctor to look you over? I can try my best, but I'm not a doctor yet."

Luna nodded her head. "Can you check my throat? It's killing me."

Cecilia nodded, moving back so she could look at her throat. She touched and poked like a true professional. Her face stayed neutral while she eyed it, being mindful of the whimpers that left Luna.

"You're definitely going to bruise," Cecilia told her. "It's already starting, and judging by the marks already, it'll be gnarly, but keep switching from cold and warm compresses to help heal it. Your voice sounds strained, so you might have damaged your vocal cords. You should see an actual doctor to check for sure. Good news, your nose doesn't look broken, but it'll bruise as well."

"What's your official diagnosis?" Luna asked, her voice quiet.

Cecilia sighed. "Your voice and neck will heal, but your brain might take longer. Be kind to yourself. It'll take time."

She looked down at the floor. Would the fear ever leave? How the hell was she supposed to get over almost being killed? The body still sat only a couple feet away, being kicked around by Augustus, who held no regard for human life.

Cecilia dropped her hand on Luna's shoulder. "I can get you some pills to help with the pain," she told her. "It'll at least make you a little bit comfortable. Besides, I'm sure Valerio will get you some anyway."

Luna nodded. She would take it if it meant that she could forget about what happened even temporarily.

"Are you allowed to write a prescription?"

Cecilia gave her a small smile. "Something like that. Let me help you on to the couch. The floor is too uncomfortable. I'll get you some ice too."

She helped Luna stand up, setting her down on the couch. Cecilia went into the kitchen, leaving Luna to listen to the boys, who talked rapidly and quietly, throwing their hands around in frustration as if they were personally offended.

All Luna wanted was Valerio, who was no doubt on his way by now. But he was still so far away. She needed his arms around her, his protection and warmth. She needed him to tell her he wouldn't let anyone touch her ever again and that he was never going to leave her side.

She closed her eyes, leaning back on the couch. She felt defeated, the exhaustion overwhelming her.

The sound of footsteps thumping around the room had her jumping up once again. Her eyes were frantic, looking around for some new intruder, but there was none to be found. Cecilia sat beside her with an ice pack in her hands, her eyes holding a comforting look. This time both Blair and Gianna sat in front of her as well with worried looks.

Luna let out a deep breath. "When did you guys get here?" She cringed at how much worse her voice sounded; it was hoarse and broken, completely different from the way she usually sounded.

"A little bit ago," Gianna said. "You were sleeping, so we decided not to wake you."

"He called a couple of minutes ago," Blair said. "He's almost here."

Luna nodded, leaning back. She must have been asleep for a little bit then. The body was gone, as were all signs of a fight in the room or blood on the floor. Allister now joined the boys sitting all around the room, taking up space wherever they could. It felt odd to see everyone together without threatening each other or pulling guns.

"We managed to clean up the blood from your face and most of your body while you were sleeping," Cecilia said, pressing the ice pack to her neck once again. "You'll probably want a nice shower when you have a chance."

So much for the relaxing bath earlier. It was funny to even consider anything from earlier in the night as relaxing. How long had he been in her apartment? Did he watch her get dressed? Did he listen to her on the phone with Valerio? Where was he hiding? A harsh throbbing returned in her temples, reminding her that stressing about the situation right now wasn't going to make any of her injuries better.

The door banging open had everyone swinging their heads around to see who it was. Luna could feel him before she saw him. It felt like everything moved in slow motion when his broad frame stomped through the doorway and into the room.

His eyes met hers, a deep frown on his lips. Luna jumped up instantly, running toward him, but he met her halfway. She threw herself into his arms, her body melting when she felt his warmth once again. He immediately enveloped her body, pulling her against his chest.

She didn't even realize she was crying until he lifted her head, wiping his thumbs underneath her cheeks. He skimmed the bruised skin of her neck and her nose, his face transforming into a murderous look. The look of vengeance in his eyes was clear, but his touch was still gentle.

"I'm sorry I wasn't here," he muttered, leaning his forehead against hers.

She shook her head. "It's not your fault."

"That doesn't outweigh the fact that I should have been here. God, your precious voice," he said. "I should have never left."

"You're here now," Luna muttered, burying herself in his chest. "Please, don't go anywhere."

"Never again," he swore. "I have a doctor coming to look at your throat. Where's the fucking body?" The question was directed toward the other men, who now stood.

"On its way to the warehouse," Allister said. "None of us could recognize who it was, but given how he managed to get in, he's a professional. And a good one at that."

Valerio's jaw clenched. He looked over at Finn. "How did you get here so quickly?"

"She called," he said. "I rushed here as soon as the call came through."

Valerio was quiet for a moment. "You saved her life when I couldn't. I owe you. Whatever you want, just name it."

Luna's eyes widened. Was this the beginning of a truce between the two of them? She could only hope so, but when Finn shook his head, reality hit her.

"She's my sister," he said. "You only proved you're incapable of taking care of her."

"How did he get in?" Valerio snarled. "My security would have never allowed this. If your father had allowed me to put my team here, I doubt we would be standing here right now contemplating how she was almost fucking killed."

"We could all go back and forth all day, but how about we focus on the fact that someone wants her dead?" Dante spoke up. "That seems more important than anything else."

"She's not married yet, so she's not under any protection," Allister said.

Luna frowned. "What are you talking about? What does that have to do with marriage?"

"Since you and Valerio aren't married, you're still in the space where there is technically a way out of the contract. If one of you dies before the legality is set, then it's like the contract never existed," Allister said.

"You think it's someone who doesn't want this union?" Blair asked.

"Why the hell would anyone care?" Augustus asked.

"I can name a few people," Cecilia said, huffing. Everyone turned to look at her. "What? Valerio did kill the man she was supposed to marry after he called off the marriage. I doubt Reece Kingsley is thrilled about having you as a son-in-law."

"My father wouldn't want his own daughter dead," Finn spit out.

"Watch it," Augustus warned him.

Luna thought about it for a bit. She didn't have the best relationship with her father, but he wouldn't actually want her dead. Besides, if he was upset about the engagement, he would have wanted Valerio dead, not Luna; she was still an asset to him.

"Either way, the apartment is compromised," Gianna said. "I don't want you guys staying here."

"Agreed," Valerio said. "You're not staying here."

Luna frowned. "I guess we could try to look for a new apartment."

"No need," he dismissed. "You'll come live with me."

Luna's eyes widened. "Move in?"

"Yes!" Gianna yelled.

"No way in hell is Cecilia staying in your house," Augustus said.

"Oh my God, leave me alone," she groaned.

"Well, I'm not separating from my best friends," Blair said.

"We have plenty of space at our house and the girls will be safe," Valerio told them. "I'll allow permission for you to visit whenever you want."

"No!" Cecilia blurted at the same time Augustus said "Yes."

She couldn't stay at their apartment. Not when the place that had once been their home was now tainted and ruined. She would never feel safe in it again. Hell, she didn't know if she would ever feel safe anywhere. Not until they figured out who did this to her.

All they had right now was a dead man, and dead men couldn't talk.

It was decided then. The girls were moving into the Vitali mansion. Luna was going to be moving in with Valerio when not too long ago she would have fought against the thought with everything she had. The girls went to their rooms, beginning to pack up what they would need for now until they could manage to get people in to pack up the rest.

Valerio grabbed Luna's suitcase, tossing it on the bed while she began filling it. He didn't take his eyes off of her for a minute, leaving her squirming under his gaze.

"I'm not going to disappear," she said. A bitter cough left her lips. "You don't have to literally keep an eye on me forever now."

"You almost did disappear," he said. "If your dumbass of a brother hadn't gotten here, you would have been dead."

Luna swallowed harshly, throwing her clothes into the bag. "I don't want to think about that."

He approached her, tracing her face with gentle hands. She leaned into his touch, relishing in it as if it could disappear at any moment. "I swear I'm going to find who did this to you, and when I do, I'm going to annihilate them. I won't stop until there's not a single trace of them left."

She shouldn't have liked the words that left his lips so much, but she did. And when his lips met hers, she accepted it. She needed him to taste the fear she'd felt before, and the safeness she had now with him.

He leaned his forehead against hers. "I swear to you, nothing like this will ever happen again."

That was exactly what she needed. His promise. One she knew he would never break.

"I know."

TWENTY-NINE
VALERIO

"ALRIGHT, well it doesn't look like anything is crushed," the doctor said, moving back from examining Luna's neck. "But the bruising will take a little longer to heal. Rest your voice as much as possible, keep a cold compress on for fifteen minutes max at a time, and use the eyedrops I'll prescribe."

Valerio nodded, taking in the instructions as if they were for him. He wouldn't forget a single detail for Luna.

"So she shouldn't talk at all?" he asked.

"Only if she wants her voice to recover quicker," the doctor said. "Emergencies and anything urgent should be fine."

He turned to her. "I'll get you a whiteboard and a marker so you can communicate."

She huffed, crossing her arms. He knew it sucked for her, but nothing was worse than her voice being permanently damaged. If there was a way to avoid it, then he would do it.

Valerio texted Dante, waiting a moment before he appeared, obnoxiously cracking his fingers. "Alright Doc, time to walk you out."

The doctor nodded, offering Luna a small smile. He dropped the prescription on the counter beside them, packing up his things. Going to an actual doctor's office would have been simpler, but they didn't want any other mafia families to find out there was a hit against Luna. Until Valerio was sure who was behind the attack, he couldn't trust anyone outside the walls of his home.

So Valerio called—or more like forced—his doctor to do a house visit. He was able to watch over him with a harsh eye, keeping his promise not to leave Luna alone.

"If you need anything else, you know where to reach me," the doctor said. He held out his hand, waiting for Valerio to set the check in it.

"Not a single word," he told him with a warning. Expensive fucking doctor, but he was the only one he could find that was willing to keep his mouth shut under the right price.

"I respect my patient's privacy," the doctor said. With that, Dante guided him out of the kitchen. Luna flopped down on the counter with a huff. Valerio knew there were a million things she wanted to say, and yet, she wasn't allowed to say any of them.

He wrapped his arms around her, resting his head on her shoulder. "I know this is going to be hard, but it's better if you're healed completely. If you want, I'll be your voice for you."

Luna gave him an unserious look.

His smirk widened. "Was that a yes?"

She let out a frustrated sigh, smacking his arm.

"Are you hungry?" he asked, walking toward the fridge. "I can make you something quick before I put you to bed."

She nodded her head.

Dante entered the room again, this time carrying a whiteboard and a pack of markers with him. "I know I kind of owe you right now, but being your assistant wasn't what I anticipated," he said, setting them in front of Luna.

She immediately ripped the pack open, scribbling something down.

"The only reason I didn't put a bullet in you was because Luna begged me not to with the last remaining voice she had,"

Valerio spit out. "So stop bitching and make sure you pick up her eye drops and pain meds."

Dante turned toward Luna, grabbing the prescription off the counter. "I'll apologize for the rest of my life if I have to."

Luna waved him off and even that simple action pissed him off. Maybe Valerio wanted her to be more pissed off and unforgiving because if Finn was even a second too late, she wouldn't be sitting in front of him right now. It was more serious than she acted like it was. More serious than she was allowing Dante to be let off the hook for. He should have checked on her, but he decided that partying and swallowing his fucking sorrows in alcohol and whatever dick he could find was more worth it than protecting Luna. So yes, he should apologize for the rest of his life, but instead Luna emphasized that if they wanted to find who did this to her, they needed to work together, not throw accusations down each other's throats.

Dante walked off, leaving the kitchen in silence again. Besides the night before, this was the only time they had been truly alone since everyone moved in. The household was chaotic and busy with Augustus's and Cecilia's arguing, Blair's and Allister's bickering, and Gianna throwing herself into the chaos just because she wanted to. It had been one night and it was already too much.

He prepared a pesto panini, putting it on the panini press to heat up. He turned toward her, reading the white board she held up.

Are you going somewhere tonight?

He nodded. "I'm going to the warehouse so I can see what I can find out about the asshole who tried to kill you. He might be dead, but people always leave some kind of clue about who they are on their bodies."

She frowned, erasing the white board with her hand and scribbling something else on it quickly. He handed her a paper towel to use as an eraser when she turned it back around.

So I'll be here alone?

"No, you'll have the girls with you. I'll only be an hour, which is entirely too long, but I assumed you wouldn't want to deal with looking at a dead body like that," he said. "If you want to come, I won't mind."

She shook her head quickly.

No thank you.

He gave a small laugh, grabbing a plate and taking the panini out. He cut it in half and set it in front of her. "No one will be allowed onto the property, so you'll be completely safe. But if anything happens at all, don't hesitate to call me. I know you can't talk, but the phone call will alert me enough. I'll come in an instant." Luna nodded, taking a small bite, but burning her tongue instead. He narrowed his eyes, grabbing a water bottle for her. "Be careful. You're supposed to get better, not worse."

She flipped him the bird, taking a sip of water. He raised his eyebrow. "So we've settled with lewd hand gestures then? I can show you one myself," he said, lifting his fingers in a "V" up to his lips.

Luna looked away the moment he stuck his tongue out. He sat beside her, letting her eat while he checked the text from Allister telling him that Finn and Augustus were planning on joining them tonight. Why? He had no fucking idea.

She tapped his hand, showing him the board.

Keep me entertained. I left my phone upstairs and I can't talk. :(

Valerio put down his phone immediately. "What should I talk about?"

She stared at him blankly. He shook his head. "Fine, how

about we talk about our wedding? I'm thinking you wear a ginormous dress that you can't walk in and we'll serve lemon cake."

Absolutely not!

"Is that a yes? Well, if you say so. Maybe I'll have to plan the entire wedding myself," he said with a grin. He didn't know shit about weddings, but watching her get angry and not being able to voice the frustrations made him laugh. She looked fucking adorable. "I'm just kidding, I would never make you give up control over that. I know you only like to give up control when I fuck you."

Her mouth dropped open before it closed back up. She blushed as she went back to eating. He kept her entertained with random stories from his childhood that at least put a smile on her face. They were the good ones with Dante and his mother. One in particular where he convinced Dante that there was a shark in the water while they were swimming and the dumbass actually believed him. They weren't even in an ocean; they were swimming in a lake.

When she finished, Valerio took the plate from her and set it in the sink. He helped her walk up the stairs, holding on to her hips from behind. He assured her it was in case she suddenly became faint. He was the perfect nurse.

But realistically, since the night he walked into her apartment and saw her pale shaken body covered in bruises and dried up blood, he found himself reaching out to her more often just to make sure she was next to him. That she was real.

She threw on one of his big shirts and slipped into their bed. Dante had brought in both prescriptions at that point and Valerio gave them to her, making sure she took plenty of water with them. Every painful swallow sent a stab to his heart, but she would get better and he would get his revenge.

Snores escaped Luna soon after. Valerio covered her body

with the comforter, tucking her in the way she liked. He pressed a kiss to her forehead, muttering an "I love you."

He left the room quickly, carefully closing the door behind him. The minute it clicked, his face changed. The ability to care for someone only existed with Luna. Valerio, at his core, was deadly, rotten.

Someone had made the grave mistake of putting their hands on what was his. They tried to kill her.

He once promised he would burn the world down for Luna. Now, it was time to come through with his promise.

Valerio's footsteps echoed against the concrete of the warehouse hallway. He walked quickly, unwilling to stay there for a moment longer than he had to while Luna slept at home.

Everyone else was already waiting for him, and that included Finn and his goon. Valerio wanted nothing to do with the most annoying Kingsley, but he'd killed the man that attacked his Luna. If Finn had any information whatsoever about what happened, then he needed to find out.

They all crowded around the center of the open room where the dead body sat on a metal table. He could already feel the rage entering him, but he had to remind himself that the man was dead.

"Did you find anything yet?" Valerio called out, directing the attention to him.

Allister was the one to answer him. "No, he's completely empty. Not a single phone, ID, or anything to identify him or the person that sent him."

"All this shows is that he was smart enough to be unidentifiable just in case he got caught," Finn said, crossing his arms.

Valerio looked at the naked dead man closely. He scanned his skin, using a pen to lift his arms and legs.

"What are you looking for?" Augustus asked with a disgusted look.

"Some kind of mark or tattoo that would show who he's connected to," Valerio said.

"Who the fuck even does that anymore?" he asked.

"Our family," Dante answered. Valerio nodded in agreement. An old tradition, but a useful one for secret missions like this.

"And mine," Finn said. "The only person I know who used to seriously use it was my great-grandpa. I don't think anyone younger does it anymore."

Valerio continued his assessment, looking over the man's neck that was covered with a thick beard. "And they're not actual members of the family either. They're assassins the family uses, certain dealers, spies, anyone with secret association to the family."

"I never understood why they needed to hide it," Dante muttered. "If you were planning on attacking, don't be a fucking coward about it."

"Because these were attacks or missions that could cause complete destruction, war. A hit on Luna Kingsley is grounds for complete annihilation. Look at who her soon-to-be husband is, her brother, her father, her father-in-law. The list goes on. They wouldn't want to come out with it full on. That would be too easy." He continued his assessment, making sure not to miss a single inch of skin. "And the hard part is telling which one belongs to which family because they make an effort to keep it a secret, so only members who carry the mark could identify each other."

"How would you even know who it belongs to if you find one?" Augustus asked.

"Well, when you have a ridiculously smart person like Valerio who makes an effort to memorize them, it's easier," Allister said.

He came up to the left ear, noticing a small little patch of ink that only showed from the bottom of the man's earlobe. His eyes narrowed as he used the pen to lift the earlobe up.

There it was. A small emblem. Valerio stopped when he noticed what it was. A small lion head with two swords crossing behind it, and faintly, nearly impossible to see if the eye wasn't trained for what it was actually looking for, was a "K" in Old English font in the lion's open mouth. To anyone else, it would have looked like just any tattoo, but he wasn't just anyone.

Valerio stood up, deathly calm.

In a split second, he grabbed Finn's neck, slamming him down onto the dead man's body, squeezing with all his might.

"What the fuck are you doing?" Augustus yelled, trying to pull Valerio off.

"Why the fuck is the Kingsley symbol on the assassin that tried to kill Luna?" Valerio screamed. He tightened his hands, choking the life out of Finn, who fought against his hands.

"Let go of him. You can't kill her brother," Dante said, trying to rip him away.

"I'll tell her the assassin woke up from the dead and got the correct Kingsley this time," Valerio spit out.

Then he thought about Luna and how fucking heartbroken she would be if he told her that her dumbass brother died. With that thought he let go, stepping away. Finn coughed and attempted to catch his breath.

"Did you have to push me against the dead man's dick?" Finn asked. He was hunched over holding his knees, taking in deep breaths.

"Explain to me why that man has your family symbol on him," Valerio said. He was seething in anger. His mind was already jumping to conclusions that he hoped weren't true for Luna's sake.

Confusion crossed Finn's face. He walked to where Valerio had seen it, looking back at him with even more confusion. "I have no fucking idea."

"If you're lying to me, I swear to God," he hissed. Dante held him back.

"I'm not lying," Finn spit out.

"Is it possible someone else hired him?" Allister asked. "Someone from a different family that wanted to frame you guys?"

"Why are we dismissing the possibility of it being your father so quickly? Maybe what Cecilia was saying about your father was true," Augustus said to Finn.

. Finn shook his head. "My father wouldn't send someone to kill his own daughter. There's no fucking way."

"How do you know?" Valerio asked.

"Because he has to have some humanity!" he screamed, running a hand through his hair. "Why would he attack his own daughter? Why not just go after you?"

"Because it would cause a full-out war if your father attempted to kill me," Valerio said. "It would be the first person my father would attack, but if Reece Kingsley harms Luna himself, he can blame whoever he wants knowing the truth. Has he mentioned anything about the contract to you?"

"No. Nothing," he said, shaking his head.

Augustus looked up with an uncertain face. "Actually, I might have heard something."

"What?" Valerio barked at him.

"I overheard him asking about legal loopholes, but my father couldn't find anything. That contact was so fucking precisely worded," Augustus said. "But I thought it was just him being a protective father. No fucking offense, but can you blame the guy for not wanting his daughter with you?"

"You didn't think that was important enough to mention?" Dante asked, rolling his eyes.

"Fuck off," Augustus spit out. "I don't get involved in this bullshit."

"Suddenly Luna stops being an asset, so he throws out keeping her alive all together. How much more evidence do you need?" Valerio asked Finn.

"None of this is evidence. It's all coincidence," he said.

"Then look through his shit. Find concrete evidence that

proves your father didn't do this because as it stands, he's the first person on my hit list right now," Valerio told him. "The only fucking loophole that all of us know of is death. He wasn't above hitting her, he wasn't above hitting you, he's not above this either. Sleep with one eye open. If he was dumb enough to attempt to murder my Luna, then you're not far from it either."

He knew Finn was shocked, his mind going through a million different thoughts. He wanted to believe his father could be good, but the truth was none of them were. Given the horrible shit both Cesare Vitali and Reece Kingsley had done, an attempted assassination on their own kids couldn't be out of the question. Not until they were proven otherwise.

Valerio wouldn't sleep until whoever did this to her was buried six feet under. And rest assured, he would find the person responsible.

"Then what's the plan?" Allister asked.

"We're going to throw our engagement party," Valerio said. "It's the only time me and Luna will be out in public together. If someone wants to target the two of us, then they'll have their chance to. We'll catch whoever is suspicious and use our usual methods to get information we need."

"Fine," Finn agreed. "When?"

"Next week," he told them. "Spread the news. I want everyone in attendance. Not a single person is off the suspect list, so keep your fucking eyes open. If you hear even a whisper or see a slight shadow that is suspicious, then you tell me right away. Got it?"

Valerio didn't wait for their responses before he turned around to leave. Ready to get back to Luna.

"What should we do with the body?" Dante asked.

"Burn it," he called out, slamming the warehouse door behind him.

THIRTY
VALERIO

I don't like that our engagement party will be used to bait dangerous people.

LUNA SAT with a frown on her face, arms crossed, and the white board on the bed once Valerio finished telling her the plan. It was the next day now and she had been in and out of sleep because of the pain medication. He'd spent the day getting work done in his study and checking in on her on the security cameras. His mind was in preparation mode, organizing the delivery of weapons and supplies to the house that he assumed they would be needing soon. That was the whole reason for the trip to Buffalo, to meet with his arms dealer away from his father's prying eyes while they were preparing themselves. Of course, now everything was escalated. His father remained a threat and so did whoever tried to kill Luna.

When she finally woke up, she demanded to know everything that happened.

For her sake, he left out the part where he believed her father set up the assassination attempt on her life. That would be far too much stress on her after everything.

"If it means keeping you safe, then we have to try," Valerio told her. He slipped his T-shirt off, throwing it over the chair of Luna's new vanity.

She cleared her throat. "I don't want to sacrifice my engagement party for it."

He cringed at how rough her voice sounded. "Don't talk."

"This is an emergency," she said.

"No, it's not," he rebutted. "Plan the engagement party to whatever extent you want. We'll catch whoever it is lowkey, so you can still enjoy the party and celebrate our engagement."

"And where will you be?" Luna asked.

He slipped off his pants, walking to throw it in the hamper inside the walk-in closet before coming back out to stand in front of the bed. It bought him a couple of seconds to build up the courage to face her because despite how sweet she was, she was the one person he was actually intimidated by.

"I will save my torture until after the party," he promised. "Now, will you join me in the shower?"

She shook her head. "You're not understanding what the issue is."

Valerio's nostrils flared. "Write it on the damn white board."

"No," she said. "It makes me feel restricted."

He sighed, sitting on the bed. "I don't want you damaging your voice."

"If I'm so damaged, how am I supposed to attend an engagement party?" She raised her brow at him, swallowing harshly.

"You'll feel better by next week."

"I don't want special events in my life to be used for your mafia affairs," she said. "We're only getting married once."

"This is only for your sake," he said. "I wouldn't be doing any of this if you weren't almost killed a couple of nights ago."

Her attitude sobered up immediately. Valerio saw the change in her demeanor, how her shoulders tensed and her face became pale.

"Can you please not remind me?" Luna asked, her voice considerably quieter than before.

Valerio's eyes softened. "I'm sorry." He grabbed her hand, pressing a kiss to the back of it. "When we catch whoever set this up, I swear to you nothing like that will ever happen again. I just need this one event and then we live in bliss."

Luna sighed. "Fine. I'm not letting you touch my wedding."

"Our wedding," he corrected with a smirk.

"We'll see about that," she said, a smile on her face. "Now, go shower. You stink."

"I can't reach my back. Care to help?" His brow was quirked up in question.

"Only because I need a shower too." She got out of bed, following him into the bathroom.

He turned on the shower, making sure it was the scalding temperature she loved while she undressed. He ran his gaze along the length of her naked body, still believing there was nothing more beautiful in the world.

He let her enter first, following in right after. They both stood under two different streams of water across from each other. He grabbed her shampoo, pouring some in his hand to lather it into her hair. His fingers massaged her hair, forcing her to let out sighs of contentment.

"I need a dress for the party." She leaned against his body with his hardening cock pressed against her ass.

"Order however many you want." He washed the shampoo out of her hair, pressing kisses against her neck. They were gentle, not rough and possessive like they usually were. But given the state of her neck, he didn't want to cause more damage.

Luna arched her back, letting his dick grind against her ass. He ran his hands down her body, grabbing a handful of her breasts in each palm. She leaned her head against his chest, reaching behind her to grab him.

His left hand drifted down, stroking through the folds of her pussy before he settled on her clit, rubbing small circles.

She turned around, connecting her lips to his. He grabbed a fistful of her ass, lifting her up and pressing her back against the shower wall. Steam covered the tight space, making everything feel hotter.

Valerio wasted no time entering her. He thrust in and out, groaning when she pulled his hair. They both needed this, one moment to forget about everything happening in their lives.

Her back arched off the tiled shower wall, pushing her impossibly closer into Valerio's body. He moved with more fervor, taking her over the edge once and for all.

Luna gasped, impaling his back with her nails. His thrusts sped up before he let out an animalistic growl, filling her until she was impossibly full.

"Good girl," he muttered, pressing a kiss against her forehead as she slumped onto his shoulder.

She could only muster up a gentle smile, leaning against him while he finished washing her hair and body. She returned the favor, lathering up the loofa before trailing it over his body, letting the soapy beads cover every crevice of his toned body. He could only watch her in awe, her touch driving him insane.

When they were done, he brought her up food, making sure she ate before she took her meds for the night. He pulled her body into his, holding her close and inhaling the sweet coconut smell that she always had in her hair.

"Are we going to be okay, Val?" she asked, her voice thick with exhaustion.

"Yes," he said without hesitation. "We'll be fine." And as she slipped off to sleep, his mind raced with a million thoughts.

He hoped for all of their sakes that they would be.

THIRTY-ONE
LUNA

THE LAST TIME Luna was at an engagement party, it was eventful to say the least.

Now, she was sporting the same uneasy feeling in her stomach as she prepared for her second engagement party—with Valerio this time. She ran her hands down the length of the dress, smoothing out the silky material.

She had to go with a halter top dress, so it would be able to cover the fading bruises from her neck. Her back was exposed, but she still kept her hair down and curled like always.

Her engagement ring sat on her finger, glimmering in the light. Maybe she would have been less nervous had there not been security at every corner waiting to see if the person who set up her assassination showed up. How they would even be able to identify the person was still a question Luna didn't understand.

They waited in the library while Valerio talked on the phone, ensuring the building was secure before they walked out. Her mind told her over and over again that this was a horrible idea. She played it off as anxiety and trauma from before, but the dread came from her gut.

It was too late to back out. They were minutes away from entering the party.

The girls had spent so much time setting up, helping to order the decorations and rent out the venue. They ended up choosing another ballroom located in the city for obvious reasons. Large cream pillars stretched across the outside of the building making the whole space feel like they were in ancient Greece. White and gold decorations were scattered around the room. It wasn't overwhelming, but it did make the space feel dreamy. Luna saw all of it earlier and was amazed at the hard work that went into setting up the space.

Then she was ushered into the library where she waited with Valerio.

He looked handsome, even with the angry snarl on his face. He ran a hand ran through his hair, the black tux molded to his body. He was undeniably beautiful, but he had always been. She wished he held the same unease he had at his birthday party or when they were at the cabin instead of the worry that laced his face now. They were supposed to be celebrating, not doing all of this.

Finally, he hung up the phone, walking over. "Are you ready?" he asked.

"Are you sure about this?"

His eyes softened. "I won't let anything happen to you. I swear." He grabbed her hand, pulling her body into him.

She wanted to believe him. She really did.

Instead, she plastered on a smile, squeezing his hand. They walked out of the library, making their way down the long hallway to the ballroom. Three bulky guards walked in front of them, two behind. It threw off the entire romantic atmosphere Luna intended to keep.

The ballroom doors opened up for them. The couple walked down the stairs, taking in the claps, cheers, and stares that were passed their way. Luna held her head up high, holding on to Valerio's hand with a death grip.

She looked around the room, noticing how a guard stood by every large window, completely armed. Her smile faltered.

Valerio promised not to let her out of his sight the entire night, which she appreciated. But it meant that before she could greet her friends, she was forced to say hello to the rich people his family worked with.

Her cheeks were killing her from the smile she kept on. And after what felt like a lifetime of mindless conversation, she finally found the girls waiting by the drink table. This time she dragged him over with her.

"You're a busy woman, Mrs. Vitali," Cecilia told her, taking a sip from her glass.

Luna snatched it out of her hand, emptying the contents. Valerio eyed her, removing the glass from her hands. "Easy on the booze," he said.

"I need this more than you know," Luna muttered, leaning against him for support. He held onto her waist, peppering a kiss in her hair.

"Have you found anyone yet?" Blair asked, shifting the conversation.

"Not yet," Valerio said. "Where are Allister and Dante?"

"I saw them by the food," Gianna said. "You should go find them."

Valerio rolled his eyes, but Luna agreed with the less than subtle hint to leave. "I'll be fine here for a few minutes."

"Fine, but I'll only be gone a second," he said, kissing her forehead again. "Watch out for her," he threatened the group.

She sighed once he walked away. "This isn't what I wanted."

"I know, but these are his people. You'll have to get used to them," Blair told her, handing her another drink. Luna took it, gulping down a good amount.

"It's not the people. I know how to act cordial with these rich assholes. I'm talking about the tension in the room. The armed guards, no one being able to relax. Everything feels off. I hate it."

Cecilia frowned. "It's just for tonight."

"Is it? I don't think anyone is going to make their move in a room full of mafia personnel, so it'll end up going into the wedding, the honeymoon, the baby shower, who fucking knows. I won't have any normal events in my life because it'll be mafia matters always," she said, choking down the lump in her throat.

"Valerio isn't normal. You knew that," Gianna said. "That's why you fell for him in the first place."

Luna sighed, knowing she was right. She didn't want normal; she wanted Valerio.

"What can I do to make this asshole act out?" Luna asked them. "That way they can take him away and I can enjoy the rest of my life."

"Don't do anything," Blair said. "Enjoy the party as much as you can and let them handle this other shit. You've been through enough."

She let out a long breath. "That seems impossible."

The girls quieted down, standing up straighter. Luna turned around, facing her mother and father, walking with their arms intertwined. They didn't smile, they didn't offer pleasantries. They looked like they would rather have been anywhere than at the party.

She knew they would be coming but seeing them here after everything felt strange. Especially since the last time she saw them, Valerio had broken her father's wrist and shot the man her father wanted her to marry. They hadn't spoken since.

Luna tensed up. "When did you get here? I would have greeted you if I knew you had arrived."

"Why did we hear about this party from your brother and not you?" Eleanora asked. She completely ignored Luna's question. Despite her attempt to keep her tone light, there was a bite to her voice she recognized immediately.

"I was busy planning it," Luna said. "Are you enjoying the party?"

"What are you thinking?" Reece Kingsley hissed. "Why are you parading this engagement around?"

She frowned. "Because we're getting married."

"I was trying to find a way out for you," her father said in a low voice. "I have a couple of suitors better fit."

Luna's eyes widened. "What are you talking about? You set this all up. You signed the contract."

He was the reason any of this was happening.

Reece grabbed her arm, his hold tight as he pulled her off to the side. Luna held in her yelp, her arm burning. Like always, no one batted an eye. They never did. But she didn't expect the girls to get involved either, not when he could turn on them.

"I refuse to come up with a truce with that family. You will not be marrying him."

"Yes, I am," Luna replied, her voice stern. "We're not doing this again."

"Watch your tone," he bit back. His hold tightened. This time, a whimper escaped her lips. Suddenly, she was a child again, completely defenseless against him. "You're not married to him. There is no heir. I can pull you out of that contract when I please."

"Why would you do that?" she whispered. "Why go through the trouble?"

"I've received better offers for you. Things that will help out the family. You know how important it is to choose family," he said. She could hear the manipulation in his voice that tried to weigh out whether Luna was still loyal to him or not. She had never been loyal to him. It was fear that kept her tied to their name, not true unwavering loyalty.

It all came down to dollars and cents with him. He wanted the highest price for his precious daughter, and if people were offering more, why would he want to refuse?

What had changed though? Why hadn't he mentioned anything before?

"It's for the best," her mother said. Her voice attempted to hold the empathy that she would have expected from a mother, but it sounded inauthentic when she did it. "We'll find someone who can take care of you, keep you safe."

"Why? So I can end up like you?" Luna said before she could stop herself.

Her mother's mask slipped for a second, showing disbelief or maybe even remorse before it was back up and stoic again.

"After the break-in the other night, you don't have a choice," Reece said. "Someone wants you dead because you are with him. It was enough of a scare to make us realize you are in danger with him."

Luna's head swirled, making her dizzy. She turned to her father. "How do you know about that?"

Everyone swore not to say anything, including Finn. He knew how important it was to stay silent. He wouldn't have betrayed her like that. He couldn't.

Then how did they know?

Pure fear rippled through her body. His face didn't change—it was her mother who let her know that he had slipped up. When her eyes widened for a fraction before they went back to normal. It was like the facade had cracked for a moment, revealing a wrinkle in the plan.

She felt a pair of arms wrap around her shoulder.

"Mr. and Mrs. Kingsley, thank you for joining us," Valerio sneered, pulling Luna into him.

"We were just giving our congrats," Eleanora said with a fake smile.

Even Valerio's warm hand on her shoulder couldn't calm down the anxiety building up inside of her. They knew something; they did something.

"We need to give our toast, so if you'll excuse us," he said, leading them away.

Luna gripped his arm with a death hold, trying to calm her mind. He must have noticed she was off.

"What did they say?" Valerio asked, walking them towards the stage.

"They knew about the assassination attempt," Luna said. The

words felt like acid in her mouth. "They want me out of the contract."

He stopped walking for a moment. "They said that?"

"Valerio, they seem so against it out of nowhere," Luna said. She looked at him with fear in her eyes, fear that he didn't seem to match but he understood. As if he already knew something she didn't. "I'm not sure if this is a good idea anymore."

"I knew the assholes had some role in it," Valerio told her. He sounded like he had been thinking that for a long time. He continued walking.

"What are you talking about?" she asked. "You think they were a part of the assassination attempt?"

He didn't say anything; he just kept walking. She pulled on his arm to stop him completely and this time he did.

"You think they did it?" she asked, this time in a whisper. Her eyes were wide, dread filling her body.

"The assassin had your family emblem tattooed on him," Valerio said. "It's suspicious that they're suddenly trying to pull you out of the contract after the attempt didn't work."

"You really think it was my father?" Even she couldn't believe it. Or maybe she didn't want to believe it.

Valerio sighed, pressing a kiss to her forehead. "We'll talk about this tonight. I promise. We need to figure out how we'll approach him now."

She nodded, but his promise did nothing to ease the anxiety in her. Why would her father want her dead when he'd just insisted on selling her off for a better deal? Her mind shifted to how deceitful he could be.

Was it so he could try to blame Cesare Vitali for this? Say that he sent the assassin after Luna and give him a way to get her out of the contract? None of this made any sense.

Unless her father knew Valerio wouldn't let her out of the contract and the only way out was through death. As soon as the marriage was legalized and an heir was on the way, the two families would be tied together forever. If her father was really keen on trying to separate the two before then, they weren't safe. Who knew what he or anyone who didn't want the marriage happening would do to make sure the two most powerful families in the world didn't merge?

There had to be a loophole. Something no one would dare harm; something that could truly unite the two families together until they could buy some time. Either way, she had to do something.

They walked up the stairs onto the stage, Valerio holding Luna's waist tightly.

She looked out at the crowd.

The separation of families so glaringly obvious. On the left side stood the Kingsleys, including her parents.

On the other side stood the Vitalis, with the grand guest of honor, Cesare Vitali. She didn't know when he had shown up, or why he did for that matter. His eyes locked on Luna's, unwavering and unblinking, devoid of any emotion and holding a promise—Luna wouldn't survive against him. It made her skin crawl, forcing her to break the contact and look away first.

Hatred had only brought on violence, and it had almost caused her death. She was sick of it.

Luna grabbed the microphone, holding it in her shaky hand. She plastered on a smile, ignoring the look Valerio gave her.

"I want to say thank you to everyone who showed up for us tonight," Luna said. "It means a lot that all of you would be willing to come out and put your differences aside to support us."

She looked at the crowd where the girls stood with Dante and Allister. Finn and Augustus stood behind them, but they all congregated in the center of the room.

She swallowed harshly. "We are excited to become a union."

She held her left hand against her belly as if something were inside.

Gasps exploded in the room. Luna looked over at Cesare,

whose eyes darkened, and then her father, who looked like he could implode.

"And welcome our baby," she said.

Then chaos broke out.

THIRTY-TWO
LUNA

IF IT WAS true that blood was thicker than water, then a baby carrying the blood of the Vitali and Kingsley families would have to pull its weight.

Only problem was that there wasn't a baby. And Luna had just declared there was.

She dropped the microphone on the stage, letting Valerio pull her away. She didn't want to see the look on his face, not when she was sure it would hold betrayal. But before they could make a true escape, they were stopped by Cesare. His smile didn't match his eyes and Luna was sure it never had.

"I think congratulations are in order," he said, blocking the path. Luna's heart beat rapidly, but she kept the look on her face neutral. "After all, a baby is a wonderful surprise."

Valerio didn't bother smiling or pretending he cared. His arm only tightened around Luna as if he could sense danger, which she appreciated. "Thank you. Maybe we can discuss things later; Luna is feeling a little bit faint."

"Of course." Cesare nodded as if he cared. "Can't let the mother of the future Vitali heir feel unwell. I hope we'll catch up soon, *Mrs. Vitali*."

"Thank you," Luna muttered, walking past him.

LEJLA MURIC

But missing one hurdle didn't help the fact there was another coming straight for them in the form of Luna's father. Valerio must have been as dazed as she was because for the first time ever, he was caught off guard by Reece Kingsley's hands around his throat.

"How fucking dare you defile her before you're married," he screamed, attempting to slam Valerio against one of the pastry tables. "I will not claim an illegitimate grandchild."

"Doesn't fucking matter what you do," Valerio growled, pushing him off. "That child is a Vitali."

Luna's brows furrowed. God, she had seriously screwed up not telling Valerio the plan before.

She stepped in, trying to ignore the guilt that broke through her. "What's done is done. Both families are united now, despite anyone wanting anything different."

"We'll see about that," Reece hissed, turning around to walk away. It wasn't a walk as much as it was a stomp, but at least he was gone.

Luna's mother approached them now. Luna expected to be screamed at, called any name possible, but instead her mother's eyes were light, excited almost. Her smile actually looked genuine for the first time in her life.

She grabbed Luna's hands, squeezing them in a motherly embrace she couldn't remember ever feeling in her life. At least not since she was a baby. It stunned her to see such a drastic change in her own mother.

Eleanora's eyes didn't leave the space of Luna's abdomen, not even when she reached her hand out to touch, but decided against it.

"I'll call you tomorrow," she said quickly. "We can talk, maybe get lunch or something. Okay?"

Luna could only nod, stunned. Then Eleanora was walking away to meet her father outside.

Valerio took her hand again. This time they were able to make their way back into the library they had been in before, only they

252

weren't alone. The room was entirely too small for all the girls, Allister, and Dante.

"So when were you planning on telling us about this?" Gianna asked.

"You didn't know either? Makes me feel better finding out at my own fucking engagement party," Valerio said sarcastically, taking off his suit jacket and throwing it on the floor. "These are things we need to plan to announce."

She opened her mouth to talk, but the door flying open with Finn and Augustus stopped her once again.

Luna expected Finn to say something threatening, something awful and horrible, but he was silent. He just looked between Luna and Valerio. He was unusually pale for the outrage that was caused a moment ago.

"Save the fucking lecture; your father already made his point known," Valerio told him, pacing the room.

Finn looked at her. "Were you pregnant when that man broke in? Did anyone know? Anyone like our father?"

Luna huffed, throwing her arms up. "I'm not pregnant."

The entire room went silent. She was sure a feather falling would be heard like an avalanche. At that moment, she wished she could be buried by an avalanche to avoid the angry gaze Valerio threw at her.

"You're not pregnant?" he asked, stalking toward her. "Then what the fuck were you thinking announcing something like that? Do you know what you've done?"

"Don't talk to me like that," Luna said. "I did what I had to do. My parents were going to do whatever they had to in order to get me out of our contract and marry me to someone else. I needed to do something to protect myself."

"You protected yourself, but what about me? We're in this together. We plan these things together," Valerio hissed, running a hand through his hair.

"It doesn't matter now. The damage is done. They're expecting a baby in nine months," Allister pointed out. "Both of the mafia leaders of two very important families are expecting a baby now."

"Fucking hell, Luna," Finn muttered. "You couldn't think of anything else?"

"Someone wants me dead!" she cried out. "Someone you promised to catch tonight and didn't. I took matters into my own hands."

"You destroyed the plan completely!" Valerio screamed back. "Do you understand the consequences of what you did?"

"It tied us to each other," Luna said.

"We would have been tied to each other when we got married. When we actually had a baby," Valerio pointed out.

"And it would have been too fucking late because someone tried to kill me," Luna hissed, her chest rising and falling rapidly. "Don't you understand? We're not safe. No one in this room is," Luna told him, walking closer. "They'll turn on any of us; they already have."

The paranoia was thick in her voice, but she saw it out there. She saw it in her father, in his. She needed to protect herself, protect Valerio. This was the only way. And it had to work because if it didn't then she just destroyed everything.

"That wasn't your call to make," he muttered, walking out onto the balcony. Luna's mouth dropped open, her shoulders falling in disbelief.

"We still have the issue of everyone expecting a baby," Dante said. "From where I'm sitting, we have a few options."

"Like what?" Blair asked. "She gets pregnant and pops a kid out?"

"That or we tell everyone she lost the baby. It's believable enough," he said.

Luna was nauseous listening to them talk. She made her way out onto the balcony where Valerio stood, gripping the white rail in a death grip with his head down.

Her heart was broken, empty. She didn't mean to cause so much heartbreak and chaos. It was miscalculated, she'd admit, but she only did what she thought she had to. If her father was willing to send someone to kill her, then what was stopping him from doing the same to Valerio? Especially after their engagement party and everything he had told her.

Reece Kingsley wouldn't harm the father of her child, wouldn't harm her while she was pregnant. At least she prayed to God he wouldn't. It bought them some time.

"I'm sorry," she told him, walking closer. "I only did what I thought would protect us."

He lifted his head slightly but still didn't acknowledge her fully. "You could have warned me. I thought you were pregnant, Luna. That really fucked with my head."

She stepped closer, running her hand along his arm. "You're right. I should have told you."

He sighed, lifting his head. "I don't know how we're going to get out of this."

"I'll get pregnant," she said. "If it'll make things easier, then we'll have a baby."

"I will not use my child as collateral in this war," Valerio said. He turned to face her now, towering over her frame with his. "We'll figure something out."

"Please don't be mad at me," she whispered, her vulnerability peeking through. "I mean, you can be mad at me all you want, but please don't leave me. I need you on my side. Please."

"I'm on your side for the rest of our lives," Valerio said, pulling her body into him. "I'm never leaving you. I've already told you as much. I wish it was true that we were expecting, but now isn't the time."

"I would never announce it to you like that either," she said. "You will be right beside me, finding out at the same moment I do."

He gave her a small smile, leaning his forehead against hers. "We need to discuss what your father said to you."

"And we need to discuss this war," she added, taking in every ounce of his warmth. "Something has changed with my father, Val. I don't trust him. I can't."

"We have some time now, as long as they believe this is true. My father, he's not to be trusted either. Something has to be done about both of them."

"What are you saying?"

"We'll talk about it later, I promise. Just remember, we're a united front," he said. "For the rest of our lives."

She pressed her lips to his, savoring the moment. It was their engagement party and they had yet to even share a kiss to celebrate. She'd destroyed the night and yet, here he was, holding her like she was going somewhere. She didn't deserve him; that much was true. Maybe she never would.

She pulled away first, immediately missing his taste. "Let's go inside. It's cold."

He nodded, letting her move first.

She had just turned her back when she caught the sound of something whooshing through the air. She watched Valerio fall onto his knees, his face filled with confusion.

Time slowed down when he held his hands in front of himself to stop the fall, but it didn't seem to matter. Not when Luna saw the blood leaking through the back of his white button-up, falling like a waterfall down his back.

She let out a bloodcurdling scream, falling to the floor to hold Valerio so his face didn't rest against the cold, dirty concrete of the balcony. She touched his back, trying to apply pressure as if she knew what she was doing.

"Dante!" she screamed and didn't stop screaming even when everyone ran out to see what was going on. Cecilia dropped to the floor, ripping Valerio's shirt off to see where he was hit.

Dante stood across from Luna on the other side of Valerio's body, too stunned to do anything. Valerio's eyes closing finally snapped him into action. He began slapping his brother's face, begging him to stay awake.

Luna let out screams and cries, desperately wanting to see Valerio's face.

"Don't move," Cecilia told her. "You're the only thing stopping him from bleeding out right now."

So Luna stayed there, pressing firmly to slow the bleeding despite how horrified she was at how much was coming out.

"We need an ambulance," Gianna said. She took out her phone with trembling hands.

"There's no time," Finn told her. "We can transport him. As long as Luna keeps pressure, it'll buy us enough time to get him there ourselves."

"There's a hospital a few blocks from here," Allister said. "We can take him there." He handed a pair of keys to Blair. "Go downstairs with Gianna and get the car pulled up to the back entrance. We'll go through there."

Blair nodded, pulling Gianna with her as they ran out of the room.

"I need you all to line up around his body," Cecilia said. "Two to support his head and shoulders and two to hold his legs, especially his torso. Be gentle. I don't know how close the bullet is to his spine."

They did exactly what she said, slowly lifting him off the ground. A groan reassured Luna that Valerio was at least a little bit conscious. That had to be a good sign.

"Please stay with me, Val," she begged him. "Please. Please."

She stood along with them, keeping her hands pressed against his back, even while they walked out of the room and down the stairs. Luna's mind was fuzzy. She had no idea how they got out of the library or into the car or even to the hospital.

The warmth she'd felt earlier was completely gone. All that was left in its wake was loneliness as she stood in the hospital hallway in her white engagement dress now soaked in the blood of her dying fiancé, watching him get wheeled away.

And she had never even told him she loved him.

THIRTY-THREE

LUNA

LUNA'S EYES snapped open to the sound of footsteps approaching. Her back ached from the uncomfortable waiting room chair, but she refused to move from that spot in the chance that the doctor would come out to speak to her.

No one had yet.

Dante sat next to her, carrying a cup of coffee in his hands. "Got this for you," he said, trying to hand it to her.

She shrugged him away. "I don't want it."

Her voice was back to being rough and raspy, but this time it was because of the screams and cries she'd let out earlier.

Oh, how she wished she was the one in the operating room and not him. Her Valerio didn't deserve it, and if he didn't make it—she stopped herself, swallowing harshly.

"Maybe you should at least wash up and change?" Dante asked.

"The girls are bringing me clothes," she said. She was still in her dress and hadn't washed the dried-up blood yet. She didn't want to leave though. The moment she turned her back, Valerio was on the floor with a bullet in him. She didn't want to turn her back on him ever again.

Dante sighed. "The nurse said it was going to be a long night."

"And I'll stay here until he's out of surgery and I get to see him. What's your fucking problem?" she snapped.

"He would want you taken care of."

"Then he can do it when he recovers and is next to me," Luna said. "I'm not leaving this spot until then."

"Then I hope you enjoy the company," he said, stretching out on the chair beside her. "The others are back at the library looking for anything that would point to who did this. They'll be back soon."

"We'll find who did this," Luna said. "And when we do, I'll put a bullet through their head myself."

He was silent for a moment. "You mentioned earlier that none of us were safe."

"And I believe it."

"You believe your father tried to kill you," Dante said. He didn't say it as a question, but more so a fact he was checking.

"I don't need you to tell me it's a wild idea," she said dryly.

"I'm not. I think he did it and so did Valerio," he said.

"He told me," she said.

"Did he also tell you about the war between him and our father? It would make sense that your father would attempt to kill you to make it look as if my father had done it. Help push Valerio into a war with our father and give him an opening to pull you out of the contract, unless of course you had actually died," Dante said. "It's kind of genius when you think about it. Too bad he didn't know Valerio's war with my father started long before any of that and now he's keen on destroying both of them."

Luna looked at him with wide eyes. "Valerio mentioned something about your father not being trusted while we were on the balcony. He didn't have a chance to say anything else, so what am I missing here?"

"A couple of weeks ago, my father threatened your life because Valerio had resigned the contract with you. He realized there was no monetary gain from the union with the Kingsleys, it was all bullshit. Valerio was in love with you. Cesare realized his heir had a liability—a weakness." Dante shook his head. "Valerio threatened to kill him. His trip down to Buffalo wasn't because my father sent him. It was because he was arming himself."

"I don't understand. You think it was your father who tried to kill me then?" Luna asked, trying to add everything up. That had to have been what he was saying. If Cesare Vitali had threatened her outright, maybe he did actually try to kill her. Maybe her father hadn't succumbed that low.

But that hope was quickly extinguished by Dante shaking his head. "No, no. That would be too easy. Valerio would know it was him right away. But tell me this, if your father tried to kill you, who do you think tried to kill Valerio?"

"Isn't it obvious?" Luna asked bitterly. "I'm still alive, so he probably moved onto his next target." That was the sick truth, wasn't it?

"What do you think is an easier situation to accept? That your father tried to kill you or that he tried to kill Valerio?"

Luna swallowed harshly. "What kind of question is that?"

"I mean, he must have felt pretty murderous after what you told everyone earlier," Dante said. "When he held Valerio down and threatened him, especially when he had plans to put you into another contract since you're not dead. Probably won't get much for you anymore since your cherry is gone. You're right about Valerio being the next perfect target with all of that in mind."

She turned to him with a murderous glare. "What the fuck is wrong with you?"

He stared at her for a long moment. "I didn't mean to upset you."

"Then shut the fuck up and let me worry in silence," she spit out.

He obliged. Luna watched nurses and doctors run around the waiting room. Her heartbeat sped up every time she thought they were finally bringing some news about Valerio, but it was always a false alarm.

"When did you fall in love with him?" Dante asked suddenly.

She sighed. "Far earlier than I thought I would."

"I had someone like that once." He looked at the hallway in front of him as if he was remembering something beautiful. "He was the love of my life. He was bright-eyed, with the whitest hair I had ever seen. I swear to God he had to have been bleaching it or something, but he denied it."

"He sounds beautiful."

"He was," Dante said, a small smile on his face. In an instant, the smile was gone. "Until I found him with a bullet in his back, tossed in a bathtub like he was a piece of trash."

Horror struck her. "I'm sorry."

"Don't be. You didn't kill him. My father did," he said.

"Why are you telling me about this?" Luna asked, her voice shaky.

Dante turned to face her. He leaned in close, his voice a low whisper. "Reece Kingsley trying to kill Valerio makes sense. Too much sense. It's almost the perfect cover-up, don't you think?" He shook his head. "There is one man I know that hides behind the easy kill, that has a specific specialty: my father."

Luna swallowed harshly. "What are you saying?"

"Cesare Vitali prefers his enemies be killed with a bullet to the back to blindside them, to make them regret turning their back on him. The minute Valerio chose you over our father, that was exactly what he did; he turned his back on the Vitali family in my father's eyes. But he wouldn't kill Valerio unless the bloodline was secured and continued."

Luna's mouth dropped open. "A baby."

"Exactly. Your pregnancy secured an heir without him needing Valerio around. The baby would be someone he could manipulate, and by blaming your own father for it, you would have no choice but to trust the Vitali empire." Dante let out a laugh of disbelief. "Even though Valerio told you not to trust our father, you still jumped on your father as being the culprit. It's genius. Both sides targeting their own children so they have a reason not to unite, so they can continue their wars."

"He tried to kill Valerio," Luna whispered. The thought made her nauseous. How had everything become so twisted that there wasn't a single soul they could trust anymore?

"You have more worth to my father as long as he believes you are pregnant," he said. "But only until the baby is born."

"There is no fucking baby," she whisper-screamed. The guilt tore through her body.

"Do you see the problem now?" Dante muttered.

"How do you even know all of this?" Luna asked. "What if you're wrong?"

"Maybe I am," he said. "But as it stands, Valerio is lying in an operating room clinging onto his life. Someone is responsible for it and there are two people who are at the front of this chaos."

She finally understood what Dante was saying. For the longest time she had been thinking they had to unite the families in order to stop the madness between them. But that wasn't what they needed.

No, they needed to do the opposite.

"You want to get rid of Reece Kingsley and Cesare Vitali?" Luna asked, her voice slow, making sure he heard every single word that came out of her mouth. What they wanted was a betrayal they couldn't turn back from. It guaranteed them death if anyone found out or if they didn't succeed. But if any of them wanted a chance at a normal life, if they wanted to start their families and avoid their children living in the same generational trauma as they all did, then they needed to change who ran things.

"I want them dead," Dante clarified. "And so do you."

Before Luna could say another word, the girls were walking toward her with a bag of clothes. They practically dragged her to the bathroom where they washed the blood off her arms and legs and put her into a pair of sweats and one of Valerio's hoodies.

She was numb, but when she came back to the waiting room

chair, something changed. There was a different energy in the air, signaling change was approaching. They could either get on it, or they could miss it and end up with bullets in all of their backs.

Whatever it was gave Luna something to focus on, something to set her mind to. Valerio would pull through; he would. And when he did, they would start taking control of their lives.

She would start with their fathers.

THIRTY-FOUR

LUNA

AS THE HOURS DRAGGED ON, Luna had yet to hear any news. Her mind wandered in a million different directions, forcing her to live out a million different scenarios on how all of this would end. The morning sun was beginning to rise, and Valerio was still in surgery.

Her head throbbed from the crying she did every time she thought about him not pulling through. It got to the point where she almost begged Augustus for a pill to make her stop feeling any of it, but she stopped herself. Valerio was the priority, not herself.

She played with the ring on her finger, twirling it around aimlessly. It was the one thing that connected her to him at that moment. Maybe they were cursed at this point, unable to enjoy a single minute of peace for their entire lives because they were defying the fact they were supposed to be enemies. Generations of war and violence between the two families wouldn't be able to end with the two of them and maybe it shouldn't.

But when she considered her life without Valerio, without his cheesy comments and affection and sometimes brutal tendencies protecting her, she realized that she didn't want a life without him. He snuck his way into her life—well, it was more like he bulldozed his way in—and now she didn't want a single moment without him.

She looked around the entire waiting room. Dante still sat beside her, his eyes closed as if he were sleeping. Allister sat next to Gianna on the wall to the left of them. She dozed off, but he typed away on his phone with a frown. Finn snored loudly in the corner, his head hanging at an uncomfortable angle. Luna wasn't sure why he had stayed; he hated Valerio. But either way, she was thankful to have even a little bit of familial support. Blair sat beside Cecilia on the other side of the room, the latter slumping on Augustus's shoulder.

Luna's eyes snapped to the doors at the end of the hall when they opened, a woman with blue scrubs and a surgical cap covering her hair walked over to them. Luna shot up to her feet, meeting the doctor midway.

"Is he okay?" she asked before the doctor could get a single word out.

"He's not out of surgery yet. I came out here to let you all know we are still doing everything we can to remove the bullet and make sure there's no permanent damage to his spine. The bullet narrowly missed it by four centimeters, but it exploded deep inside the muscle leaving fragments," the doctor said. "With that being said, I think it's important to start preparing for the worst-case scenario."

Luna's heart dropped.

"What the hell do you mean? You just said that the bullet missed his spine. That should be a good thing," Dante said, his face contorted in misaligned anger and confusion.

"And that is a good thing, but it is risky trying to pull it out. His blood pressure dropped dangerously low on two separate occasions, and on the latest one we had to prepare the defibrillator and do minor compressions. He returned back to normal, but there is a possibility of him not coming back if it happens again," she said. "We will continue doing everything we can, but I thought it would be wise to warn you just in case."

"Please," Luna whispered, wiping away the tears that slipped out of her eyes. "Please do everything you can."

The doctor gave her a small smile, one of comfort. "I promise I will try my best."

Luna nodded, her voice too weak to say anything else at the moment.

"I also wanted to give this to you, so it doesn't get lost in the chaos," the doctor said. She handed Luna the chain that she had given him on his birthday. A sob escaped her as she grabbed it and pressed it against her lips. "I'll be back out to give you guys another update as soon as I can."

Luna turned around, trying to walk back to her seat when her legs buckled underneath her. She fell to the floor, letting the choked sobs claw their way out from her chest once again. She clutched the necklace in her hands, praying for a miracle. Something, anything.

"He's going to be okay," Blair told her, stroking her back in comfort.

"He's strong," Gianna said.

"And he would never want to leave you alone," Cecilia confirmed.

But what if he did?

They managed to get Luna back onto the chair, but she kept her head in her hands, whispering prayers over and over again. Her eyes itched and burned from the tears she had shed at that point, but they refused to stop no matter how hard she tried.

"Luna, there's a lawyer here. He needs you included in the conversation," Allister said, standing directly in front of her. "I know you don't want to do this now—"

"Are you serious?" Blair asked, her voice raised. "Can you read the fucking room?"

"I'm being practical," he said. "Valerio had these things set up in case anything ever happened. I'm only following his directions."

"Send him away," Luna muttered. She closed her eyes tightly.

"We're all hurting," he said. "But no matter what, he would want you taken care of. Think about what he wanted."

Luna snapped her head up. "All I've been fucking doing is thinking about him."

The lawyer stood only a few feet away, looking uncomfortable being in the middle of such a stressful situation. Luna didn't care. The man didn't deserve any comfort.

"I won't talk to him," she concluded. Maybe it was because she didn't want to hear all the legal jargon talking about Valerio's life as a transaction.

Allister looked over at the lawyer, grabbing the papers from him instead. "Then I'll go through it with you." He motioned for the lawyer to leave the waiting room, and luckily, the man took the cue.

"Whatever," Luna muttered, leaning her head on Blair's shoulder. Cecilia held her hand tightly, while Gianna kept a hand on her back.

Allister sighed, pulling a chair up in front of the girls. Dante leaned against the armrest. He opened up the first page, clearing his throat. "There's a letter he wrote here; do you want me to read it out loud?" Allister asked.

Luna shook her head frantically. "No, he's not dead. Just go over what you have to."

"Well then, the most important factor would be who he set as his power of attorney in case he couldn't make the decision for himself on what to do with his health," he said.

"Who does that typically fall on?" Gianna asked with a frown.

"Depends on the situation. Usually when you're married, your spouse makes the decisions for you, or you can set it as someone else if you choose to do so legally," Allister said.

"Please just tell me it isn't our father," Dante said.

Luna prayed that Cesare wasn't named as power of attorney. If it was true that he did put the bullet in Valerio's back, then there was no doubt he would do anything to make sure Valerio no longer existed.

"No, it's good news," Allister said, sighing in relief. "He named Luna first and then Dante in case she didn't want the responsibility."

"What does that mean?" Luna asked.

"It means you will be making the decisions on what to do with his health," he said. "It also means your word speaks for him in relation to everything else in his life when he's unable to lead himself."

She furrowed her brows. "Again, what do you mean by that?"

Dante cleared his throat. "It means you're in charge of his assets, businesses, estates, everything if he's unable to."

Luna's eyes widened. They weren't even married. Until recently, they hadn't even been in a stable enough relationship. And yet, he had entrusted her to make decisions on his behalf. He chose her over Dante and Allister, over anyone else in his life.

"When did he appoint me?" she asked.

Allister looked her dead in the eye. "Seven years ago."

Seven years ago had been when they were first put into their marriage contract together. Seven years ago Luna hated Valerio for taking her choice away. And even knowing her feelings toward him, he left everything to her. He wanted her taken care of in case anything happened.

A sharp pain rang through her chest.

He had truly loved her all along.

And she had waited to say those same words to him and now she might have missed her chance completely.

She wouldn't do wrong by him this time. She couldn't change how they had started out their relationship, but she could change how it continued. He chose her. They were a team.

That meant she would do everything she could to protect him, take care of him, and bring him back to her.

Luna wiped the tears that slipped from her eyes. "Call Finn over here."

Dante's eyes narrowed, as if he knew exactly what was going

through Luna's mind. As if he had been waiting for her to gain control of herself once again since everything had gone down.

He whistled, motioning for Finn and Augustus to come closer to them.

"What happened?" Finn asked, unsure.

"Before I say anything, I need everyone here to swear that not a word of this will leave any of your lips," Luna told them.

"Why?" Blair asked, her eyes wide in worry.

"Because we're going to take down Cesare Vitali and Reece Kingsley."

THIRTY-FIVE
VALERIO

VALERIO GROANED. His entire body ached, and the slightest bit of movement sent a stab of pain throughout his body from his back. The lights were dimmed, and the constant beeping from the different machines was beginning to annoy him.

He was in the hospital. And he wasn't dead.

There were voices coming from outside the room—a mix of feminine and masculine. Valerio tried to listen in, but the voices were far too muffled. He attempted to sit up, but the pain was unbearable once again. He found the IV connected to his arm, tracing his fingers up to find it was connected to an IV bag with morphine mixed inside of it. He turned the clamp, increasing the flow of the fluid to medicate him quicker.

The door opened, letting in only a sliver of the bright white hospital light before it was closed quickly once again. Valerio's eyes snapped up, connecting with a familiar pair of green eyes he had come to fall in love with.

Her eyes widened and she stood in shock.

"Hi baby," he said, his voice hardly more than a whisper. His heart swelled with happiness at the prospect of being reunited with her once again.

Luna walked closer to him, as if she was unsure if it was real or not. "You're awake?" she asked. Her hand hovered over his arm, scared to touch him. Valerio reached for it, feeling the same sparks when his hand touched hers.

"I'm awake," he said.

The sob that escaped her was unexpected. Luna grabbed his face, feeling the warmth of his skin under cold hands. She pressed messy kisses around his face.

"I thought I lost you," she whispered, leaning her forehead against his.

"You will never lose me," he promised her.

Maybe that was the only promise Luna needed to hear at the moment because she wasted no time in pressing their lips together.

He wiped the tears from under her eyes before pulling her onto the bed beside him. She refused, trying to get back up. "You're hurt," she told him. "I don't want to make it worse."

"Hush," he muttered, making space for her to lay down. He held back the groan of pain that threatened to escape. "I need this and so do you."

That seemed to muffle any of the fight from her as she finally settled in beside him. She brushed a piece of his wavy hair away, running her other hand against the stubble that had begun growing on his face.

"You don't know how happy I feel right now," she told him. "There was a time when I thought I wouldn't have this moment."

"Don't say that. I told you I was strong, remember?" he asked, trying to lighten the mood.

She nodded with a small smile. "I do remember."

He grabbed her hand, pressing a kiss to the back of it. "How long was I out for?"

"Six days. They operated on you for almost nineteen hours. They assumed the comatose state was because of the trauma your body had gone through, but they weren't sure when you'd wake up." She sniffled, squeezing his hand. "But you did wake up."

He tried to move his head for a kiss but wasn't able to without his back killing him. "Give me a kiss," Valerio said. "I need to show you that I'm never leaving you."

She shook her head with a small laugh but still kissed him. "You have a lot of kisses to make up for, but I'll excuse it for now."

"I'll spend the rest of my life making up for it," he said. "What happened with everything? What's been going on?"

Someone had tried to kill her, and kill him. As much as he wanted to lay in bed to recover, he couldn't. There were lives that needed to be taken care of and he needed to get on it. The sooner he could find out he missed and begin working on everything, the sooner he could fucking annihilate everyone involved.

"Don't think about any of that for now," Luna told him. "Your body needs rest. And besides, I've been taking care of everything."

His brows shot up his forehead. "What does that mean?"

She sighed, sitting up. "It means that not a single person knows you've been in the hospital. Not even your father."

"Why would it matter if he knew or not?" Valerio asked. "What do you know, my little moon?"

Luna stood, walking to the end of the bed. "Can you feel your feet, wiggle your toes?"

Valerio did just that. They felt sore, but he felt every little movement. "Yes, why?"

She ignored him, grabbing her phone out of her pocket and typing something out before she put it back in her pocket. "I swear I will answer all of your questions once we get you home."

The door opened again, and this time it was Dante and Allister pushing their way into the room. Luna took her spot beside him once again, grabbing his hand.

"Good to see you again, brother," Dante muttered, pulling him in a small hug. Allister did the same, and it was clear there was balance brought back to the group with all of them reunited once again.

But it was also clear that they were keeping something from

Valerio, and it was driving him insane to be kept out of the loop. He wasn't ever kept out of the loop. Usually, he was the one who was doing the planning and scheming of everything.

"Everything is ready for us to go," Allister told Luna. "I have the discharge paperwork, and all of the hospital staff have signed NDAs. A nurse will come in here to get him unwrapped and the doctor is waiting at home."

Luna nodded. She opened her mouth to say something, but a nurse coming in with gauze and other equipment had her shutting up. Valerio took it as his cue to also not ask any questions until they were alone. He picked up on the stiffness in the room. Something had definitely changed, and he wasn't just talking about the dynamic in the three people he trusted more than anything in the world.

The nurse moved quickly, taking out the IV and making sure the wound on his back was properly wrapped. Sitting up caused another sharp stab of pain to travel throughout his back, forcing out a groan.

Luna squeezed his hand tightly and it gave him comfort. Being around her always did.

The nurse left without a word, not looking at anyone as she left. Probably smart not to remember any of their faces.

"Do I get any answers now?" Valerio asked, throwing the blanket off himself. Luna helped him sit up, pulling his legs so they hung over the edge of the bed.

"It's just safer if we get you home first," Dante told him. "You were shot, remember?"

"Of course I remember, dumbass, but you guys aren't telling me something," he said. He slid the hospital gown off his shoulders, lifting his arms so that Luna could help him slide a T-shirt on.

When he let out a particularly painful groan, she stopped completely. "Maybe we should just leave him at the hospital to heal? We'll secure it and have guards standing at every entrance."

"We can't. He's already been here far longer than he should have been," Allister said, rolling a wheelchair over by the bed.

Luna's face was drawn into a look of worry and frustration. Valerio grabbed her hands, placing tender kisses on the backs of them. "Do you think it's dangerous for me to stay here?" he asked.

She slowly nodded her head. "I know it is."

"Then let's get me home and you can be my personal nurse in the comfort of our bedroom," he said, giving her a small smile. "I can push through a little bit of pain."

That seemed to give her the confidence she needed. It also raised every single alarm in his body. How much did Luna know that now she was able to weigh in on these types of matters?

With Allister's and Dante's help, they were able to get him standing. Luna helped slide the sweatpants up his legs.

Walking to the wheelchair was hell. His legs were like lead, heavy and unwilling to move after being stuck in bed for the past week. Sitting back down was even worse, putting more pressure on his back than was necessary. His body heated up from the pain.

"We have pain meds at home," Luna said quickly. "As soon as we're there we'll get another IV started."

"I'll be okay," he groaned, taking deep breaths. He had a higher pain tolerance than most, which meant he could handle being beat and bruised with no problem. But this was worse than anything he had experienced before.

The worry on her face was enough for him to pretend that he wasn't in pain. He hated seeing her so concerned and distraught. He could only imagine the hell she had been in the past week, so if he could ease her mind now, he would do so.

After checking the room to make sure nothing else was left behind, they forced him into a pair of sunglasses and a hat that managed to cover his face enough.

"Now no one will know who I am," he said sarcastically. "Great distraction."

"It's just a precaution. This wing of the hospital should be empty by now, so we'll be able to get into the utility elevators without being seen," Allister told him. "Camera feed has been cut as well, and all documents have been seized. Your stay here no longer exists."

Luna pushed him out of the room, moving quickly so they weren't seen. Luckily, they were right. The floor seemed deserted as well as the elevator.

But once they got to the ground floor, everyone seemed to be on high alert all over again. They traveled through the hospital staff-only halls, following Allister out to one of the back entrances.

To his surprise, Finn was out back waiting for them with a cigarette hanging from his lips.

"What the fuck are you doing here?" Valerio asked, his eyes narrowed in confusion. He was out for six days. What happened in that time that Finn was suddenly his personal chauffeur?

"Glad to see that you're alive and well," Finn said, his voice full of sarcasm. He threw the cigarette on the ground, opening the car door for them. "Get in."

Luna and Dante helped him up, trying to get him into the car with the least amount of damage they could manage. Only once he was situated were they driving home. Valerio barked out curse words whenever Finn hit every single pothole that existed.

"They should really invest in fixing these roads." Finn smirked.

Luna slapped his shoulder. "Knock it off."

Valerio didn't want to admit it, but it was satisfying to see her sticking up for him.

When they pulled up to the house, he was shocked to see how much of it was a ghost town. The usual guards were gone; no one stood by the gates to let them in. What the hell happened?

Allister opened the fence for them through his phone.

They drove up the paved pathway, parking in front of the entrance to the house. Instead of any of his usual house staff greeting him like they usually would, Augustus came out with a machine gun strapped to his back, looking like someone who was going to war.

"What the hell are you wearing?" Allister asked.

"Just staying protected," he answered, a cocky smile on his face. "I got my girl in there; I'm not risking shit."

When they managed to get Valerio out of the car and into the house, they came across another hurdle.

"How did we not remember there were fucking stairs in this house?" Dante asked, throwing his arms up.

"I can set up a spot on the couch for you?" Luna asked Valerio.

"No, I want our bed," he told them. "Just help me up. I'll manage."

"That's a lot of steps."

"I can carry you up," Dante suggested.

"I can fucking kill you," he rebutted.

She and Dante helped him out of the wheelchair, supporting both sides of him while they slowly walked up the stairs. With every step, he could feel his back stretching and pulling uncomfortably. The medicine had to be completely out of his system because it did nothing to ease the pain. Instead, everything felt intensified. From his toes to his head, he felt like his body was on fire. By the time they reached the top, Valerio thought he was going to pass out from the dangerously intense pressure in his back.

Allister brought the wheelchair up with him, letting Valerio throw himself onto it. He gasped for air, desperately trying to soothe the pain away but there was no use. The only thing that brought some relief was seeing the doctor waiting in their bedroom.

"Give me a fucking IV," he growled, forcing the doctor into action. That seemed to have done it because soon the needle was going through his vein, sending the morphine into his body and soothing the pain immediately.

He finally laid on the bed, breathing in deeply. They talked about some pills for him to take for additional pain relief and to help avoid infection, but he didn't listen to any of it. He could care less. He wanted everyone out of his room and Luna in the bed right beside him.

Luna kicked everyone out, finally giving him the peace he craved. "Thank you," he said, opening his eyes. The bed dipped beside him when Luna curled up at his side.

"Anything you need, just let me know," she told him, pressing a kiss to his jaw.

"I want to know what you're all keeping secret from me," Valerio said, but his voice was far too groggy. "What happened while I was out?"

She took a deep breath, running her fingers through his hair. It only lulled him further into peace, forcing his eyes closed once more. Her entire presence always did that. The softness in her voice, her gentle touch, her smell, just her. It made him feel like going to sleep again was okay.

"While you were out, we decided on a couple of things. We're tired of the violence, of the uncertainty and the control our parents hold in our lives," Luna said. "I don't know if you'll agree with this or not, but we're taking down my father and yours."

And then Valerio fell asleep.

THIRTY-SIX

LUNA

THE BLINDS WERE THROWN OPEN, exposing the morning sun to the once dark room. Luna moved over to Valerio, pressing soft kisses to his face to wake him up. He groaned, stirring awake. He reached up to cup her face and kissed her.

"I can get used to being woken up like that." He smirked, pressing one more kiss to her lips. "I would also prefer to wake up with your cunt choking my dick, but we have time to test that method."

Luna shook her head. "Until you're healed, that won't be happening."

"That's the only way I'll heal." He reached out to pinch her ass, causing her to swat away his hands.

She helped him sit up, setting the pillow to support his back. Then she grabbed the tray from the desk, setting it on his lap.

"What is all this?" he asked.

She got into bed beside him. "I made us breakfast. There's eggs, fruit, potatoes, and bacon."

"You don't like bacon," he said, grabbing one of the plates.

"But you do," she said, giving him a small smile. "Was it disgusting to cook? Yes. But if it'll miraculously help you heal, then I'm willing to cook it."

He kissed her cheek, letting his lips linger there. "Thank you. Seriously, you don't have to do all of this for me."

"Yes, I do. I know you would do the same for me if the roles were reversed—actually, you did do it for me," she said, grabbing her plate. "Now eat. The doctor said he was going to stop by later to check on your back. Make sure it's not infected or anything. I think he also might suggest you start walking, so fuel up."

He ate his entire plate, taking bites off of hers as well. She let him, overly grateful for the fact he was alive and right beside her.

A knock came at the door. Before either of them could invite the person in, the door was being thrown open by Dante.

"Good morning, lovebirds. Hope I wasn't interrupting anything." He grinned, walking over and plopping down on the foot of the bed.

"There's nothing to interrupt. I can't fuck until I'm healed," Valerio said, crossing his arms. Luna took the tray off the bed, setting it on the desk again. "Or at least that's what my nurse says."

She shook her head, sitting back on the bed. "You'll be fine." His vulgar mouth was doing things to her body she couldn't act on either, but she couldn't tell him. Somehow he would muster up superhuman strength to fuck her, and she wasn't going to allow him to risk any harm to his healing body.

Dante let out a small chuckle. "How are you feeling?"

"The pain meds are working, that's for sure," Valerio said.

Allister peeked his head into the room before entering. "Good, you're awake. Given how light the room feels, is it safe to assume you haven't told him anything yet?"

Luna shook her head, rolling her eyes. "No, Allister. I haven't, but now I will."

Valerio looked between the three of them. "You mentioned something last night. I barely heard it before I passed out."

She bit her lip, looking at the other two men in the room. There was no good way to say the plan. Really, she just had to rip off the Band-Aid, so that was exactly what she did. "We want to get rid of our fathers. Both of them."

Valerio was silent for a moment. She could see the thoughts swirling in his eyes as he looked at her. She had always admired his intelligence and his knack for figuring out people's intentions, so revealing their plan to him made her nervous. Would he agree with it? Would he fight it? She wasn't sure, especially when his face gave no indication of what he thought.

"Why?" he asked slowly. "I feel like I'm missing a couple of key components, so I need you all to explain this to me in detail."

This time Dante took the lead. "Luna's father tried to kill her, our father tried to kill you. It's quite simple when you think about it. We need to eliminate the threat before the threat eliminates us."

"So Finn confirmed it was her father?" Valerio asked.

"Well, no. Not exactly. Finn wasn't able to find anything yet," Allister said. "But you had thought it was him before, without any clear evidence."

"I did. I am willing to go head-to-head with that son of a bitch if I have to, but I gave Finn a chance to prove me otherwise. Now you're claiming that our father tried to kill me. What makes you think that?"

"You're not his only heir. At least not while he thinks I'm pregnant," Luna said. "Your father knew you weren't on his side anymore. Your loyalty had shifted, but while there was someone else carrying Vitali blood, maybe he could shape the baby into someone whose loyalty wouldn't waver."

"That's not proof though," Valerio said, shaking his head. "I understand what you're saying, but there isn't a baby. He would want more proof before he ever tried anything like that."

"You were shot in the back. From what Luna told us, you were out on that balcony for a long time. Both of you were. You could have been shot in the chest when you were looking out directly, but you weren't. You were shot when you turned your back," Dante told him. "Luna wasn't shot either. If they wanted both of you out, why not get you both while you were open. Unless Luna had something of importance. You know our father."

Valerio's jaw clenched. Luna knew what was going on in his mind: the denial, the refusal, the betrayal. She had gone through it herself. She didn't want it to be true either, but it was. That was why they needed to do something about it.

"Has he tried contacting any of you?" Valerio asked.

"I made sure no one knew you were in the hospital. If he contacted us asking about you, that would be the only proof I needed," Luna said. "I know you don't want to believe this, but I seriously think it's the truth."

"I'm not denying it," Valerio said. "He's not above it. Neither of our fathers are. I just never thought I would be on the receiving end of it."

Allister sighed. "Even if we don't know one hundred percent for sure, look at the facts. As long as both the Kingsley don and the Vitali don are alive, you don't get a moment of peace in either of your lives. Both of your fathers have allegedly tried to have you killed. What kind of life does that leave for you? Or perhaps for your children? Will they take one child as the Vitali heir and another for the Kingsleys?"

Luna swallowed hard. "I won't let anyone else suffer because of them."

"We need to think about this. Come up with an actual plan before we even think about going in guns blazing. So much could go wrong. If they find out who did it, we're dead. All of us," Valerio said.

Luna held her breath. She couldn't do it if he didn't agree. She didn't know where to start or how to lead or get organized. But he did. He was strong and powerful and confident. Without him, the plan would fail.

He sighed, grabbing Luna's hand. "But that doesn't mean you guys aren't right. I almost lost you, Luna. You almost lost me. They won't stop, I know they won't."

"With you leading the Vitali empire, and Finn leading the Kingsley empire, we can actually change this shit once and for all," Dante said. While he tried to empower Valerio, his voice betrayed him with a slight quiver at the end. "Think about our mother, what she would have wanted."

Luna swallowed harshly. Too many people had suffered for far too long.

Valerio pushed a strand of her hair back, his eyes glossing over as if he was remembering something painful. "We all have to understand what this means. Once we reach that point, there is no going back. Not anymore."

"I'm ready for it," Luna muttered, closing her eyes in relief.

Things would either change or they would die trying.

THIRTY-SEVEN

LUNA

LUNA STOOD BY THE DOOR, watching as the physical therapist and nurse helped Valerio take a few steps. He was expected to walk from the bed to the bathroom a couple times a day, but he had already advanced past that. Now, he walked up and down the hallway, pushing himself even though he should have been recovering and resting.

She knew it was because he wanted his strength back. After the conversation a week ago when they finally revealed what their plans were, he was anxious to get moving again. The first time Luna saw him trying to get up by himself, she nearly had a heart attack.

He was perfectly capable of deciding what he wanted to do for his health on his own, but she had become particularly protective of him lately. For the past two weeks, while he was in the hospital and back at home, she'd had the same recurring nightmare. The one where she was forced to watch him bleed out, only this time he didn't wake up. When she awoke, she rushed to the bathroom to wash her hands until they were red and dry to the point of peeling. She swore she could still feel his blood on her hands, but in the light it was never there.

She only managed to get a couple hours of sleep a night.

Between the nightmares and putting her ear against his lips to feel his deep breaths, she was on edge constantly. It seemed like everyone in the house was on edge more than usual.

When Finn and Valerio had finally talked the other night, they didn't even bother to fight or bicker like they usually would. Instead, the conversation between them was direct and surrounded their plans for their fathers. It was almost as if they had reached a mutual understanding, that once their fathers were gone, they would be the ones running everything. Either they ended the cycle of abuse and violence or they let it keep going.

"You're going to overexert yourself," the nurse told Valerio.

"I'm fine," he said, dismissing her. "I can do a couple more laps."

Luna shook her head, approaching the group in the hallway. "Let's pick this up later. You're not going to get better if you don't give yourself rest."

"I've been resting," Valerio muttered.

"Have you always been this stubborn?" the doctor asked.

"Yes," Luna answered before anyone else could. "It's getting late. You guys can go. I'll help him back into bed."

She ignored the way Valerio rolled his eyes and instead focused on scheduling a time for them to come back tomorrow. She turned to him, grabbing his arm.

"I love when you play nurse, but I'm seriously fine," he said. With careful steps, they made their way back into the bedroom. He let out a loud sigh when he finally sat back down on the bed.

Luna narrowed her eyes. "That doesn't sound fine."

"What can I say, you take my breath away," he said with a small smirk.

This time Luna was rolling her eyes. "Very smooth."

He grabbed her hands, pulling her down to sit on his lap. She immediately fell into his warmth, finding peace in his heartbeat against her back. "I know you're worried," he said, surrounding her with his arms. "You have every right to feel that way. But remember, I'm not going anywhere."

She shut her eyes. She wanted to tell him he almost did go somewhere, that she was worried because she believed that at any moment he would be ripped from her arms again. Instead, she nodded. "I know."

He pressed a kiss to her forehead, allowing it to linger. "Let's go downstairs to eat. I'm starving," he told her.

"I can bring it up," she suggested, standing.

He shook his head. "It should be me bringing you food in bed, not the other way around."

"You'll have your entire life to do it," she said, helping him off the bed.

Despite Luna's protests, Valerio made his way down the stairs. She could see the improvements, but something in her mind refused to believe it was real. She kept her arms on him the entire time, providing the support she knew he needed but was too stubborn to admit to.

They hadn't even approached the kitchen yet when loud laughs rang through the halls, reminding them of the full house at the moment. They walked to the kitchen table, ignoring the arguing going on between Augustus and Cecilia. It happened far more often than Luna would have liked.

"Look who decided to join us," Gianna mused from the kitchen counter.

Valerio pulled out a chair for Luna, forcing her to sit down first. She sent him a glare, but he pretended not to see it. Instead, he approached the stove to grab whatever food had been made.

"He refuses to rest," Luna told her, rubbing at her eyes. They burned and ached with exhaustion.

"You look like you haven't slept in weeks," Blair said, a frown on her face as she took the seat beside Luna. "Are you okay?"

She nodded. "Yeah, I just haven't been sleeping well. Why are they going at it again?" It was an easy way to move the conversation away from herself.

Blair snorted. "You know how they are. This is their foreplay."

Luna's eyes drifted back to Valerio, who was nodding his head at something Allister was telling him. He shifted slightly on his legs. Not noticeable to anyone else, but Luna wasn't anyone else. She knew he should be sitting down instead of moving around like he wasn't shot in the back two weeks ago.

She moved to stand up, but Valerio was already turning around to walk back to her. He set two bowls on the table, some kind of pasta with marinara sauce. "Apparently Dante made it. Not sure how good it'll taste," he told her, taking the seat to her right.

"Hey, fuck you. I know how to cook." Dante grinned, slapping Valerio on the shoulder. Luna flinched as if it had impacted her.

Cecilia stormed over to the table. "God, I can't stand men," she said with a huff.

"Trust me, I know," Gianna said, taking a seat. "There's too much testosterone around here. I'm suffocating."

"I thought this was your dream scenario," Dante said, cackling at his own joke.

"It would be if the people I'm related to weren't here as well," she said, rolling her eyes.

Luna watched Valerio eat his food, holding the hand he'd placed on her thigh tightly. She grabbed a bite herself, forcing it past her lips. The pasta could have been delicious, but anything going into her stomach tasted like acid these days.

The feeling only got worse when Finn walked over to them, a somber look on his face. "Father called," he said, taking the seat directly across from Luna.

She dropped the fork on the table. "What did he say?"

The simultaneous dread and fear that filled her came over her so quickly that if she was standing, she was sure she would have fallen over. Valerio tightened his hand on her thigh.

"He was asking about the baby, how you're feeling," Finn said, tapping his fingers on the table. "Mom was wondering why you haven't called or met up with her. She wants to go with you to one of your appointments."

"What did you tell them?" Valerio asked, his voice hard. His eyes narrowed harshly at Finn.

Finn rolled his eyes. "I told them she was sick with morning sickness. Said you've been resting for the baby."

It was silent for a few moments until Dante spoke up. "So, there is no baby. I just wanted to remind everyone in case we forgot."

"Yeah, we fucking know," Luna muttered, rubbing her hand over her forehead. "Does it even matter anymore?"

"Well, if we're planning to get rid of them, then no, I guess it doesn't," he said, shrugging.

"They seem caring enough now," Finn said. "Maybe we don't have to do anything drastic. Maybe there's a possibility an actual child could do what we need done."

Luna shook her head frantically. "No."

"I don't see how having a child is any worse than killing our father or his father," Finn said, pointing at Valerio. "I mean, you can't possibly want your father dead. Are you willing to pull the trigger?"

"Don't tell me you're getting cold feet," Allister said.

"You can't fucking talk. No one is telling you to kill your fucking father," Finn spit out.

"Don't be naive," Luna told him.

"I'm naive? Are you kidding me?" he said. "You're naive for thinking you have the fucking guts to kill your own father."

"Why would a grandchild change any of their minds? They had their own fucking children and still managed to be the worst people in the world. No baby is going to change that, ever. And I'm not risking it," Luna bit back.

Finn ignored her completely, turning his attention to Valerio. "What do you think about this?"

"It's a complicated situation," he said.

Luna looked at him, trying to find some—any—indication of what he was thinking. Yes, it was complicated, but he couldn't change his mind now. Not after everything.

"What does that mean?" she asked.

"It means that this shouldn't be a rushed decision," Valerio said. "We need to make sure we know what we're doing, as I mentioned before."

Luna tensed. Her eyes met Dante's, who looked at her with a look that seemed to think the same: they were pulling out. The fear was back. Valerio wasn't on her side. Why wasn't he on her side? Why would he agree to everything, seeming like he cared, just to pull back?

Exhaustion crept up with the paralyzing feeling of betrayal. Not Valerio; he couldn't do it to her. Their parents already had; she couldn't handle it if he did too.

"Did they think before they decided to shoot you in the back?" Luna asked, her voice no more than a whisper. "Did they think before they sent a man to nearly strangle me to death in my apartment?"

"Luna," Valerio said softly.

It was too late.

She was already grabbing the bowl, sending it crashing against the wall beside them. "Did any of them think before they ruined our lives? No, they didn't. They don't deserve a single thought more. They deserve to be brought to their knees, forced to stare at the barrel of a gun before they're sent straight to hell for what they've done."

Her screams echoed through the kitchen, causing an eerie silence. She stood, pulling at her hair. "My hands were soaked in your blood while I tried to save your life. You almost died! Don't you care about that even a little bit?"

"Of course I do," Valerio said, attempting to stand up.

"I can't sleep, I can't eat, I can't fucking breathe. As long as they're living, breathing, and plotting, I will not know a moment of peace. I need them gone forever," Luna screamed.

"You haven't been sleeping or eating?" he asked, his eyes narrowed. "Why didn't you tell me?"

"Because you need to get better," she told him, her shoulders falling. "Because a couple weeks ago I was sure you were going to die. A couple weeks before that, I was sure I was going to die. A few months before that, my father was willing to sell me off to anyone who offered him the most money. My entire life before that I never got to make a single choice for myself because of *him*. He doesn't deserve the option of staying alive, not after everything he did to me."

Her chest heaved with every breath she took. The truth was out there, seeping into each and every one of them now.

She needed a minute where she didn't think about anything. Just one moment of peace, true peace. Until then, she could feel herself slipping deeper and deeper into her own misery, one she wasn't sure she could get out of.

THIRTY-EIGHT
VALERIO

VALERIO WAS STILL COMING to learn who Luna was, but one thing he was learning quickly was that she was eerily good at showing people the emotions she wanted them to see. He thought they were past the point of hiding the bullshit and could be fully transparent, but maybe he was wrong.

He couldn't remember much of the night when he was shot. After the bullet hit him, everything just kind of went black. There were times when he would remember seeing their faces: Luna's, Dante's, Allister's. It was for a split second before everything would become blurry and go completely black once again. There was no way for him to figure out whether it was snapshots of that night or not, but after hearing her words, he realized it was real. It wasn't just his mind showing him fragments of the people he loved and trusted the most in the world. They were actually covered in his blood, screaming out orders in a rush of pure fear.

Valerio stood from his chair, slower than he would have liked, but he managed to do it alone, waving off Dante's help. He didn't need his help, or anyone else's for that matter.

After a week of practicing walking, his steps felt less heavy, but he missed how quick he used to be on his feet. He missed his own strength. Now, he felt like a stranger in his own body, feeling betrayed by his own weakness.

People jumping out to help him at every second only made the feeling worse. He hated needing help ever since he was a child. It made him feel weak, made him feel vulnerable, and that was exactly what got people killed in their world.

Maybe that was his issue; he had too many weaknesses. He would destroy the world for Luna, he was fiercely protective over his brothers, and he kept loyalty sacred.

And within that loyalty remained a sliver for his father.

He hated the man. Hell, he couldn't remember a time in his life when he didn't. But that was the only parent he and Dante had left. He tried to convince himself that if his mother was able to see something in him to stay as long as she did, then maybe there was something redeemable about Cesare Vitali.

Then, Valerio remembered every single thing his father did to him and suddenly he didn't care if the man lived or died. He remembered his father forcing him to kill a man on his thirteenth birthday because he needed to learn how to run the business. He remembered his father taking a belt to his ass at nine years old when he would wake up with nightmares at night after his mother had died and he would cry out for her, waking up the house. He remembered his father forcing him to go to Italy when he was seventeen years old because he thought Valerio was getting too soft being at home. There wasn't a single good memory there.

And yet, he found himself at a crossroads, justifying everything like he always did by saying it made him the person he was today. There might have been a point in time when he would have chosen his Vitali loyalty over anything else. Probably at a time when his life looked lonely, loveless, and bleak. When he thought it was the honorable thing to do to continue the legacy.

But he found Luna. She was his everything.

In this war, it was between Luna and his father. And Valerio knew for a fact she wasn't going anywhere.

He found her in the library. Only a single lit up lamp on a small side table let him know that someone was in there. She sat with her legs pulled up to her chest, the chair only a few feet from the window where the full moon glowed vibrantly. A muffled sob escaped her lips and suddenly there was clearance for his crossroads.

It was so painfully obvious he would always choose her, that any threat against her was a threat against him. They were one in the same.

"When I put this library together, the vision of you in here was at the forefront of my mind. I always knew you would look absolutely beautiful inside of it," he said, finally approaching her from the shadows.

She gasped, wiping her cheeks and turning her head to look at him. She began standing up. "You shouldn't be walking without any help."

He pulled a chair beside her before she could get up. "I thought about all the books you read and knew I needed to fill it. I figured since I got to design this library, you would get to design the next one."

He took a seat, grabbing her cold hands in his. "I like this library," she said, squeezing his hand tightly. "But I might make the next one a little less dark."

Valerio let out a small chuckle. "I guess I can let you mess up my dark and mysterious aesthetic."

Luna took a deep breath. "I shouldn't force you to—"

"Hush," he said, pushing a strand of hair behind her ear. "You can do whatever you want."

She shook her head. "No. I can't ask you to choose your father over me, let alone kill him. That's not right. We can figure something else out."

"You're right about everything," Valerio told her. "The threat they pose is too high to not take care of. It's us or them, and I'll slaughter them before they lay another finger on you."

Another tear slipped out, but this time, Valerio was there to wipe it away. "I don't want you to hate me for it or to regret choosing me because of it."

His chest squeezed painfully as if something was stabbing right through it. "Do you really think I could ever hate you?"

"It's not impossible," she whispered.

"I'm not capable of hating you. I've never been. Even at our worst, I couldn't find myself hating you. It would feel like I was hating a piece of myself. I don't think there's a single thing you could do that would ever make me not forgive you," Valerio admitted.

"That feels terrifying."

"It is terrifying." And it was. Knowing he was in so deep that no matter what she did, he would be able to forgive and still be able to love her, it scared him. It also empowered him in a way he didn't know it could.

"But you still feel that way despite how scary it feels?"

"I do because I know you're a good person, Luna. I know you would never hurt me and I know you would never want to hurt anyone you love. And because of that, I find myself able to trust you with every fiber of my being," he said.

"What if I'm not so good?" she asked. She sniffled, attempting to turn her face away, but he held her chin. Her eyes broke through every wall he could ever imagine putting up. "Would you still love me?"

He couldn't help the small smirk that found his lips. The way she questioned his love for her was humorous. "You could stab me in the chest with an actual knife and I would still love you. I would say I'll love you for the rest of our lives, but I know I'll love you long after that too."

"Swear that you'll never change that answer," she begged. "Tell me that no matter what happens, you'll always feel that way."

The raw vulnerability in her voice pushed murderous intent through his veins. The way she had loved so many people just to be burned by them had made her this person: someone who was scared to trust and to love. He would always be there to mend the broken pieces, and to love and defend her with every inch of his soul he had to give.

"I swear it," he said. "I love you, now and always."

"I love you too," she said in a whisper.

Valerio's eyes widened, his heart skipping a beat. "What did you say?"

"I said I love you too," she said, louder this time. "I hated thinking that you would never get to hear me say it and I won't live with regrets anymore. Whatever happens, I love you, Valerio Vitali."

There were a handful of days that meant something to Valerio. All of them included Luna, but this moment, right here, was by far his favorite. He had known she'd felt this way far longer than she tried to let on, but she needed time. He refused to force it on her. But now, it was real.

She loved him. Luna loved him.

He couldn't stop himself from kissing her, sealing her admittance the only way he could think of. He wouldn't let her take it back now, no way in hell.

"I love you," he said, pressing another kiss to her lips. "I love you." A kiss to her left cheek. "I love you." A kiss to the right cheek. "I love you." A kiss to her nose. "I love you." A kiss on her lips.

"Wait, remind me one more time," she said. The glow in her eyes brought her back to life.

"I'll remind you for the rest of our lives," he said. "Say it one more time."

"I love you."

"Okay, one more time."

"I love you." She laughed, kissing him. "Now you can't leave me, ever."

"Never," he promised. "Our lives are going to change. I promise you what happened that night will never happen again."

The smile fell off her face. "In this world, you can't promise that it won't happen again."

"I can. I let my guard down, but it won't happen again," he said. "I will take care of my father. As for yours, just say the word."

She swallowed hard. "Please, think it through."

"I already have. I have waited what seems like a lifetime to be with you, Luna. To give you the life we both want. I'm not waiting anymore."

"What are you talking about?" she asked, watching as he stood. "Where are you going?"

"Come on, Mrs. Vitali," he said, helping her up. "We have a wedding to plan."

THIRTY-NINE
VALERIO

"ARE YOU KIDDING ME? I told you to hang the fabric elegantly, not half assed," Gianna screamed at Dante, throwing her hands up in the air. "Useless, all of you."

He rolled his eyes. "That's why I chose a life of crime, not wedding planning."

Valerio watched the interaction, shaking his head. Somehow, Gianna had self-selected herself to be the wedding planner, and despite her barking at everyone, she was getting things done on the tight deadline.

"If she's this bad as a wedding planner, I'm scared to see how she'll be as an actual bride," Allister said.

"I'll send a prayer for the idiot that falls for her. He'll need it," Valerio said.

"Where's Luna anyway?" he asked. "Shouldn't she be the one deciding where all this shit goes?" He picked up some fabric, tossing it back on the table.

"She's making the others carry in the rest of the decorations," Valerio said.

"And what are you doing then?"

"I'm the groom. I wait until my bride calls for me." He gave him a grin.

"Allister! Come help this idiot hang these drapes," Gianna screamed from across the room. He muttered a curse word, begrudgingly making his way over.

They'd only had a couple of days to set everything up, but in that time the second living room had been transformed. All the furniture was taken out of the room, replaced with white chairs that had white satin bows tied to the back of them. The guest list was small, so four chairs sat on either side, creating a small aisle that Luna would walk down.

Dante, and now Allister, were in the middle of draping the ceiling with white fabric before they lined it with warm fairy lights. They could have hired companies for everything, but any indication of wedding planning to certain outside forces would have raised suspicions. That left them to do everything themselves.

Tomorrow was the big day though. Tomorrow they would officially be married, and Valerio couldn't fucking wait. Sure, he had always imagined his wedding would host hundreds of people, most just associates or people he had come across a handful of times, but he preferred this more. As long as Luna was walking down the aisle to him, he didn't care who showed up or who didn't.

Valerio made his way back to the dining room, which was now the official reception room. The table had been covered in a thick white tablecloth with white candles lined up in the center. Two floral arrangements sat on either side of the table.

Finn was setting down plates and silverware. The dining room's ceiling had already been draped, so Augustus added the lights to decorate the ceiling.

Blair and Cecilia laid out the glasses and the many bottles of alcohol on the counter. But Valerio cared most about his bride-to-be, who sat tying her bouquet together. She cut the extra pieces of ribbon off, holding it up to herself with a smile.

"It looks beautiful," he told her, pressing a kiss to her cheek.

"Thank you. I'm glad the flowers in the greenhouse will get some use," she said with a smile. "Did you lay out the tuxes?"

"They're upstairs in the spare bedroom."

"And the food?"

"Ready to be dropped off tomorrow morning."

"What about the music? Has anyone tried to connect it yet?"

"It's all figured out," Valerio said, easing her mind. "Everything is going perfectly."

"I feel like we're missing something. I can't put my finger on it," Luna said, biting her lip. She absentmindedly played with the ring on her finger before her eyes widened. "Oh my God, the rings. How did I forget the rings?"

Valerio smiled. "I already took care of it."

Her shoulders slumped. "Oh, thank God."

"All you need to do now is enjoy your bachelorette party," he told her. "And then show up to our wedding tomorrow."

"I wouldn't miss it for the world," Luna said, grinning. "I'm curious to know how your bachelor party will go. I bet you never imagined my brother would be attending it."

"I can't say that he was on my list, but life is full of surprises," he said.

"I wish we were running off to some honeymoon afterwards," she said, wrapping her arms around his neck. "Somewhere tropical, where clothes aren't necessary."

"If you want a private island, all you have to do is ask," he said, his voice now low and seductive. "But I do have something planned."

"Does it include leaving this house?"

"Only if you're a good girl," he said.

Her cheeks flared red. "I thought I already was your good girl."

"You are." He kissed her, letting it linger. "You're my perfect fucking good girl."

It had been too many long fucking weeks at this point. And sure, they could have fucked anytime in the past week, but why not save it for their wedding? The idea was smart five days ago when they decided on it. Now, it was fucking torture.

"I need to talk to your asshole fiancé," Finn said, interrupting their moment.

Luna rolled her eyes. As if out of instinct, Valerio's hands clenched up into fists. She was there in no time unclenching them for him. "Sure. I'm going to go check in with Gianna."

She got up, leaving him with a lingering look as she walked away. Valerio crossed his arms, waiting for Finn to begin. "Start talking, I have shit to do."

"Can we go somewhere private?" he asked.

Valerio clenched his jaw, resisting the urge to roll his eyes at the dramatics. "Sure."

They moved out into the hallway, away from the chaos and Gianna's yelling from the living room. Valerio wanted to remind himself that this was Luna's brother, that he shouldn't have had his guard up the way he did, but he never trusted Finn. He never had a reason to. From the moment they had been born, they had been groomed to hate each other. Valerio marrying his sister was an attempt to soothe out that hatred, but after generations, it seemed impossible to do.

"So, what was so important you had to pull me away from Luna?" he asked, leaning against the wall. "Don't tell me you're trying to object to the wedding now."

"I don't think it would make a difference either way," Finn said. "She has big plans for what our future can look like."

"And you don't agree with them?" Valerio raised his brow.

Finn snorted. "Don't tell me you actually think there is a world where we don't hate each other. It would never happen."

"Why?"

"Because you love your name and I love mine. We exist far better in a world where we don't find the need to work together," Finn said. "I'll coexist for the sake of Luna, but anything else is off the table for me."

"I always knew you were a fucking idiot. I just didn't know

the extent of it," Valerio said, shaking his head sarcastically. "Remind me again why you're staying in my house?"

Finn clenched his jaw. "I came to support my sister."

"You could have texted or called, not sat in the hospital waiting room," he pointed out. "I wonder if it has anything to do with your fear that your father might turn on you the same way he turned on Luna."

Finn shrugged. "I'm protecting myself. She was almost killed, you were almost killed. It seems like I'm next in line."

"You're his perfect little loyal heir. Why would he want you killed?"

"Why did yours want you dead?" Finn asked.

It was silent. He stared at him, trying to figure out who the hell he was. "If you suspect your father wants you dead, why not get rid of him first? Why are you so against Luna's plans?"

"Because as fucking horrible as he is, I can't find myself willing to put a bullet in him. At the end of the day, he's still my father." Finn's voice was just over a whisper, as if he were scared to admit it not only to Valerio, but to himself as well. It looked like he had a weakness too, the same one that kept him up at night.

How fucking tragic, Valerio had so much in common with someone he hated so badly.

"Then it's a good thing I'm willing to do it for Luna myself," Valerio said, pushing himself off the wall. He stopped for a moment. "If you need a real reason to hate me, you'll have it. I'll be the one murdering your father, not a Kingsley, not Luna—me, a Vitali. I'll give your sister the justice she deserves. Hell, I'll even give you the justice you deserve but you're too much of a fucking coward to go out and get yourself." He shook his head. "It's a shame you don't want to work together in the future. You could have genuinely been a good asset if you didn't let it all go to waste."

With that, he left the room. Finn coming to the harsh realization of what this life actually was could only be done with him and him alone. Valerio had dealt with true loss before, so he was able to understand that nothing was more valuable than true love. That was why he was willing to fight for it.

He wanted to consider that their conversation had held some hope, but all it showed him was that Finn was a liability. He needed to listen to his gut, but he would worry about it after his wedding.

He deserved at least one bit of happiness before the war had begun.

FORTY

LUNA

"IT'S ALMOST TIME," Finn announced, walking into Luna's bedroom that was now the official bridal suite. She looked at him through the mirror, noticing how much older he looked when he dressed up in a tux and tamed his crazy hair.

Once upon a time, Finn would have hated her being at the Vitali mansion. Now, he was prepared to walk her down the aisle to the Vitali heir himself.

Luna nodded, allowing Blair to fix one of her curls. On short notice, Luna was able to get the perfect dress. A satin A-line dress with small straps that sat on her shoulders. The back was cut out with a white bow attached to her lower back. The dress cinched at her waist before it flowed out and down her body.

With the dress on, hair and makeup done, the girls helped her slide the satin gloves up her arms, finishing the traditionally elegant bridal look.

She had never been the type of person to plan her wedding in extensive detail, mostly because she'd always dreaded the day it would come. Today, however, that dread wasn't present, and because of that, she now wished that she had more time to plan it the way she wanted. But the number one thing she asked of the girls was to make her feel beautiful. And she did.

"She's ready," Cecilia said. She straightened out the silky dusty rose dress that all of the girls wore. Hers was fitted at the chest, the straps hanging off her shoulders. Blair's was in a halter top style, pinned at the back of her neck. Gianna's was strapless, a large slit down her right leg.

"You guys can go have a seat," Luna told them. "I think I can manage to get myself down there."

Gianna pressed a kiss to her head. "We'll see you out there."

Luna let out a deep breath once it was just her and Finn in the room. A new emotion came over her. She used to imagine a world where her father changed his ways and decided to let her marry whoever she wanted rather than forcing her. Her mother would help her plan the wedding and shop for the wedding dress, while her father, despite his flaws, walked her down the aisle. She could forgive them both because they were capable of change and proved they loved Luna.

Again, it was just a dream.

It was tragic how she'd managed to gain someone she loved deeply but lose someone simultaneously. Her father had done the damage though. He sent someone to kill her. He wanted her dead. If she didn't fight back, that exact thing would happen. Those were the things she had to tell herself every time her dreams pushed on her naivety, forcing her into the same startling reality check repeatedly.

On the bright side, she had her brother there. The one blood relative she had left.

"Thanks for walking me down the aisle," Luna said, turning to face him. "I know you'll never like Valerio, but it means the world to me that you're here."

Finn shrugged. "You're my sister."

"You're not obligated to stay and help me just because we're siblings."

"You're not the only one who lost their family. I don't think any of us are allowed back home. Definitely not once Father finds I've betrayed him."

"You could still go home," Luna said. "I'll tell you what I told Valerio: I'm not going to force you to have any part of this. I'm definitely not asking you to pull the trigger. If you want to keep your innocence, you can go home, but I'm letting you know that I'm still going through with it."

Finn looked at her, confused. "Why are you doing it?"

"Because I want my justice." She shook her head. "No, I deserve my justice. Because of him, my life could have been so much worse than it is right now. I got lucky. Somehow, someway, I did. I could have been dead, I could have been in the worst marriage of my life, I could have been trapped in a cage. There are so many ways my life could have played out because of him. He deserves worse, but this is all I can give him. You don't have to understand or agree, but that is my truth."

"And yet you're still willing to let me go?" Finn asked, almost in disbelief. "What if I ran back to him and told him everything? Would you still be so kind to me?"

"I'm not him, Finn. I never want to be him," Luna said. "Forcing you to do what I say is what he would have done. I won't take that choice away from you, away from anyone." She forced a small smile onto her face. "I just ask that you still walk me down the aisle."

He stared at her for a long moment, completely silent. She couldn't tell what he was thinking based on the stoic look on his face. That was her brother. Always good at hiding what he felt. Finn approached her, allowing her arm to grab onto his.

"I'm not going anywhere," he decided.

She felt the unease leave her body. "Thank you," she whispered.

They walked out of the room, their footsteps being heard in the hallway.

"I know you said you wouldn't work with us after all of this is over," Luna said.

"Of course, that prick told you about our conversation," he said, rolling his eyes.

"He tells me everything. But I just want you to know that you're smart, Finn. You could do some good in the world, some good for yourself, for the Kingsley name. Don't let your stubbornness get in the way of that," she said.

Finn snorted. "Fucking doubtful."

Luna shook her head, freezing when they approached the doors to enter the living room. She could hear the light lull of music, an orchestral rendition of one of her favorite songs. She took a deep breath, squeezing Finn's arm.

"You'll be fine," he said. "Just don't fall."

"Shut up," she muttered.

With that, they walked through the doorway. Luna swore her heart stopped when she saw Valerio standing under the floral arch, adorned in a black tux and his hair gelled back.

Her chest rose and fell rhythmically, matching every step she took down the aisle. Everyone had already stood up to watch her entrance, but her gaze stayed on him like a moth to a flame.

When they reached the end of the altar, Finn handed her off, pressing a small kiss to her forehead. He acknowledged Valerio with an awkward nod that was returned, before he took his seat beside Gianna. Everyone else took the cue to be seated as well, all except for Dante, who walked to the altar. Ironically, he was the only person who was officiated to marry people. He got it on a dare once upon a time, but it worked out in a moment like this.

"You look perfect," Valerio whispered. He grabbed her hands, running his thumbs along the tops of them.

"Thank you." Her blush was ever present.

"Dearly beloved, we are gathered today to celebrate the coming together of two of the best people I have ever met in my life," Dante began, his voice confident and compassionate. "Luna and Valerio came together unconventionally, some might say tragically, and still managed to find respect, love, and mutual pining for each other. It's because of them we are all here today, and it's because of them we find ourselves believing in love."

She hadn't listened to Dante's speech beforehand, just prayed it was appropriate. Hearing it now, she was thankful she had used waterproof makeup.

"I'll let you guys get on with your vows," Dante said.

Valerio cleared his throat, giving Luna a small smile. He was nervous. "All it takes is one person who sees you for who you are, for who you want to be, to change your mind on love. You've always been compared to the moon, but to me, you've always felt like the sun. A body of light that warms up the people around you. And even though for most of my life I was lost in a labyrinth of darkness, you came and shined a pathway leading me out. I have done so much wrong in my life, but by far the greatest thing I have ever done in my life is love you. Everything I am, everything I want to be, is for you. I vow to protect you, to honor you, and cherish you every moment for the rest of my life. In this lifetime, and the next, you will forever be mine, and I yours. I love you, Luna."

Nothing could have prepared her for the speech. His admittance of love was pure and kind, everything he believed himself not to be. She was breathless, speechless. The tears fell from her eyes, but Valerio reached up to wipe them before she could. She squeezed the hand that still held hers, silently thanking him for every word he said. It was the truth, the absolute truth, and she knew it.

"Luna, it's your turn," Dante told her.

She nodded, taking a deep breath. "The first real decision I had made for myself was accepting that I loved you. It didn't come without a fight, but when I think about everything in my life leading up to this, I would do it all over again if it meant I would come right back to you. In the middle of the night when your warmth finds me while you're deep asleep, when you're having a conversation and you press a kiss to my forehead without realizing, when you start making me food without even asking if I'm hungry, when you ease the chaos from my mind the moment you're close—it was the best decision I had ever made in my life. Now, on my darkest days, on the days when I hate myself the most, I find myself running to you. I don't know how long we have together, but I promise to love you for the rest of this life-time, and the one after it. I love you, Valerio."

A single tear slipped from his eye. Quick and almost invisible, but she caught it. He didn't turn away to hide it; he let her see it. He felt her hurt and he felt her love, and he embraced it fully.

They took their time saying "I do" and sliding the rings on each other. All that was left was for Dante to officially pronounce them husband and wife. The words had barely left his mouth when Valerio wrapped his arms around Luna's waist, crushing her to him. It was a heated kiss, one that devoured her and left her wanting more. Time ceased to exist for a moment, leaving them in pure, unimaginable bliss. For once, their reality was as good as their dreams.

When they finally pulled away, there were claps and cheers from the small crowd, reminding them that they weren't alone.

Luna gave him a big smile and one more kiss. He held onto her waist.

They all made their way into the kitchen turned reception room, immediately popping open a bottle of champagne. Luna hugged her best friends, reveling in their congratulations. Someone turned on the music, playing the specific playlist she had curated just for her wedding day. They uncovered the food, filled their plates, laughed, drank, danced, and sang to forget everything wrong with the world for a moment.

Luna looked around the room, taking time to acknowledge everyone who was there for her. When her eyes fell on her husband, the love of her life, she knew then that she would do whatever necessary to protect every single one of them.

Even if it killed her.

FORTY-ONE
LUNA

VALERIO TALKED to Allister and Dante in a hushed voice, nodding and keeping a stern look on his face. They partied for the past couple of hours, which meant that almost everyone was incredibly drunk except for Luna, Valerio, and Allister. Well, Luna might have had a couple of drinks, but Valerio kept it minimal saying that he needed his sobriety for the drive later in the night. Allister was on security duty, so he didn't have more than a beer earlier.

Luna approached the boys, grabbing Valerio's arm. "What are you guys talking about?"

"Safety," he said. "They'll be keeping an eye on us and the car until we get to where we're going."

"Allister will be doing most of the work." Dante grinned, his eyes shining with inebriation.

"Let's consider it your wedding present," Allister said.

"Well, thanks for doing it," Luna told him.

"He has no choice." Valerio gave him a warning look, earning him an eye roll from Allister. He turned to her. "We should head out before it gets too late."

"Wait, should I change out of my wedding dress?" she asked.

It was starting to get a little too heavy to keep dragging everywhere.

"No," Valerio said without hesitation. "I want to take it off of you."

"Gross. Keep your fantasies to yourself," Allister muttered, trying to hold up a drunk Dante who slumped on him.

Luna laughed. "Let's go," she said. "Please keep an eye out on the girls. They're incredibly drunk and I don't want them to make any decisions they'll regret."

"Promise," Allister said. He waved them off, letting Dante fall to the floor.

Valerio grabbed her hand and their bag—a small overnight duffle with a few things. They made their way to the garage, walking to the black SUV. He helped her in, trying to keep the dress from getting dirty or destroyed. Then he walked over to the counter by the entrance of the garage where a couple bottles of oil and windshield wiper fluid sat, and picked up the four guns that were sitting there. He made sure they were all loaded, placing the smallest in his suit jacket and carrying the other three to place in the back seat.

She tried to ignore it so it wouldn't put a damper on the perfect day, but that was their life now. It was better that they were safe.

He got into the driver's seat, letting the car purr to life. She said a little prayer as soon as they received confirmation from Allister that they could head out. He kept the headlights off until they got to the main road where it was easier to blend in with everyone else driving.

He drove quickly, constantly checking the mirrors to make sure no one was following them. She held her breath the entire time, her shoulders tensed, and her eyes peeled for anything suspicious even though she didn't know what she would be looking for. Only once they entered the remote road to the familiar woods did the anxiety start to wear off.

"We're going to the cabin?" she asked, a small smile on her face.

He nodded. "I would have taken you somewhere nicer, but I figured just getting out of that house was enough for now."

"It's perfect."

He grabbed her hand, placing a kiss to the back of it. He parked the car right beside the cabin, texting Allister that they had arrived. Like a gentleman, he helped her out of the car, only to sweep her off her feet and into his arms.

"What are you doing?" she asked, laughing.

"Carrying my wife over the threshold."

"You're supposed to do that in our new home." She opened the door for them. "Besides, you need to take it easy. You just started recovering."

"My back is fine," he promised, giving her a quick kiss to presumably shut her up. "You know I can't resist any reason to hold you." He placed her on the couch before running off to grab their bag and the other guns.

Luna fell back with a small smile of contentment. The cabin was exactly how they had left it from the last time they were there, almost as if it was frozen in time from when things seemed simpler. Now, it was her favorite place in the world, and a place they would return to once the war was over. Simpler times would come that was what she had to remind herself.

Valerio dropped the stuff on the small table, locking the door behind him. He peeled the tux jacket off and ripped the bow tie from his neck, moving with precision to the fireplace.

Her eyes followed his every movement in a daze. Even though his body took up most of the space in whatever room he was in, he still moved with such an elegance that she couldn't understand. He was never clumsy; everything was always done with certainty. She was fascinated by it.

He kneeled down, placing logs of wood into the fireplace and igniting a single match to get it going. With a sigh, he stood back up, stretching his back out as he turned around to face Luna once again.

"It'll warm up soon," he said.

She could hardly register the coldness in the cabin from the overwhelmingly hot temperature of her body.

"Come sit with me." She patted the spot next to her on the couch.

He shook his head with a smirk but still complied. She turned her back to him, exposing the zipper of the dress. "Mind getting that for me?" she asked innocently. "It's a bit uncomfortable."

"Anything for you, Mrs. Vitali," he told her. He traced along her spine, finding the zipper with ease.

He pulled the zipper down slowly, cherishing the moment before moving onto her shoulders next to push the straps off. His lips had just barely grazed her neck when she suddenly stood up. She let her dress fall into a pile on the floor. All she stood in was a lacy white bra and underwear set with a garter strapped to her upper thigh.

"That's more comfortable," she said, stepping out of the dress. The way his eyes watched her sent goosebumps along her body. He hadn't even touched her yet, and she was already soaking between her thighs.

He reached out, setting her on his lap. Immediately, his fingers traced the garter. "What is this?" he asked.

"I think you're supposed to remove it," Luna said. "With your mouth."

"Is that what tradition says?" Valerio asked, raising an eyebrow in question.

Luna nodded. "I don't make the rules."

"Then I guess I don't have a choice." He shrugged, setting her on the couch beside him. Without a moment of hesitation, he dropped to his knees in front of her, using his hands to part her legs open. He kissed up her thigh, biting on the skin softly before he finally landed on the garter.

Her breath hitched. He was so close to her aching pussy.

But he didn't move any higher. He placed an openmouthed kiss on the garter and then pulled it with his teeth all the way down her leg. The heels she wore all night were still strapped to her feet, so with careful movements he slipped them off, laying small kisses to her ankles. She settled her feet on his shoulders, letting him pull the lacy white thong down her legs. The way he removed each leftover piece of clothing slowly was driving her mad.

His patience was both incredibly hot and incredibly annoying. She needed him to touch her, taste her, fuck her, but he moved like he had all the time in the world.

"Stop teasing," she begged.

He stopped all movements. "I thought you were my patient, good girl."

She nodded her head. "I am. Please."

He shook his head. "Your begging is so sexy, but I think you might be greedy."

"Please, Val."

He grinned, throwing her underwear to the side. "I don't reward bad girls." He draped her legs over his shoulders, pulling her to the edge of the couch. His mouth met her slick cunt, giving her one single lick. Luna moaned, thrusting her hips for more. "I punish them," he said. His eyes held a wicked gleam in them, one that nearly had her panting.

With that he began devouring her, licking and sucking on her clit, forcing her closer and closer to her climax. Luna bucked wildly, feeling herself at the edge when he stopped completely. She cried out, trying to push his head back in, but he refused.

"Bad girl," he muttered, slapping her pussy.

"Please stop teasing me," Luna begged. "Please, I'm your wife. I love you."

"Say it again," Valerio said.

"I love you," she cried out, delirious from needing to come.

"Whose pussy is this?" he asked, grabbing her cunt with his hand.

"Yours," she said.

"Who do you belong to?" He waited for the answer, his eyes darkening when it finally came.

"You."

"Forever now," he muttered, diving back in between her legs. He slipped two fingers inside her, continuing his torture with his tongue while he thrusted his fingers in and out.

Luna could feel it coming, harder than it had in so long. She gripped his hair, holding him in place while she came. Her eyes closed while she spit out moans. Her chest moved rapidly, leaving her crashing.

She didn't get a second to recover before Valerio pounced on her. She tasted herself on him, desperately trying to keep up with the maddening kiss he gave her. The possession, the obsession—it was all there, willing to destroy her.

He carried her into the bedroom. Quickly, she undid her bra, throwing it somewhere in the room before he could rip it apart. She actually wanted to cherish this lingerie. He took the chance to bite and pull on her nipples, mixing pleasure with pain in an intoxicating concoction. Every touch lit up her body all over again.

Valerio threw her on the bed, ripping his shirt off. The buttons went flying, scattering around the room. He pulled his belt off in a haste, stripping himself of the rest of his clothes until he stood before her in his naked glory.

She would never get tired of seeing his healthy, toned body. And she especially wouldn't get tired of the stiff cock between his legs.

Valerio spit on his hand, moving it slowly up and down his cock. Luna watched in awe at the way his abdomen flexed, the way he looked at her to make sure she was watching him.

"I want a taste," she said, sitting up on her knees. He approached the bed, leaning one knee on the edge.

"Take what's yours, baby," he said, grabbing hold of her hair when she leaned over. Her tongue found him first, trailing along the shaft before circling the tip. She opened her mouth, swallowing him before pulling him out again.

He cursed as he guided her head up and down his cock. "Such a good girl," he moaned, throwing his head back. "My perfect girl."

Luna's body sang at the praise as she moved her head frantically. He pulled out before she could take his cum down her throat.

"On your back," he said, letting go of her hair.

She did as he said, savoring when he fell on top of her, his lips on hers all over again. His tongue fought with hers, tasting her mouth the same way she did to him. She could stay there like that for the rest of her life—kissing him into oblivion.

Instead, his hand reached down, finally guiding his cock inside her.

She gasped, the full feeling overstimulating every nerve ending. He stopped for a second, allowing her to take it in, so she could savor her husband. As soon as her nails trailed down his back, he began thrusting, letting her ride his cock.

Sweat built up on their skin, their moans getting louder as Valerio's hips moved quicker. He lifted her legs over his shoulders, fucking her and rubbing circles on her clit with his thumb at the same time.

Luna's legs shook as she came again, her body completely falling apart. He came shortly after, a groan leaving his lips as his eyes locked on hers. He fell on top of her, letting his dick soak in her pussy as he stared at her with an emotion she finally understood: Love.

She couldn't stop herself from kissing him again, as if they hadn't been doing it all night, as if she wouldn't be doing it for the rest of her life. She flipped them over so he was on his back this time, never disconnecting their bodies.

"Already?" he asked, his cock becoming hard with the movement of her hips.

"Can't handle it?" she asked mockingly.

That seemed to do the trick for him, and once again they got lost in each other.

Again and again and again.

FORTY-TWO
LUNA

LUNA STIRRED AWAKE, sore and exhausted. Her body still hummed from last night.

Valerio's arm held her down to the bed, pulling her impossibly close to his own. He looked so peaceful and serene with his little snores. It made him look so much younger than he was. She was honestly just glad that he was able to get some sleep, and from what she could tell, it was some good sleep.

She traced her finger along his cheekbones, his slightly crooked nose, over the long eyelashes that coated the most beautiful eyes in the world. His beauty had always called to her even when she had a crush on him all those years ago. It was a dangerous beauty, one that promised to sweep her off her feet. Obviously, it worked.

A small smile graced his lips. "Keep going. It feels good."

"I didn't mean to wake you up."

"I don't mind," he said. "How do you feel?"

"Sore," she said. "How do you feel?"

"Like someone scratched the shit out of my back." The grin on his face only seemed to grow.

Luna rolled her eyes, fighting her own. All she did these days was smile with him. "It was deserved."

"Hey, I'm not complaining. Mark me up, baby."

Luna shook her head, sitting up. "We should head out before it gets too late in the day."

Valerio groaned, sitting up as well. "Yeah, I know. I wish we could just stay here, not face anything back at home."

Luna was silent. Going home meant they had to face reality. Going home meant they had to begin their plans, whatever that was going to look like.

Luna grabbed his hand, squeezing it. "I love you," she told him.

"I love you too, always."

They changed into some comfortable clothes they had packed, not bothering with breakfast and not wanting to wait another moment longer.

When they finally took off, the sky was dark and gray—mean looking. The temperature had fallen to freezing, seeping into Luna's soul. She held onto Valerio the entire time, selfishly trying to steal his warmth from him.

They pulled into the garage of the house in no time, sitting there for some time before they decided to finally get out of the car. "We have to clean up the house," Luna said.

"It'll be okay for a couple of days."

"Maybe we can put everything into a box to save it," she suggested. "And get the pictures printed so we can hang them up."

"Anything you want to do," he said. Valerio cupped her cheek, bringing her closer. "We'll be okay."

She knew he could see right through her. She wanted to appear strong and brave, having been the one to command everyone and tell them they needed to get rid of their fathers. Now, when the moment was fast approaching, Luna felt weak. She desperately searched for any ounce of strength she could muster up, but it seemed useless.

There was a fear that she couldn't get rid of. One that kept reminding her of everything that could go wrong—of everything she had to lose.

Instead of voicing it, she gave him a kiss, memorizing the feel of it into her mind. If he promised they would be okay, then she had to believe that they would be. With that, she opened the car door and got out. Luna carried in the dress while Valerio carried their bag. "I'll make us some breakfast," he said.

She nodded. "I'm going to put my dress upstairs."

Luna climbed up the stairs, taking in the silence of the house. It seemed like everyone was still sleeping, most likely hungover and oblivious to the ominous feeling that surrounded the air now.

She opened the door to the closet and grabbed the same hook that had held her dress yesterday. She would have to send the dress to get dry cleaned, but that could probably wait as could all the things she actually wanted to do. Her list of to-do items grew longer and longer, but she desperately tried not to overwhelm herself.

Her phone rang, pulling her out of her thoughts. Luna took it out of her pocket but didn't recognize the number. She answered, wondering if it was any of the companies from yesterday contacting her about something.

"Hello?" Luna asked, answering the call.

"Luna?" the soft feminine voice asked, unsure if she had the right number.

It was her mother.

"Mom?" Luna asked. "Why are you calling me off a different number?"

"I didn't know if you had me blocked or something. I've been trying to call you," Eleanora said. Her voice was unusually kind. Similar to the voice she'd used when she would comfort Luna as a child. It was rare, but it did happen.

"I've been busy," she said, lying.

"Oh. Well, how have you been feeling?"

Luna closed her eyes, suddenly feeling immensely guilty for carrying out the lie. "I haven't been good."

"Why is that? Have you seen a doctor?" Eleanora asked, her voice sounding like she was actually worried. Luna couldn't remember a time her mother cared this much about anything.

"No, I haven't needed to," Luna told her. "There's no baby."

She chose to rip off the Band-Aid and tell the truth. Maybe it was risky to tell the truth, but lies would only do so much. Even if her mother decided to run back to Luna's father and tell him everything, they would handle it. At least she wouldn't be carrying the sick lie with her anymore.

It was silent on the other line, so much so that Luna thought her mother hung up until she heard a deep breath. "Did your father cause this? With what he said at the engagement party?"

Tears filled her eyes. She sat on the floor, bracing her back against the cabinets. "As long as he is around to hurt me or Valerio, there will be no baby. Did you know about what he did to me? How he hired someone to hurt me?"

"I knew he hired someone. I didn't know it was to harm you. I would never want you harmed."

Luna's heart broke. She swallowed down the sob, unwilling to let her mother hear her breakdown. "I almost died. How could you let him do that to me? How could you be willing to let him sell me off to a horrible man? How could you try to push me to leave Valerio knowing the alternative? You're my mother; you should be protecting me. I would never let anything like that happen to my daughter, ever." Her voice was full of venom, full of the hurt she had been feeling since she was a child herself when her mother chose to leave her with random staff and nannies rather than support her children.

"I know I failed you. I know that. But I did what I had to do to survive," Eleanora cried out, the biggest reaction Luna had ever heard from her.

She laughed sinisterly. "And where did that get you?"

"I never had a choice in anything either, Luna. I was younger than you, but I was completely alone. I had to adapt and learn everything on my own. If he knew that I loved my own children, he would have used you against me. Don't you understand that? Everything is a game to him. I was playing it just like you were." Luna heard the sob on the other end. "Please don't blame me. Please, how can I fix it? Tell me, what can I do?"

She looked down at the rings on her finger: her engagement ring and her wedding band.

She took a sharp breath. "There's nothing to be done. As long as he is alive and you continue standing by his side, you will never see me. Goodbye."

Luna hung up without another word, finally allowing the tears to escape her eyes and the sobs to find their way out of her chest. She cried for the little girl who always needed her mother, and now for the twenty-three-year-old who wanted her mother, but would never have her.

When arms wrapped around her, she knew it was Valerio. He didn't say a word. He just held her as if he could make up for the loss she had felt throughout her life.

"She's been hurt herself," Valerio said. "That doesn't excuse what she has done, but it means she knows what it feels like to hurt, to feel hopeless."

"She'll never change," she said, leaning on his chest for support. "None of them will."

"Maybe she will," he said. He ran his fingers through her hair, soothing her. "People have a way of surprising us."

Only time would tell.

FORTY-THREE
LUNA

"OUR FATHER WILL BE BACK from his trip to Italy tomorrow," Dante said. "It'll be a good chance to surround him. He won't see it coming."

Valerio shook his head, leaning on the table. "He'll still see us coming. He has security everywhere. Probably even more so now."

"Does he think you're alive or dead? I mean, have you heard anything from him?" Finn asked.

Luna listened in, her head already pounding from the hours of planning they had been doing. They enjoyed one night off just to be thrown into the thick of it.

"Not a single word," Valerio confirmed.

"Same here," Dante said.

"We have to assume he thinks I'm dead, or at the very least severely injured," he said.

"Then he wouldn't expect to see you, but he would expect to see Dante," Allister said, tapping a pen against his lip.

"If Allister and I go in first, maybe we could disarm the system," Dante said. "And then you could sneak in or something."

"How high tech is the system?" Blair asked. She had her arms crossed, a serious look on her face. The fact the girls wanted any part of the planning meant a lot to Luna. It wasn't an easy subject and she wouldn't have blamed them if they decided to ditch it for their own peace of mind. "Maybe Augustus could disarm it himself?"

He snorted. "Uh, yeah, if I had a million hours to work on it."

"You've hacked through sketchier shit before," Finn said.

Augustus pushed him. "And I'm not trying to go to prison for it, so shut the fuck up."

"I could help you get through most of it, since I'm the most familiar with it," Valerio told him. "At least until I have to leave."

"That should work," he said. "As long as the system is out before you enter the house, you should be fine. If not, we'll be planning our funerals."

Luna swallowed harshly, ignoring the rush of anxiety that swept through her with those words.

"What do you do about the fallout?" Gianna asked. "He has guards all over the house. If they hear a gunshot, they'll come after you. If there's only three of you and like dozens of them, it's not hard to assume who would win."

"You have to take out whoever you see," Finn said. "Unless they decide to side with you, but you can't ensure their loyalty either way."

Luna shook her head immediately. "Those are innocent people. They don't deserve to die."

"No one is innocent in our world," Finn said. "They all knew what they were getting into."

"I won't kill anyone who pledges their loyalty to me," Valerio said, giving her a look of confirmation. "I'll try to keep the death count to a minimum."

"We'll prepare everything tonight then," Allister said. "Now, we have to decide what the Kingsleys are going to do."

"I'm meeting my father tomorrow to talk," Finn said, sitting up now. "I'll do it then."

Luna looked confused. "That's all? That doesn't seem

thought out in the slightest. Won't he be suspicious that you brought me?"

Finn and Valerio shared a look, but it was the latter who spoke up. "You won't be there. I won't risk your safety."

She shook her head immediately. "I'm not letting Finn go in there alone."

"He can have Augustus," Cecilia said. "Send him in after he figures out the stuff with the security system."

"Sorry to burst your cold little heart, but there's no way I can do both," Augustus said. He blew Cecilia a kiss after she rolled her eyes.

"Perfect, then I'll go in," Luna said.

Valerio shook his head. "No."

"We are plotting to kill my father. You can't ask me to not be there," she said. She was growing increasingly frustrated. Valerio couldn't possibly believe that she was actually going to be sitting this out.

"Do you think you could actually handle seeing your father take his last breath or watch him bleed out?" Valerio asked. "That will destroy your life; you will never be the same."

"It won't destroy my life any more than he tried to," she bit back. Luna turned to Finn. "What do you think about this?"

"I'm not getting involved," he said, raising his hands in surrender. "I just don't want any distractions."

"I can't be sure you'll actually do it," Luna said. "How do I know you won't change your mind while you're there? Just the other day you were convincing us not to do this."

"I guess you'll just have to trust me," Finn said.

She did trust him. Not with this though. Not when he could be swayed by their father.

"She'll stay here then," Gianna said, interrupting Luna. "We'll make sure she doesn't leave."

She gave Gianna a look of disbelief. "What the hell are you talking about?"

"I'm trusting you, Gianna," Valerio said, ignoring Luna.

"Plan whatever you want then," she hissed, letting her chair screech across the floor as she got up. "You don't need me here for any of it anymore."

Maybe it was immature leaving the room during such an important moment the way she did, but the frustration was too much. She was already on edge as it was. If one little thing went wrong, anything, then any of them could lose their lives.

She couldn't live with herself if something really happened to any of them.

She almost made it back to the bedroom, when Gianna came running up behind her, trying to get her to stop. Luna ignored her. "I don't want to talk to you right now."

"Well, you should, dummy. I only said that so they would leave it alone," Gianna told her, yanking her shoulder so Luna could turn around. It worked. The blonde was stronger than she looked.

"What are you talking about?" she asked, crossing her arms.

"Valerio would never agree to let you go, especially if he thinks Finn is dodgy. But if he thinks you're here protected tomorrow, then he won't have to worry about you. It gives you the chance to sneak out with Finn," Gianna said.

"Why would you want me to go?" Luna asked, testing the waters. It felt almost too good to be true that she would willingly want her to go off into danger.

"Because you deserve to get your justice." She grabbed Luna's shoulders, looking her dead in the eyes. "Get your revenge for everything he did to you. For wanting you dead, for trying to sell you off. Do it for all the girls that never had the same chance."

Luna felt like someone had kicked her in the chest. It made sense. She wasn't doing this just for herself and everything she had ever been through in her life. She was doing it for every girl in their world that lived the way she had. Who were sheltered, forced to miss out on moments of their life for the sake of keeping their purity. Who contemplated ending everything to avoid the very fate that put them in the hands of abusers and predators.

Luna nodded her head. "Okay."

Gianna nodded, pulling her along with her to her bedroom so they could discuss just how far Luna was willing to go.

Even if Finn didn't do it, she would be there, landing the final blow.

FORTY-FOUR

LUNA

IT WAS A QUIET NIGHT. After Blair and Cecilia had filled Luna in on Finn's plan, they decided to take it easy. They all sat on the couch, oddly quiet. But what would come tomorrow hung over all of their shoulders.

Tomorrow she would kill someone. Tomorrow, they hoped change would come.

The thought made Luna feel nauseous. She decided that planning the actual event must have been worse than actually doing it. Knowing what was going to be done, reliving the scenario in her head over and over again, it was horrifying. It wasn't just thinking about killing her father, it was thinking about everything that could go wrong that left her feeling haunted.

Valerio kept a strong face, and she wanted to know whether it was an act or if it was genuine. It wasn't the first time he would kill someone, but this wasn't just someone.

"Let's go outside," Luna whispered to Valerio. "I want to see if the stars are out."

He nodded absently. It was like he was there, but he wasn't. He stood, allowing her to pull him with her.

They walked out the sliding door that led to the backyard.

The sky had already begun to drop small flecks of snow onto the ground, promising for more.

"It's cold out here," Valerio said, immediately taking his sweater off to hand to her. "I don't want you to get sick."

"I'll be fine for a little bit," she told him. He still helped her get it over her head. It was covered in his warmth, making the cold of the night seem impenetrable.

Valerio stared back out in the horizon, getting lost in his thoughts all over again.

"Are you okay?" Luna asked.

He nodded. "I haven't done anything yet. There's no reason not to be."

"You have every reason to not feel okay if that's how you feel," Luna said. She placed her hand on his back. "I'm terrified for tomorrow. I'm terrified for you. Of you getting hurt, but mostly of you afterwards."

Valerio shook his head. "Don't be. I've killed people before. We have a solid plan. It'll all go how it should."

"I know you're not used to people caring about you and your wellbeing, but I do. I can see you're not okay, and that's okay. You will be eventually." Luna wrapped her arms around herself. "You don't have to be strong around me." She whispered the second part, looking out into the distance herself.

Valerio wrapped an arm around her, pulling her close. His lips were close to her ear, almost as if he wanted to be sure only she could hear him. "I am terrified for tomorrow. I am terrified of killing my father, of doing what I have dreamed about doing my entire life. I am terrified I won't be able to do it, that I'll fail you, that I'll fail my own mother."

"Your mother would never be disappointed in you," Luna said. Her eyes were wide, swallowing the admission.

"I know that. It's not my mother I'm truly worried about," he said, looking down at Luna. "I'm terrified you'll look at me differently. If I choke and I put you at risk, I will never forgive myself."

"You could never disappoint me." She held her hand to his cheek. "I would never blame you for anything."

He was always so confident, so sure of himself that Luna wouldn't have ever known he was this terrified. But she saw who he was at that moment. A young boy trying to avenge his mother's death and make a difference in his life.

And he would. Luna knew he would.

"I need to believe you," he said in a voice so quiet, she almost didn't hear him herself. "I need to believe in myself. You're right about me never having someone who cared about me like this, and that's why the thought of disappointing you terrifies me. If I don't have you, I have no one. That's why I need to ask you not to go tomorrow. I can't be there to protect you and I don't know if Finn will change his mind. I can't have anything happen to you."

"You will never lose me, I swear," she promised. Guilt tore through her knowing that come tomorrow, she would break his heart going with Finn, putting herself in danger to make sure her father never took another breath again. Instead of saying anything else, she pressed herself deeper into him.

He pressed a kiss to her forehead, standing with her in his arms a little longer. The snow continued falling and she imagined someone looking at them through a snow globe. The scene looked perfect, a beautiful young couple in love, holding each other in the cold.

No one would know of the horrors that haunted them.

But come morning, those demons would be expelled, freeing them from that very confinement.

FORTY-FIVE
LUNA

LUNA HADN'T SLEPT a wink all night. Her mind and body wouldn't let her, constantly waking her with nightmares instead. It was horrible, but even worse was the realization the sun was up.

Valerio got dressed in thick black cargo pants. On top, he wore a black long-sleeve shirt, and then a black quarter zip on top to keep out the cold. He was dressed like he was a spy going on some top-secret mission.

Luna wore something similar. A black sweatshirt and black leggings. Wearing any other color felt wrong. They walked downstairs together, running into Dante who was already sitting at the table with a coffee in his hands.

"Good morning," he said.

"How long have you been awake?" Valerio asked, grabbing two mugs.

"I haven't slept," Dante said.

"Neither have I," Luna admitted, taking a seat at the table.

"I would have been surprised if you did," he said, taking a sip of his coffee. Valerio came back, handing her a mug.

"We'll leave soon," Valerio said, taking a seat. "The sooner it's finished, the better."

They sat in silence after that, watching as one by one everyone came downstairs. First, Allister, followed by Blair and Cecilia. Finn and Augustus walked down together, leaving Gianna as the last one to wake up.

Valerio and Augustus set up some monitors and different computer systems that Luna knew nothing about. Once that was done, everyone got to work.

Dante and Finn checked the guns, making sure each was fully loaded and ready to go. Allister got out the other equipment, setting it out for all of them. Cecilia packed a first aid kit for each of them, Blair and Gianna helping her set up a station so that if anyone came home with cuts or worse, she could work on it right away.

Valerio and Augustus typed furiously on their computers, speaking to each other in some code that Luna found strangely attractive.

An hour had passed before they finally announced that they were ready to head out.

The mood in the house changed after that.

The nerves were still ever present, but now, the determination set in. Valerio grabbed one of the bulletproof vests Allister had set out, strapping himself in. It was hard not to watch him, memorize everything about him. She tried to tell herself to stop, that he would come home and everything would be alright, but her mind worked against her, savoring the moment nonetheless.

He grabbed two guns, putting them in his holster and holding the assault rifle over his shoulder. "You look terrifying," Luna told him.

"I don't prefer to wear things like this every day," he said, cracking a small smile.

Luna couldn't return it. "After today, I hope you never have to."

"I'll be okay," he said. "Everything will go according to plan."

She nodded, begging herself to keep her composure. But as she stared into his blue eyes, the same ones she had fallen so deeply in love with and the same ones she now called her husband, she couldn't help the tear that slipped out her eye and down her cheek. "Please just come back to me."

Valerio set down the rifle, pulling her into his arms. She held on to him as tightly as she could, unwilling to let him go. She wanted to just say fuck it to the plans, to keep him at home where she knew he would be safe. But this was bigger than her, it was bigger than him.

"I will always come back to you," Valerio said.

"I love you," Luna said. "I love you so, so much."

"I love you too, my little moon," he whispered. "I love you more than you'll ever know."

He pulled back for a second, only to kiss her. It was perfect, like all kisses they ever shared. This one held nothing but love and hope. They were desperate to make it last as long as possible, but it was the lack of air that forced them apart. Her heart had never felt as empty as it did when he pulled away.

"I will see you after," he told her with one more kiss. "I swear."

Luna wiped a single tear that slipped from her eye. She stepped away from him completely, wrapping her arms around herself to stop her from reaching out and pulling him back to her. He stared at her for a long moment, flexing his hands as if he wanted to do the same to her.

Then he grabbed the rifle and walked outside with Allister.

Luna turned to Dante, who stood there watching them. "Good luck, Dante," she said, grabbing his hand. "And when all of this is over, I hope you can find your own happiness."

"Despite how much of a dick I was to you before, I couldn't imagine life without you in it," Dante said, squeezing her hand. He gave a small smile that didn't reach his eyes. "I'll make sure nothing happens to him."

She could only nod, the emotion thick in her throat. He walked out as well to join the other two.

It was just her, the girls, Finn, and Augustus who remained now. "When are you going?" Luna asked Finn.

"Any minute now," he said, fastening himself into the bulletproof vest.

"Be careful," Luna said.

"I kind of figured." He snorted.

She grabbed his arm. "I'm being serious. Be careful, Finn, more careful than you've ever been in your life. You need to come back."

The seriousness settled onto his face after that. "I'll come back." He pulled Luna into a hug. It had to have been the first one he had given her since they were children, making the moment all that much more bittersweet.

When they finally pulled away, Luna let the words she had been waiting to say all morning leave her lips. "Let me come with you."

"Valerio doesn't want you there," Finn said, pulling back completely.

"I know he doesn't. But I need to be there. Please. You can't go in there alone."

He was silent, his jaw clenched. "Fine, but if he asks, you jumped into the fucking car when I wasn't looking."

Luna nodded quickly, not expecting him to have agreed. Her Plan B was to do exactly that, but now she wouldn't have to.

She put a bulletproof vest on, one that was entirely too big but would do the job. She was in a rush, but still stopped to share a group hug with the girls beforehand.

"You're stronger than you know," Gianna said, pressing a kiss to her forehead. "You're my hero, Luna."

"Stay with Finn. If anything happens though, run like hell," Blair said, fixing Luna's hair. Luna could only nod, attempting to seem confident.

"Please come back to us," Cecilia said. "You need to, okay? I can't live without you."

"I can't live without any of you," Luna said. "I promise I'll come home."

With one more hug, they were pulling away. She and Finn got into the car, driving to their parents' home. The place they grew up, the place they left, not realizing they would never return, and the place where they would take their father's life.

FORTY-SIX

LUNA

THE CAR RIDE WAS SILENT. There wasn't a single conversation that would have been appropriate for the moment they were in. Silence was the best option for the overbearing tension.

Overnight, the sky had dumped almost a foot of snow on the streets, leaving it difficult to drive. Most of the snow was untouched, pure and white. Come later in the day, it would be black and gray from the dirt of cars as they drove by. Cold, dry air accompanied the snow, leaving the dreary sky to feel like an omen of sorts.

She took in long, deep breaths, trying to keep herself grounded. By the time they were pulling into the driveway of their childhood home, her breathing was frantic once again.

Finn drove slowly, surveying the area around them. "Where the hell is everyone?"

Luna gave him a confused look, trying to figure out what he meant. That was when she realized it too. There was no security guard at the gate; in fact, the gate was wide open, allowing anyone to pass through. No guards walked around outside patrolling the area. No one even stood by the front door, waiting to greet people.

Her father was always the type of man to be fully armed at all times, his paranoia forcing him to believe he was never safe. There was no way in hell that he would leave his home completely unattended if he was there too.

"Are you sure you were supposed to meet with him today?" Luna asked. Her unease was growing by the second.

"Yes. He wouldn't bail on me like this," Finn said, his brows furrowed.

He parked the car, getting out and leaving Luna to follow after him. She didn't have a gun of her own, so she trailed closely behind him. He kicked at the front door, smashing it open with brute strength. It was silent in the house.

Finn held up the gun, holding it in front of him in defense. Luna's eyes were wide, taking in every inch of the home. It looked like her house; everything was still where it was her entire life. The only difference was that the house felt void of life. It was never a comforting home that exuded warmth and happiness, and Luna frequently referred to it as her cage. This feeling, however, was unusually still for their house.

Finn walked into the living room, while Luna decided to take the other side where the dining room was. The nice china was laid out, four plates with the accompanying silverware sitting on a piece of white linen tablecloth. It was completely dark inside the dining room with the blinds pulled down, but a small patch of light from the gray skies outside seeped in from one of the windows where the blinds hung haphazardly. Luna looked to the side, noticing little droplets of some sort of liquid leading into the kitchen.

Luna followed the trail, her blood running cold at the bloody handprints stamped on the walls of the kitchen. Blood was smeared on the floors and on the cabinets. The metallic smell brought bile up her throat.

"Finn," Luna called out, fear in her voice.

He didn't answer back. Immediately, panic set in her, forcing her to run back toward the living room.

He stood there in silence.

Her mother sat on the couch with blood covering her hands and most of her nightdress. Her hands shook as she lifted her head to look at Luna.

On the floor lay her father's dead body. His eyes wide and lifeless, his white button-up completely soaked in the crimson liquid.

"What did you do?" Luna whispered, her eyes wide. "What happened?"

"I did what I had to do," Eleanora said, her voice shaky. "I did it for all of us."

"You killed him," Luna said, clutching her stomach. "He's dead."

"You needed him out of our lives, and now he is," her mother said, standing. "Now, I can see you."

Luna couldn't stop herself from turning around, throwing up everything in her stomach. The smell, God, the smell was worse than anything she had ever smelled in her life.

The image of him lying in his own blood, not a single breath escaping his lips anymore, was forcefully engraved in her brain. Her father was dead. Her mother killed him.

"You need to get out of here," Finn said, snapping out of his daze. "If anyone finds out what you did, they will kill you."

"You're in charge now," Eleanora said. "You make the rules."

He shook his head. "You need to leave now. Where is your passport?"

"They'll find me. It's no use," Eleanora said, walking closer to them.

Luna wiped her mouth, turning back around now. "You can't stay here. Not now at least."

"We'll send you somewhere, to one of the properties," Finn said, running a hand through his hair. "There must be a place he kept secret from his men."

"I don't want to go anywhere," Eleanora insisted.

"You don't have a choice. You killed the don," Finn screamed. "None of us get a choice in anything anymore."

"You were coming here to do it as well," she said. "I know you were. I just beat you to it."

"What changed?" Luna asked, shaking her head.

"I won't go my entire life without seeing my children or my grandchildren," Eleanora said. "I've suffered enough, don't you think?"

For most of Luna's life, her mother had remained emotionless, numb. She did whatever her husband asked of her, choosing him over her own children. It drove Luna wild, making her wish she had some family on her side for once.

Now she did.

Finn turned to Luna this time. "Take her upstairs and get her cleaned up. Pack her some clothes. I'll find her documents, arrange a flight for her."

Luna nodded, grabbing her mother's hand smothered in her father's blood. She pulled her along and up the stairs to the bathroom, forcing her out of the stained dress. She turned on the water, instructing her to scrub every inch of blood off her.

Luna made her way into the closet, grabbing a duffle and filling it with the essentials. She threw in some of the important jewelry, leaving all of the fancy dresses her mother used to wear.

Luna helped her mother out of the shower, getting her dried off and dressed.

She stopped for a moment to stare at her, seeing someone so broken. She wanted to cry out for the woman her mother once was, but it was no use. She would never be that person again and maybe that was a good thing.

This way she could start fresh. Find out who she was when she wasn't married or in the life of crime. She could get the new beginning women in their world only dreamed of.

Luna realized that while she needed her revenge, her mother deserved it far more than she did. She never had the support to make it out the way she did. She had taken it into her own hands.

They both deserved fresh starts.

A part of her still felt bitter, wishing the woman in front of her had done more in their lives, but Luna would never get those years back. She could either let it hang on her shoulders like a burden for the rest of her life, or she could move on from it.

"Look at the woman you have become," Eleanora whispered, pushing back a piece of Luna's hair. "You look just like me."

"I've been told that a lot."

She grabbed Luna's hand, looking at the two rings on her left hand. "You got married?"

"I did," she said, pulling her hand back. "I'm sorry you couldn't have been there."

"I don't want to miss any more events," Eleanora said, holding her hands together. "Please."

"We'll see what the future looks like," she told her. It was difficult to promise anything. Maybe once everything was done and settled, she could consider what that would look like in her life.

"Don't ever settle for less." Eleanora shook her head, her eyes glazing over. "Whatever you do, never settle for the abuse, for the hurt, for everything you don't deserve."

Luna didn't expect the first sob that escaped her mother's mouth, or the second, but by the third she wrapped her arms around her, holding her the way she wished she had been held her whole life. They cried together, mother and daughter, the only two people that would ever truly understand what the other had been through in their life.

"Thank you," Eleanora whispered, wiping her eyes and pulling away from Luna.

"For what?"

Her mother gave her a small smile. "You know what."

With that, Luna led her down the stairs, finding Finn waiting. He looked up from his phone, holding a passport in his hand. "I put you on a flight on the jet. You're going to Munich for now. Once everything is settled, we'll consider you coming back," Finn told her. "This is the safest option for you."

Eleanora nodded. "I understand."

"Grab anything else you need," he said. "You won't be returning to this house."

"I have everything I need," she said, holding tightly to the handle of her duffle bag.

As a new family of three, they walked out of the house. It was only then that Luna smelt the gasoline, a bottle of it sitting on the front porch. Finn helped Eleanora into the back seat, while Luna climbed in the passenger seat. He got in himself, opening the window and tossing a match out. Luna saw the trail of fire lead up to the front door before it was completely engulfed in flames.

They drove away, leaving the fire behind them. Soon, not a single trace of the home would remain. Her childhood and her father would both be ash, just a distant reminder. She closed her eyes, letting the tears run freely.

It was done. She was finally free.

FORTY-SEVEN
VALERIO

DISARMING the security system allowed Valerio, Dante, and Allister to enter the woods behind the home to find the underground tunnels.

These tunnels were the same way that Valerio used to sneak from his home to the cabin, especially after he lost his mom and before he was sent to Italy. His father knew about the tunnels, but since his property was already protected, he never considered it a big enough threat to close them up.

Good thing for Valerio.

He kicked down the door, quickly climbing up the steep steps to the room that led into the basement. It was more like a cellar, used as a room where "business" took place back in the old days.

He gave Dante and Allister a lasting look, making sure they were prepared for what they were about to do. They only nodded their heads in confirmation, communicating without needing words.

With that, they navigated the long halls and stairways to get to the main floor. Valerio entered first, holding the gun up in defense in case anyone caught them. The hallway was clear.

The three of them took quiet, quick steps, making their way to the study on the second floor. After any trip, his father always spent time there, attempting to catch up on work that he missed. He just hoped his father was still a man of habit.

Two guards stood outside of the study, both armed and dangerous. Without a second thought, Valerio lifted his gun and fired at both, the noise canceled out by the muffler. They fell to the ground in instant, perfect shots to the head.

"I don't think there's anyone else here," Valerio told them. "But keep your eyes peeled. We'll carry the bodies into the study so that if someone walks by, they won't see them and be alerted."

"They'll see the blood," Dante pointed out.

"Harder to see blood on the floor than it is to see two bodies," Valerio said.

"I'll stay out here while you guys go inside," Allister said. "You need that moment alone."

He was right. This was justice Valerio and Dante needed to take alone.

"Stay hidden. Holler if you need backup." Valerio clapped him on the arm. He knew Allister was good enough to hold his own, but he would never leave his best friend out there alone.

Valerio and Dante grabbed hold of the two dead guards and with another swift kick, forced their way into the study. He surveyed the room in an instant, finding no one else there but his father.

They pulled the dead men in, closing the door behind them.

Cesare lifted his head, appearing unfazed until he saw it was Valerio standing in front of him. "What the fuck are you doing here?" he asked, clutching the pen in his hands.

"Don't act so surprised," Valerio said. "You had to have known this was coming. Or are you surprised I managed to survive the bullet to the back that you sent me?"

"I don't know what you're talking about," Cesare said, his tone disingenuous.

"Don't lie to me!" he screamed, losing all cool. "For once in your life you are going to tell the truth."

"And if I don't? What will you do? Kill me?" Cesare asked,

crossing his arms. "I have guards posted everywhere in this house."

"I don't care," Valerio said. "To see you dead would be worth a bullet to the head."

"You're fools, both of you. I never thought I raised coward sons, but here you are. Following in on the same suicide pact your mother had," Cesare hissed.

Valerio slammed the butt of the gun against his nose, hearing a sickening crack. "Watch your mouth about my mother."

Dante stepped up. "The first thing you are going to do is confess to killing Alec."

Valerio eyed his brother. Alec was someone Dante hardly ever brought up, but he remembered how his brother looked after he found the body. He didn't sleep, he didn't eat, he didn't move; he was practically a zombie of a person. He was never the same after it. The smile never matched his eyes again. Valerio never even knew about the relationship until after Alec's death, but he would have protected his brother and supported him one hundred percent, back then and now.

"You already know I did," Cesare said. He held his bloody nose in his hand with a sickening grin.

"Why? He was innocent," Dante growled.

"No son of mine, no matter how much of a disappointment, is going to ever be with a man. Not in this lifetime," Cesare bit back. "You should be thankful. I saved your reputation."

"You killed the man I loved," Dante screamed. "But you don't feel any remorse; you never did."

"And I never will," Cesare said.

Valerio took a deep breath, calming himself enough to get all the answers before he shot his father in the head. "Why did you try to kill me? Your own son, your fucking heir!"

Cesare's eyes hardened. "I had no use for you. Your loyalties have shifted."

"So I was better off dead?" he asked.

"As long as that girl carried your child, I had no use for you," Cesare said.

"I am your son. Your blood. You were willing to kill me off just like that? What the fuck is wrong with you?"

"The same thing that's wrong with all of you. You know what comes along with this life. Don't act so surprised now. I did what was right for the Vitali name," Cesare said, standing up. He wiped the blood on his hand on his suit jacket. "Which is what the two of you should have done if you cared about this empire at all."

"What about my mother? What did she do?" Dante asked.

"She killed herself," Cesare said.

"Because of you," Valerio told him.

"Because of all of us!" Cesare screamed, slamming his hand on the desk. "She wanted to leave, she wanted to run away. I wasn't going to let her leave us."

"So you enabled the same misery that killed her. You could have let her go," Valerio hissed.

"See if you would ever let that Kingsley girl go," Cesare said, his voice full of malice. "Tell me you wouldn't keep her locked up."

"I wouldn't because I'm nothing like you," he spit out.

"You fool! Have you learned nothing? You are me." Cesare laughed hysterically.

"I will never become the man you are—willing to sacrifice my son, willing to kill someone he loved, willing to take an innocent grandchild and manipulate it into a monster. You're not powerful. You're a coward," Valerio screamed. "You're nothing."

"Fuck you," Cesare bellowed. He reached for the gun on his desk, but Dante was quick with it, shooting him in the arm before he could.

"Enough!" he cried out. He rushed up to his father, forcing him onto his knees and pulling out one of the smaller guns he had stowed away. He shoved it into Cesare's mouth, forcing him still as soon as he cocked the gun.

"I won't shoot you in the back. I'll look you dead in the eyes when I shoot you. I'll make sure you remember the face of the bastard son you hated, remembering he was the one who took your life. You won't get a tombstone, you won't get buried six feet under. You'll get thrown into some random body of water, a promise that no one will find you and no one will remember you," Dante told him, his voice calm despite the situation. "See you in hell."

Valerio watched his father's wide eyes, his head shaking back and forth trying to spit out words but unable to do so. He expected to feel something, anything, but instead he felt nothing.

The shot rang out in the room, silence following afterward. Dante let the body fall forward, hiding behind the desk. His shoulders moved frantically before a sob tore through his chest.

Valerio pulled Dante over, wrapping his arms around him. He needed it more than he did. His entire life he had been made a spectacle, losing everyone he loved one by one. Almost losing Valerio was the last straw, it seemed.

He had made it his life's mission to protect his younger brother. And today, it was Dante who protected him.

"You're going to be okay," Valerio promised him. "It's all going to be okay."

And finally, they both knew it would be.

Allister opened the door to the study, looking at the two of them in question. Valerio only nodded his head, letting him know that it was done. Cesare Vitali was dead.

Dante dragged the body downstairs as they all made their way to the living room. He wanted to do it himself, not letting Valerio anywhere near it. With confirmation that the former don was dead, all guards around the house were quick to pledge their loyalty to Valerio. There was no hesitation for them to take a knee and bow their heads. They knew his character. He was different from his father, fair and honest.

They had a couple of the guards take the body to the ware-

LEJLA MURIC

house, waiting for it to be thrown into the water as Dante had promised.

But for now, it was time to go home.

FORTY-EIGHT
VALERIO

VALERIO FOUND Luna sitting outside in the backyard gazebo, looking out into the city. He approached her, sitting down on the small bench. It was freezing, but the cold was a relief for once.

"My father's dead," Luna said, not bothering to turn to him. "My mother killed him. She snapped. Now, she's on a plane to Germany. Finn burned the house down. It doesn't exist anymore."

Valerio listened, grabbing her hand in his.

"I cried with her, and I held her. For the first time in my life, I actually understood her," she said, shaking her head. "I wish it had happened years ago, but maybe it was better that it happened now." She turned to him now. "You're okay?"

"I'm okay," he said. "Dante killed him. Shot him in the mouth. We got control of the house. Everyone there pledged their loyalty, but there's more work to be done."

"How is Dante?" she asked.

"He'll be okay. Are you okay?" he asked, squeezing her hand.

"I didn't expect it to hurt as much as it does," she said. "Why does it hurt?"

"It only hurts for a little bit. One day you'll wake up, and it won't hurt so much. That's how you'll know you're healing,"

Valerio said. His voice held promise, having experienced grief in his own life for far too long. "For now, let it hurt. It's good to hurt."

"Does it still hurt you?" Luna asked, turning to face him.

"It'll probably hurt for the rest of my life," he told her. "But I can live with it."

"Once everything settles," she started. "I want the house, the kids, the honeymoon. I want it all."

Valerio nodded his head. He absolutely wanted it all too, every single part of it. "And for now?" he asked.

"For now, I just want you," she said, leaning her head in. "All I need right now is you."

They would get the kids, the house, the love story they always deserved. They would establish their lives, find out who they were as Luna and Valerio Vitali. They would heal together, confide in each other in the darkest moments. They would hold each other on the happy days and the hard ones. They would tell tales about how they survived the war and how they never stopped loving each other.

For now, however, they would simply exist there, in each other's embrace.

And just like that, the dark snowy clouds cleared, and finally the sun had come out.

FORTY-NINE

LUNA

TWO MONTHS LATER

"I CAN'T BELIEVE you're actually moving out," Gianna said, dropping a box on the floor. "This is a sad day."

Luna shook her head. "You guys are literally in the house next door. We'll still see each other every day."

"Not every day," Valerio cut in, wrapping his arm around her. "I need some proper time with my wife."

"We hear your proper time almost every night," Blair said, pretending to gag. "Believe me, we're more than happy for you to have your own place."

Luna blushed a bright red, pushing herself into Valerio's side. "I tried to be quiet."

"Now we don't have to," he declared, pressing a kiss to her forehead.

"So where's my room?" Dante asked, clapping his hands. "I think I deserve the master bedroom, but I guess I could negotiate."

"Hell no," Valerio told him.

"We'll dedicate a guest room to you," Luna told him. "But you're limited on how often you can stay here."

After everything that happened, everyone relied on each other. Dante had the hardest time, waking up from nightmares to not sleeping at all, to not eating, before finally Valerio was able to force him into a healthy routine. It helped him, and slowly they were getting him back.

"Deal," he grinned. "I can have some sick ass parties here."

"No," Valerio shouted immediately. "No parties here, ever."

"Still not sure why the two of you needed such a big ass house," Allister said, dropping a box on the counter.

"I'm picky," Valerio said.

"I told him it was too much space," Luna said. "He said we would use it all effectively."

"Oh, eww," Gianna muttered.

Cecilia walked in, a scared look on her face. "So, I may have broken a lamp outside, but I don't think it was an important one."

"This is why I said we should get movers," Valerio groaned.

"It's fine," Luna said, waving him off. "This is more fun anyway."

"I might as well offer you all a drink since I'm not paying you," he said, walking into the kitchen.

"What the fuck? I was promised money," Dante said, following after him. Allister shook his head, headed in the same direction.

Luna turned back to Cecilia. "Has Augustus heard from Finn?"

She gave her a sorry look. "No, but he does know the general location of where your brother is. He'll come home when he's ready."

Luna sighed, her worry setting back in. As soon as they got home, Finn left, claiming he needed some time alone. Luna knew he was taking it hard; she just wished he would talk to her.

"Who is taking care of the Kingsley assets?" Blair asked.

"Me and Valerio for now," Luna said. "I just want Finn home. I know he could handle it. Besides, it's too much for Valerio. Between handling the transfers of all the Vitali businesses to everything going on around here, he now has to focus on what Finn should be doing as well."

Gianna frowned. "He'll come back home soon."

"I can only hope so."

The boys came back into the room, handing the girls their drinks. They all cheered, wishing the happy couple all the best in their new home. They would have stayed longer too had Valerio not kicked them out, claiming he had enough of all of them.

They managed to get one box opened, not even emptied, before they decided it was enough for the night. Returning back to the mundane was exactly what she needed. She struggled with her own nightmares, some worse than others. But every night, she woke up in Valerio's arms and slowly everything became easier.

"What are you doing? I thought we were celebrating all night," he said with a grin, getting onto the bed.

Luna groaned. "Moving is exhausting."

"Come here," he said, pulling her into his arms. "Let me draw you a bath. It'll help you relax."

"Just a bath?" Luna asked, raising her brows.

Valerio leaned in with a seductive grin. "You know, I picked this house specifically for how much open woods we have behind us. What do you say for a quick run? Unless, of course, you're too exhausted for that."

Luna let out a breathless laugh. "I think I can manage."

Valerio lifted her off the bed, walking them down the stairs. She managed to get to the tree line before he was behind her, tackling her to the floor on her stomach. He ripped the jeans off her legs, exposing her pussy to the cold February night air, but luckily, there was no snow on the ground. Without hesitation, he entered her, thrusting and fucking her until he was sure the new neighbors could hear her moans. She came harshly, her body shaking before he came right after, filling her.

"My perfect good girl," he muttered, carrying her inside their home. "I love you." He kissed her again and again.

"I love you too," she told him. "Is that bath still available?"

"For you? Always." He gave her the same grin she had fallen in love with, carrying her up into the bathroom.

They didn't have any furniture out yet and the home didn't quite feel like them, but it would soon. This was a new start for them. One that they got to shape together.

And that was perfect.

ACKNOWLEDGMENTS

Thank you for opening the pages of this book and deciding to follow Luna and Valerio's journey. These characters have haunted me since 2022, when I finally decided to start writing their story. I rewrote this book more times than I can count, beginning and then scrapping the entire thing until in the darkest moment of my life, the story bloomed. This book and these characters saved me in more ways than I can even begin to explain, and this world is one I cannot wait to continue writing and sharing.

This book couldn't have been possible without the support of a couple of people. My sisters—Amanda, Belma, and Adelisa. You all have listened to me talk about how much writing was my dream and supported me endlessly. For that, I am beyond thankful to get to call you all my sisters and my lifelong best friends.

I also want to say thank you to my mom and my dad. Thank you for showing me what it means to always follow my dreams. Thank you to my grandma and my grandpa for being here for this journey. I kind of hope you four don't read this book!

I want to thank the lovely editors that I worked with on this book, Misha and Gabby. You both were incredibly kind and helpful in helping me prepare this story for publishing.

Ellie, thank you for all your help with setting up the ARCs and figuring all that stuff out. I'm beyond thankful that you took me on so last minute and that you were able to take that load off my shoulders.

Thank you to everyone else in my life who had supported me

and helped make this possible. I'm forever grateful for every single one of you.

While Luna's and Valerio's story is over, you'll continue seeing them in the next book coming out later this year (fingers crossed)!

With that being said, stay tuned for the next book with new couples in this world!

ALSO BY LEJLA MURIC

Heir of Darkness

Book 2 (Coming Soon)

ABOUT THE AUTHOR

instagram.com/authorlejlamuric

tiktok.com/@laymur55

https://www.threads.com/@authorlejlamuric

amazon.com/author/lejlamuric1